*Re*Minder

REMINDER

DENNIS WATERMAN
With Jill Arlon

HUTCHINSON
LONDON

First published in the United Kingdom in 2000 by Hutchinson

The Random House Group Limited
20 Vauxhall Bridge Road, London SW1V 2SA

Random House Australia (Pty) Limited
20 Alfred Street, Milsons Point, Sydney
New South Wales 2016, Australia

Random House New Zealand Limited
18 Poland Road, Glenfield
Auckland 10, New Zealand

Random House (Pty) Limited
Endulini, 5A Jubilee Road, Parktown 2193, South Africa

The Random House Group Limited Reg. No. 954009
www.randomhouse.co.uk

A CIP catalogue record for this book is available from the British Library

Papers used by Random House are natural, recyclable products made
from wood grown in sustainable forests. The manufacturing
processes conform to the environmental regulations of the
country of origin

ISBN 0 09 180108 7

Typeset in Plantin by SX Composing DTP, Rayleigh, Essex
Printed and bound in Great Britain by
Clays Ltd, St. Ives plc

CONTENTS

I have so many people to thank for their contribution to this book, but if I were to name names, I would have to provide another book. Simply, I have to say, thank you so much to all my family, friends and colleagues who gave up their precious time to be interrogated in order to (in my humble opinion) make this a much more interesting book than if it had been left solely to me.

While thanking the 'interrogees' I must also thank Jill Arlon, the interrogator. When asked to write this tome, I asked Jill if she would help me. Not really knowing how I would go about it. I thought maybe she would sort of ghost it with me, but I have always hated being interviewed, so it came to pass that I wrote it all myself. I came up with the idea that it might be interesting to have other people's views on certain events. Basically, I made sure that Jill did at least as much work as I did. In addition to finding and interviewing dozens of people she also had the unenviable task of getting me to abandon my usual lethargy and keep typing. She then basically edited the whole thing. Dear Jill, thank you so much and I know you're as amazed, not to say thankful, as I am, that we actually did it. On a more personal side, this book would never have been finished without the support of my wonderful lady, Pam – not only stopping me from throwing this bloody computer out of the window several times, but just encouraging, assisting, feeding and watering, and dare I say it, loving me. Thank you all so, so much.

This book is dedicated to the two most beautiful women in my life: Big H and Jules – Hannah and Julia Waterman.

Dennis Waterman

FOREWORD

By Eric Sykes

I am extremely fortunate in counting Dennis Waterman as one of my friends. Mostly we meet during charity golf matches, and have our usual fiver bet. Sadly he wins more often than I'd like, but pride eggs me on to bet again during the next match even though I may have to move to a smaller house. Dennis will get a shock when he sees his book in print and an even bigger one when he discovers I have written the foreword. I was thrilled and honoured when his agent rang and asked me if I would be free to do it. I immediately rang him back and told him that with good behaviour I'd be out in three weeks. It was only later that I discovered I was second choice; they'd tried for Edgar Wallace, but his widow told them he'd given up writing.

I hope the reader will overlook the fact that I have not mentioned the content of the book. For this I apologise. Due to failing eyesight I am unable to read (you might add after going through this lot that I can't write either). However, I'm eagerly waiting for someone to come along and read *ReMinder* to me.

Whatever happens, I will buy a copy of the book because, knowing Dennis, it will be interesting, lovely, truthful and above all entertaining. From one of his most devoted fans.

INTRODUCTION

Tuesday 24 February, 1998
I have just played some of the best golf of my life; unfortunately, I also played some of the worst golf of my life.

Twenty-two points on the front nine (the good bit) and a bloody nine on the back. Pathetic, absolutely pathetic.

But I didn't care. No, I didn't give a monkey's. Now, for someone who is famous for going on to the practice ground just to ensure that my shouting and swearing is up to scratch, this was something special. But then it *was* something special.

Tuesday 24 February 1998 was my fiftieth birthday. Having been born in 1948 I was what was at one time called a bomb baby. We were brought up with news of the Cold War, the Berlin Wall, the Cuban crisis and Bob Dylan singing, 'A Hard Rain's Gonna Fall', and we all knew what that meant. We didn't plan anything after tomorrow, and reaching twenty was a remote outside bet. Yet here I was, fifty and thrilled. Not just for reaching such a ripe old age, but I was back in the bar of my beloved Lambourne Golf Club, surrounded by some of my greatest mates.

Deke Arlon. My manager, partner, protector, father confessor, wine adviser and friend.

Dave (Tubbsy) Tubb. Duke of Dropmore, fourth Baron of Burnham! Actually he's the chairman of the club, insofar as he made the chairs. A real native of Buckinghamshire, poacher turned environmentalist, publican, know all, piss-artist and hater of the press. A true mate.

Sally and Chris Walford. Chris let me live in his house for a while during 'early Rula'. A stalwart of the Dennis Waterman XI. A fine left back and even better drunk! Now lives in Battersea, which he insists on calling South Chelsea. An Old Reptonian but seems to be able to mix quite comfortably with us 'oiks'. Much to his chagrin his beautiful wife Sally nearly won third prize, and she's only been playing for a year or two.

John Taylor. Ex British Lion, captain of one of the great Welsh sides of the seventies. Read *The Faraway Tree* to my daughter Hannah on a super holiday in Portugal many moons ago. Great rugby correspondent and commentator. We rather rashly became the second and third quarter owners of a villa in Spain. Money under the bridge.

Barry (Fitzy) Fitzpatrick. Golf tourist extraordinaire, self-made man, but keeps forgetting what or how. Would forget his own head if his mouth wasn't attached to it.

Chris Treacy. South London rocker. Now vice president of the Golfclub-Makers' Union or whatever it's called. A very handy person to know, and very funny. He came first, he won! Bastard.

Two old pals from the West Midlands. Keith (the Teeth) Mason. Will put you up at the drop of a hat as long as you can play guitar, keyboard, and mouth organ or pull a bird for him. A fine golfer . . . Better dentist. And Jan (Squatter) Webster. Must be the smallest and nicest scrum half ever to play for Moseley and England.

Graham and Barbara Jones from Sowerby Bridge. He was the carpenter on *Stay Lucky*, one of the magnificent crew from YTV. He and Barbara encouraged my golf in the early years and were wonderful hosts on many occasions.

Ducker and diver Don Hockman . . . 'This one's really going to take off!' An Arsenal supporter since birth, but a fine chap nevertheless. Likes a Guinness and has become a very good loser at golf.

Tony McGrogan. Tour manager par excellence. Worked with the best . . . and me. I bet David Bowie didn't play eighteen holes with him every day.

Stuart Tosh. Great singer and drummer and more importantly a member of Wentworth Golf Club. Super to work with, smashing to play with.

Mike Higgins. A new friend, but one who arranged a fantastic golfing weekend in Dubai.

Tanya Pel. Her husband Roger wanted to play, but I said no members. But Tanya can. He was chuffed! She is Pam's golf and computer guru, and, incidentally, very tasty . . .

Matt Chuter. The most natural swing attached to a body just jangling with fear. And his mum, my lady, Pam. Obsessive golfer, computer crazy, fantastic mixer, habitual laugher and wonderful lover. She, with the help of Ali and Helen at Deke's office, had basically arranged this whole day, not to mention the night.

We were supposed to play golf and then go back home or to the hotel and get ready for the real celebrations in the evening, but you know what it's like . . . 'How'd you play?' 'Not bad. You?' 'I was hitting the ball OK. I just couldn't putt, pitch, chip. Fancy a pint?' 'No, I've got to get back and change . . . all right, just the one.' Ho, ho, ho.

I think I was supposed to be back in the club to welcome the 120-ish guests at about seven thirty. At about seven the late golfers were still there and the early arrivals were starting to wander in. Among those I noticed was my sister, Joy. She huddled for a moment in the doorway, like a posh bag lady.

'You're early,' I said.

'No, I think you're late,' she replied, her mind clearly on other things.

'Well, come in.'

'Erm, yes.'

Just behind Joy and her daughter, Melanie, there was a tall, greying half-Cherokee and his wife, my youngest sister, Myrna. She and Jim had flown in secretly from California for the party. In fact I'd had a deep suspicion that they would because they hadn't answered the invitation and I hadn't received a card. But it was a wonderful surprise nevertheless, a real birthday treat. And I was about to get loads more before the evening was out.

I was back shortly, changed and charming – well, clean at least – and the place was heaving.

Now I know how boring it can be to sit through a litany of names of people you've never met, but here were the most important people in my whole life gathered for once in one room. And a bar room at that! And friends who have known me for over thirty years. Robert Powell and Tim Carlton from our Royal Court days. Paul Young, all the way from Glasgow, who remembered one of his birthdays while staying with me in Hammersmith. Tim was in a play at the Mermaid Theatre and we decided to visit. After the show, Paul had decided that we must have a vodka for every year he'd been alive. Luckily it was only his twenty-sixth. Don't tell me public school isn't good for something.

John Foster showed up too. He had heard Cliff Richard singing in a pub in Hoddesdon, took him to the Two Eyes coffee bar in Soho and introduced him to Hank Marvin and Bruce Welch. He wasn't quite as successful with me, but he did get me playing with the Showbiz XI, introduced me to Les Dawson and set up my first recording deal.

Some may not thank him! But what a mate he's been for well over twenty years.

Tony McGrogan. I'd met him playing football and later when he was Artist Liaison Manager at RCA. working mainly with Bowie. Then on the road with Sheena Easton, Gerard Kenny and me. And finally taking a play to Australia and explaining to an inquisitive member of the stage crew in Brisbane that he was in fact not my understudy but my GP. 'You're his doctor?' 'No, you prat, his golf partner.'

Chris Lewis.We met in a pub in the late sixties with Mike Pennington. Chris was working for the sports department of the BBC, and indeed still is. He was called many things, mostly 'Ginger Tom'. Obviously because of his colouring, but also his innate ability to sniff out any woman on heat. As our goalkeeper, he was 'The Plunging Carrot'.

Warren Clarke, straight from location and looking like shit. Not only a best buddy, but a great actor and, more importantly to us, one of the funniest people on earth.

I have never seen so many of my hard-living male friends go so totally ga-ga as when the ridiculously delicious Jan Francis arrived. She was accompanied by my favourite employer, David Reynolds, who'd taken us to YTV for some of the happiest filming imaginable.

Brian 'Benbo' Bennett made it out of his studio. The drummer with the Shadows, producer and co-writer of my first two albums.

If you've ever believed that pessimists are boring, then you've never met Frank 'You're skint' Coachworth, my loyal bookkeeper. I could see him looking at everything being consumed, and thinking, 'He'd better get another TV series, and soon.' His beautiful wife, Jo, seemed less concerned. Ned Sherrin waltzed in and gave me a large kiss, not something you see at Lambourne very often.

And what joy to see Barry (Barrel) Summerford, who has worked as my stand-in since early *Sweeney*, and Jacqui, his ever-patient wife. My other record producer, Chris Neil, was there with his totally huggable wife, Jenny. Without doubt the youngest-looking couple in Bucks.

The guest list also included some newer friends like Sarah and Poo Prodow. Then there were loads of members of the golf club and, of course, my family. Joy, my eldest sister, with her daughter Melanie (who won Most Pissed Person at the party, standing on her head, but then couldn't stand on her feet. I have to say there were many many contenders for this prestigious prize).

My brother Ken and his wife Anne, as always a bit quizzical about the more overt showbizzy goings-on. My ex-wife Pat looked as though she was having a great time, while her husband, Jeremy the Judge, observed the spectacle somewhat sceptically.

Last, and very far from least, my two stunning daughters. Julia, nineteen, with a school friend of hers, who had done a super portrait of Jules and Hannah which Julia had commissioned. In a few days' time Jules would be embarking on her pre-university travels, Australia and Thailand, which doesn't really thrill Pat and me, but we know it's what happens these days. My older daughter Hannah was accompanied by her chap, Phil, who for some reason insisted on keeping his large black overcoat on, even when dancing, while everybody else was melting! Hannah had something of an advantage over the other non-members because she had worked behind the bar one summer, so she knew absolutely everybody. I don't think I've encountered a twenty-two-year-old who is so liked by so many age groups. But then I am totally biased.

The spread was fantastic and everybody was going for everything with mucho gusto.

Inevitably the band were talked into asking me to sing. Probably by my manager Deke and his wife Jill (who incidentally is helping with this book). He just hates to see me not working. Unusually, and this *is* unusual, I didn't hesitate. Normally I hum and ha (not unlike my singing) and generally need the protection of a guitar between the audience and me. For some reason, this particular evening I thought, 'Bollocks' and went for it. It was dynamite, not necessarily the performance, but the atmosphere. Everybody seriously hit the dance floor. Julia came up and we sang together, probably for the first time since she was tiny. It was great. Although I ended up as perhaps the most sober person at the party, I had had a seriously good time. At around three o'clock Myrna, Jim, Joy, Pam and I went home, had a drink and opened all my presents.

I can honestly say I can't wait to be fifty again!

ONE

CHILDHOOD

24 February 1948, South London Maternity Hospital
A child is born to Rose and Harry Waterman. They may not have been that thrilled. Rose and Harry were a working-class south London couple, forty-five years old, and this was their ninth baby. Six years after their last, I made my first unexpected grand entrance and I was taken home to 2, Elms Road, Clapham Common South Side. A huge house owned by the council, split into large flats. We were on the second floor. I lived there with my parents and my siblings Ken, Peter, Stella, Norma and Myrna. My two older sisters, Joy and Vera, had already left, having got married. Another brother named Allen had died early in childhood a long time before I was born.

JOY: Nobody took any notice of babies in our house because Mum was always having them.

KEN: I'll never know how two people who disliked each other so much could produce so many kids, but along one came every two or three years.

JOY: Amazing really how we just accepted it as normal. I was the eldest, then came Vera, Ken and Peter. Stella was born the year before war broke out and we four were all evacuated. We'd come home on a visit or for the school holidays and there would be another new baby. First there was Norma. She was beautiful. Then, a couple of years later, there was Myrna, plump and gorgeous with a mass of black hair. Mother had them both when she was evacuated to Ottershaw into a flat specially provided for evacuated families. We all joined her there. She made so little of it, all those babies – that is until the end of the war and the big move back. That was a dreadful time.

Father had joined the RAF as soon as war broke out, worked on barrage balloons first then became a medical orderly. He was a fastidious little man, very good-looking, a real extrovert, with a vile temper.

He'd gone off to war with one family. He came back to even more. Even though we were his kids he couldn't cope with such a chaotic household. He wouldn't get out of bed except to go to the dogs . . . He showed no interest in any of us, save to get us out to work and earning. In retrospect, I suppose I knew all along things were bad for Mum, but when you're young, rushing about . . . I just remember her face – so drawn, tired, poor thing. I'd come in from work, she'd be in her dressing gown and he'd still be in bed.

NORMA: It was a tough time. We all lived in this big flat in Clapham with ghastly gas lighting. I didn't realise just how poor we were at the time but looking back there was never enough food and no money. The school used to feed me malt I was so undernourished. Like lots of families then we relied on free school dinners.

JOY: Dennis came as a surprise six years after Myrna, but then again I don't think any of us were planned. I doubt Mother knew much about contraceptives; people didn't discuss such things in those days and she was a shy person. She certainly never told us children anything. Sex was something secretive and scary.

STELLA: I had no idea my mother was pregnant, or if I did, I blanked it out. Mother was always heavy. I was ten, the middle one, lost in a big family, the 'lone wolf' my father used to call me. I'd been home sick from school with something or other. Joy sent me back to school with a note for the teacher, telling him the news. He knew our family well, he'd taught us all. He made me stand up while he told the whole class that I had a new baby brother. I was so embarrassed, the most embarrassed I've been in my whole life.

MYRNA: When Dennis was born we all went up to the South London Hospital. We weren't allowed in but it was arranged that Mummy would hold him up at the window, which she did. He was just a dot.

JOY: Dennis came as a lovely ray of light into our lives. He was just so beautiful, with lovely golden-red hair.

None of us have middle names. My father either planned to have loads of kids or he was a prophet. Years later he explained to me that when you sign on the dole, you have to put the full names of your dependants on all the forms and it would have taken too long with middle names. Dad was a short, dapper man, rather conceited and probably quite handsome. He had been an upholsterer (considered in those days to be a very good job). He had worked in the scenery department on several films, and had been greatly impressed, especially with Marlene Dietrich and Robert Taylor. Not only for their glamour, but the way they mixed so easily with the film crews.

He had been an excellent ballroom dancer and had apparently been courted to turn professional. He was also an inveterate gambler. By the time I turned up, he was a British Rail ticket collector.

I don't remember feeling anything about him particularly, and I remember very little about Clapham. But I do remember the endless rows between my parents, which basically continued until my mother died. And I can recall an occasion in the kitchen where my brother Ken was tying his tie standing between my parents, while one threatened the other with a bread knife. My only feeling was how cool Ken was. For some reason the arguments didn't seem to affect me at all. Maybe this explains my reticence about getting involved in showdowns in later life. No violence was ever aimed at me. But then I was the Golden Child, spoilt to death by everybody.

JOY: One time, when Dennis was just a toddler, he managed to scramble out of my bedroom window and drop down on to the flat roof of a big bay window jutting out below. Dad moved quickly then. But there was no affection in the house, no physical show of affection. Can you imagine, no one ever kissed us! Only when I saw my husband with his family did I see affection displayed when they kissed each other hello and goodbye.

Mother loved us as babies, but once you were on your feet, that was it. With Dennis she'd keep him on her lap until very late at night, long after he should have been in bed. The others she'd send away, but Dennis she hung on to, almost as her comfort I suppose. But Father was a mean-spirited man. He took it out on all of us. Ken and Peter, in particular, suffered dreadfully.

STELLA: It wasn't until I moved to the States to work for a family-orientated firm and heard my boss say to his father on the phone, 'I love you, Dad' and his kids say, 'Love you' to one another that I knew people did that. It made me cringe.

As kids we would help and protect each other in times of need, although half the time you'd never dream of asking for it. We learned to rely on ourselves. Thrown out too young, I suppose. We all grew up used to being hurt without even knowing it. The only affectionate comment I ever remember my mother making about my father was 'Your dad was as good a dancer as Fred Astaire.'

He taught us all to dance. He'd line us up and show us the steps.

Rose Julliana Waterman, née Saunders was a pretty, plumpish little East Ender. My father had been born in the West End, thus territorial wars were commonplace: 'Gertcha, you East End guttersnipe.' 'You West End tripehound', etc. For as long as I can remember she worked as a curtain- and loose-cover-maker. She could bang out self-taught songs on the piano, and I mean bang, so I suppose with her playing and singing and the old man's dancing talent, it's not as surprising as it seems that the kids grew up to love the theatre.

MYRNA: We all used to sing. Everyone. Father loved music. Birthdays, Christmases we'd all have to perform. Joy, although married, was still living at home. Ted, her husband, would play the piano and together with Vera they'd sing bits from *The Merry Widow*. Mother had a sweet voice and Father I believe always wanted to act. He saw himself as John Barrymore or Lionel Barrymore, I'm not sure which. He had a big, overpowering personality, very demanding. He instilled competitiveness in all of us. He'd make us stand behind the curtains in the living room and then come out and perform. Both Ken and Peter had really good voices. Dennis used to sing too, but only in the bathroom.

NORMA: We learned a lot from Joy and Vera. They brought music and drama into our lives. They used to do these gorgeous lavish musical productions, amateur of course, but still wonderful, with fantastic costumes.

All the girls were members of Fayes Follies (maybe with the exception of Stella), all were terrific singers and Norma became a wonderful dancer. Joy ran her own amateur dramatic group, in which everybody was involved at one time or another. I remember Peter was inveigled into *Our Town* after he had won the British welterweight title. He was my boyhood hero, but not only mine. That fine comic actor Melvin Hayes told me years later that Peter had been his 'minder' at primary school when being Jewish wasn't acceptable to everybody, even at that age. One of the great embarrassments to us kids was that our father had marched with Mosley. This gene has not been passed on.

So there we were, eight of us living in this big flat in Clapham. How or where we slept I have no recollection. There are various legends about this period: Joy, having contracted polio, going to a faith healer and next day calmly walking down the stairs; Peter leaving me outside a shop all afternoon; the pupils of Henry Thornton Grammar School, including my two brothers, throwing stones at the window and shouting in an effort to wake up the old man, which eventually they did, just in time for him to grab my nappy and stop me falling from the balcony, hopefully into the arms of the boys two flights down.

I do remember being looked after by a baby-minder in Clapham North Side, while everybody went to work. I also remember getting up in the middle of the night, one Christmas Eve, to find everybody packing the presents and them all panicking about me finding out that it wasn't Father Christmas. Personally I didn't give a monkey's as long as I got loads of presents, and when you've got five sisters and two brothers you do get loads. One Christmas I spent in hospital, with a burst eardrum. Two particular things stand out. I got a toy farm, which I loved, and two huge penicillin needles, which I didn't at all! Ironically I recollect there was only one nurse who could inject me without the usual screams and tears. She was a beautiful redhead. Funny, that . . .

I used to go to the Tucker family's place quite often. We would stand on the kitchen table and listen to a radio which was on a ledge above our heads. We would listen to *Journey into Space* and *Riders of the Range* and *Dick Barton*. For some reason we also used to stick implements into electric sockets and get a small shock. I don't think we had electricity in our flat. I went to Bonnieville Primary School, and don't remember having any great problems. They were all to come.

TWO

PUTNEY

I was about eight when we moved to the Ashburton Estate. It wasn't typical of the monolithic high-rise blocks of flats which were thrown up in the sixties. Although it was a council estate it had obviously been designed by somebody who didn't just want to wreck the environment by building giant hutches for humans. It had probably been rather a grand house with land, and a large number of the old trees and hillocks had been retained to make a very attractive green environment. Unfortunately, because the 'old people' appreciated the place so much, the grass had to be protected from the sports-mad kids. We didn't totally agree with this policy, and I have to admit that I was one of the brave 'commandos' whose nocturnal manoeuvres obliterated several floral balconies and window boxes of the most stalwart of the grass guardians. I take no great pride in this, but it does seem ridiculous when there were lots of young families that the kids were only allowed to play in the playgrounds, where there were swings, seesaws, roundabouts and monkey bars. We wanted space for football and cricket.

Strangely enough, with this estate bursting with high-spirited young people, I can't remember anyone getting into any real trouble. A group of us were brought home by the police at one time having been caught in a large house that had always been empty. 'The Haunted House', we called it. There was no vandalism; we were just testing our courage. But the police turned up and told us that it belonged to somebody and we were trespassing. They then took us back to our parents and explained our crime. In my case this resulted in a hefty clump round the ear for embarrassing the family. I don't recall any other guidance about law and order, but, apart from scrumping and the occasional lifted Mars bar, all any of us wanted to do was play some sport, any sport. Basically I've been the same ever since.

We lived at 8 Wharncliffe House, Chartfield Avenue, a maisonette on the second floor, which was very handy for practising my climbing skills. My mum used to go crackers, because my alternative mode of entry was up the drainpipe and in through the French windows. It was a four-bedroomed flat, which meant the girls had a great deal more room, and even I had my own bedroom. Peter was doing his National Service, and as my parents failed to mention to him that we were moving, went 'home' to Clapham to find an empty flat! He was just about to turn professional, having been the youngest person ever to box for England, in the 1952 Olympics in Helsinki. He figured it might be time to get his own place anyway. So that left Stella, Norma, Myrna, Mum and Dad and me.

Next door were the Thomases – Trevor and his older brother Brian, who went on to become a lighting technician in the theatre. I was later to meet him at the Royal Court. Although we were all friends, they were considered quite strange, because they went to a rugby-playing school. Downstairs at number 5 was Kenny Owen. He was an only child of slightly older parents and always had a good football, new boots and even Subbuteo. A good bloke to know! These were my near neighbours, but there were always loads of team mates who would turn up at the drop of a ball.

A few flats along lived Ann King. I suppose she was my first girlfriend. An absolutely beautiful blonde. We saw each other on and off into our late teens. Purely platonic, although I'm sure that in the teen years I must have had secret desires and designs, but she had super parents and, unfortunately, a severely handicapped older sister. They used to invite me for tea and things. This was something that was totally alien to me. Obviously we had tea in our house, but because everybody at my place was working there was no one to make it. I let myself in and out with a key that was hanging behind the door which you pulled on a string through the letterbox. Later in life, I discovered that I had been a 'latchkey kid'. It didn't affect me a great deal except when it was tea time and all the kids were called in. I would go back home and watch the telly on my own. I will never forget the smell of egg and chips wafting from the Owen household. My mum came back from work at about half past six, so I was never likely to starve, but I certainly did feel different from the rest of my mates. Also, because of my old man's mood shifts and the constant uncertainty of his reactions to anything, it was never encouraged to even think of asking anybody home. There was a time when Brian from next door would come in and Dad would get us to spar. I went to Caius Boxing Club from the age of about ten and Brian went to a school where they still had boxing on their curriculum. So under the supervision of my father we'd put on these huge boxing gloves and bash each other up. Brian had a very fast and hard straight left.

KEN: Father had been a keen amateur boxer. The sudden death of his own father had forced him to leave school at an early age, something he always bitterly regretted, to help support his mother and siblings. Boxing, I believe, was a way of earning vouchers for clothes and food. He liked to show off his skills and he certainly made sure we got the rough end when he sparred with us!

JOY: He may not have been a great sportsman but he was a complete sports fanatic, with an enormous knowledge. Whatever he read he retained and passed on to the family. I see the identical ability in Dennis. He has the same phenomenal memory and interest in everything. We all knew everything about boxing from a very early age. You would have expected him to be so proud of Peter, but he never was or he never showed it. He was always critical of all of us, whatever we did or achieved. In fact I've never known two parents less interested in their children. Maybe that's what made us strive for attention. Father saw us only as a means of bringing in money. Everyone suffered from his verbal abuse, Ken and Peter in particular. Both boys were bright but Ken was especially studious and clever. Homework time was a nightmare. Father would scream abuse at him, haranguing him to get out to work to make money, all to feed his gambling habit. Even Peter, when he was training for the Olympics, was forced to leave home to live with a friend so that he could eat properly to keep up his strength. Father's only comment had been 'Let him eat cornflakes.'

MYRNA: Years later, after Mummy died, the doctor asked if Father was a manic depressive. If he was, he was never treated. But it would explain a lot. One minute he'd be the life and soul of the party then, in a second, switch to a foul-tempered brute. I remember Peter, who was the kindest of people, saying to him once, 'Don't you think we'd all like to have had a normal father?' It was rough but I don't think it was that rough for Dennis. And as kids, it did make us very close and supportive. Joy was great with Norma. She paid for her to go to dancing lessons at Crystal Palace while Peter really encouraged me to sing. Vera had the chance to become an actress after she won a beauty contest; her impending marriage took preference but she never stopped encouraging all the rest of us.

I suppose I spent marginally more time on my own than the others, but it was only a real problem in the winter months, when it would be dark by four thirty. Then it was lonely because you can't play football in the dark, although we did try. Presumably this is where my addiction to television comes from. I seem to remember that I loved *Junior Criss Cross Quiz* and a programme that Desmond Morris did about animals, I think it was called *Zoo Time*. I couldn't stand that dopey Johnny Morris. Looking back, it seems I preferred factual TV, I don't remember ever liking cartoons. Maybe I just can't remember that far back. I can't even remember when we got a television set. It must have been quite a big deal because we certainly didn't have one at Clapham. I went to Jennifer Wilson's to watch the Coronation. It's strange that I remember her name, because she doesn't crop up in my memory anywhere else at all. Sorry, Jennifer!

My new school was Granard Primary. It had a fantastic cedar tree right in the middle of the playground, and that was on our badge. We all wore uniforms in those days. Which didn't thrill my mum, because it had to be bought and washed and ironed. My first teacher was Miss Jones, my first 'older woman'. A couple of us used to wait for her every morning and walk her to school. She was lovely. We were quite shocked when she left because she was getting married . . . to someone else! Then I had the great good luck to be taught by Miss Mason. Miss Mason put me in all the school shows that were ever done. Because my mum was working, Joy would stand in for her and come and see everything we did. A lot of people thought she was my mother. It must have been because of these school plays and shows that she decided to put me in her productions. I don't recall her asking, just deciding.

JOY: I got into drama through my husband. Not a drama club as such, more a class, but we took part in various festivals. And a few years later I was persuaded to direct.

Dennis was seven when he played Mamillius in *The Winter's Tale* at the Southwark Shakespeare Festival. Myrna would bring him on the bus to rehearsals. Even then he was so amusing to be with, a great little raconteur, with an outgoing personality. He kept all the adults amused. He would sit in rehearsals totally absorbed in what everyone was doing. He had wonderful write-ups, he was so good. He had charisma even then and his connection with the audience was instant. Whatever it was, he had it.

From then on I called him into all the productions that needed a child.

At nine or whatever, I was playing Moth in Shakespeare's *Love's Labour's Lost*, a rather large part for someone who had absolutely no idea what he was spouting about. Another big hit was *The Winter's Tale*. My sister Myrna played Perdita, Joy was Hermione and her husband Ted Leontes. He was considered a really fine amateur actor, as indeed was Joy. Myrna was terrific and a great singer. She had a residency at the Purley Ballroom but had no confidence in her own ability. A great waste and a bigger shame. I don't remember Stella being involved as much as the rest of us in our theatricals, and eventually she did the incredibly grown-up thing of getting her own flat in Kensington. I was deeply impressed.

For some reason, we very rarely went on summer holidays, lack of money, I suppose. Though we did go to Sandbanks once to a house that was owned by my brother-in-law Den Cowan's mother. I have a niece, Frances, who is only three years younger than me, and apparently we had a wonderful time. It's all a bit dim and distant. And then there was another occasion when Norma, Myrna, Mum and I went to Hastings for a couple of weeks. But that was it except for a trip once to Butlin's. I have pictures of us in our raincoats. Most of the holiday was spent with my mum trying to get Norma to come back to the chalet at a reasonable time. She was sixteen and strong-willed. Shortly after this trip she dyed her auburn hair blonde and ran away to Paris to join the Bluebell dancing group. She was (and still is) five foot ten and seriously attractive. I don't know how she found out about the Bluebells, but she auditioned secretly, got the job and told us that she was going to France to be a dancer. This caused no little distress in our household but most of that was caused by 'the hair'. There was no way of deterring her, so Mum and I went along to Victoria station and waved her off on her way to a hugely successful career.

NORMA: I didn't exactly run away to Paris. I ran away to Stella's once but that was to escape the violence and the shouting at home. With the Bluebells I was bloody lucky to be picked. I got a passport in a day. Joy had always wanted me to be a classical dancer but she took me to the audition. It came down to two of us. The other girl was an expert in point style but I was tall and they said I had style. I was just sixteen. I didn't understand what style meant but they chose me on condition I dyed my hair blonde. They already had a redhead. I didn't hesitate. Wonderful Peter, who'd encouraged me and paid for all my dancing lessons, stepped in with the money for a new suit and my passport. I was shipped off in two days. I got off the train in Paris not knowing a soul or speaking a word of French. A girl met me. She said, 'You must be Norma.' I said, 'How do you know?' 'Because you look very lost and very tall.' I thought I was tall; she was a giant.

Madame Bluebell was north-country, very strict, very straight and very tough. She ran the troupe like nuns in a nunnery. I was shoved in with all these older girls.

The Bluebells took Norma all round the world, ending in Las Vegas where she married pianist Don Randi. They now live in Los Angeles. Three kids and several adoptees later.

It was Norma who was the most responsible for me becoming a professional actor. During her travels she had met several people whose kids went to a stage school called Corona Academy. In fact on our estate there lived a stuntman called Larry Taylor, whose daughter Siobhan went there. She was in the TV version of *Heidi*. Many years later I was to arrest, beat up, and play football and golf with his son, Rocky, also a highly successful stuntman. So Norma suggested that I audition for Corona.

NORMA: I was working at the Prince of Wales. After the show we all used to hang out at Le Grand Café opposite Ronnie Scott's. Everyone went there – actors, dancers, and Larry Taylor. We used to travel back to Putney together, and he told me all about his daughter and Corona. And he helped me set up the audition for Dennis. Dennis was such a natural talent, great sense of humour, funny, joyous. I was determined to get him there and to pay for it myself. It was expensive but I didn't care. Dennis could not only act, he could sing. It was all very well being a natural but I was aware of my own lack of training. I was having to learn as I went along on stage. I recognised the importance of training. I wanted Dennis to have it too.

I was away dancing in Paris, so Joy coached him ready for the audition.

This all coincided with me failing my eleven-plus, which excluded me from going to Henry Thornton Grammar School, my brothers' alma mater. I've never quite understood how I failed the exam. I wasn't thick and I actually rather liked school. But as luck would have it I did fail, which meant I had to find another school. I went for an interview at Wandsworth Secondary, where for some reason my mum decided that I should tell them that I wanted to be a teacher! Absolute codswallop. I suppose she thought that it would impress them. I also auditioned for Corona. The one big stumbling block was that this was a private school, which meant it cost quite a lot of money. Norma offered to pay all the fees, an amazing offer from a big sister. As it happened she didn't have to, because once at Corona I was lucky enough to be selected for a number of professional acting jobs, which meant I was able to pay for all my tuition myself.

For my entrance audition I recited one of the Shakespearean speeches I had already performed and I learnt a piece from *Toad of Toad Hall*. I was actually on a school trip when the audition was scheduled. I was having a whale of a time at a camp at Sayers Croft, when I was told my mother would be coming to take me back to London for the interview. I wasn't particularly thrilled. But I did my speeches and was accepted.

My brother Ken was also very good to me when I was young. He gave me a Saturday sixpence (generally spent on a Mars bar) and took me to football, Fulham one week and my beloved Chelsea the next, and he used to take me to Caius Boxing Club where both he and Peter were also members.

KEN: I first took Dennis boxing when he was three. It was 1951, I'd just finished my term of National Service with the RAF where I'd done pretty well as an amateur boxer. I came out and joined the same club as Peter. Caius was our local club. It had been set up as a charity organisation by Caius College, Cambridge, and we boxed wearing blue. However, some of the blokes there were ex-policemen who had access to a gym at Old Scotland Yard, which they allowed us to use on Sunday mornings. This was where I took Dennis. He used to come along and watch us spar and train, and when we'd finished, he'd jump in the ring and copy us. However the routine he loved best, and where he most excelled, was 'spitting in the bucket'. He loved that!

Peter was the most magnificent person I ever knew. He looked like a god, a dark-haired Paul Newman. He had unbelievable talent. He had actually wanted to go to art school, but at that time you weren't acceptable if you were left-handed. He played for Henry Thornton at several sports but eventually concentrated on boxing. He had a wonderful amateur career, culminating in being the youngest boxer to represent Britain, in the 1952 Olympics in Helsinki, at the age of sixteen. Our dear father, for some reason, having just watched him

win another title, called him 'a punch drunk so-and-so'. Peter
apparently told him to fuck off, and was immediately censured by the
ABA. I would have thought he should have been congratulated.

After doing his National Service in the air force, Peter turned
professional. He was hugely successful and very popular. It was quite
rare for a fighter to be a grammar school boy, let alone an articulate
artist. He even had his own television series, which was extraordinary
in those days. During this period he met and married Gillian, and the
wedding was televised too. Soon they had a little boy, Frazer. Sadly,
Peter was to be the first Waterman to go through a divorce. Equally
sadly, he wouldn't be the last.

He won the British welterweight title from Wally Thom and the
European title from Marconi in Italy. As they used to say, 'You had
to knock them out to get a draw over there.' At twenty-one he was a
contender for the world championship. He had two epic bouts with
Kid Gavillan, who had just been dethroned from the title. They
finished honours even, although strangely enough, Peter was certain
that he had lost the fight where he got the verdict, and won the fight
he lost. Forty-eight fights and just two defeats. The fateful forty-
ninth fight was to be a catchweight contest against Dave Charnley,
the middleweight champion. It was a fight everybody wanted to see,
a money-spinner, but totally unnecessary. I can't remember in which
round it finished, but Peter took a real beating and was rushed
straight to hospital. He was diagnosed with serious brain damage and
operated on immediately. I hadn't been present at the fight, but
listened to it on the radio. Somehow this made it all the more
horrifying. And then there was the unbearable wait to hear if the
operation had been successful. It was, in as far as we didn't lose him,
but my hero would never be the same again. Of course there followed
the usual uproar about boxing being banned, but Peter's neuro-
surgeon insisted that it could have been a genetic problem. The fact
that Peter wrote and painted with his left hand but didn't box
southpaw, and at cricket would bowl with his left hand and bat with
his other, seemed to suggest that there might have been an
imbalance. I had always thought of my brother as invincible, yet here
he was in hospital, unconscious, his head swathed in bandages and
in deep peril. Slowly, he pulled through. A twenty-one-year-old
athlete, a champion in his prime, his life and career in tatters. The
long-term effects were as if he had suffered a stroke down his left
side, and, most annoying to him, slurred speech. But he handled it
all. Without a hint of bitterness or self-pity, he just set about making
a new life for himself, and succeeded.

In January 1986, Peter suffered a massive heart attack and died. He was fifty-two years old. We were devastated.

But back then not only was I a celebrity by proxy at the club, I had all the best gear. And I had my own, my very own hero. Every Tuesday night Kenny would come to the flat and take me to the club on his scooter. Apparently I was considered quite good. But I must have looked fairly flash in all my Lonsdale gear. Whenever there was a new load of prospective members, three or four of us 'veterans' would be put in two corners and the newcomers in the other two. We would spar with them for a few minutes each so they could be assessed. So there I was in my proper boxing boots and dark blue club colours, for all the world a prospective world champ, and in the opposite corner was this lanky kid in horrible khaki shorts, grey socks and dopey little black plimsolls. This kid had absolutely no idea. He didn't seem to understand that you're supposed to throw a straight left followed by a right hook and dance about a bit. He threw a straight left followed immediately by a straight right. Every time he moved forward he hit me. It was like trying to fight two pistons. He bashed me all round the ring. When you're ten, it's very difficult to look like you're not crying when your eyes are streaming because this maniac is bashing you on the nose non stop.

NORMA: Father wanted Dennis to be a fighter too. We girls tried to steer him away from it. We'd had enough worrying over Peter. I was working in London at the Prince of Wales Theatre with Dickie Henderson and Shirley Bassey when news came over the radio that Peter had lost a fight. I burst into tears, I just hated the thought of him being hurt. We all did. We girls rarely went to see him in the ring, even though we were proud of him and of what he'd achieved, but we did sometimes hear his fights broadcast on the radio and felt every punch. Horrible. We didn't want that for Dennis. It was fine for him to use the gym for fitness and boxing as a work-out but no way was he going to be a fighter. He was not cut out for it, he was too sensitive.

I gave up boxing lessons when I began to do more work. It was decided that a broken nose wouldn't necessarily help my career. But it certainly stood me in good stead later on, both professionally and with the paparazzi, whom everybody should be allowed to thump at regular intervals. By now I had left Granard. It was the summer of 1959. I was going to Corona in the autumn term. The deal with this school was that while they teach you, they also act as your agent and send you out for interviews. Much to my surprise I was told to go for an interview before I had even been to the school. I had to go up to Kensington and meet the director and producer of a film. I went to this very posh mansion block by the Royal Albert Hall. The producers were the Danzigger brothers, who were a couple of Americans who became quite famous for making low-budget black-and-white movies. I can't recall who the director was. I got the part. The film was called *Night Train to Inverness*, and I was to play the son of Norman Wooland and Jean Kent, who are divorced. The father has been to prison for some reason and wants to be with his son, so he kidnaps him, gently. What he doesn't know is that while he has been in prison the child has been diagnosed as diabetic. So I spent the majority of the film breathing very heavily and getting paler and paler, while the father and the rest of the travellers panicked about me. In the end, the child's illness brings the parents back together and we all live happily ever after. So, with no film-making experience whatsoever, here I was, thrust into the midst of some very knowledgeable and well-known grown-up actors. Apart from the fact that somehow I had to get to Beaconsfield Studios from Putney by half past seven, I enjoyed it immensely. Child actors always have chaperones, typically mothers of other kids at Corona. This particular one lived in Chiswick, so it was decided we would meet at Uxbridge station and then catch the bus to the studios. It took hours. I had to leave at about five thirty. I've had no trouble getting up ever since. It also shows how times have changed. I would not even consider letting an eleven-year-old travel alone that distance at that sort of time, but in the 'good old days' there was no problem. Also, strangely, for the last seventeen or so years I have lived very near Beaconsfield Studios and of course have never worked there since.

THREE

CORONA ACADEMY

The school was run by three sisters – Rhona, Muriel and Hazel. If my memory serves me right, their mother cooked our lunches. Rhona was the principal. I became quite close to her years later, when she chaperoned me in Hollywood. I don't know if she had been an actress or had trained as a teacher, but she had a huge knowledge and love of the theatre. Muriel was our tap teacher, a natural bully who petrified everybody. Nevertheless, she didn't frighten me enough for me ever to learn 'the second tap routine'. Hazel, known as Mrs Malone, was our agent. She was rather more glamorous than the other two, and had to be treated with the utmost respect. It took me many years to come to terms with the fact that actors employ agents and not the other way around.

We started school every morning at ten o'clock and had the usual curriculum until one, then lunch followed by a quick game of football in the playground – until a couple of years later when footy was replaced by a quick game with the girls! The afternoon was taken up with theatre training. Tap, ballet, modern ballet, voice training, fencing and stage fighting. We had some very good teachers. Miss Florence, the archetypal ballet mistress, feet constantly in second position, white hair elegantly swept into a bun, and, of course, a walking stick. We also had a German modern dance teacher, who made us realise just how fit dancers had to be. He had a training routine worked out that crippled us. A lot of the other teachers were out-of-work actors, ex-pupils, or quite often, both. All of these lessons were to be of great benefit to me throughout the rest of my working life. But it would be fair to say the same cannot be said of the academic standards I achieved.

I did, however, learn how to appear ten years older than my real age (or so I thought), how to drink and how to . . . well . . . have sex. I may not have become an expert at this stage but it gave me a good early start. I was to become deeply enamoured of a young lady called Pamela Tagg. Her parents ran the Ravenscourt Arms. This could have been the apex of my short life, but, before we got past platonic, she fell for an older man. He was nineteen.

I don't recall any great difficulties getting into the swim at Corona. I just went with the flow, which is basically what I've been doing ever since. I wasn't aware of any great ambition, other than to keep working. It must have quite amusing for grown-ups to overhear a group of schoolchildren asking each other, 'Are you working?' 'No, but I've got an audition for a musical and an advert! You?' 'Yeah, I'm doing a film.' We were the lucky ones. A large number of kids were forced to drop out. Not from the school itself, but from 'the business'.

There were all sorts of reasons why children wound up at Corona. Some went there as young as five, so presumably never had any other formal education. Some had rather frightening stage parents who believed their little darlings should be film or television stars. Some were problem kids who couldn't make it in 'real' schools. And some of us were just ordinary kids whose talent seemed worth nurturing.

I was part of a bit of a wonderful era at the school. Richard O'Sullivan, Francesca Annis (for some years 'the golden couple'), Frazer Hines, Michelle Dotrice, Judy Geeson, Susan George, Robin Askwith, John (Mitch) Mitchell, who didn't get into our rock group, but did manage to become a huge success as Jimi Hendrix's drummer in the Experience. We were the lucky group who made the transformation from child actors to an adult career. It must have been heartbreaking for those kids who were called child stars and never made it above fifteen. I don't think there was any 'star system'. You were either lucky enough to get a job or you weren't. Obviously you looked up to the likes of Richard and Francesca, because they were excellent, and they were successful. The biggest fuss made of any of the students was when one of the girls, who had done an enviable amount of work, decided she wanted to take her O levels. We thought she was either brilliant or bonkers.

Although I was many years younger than him (which still gets up his nose), I became a lifelong friend of Richard's and have rarely met a nicer, funnier, more talented bloke. While we were still at school, Richard and Francesca got small parts in Elizabeth Taylor's *Cleopatra*. This entailed months and months of hanging around in Rome, while earning a fortune. But Richard used to come home every now and again just to watch Chelsea.

RICHARD O'SULLIVAN: Not so many years younger, you old sod! The main reason we didn't really meet at Corona was because we were both always bloody working. Dennis was about fourteen and I was about seventeen. He'd been off in Hollywood making a television series, *Fair Exchange*. I'd been in Rome for eight months waiting to work on *Cleopatra*, eight months there for eight days' work! Bliss! But then I came back and was out of work for eighteen months. At that age it didn't matter much as I was still enrolled as a drama student at Corona.

I actually don't like actors too much as company. Dennis was straightforward, he loved cricket and football, he didn't talk about acting, or precious things like work, etc. We were far more balanced. We talked of serious things, like women and sport. Acting was our 'job', not some 'aspiring art' with airs and graces. Corona or rather Mrs Malone, one of the sisters, did not encourage that. Like Dennis, I'd had to pay my own way through school. Acting was not a calling but a job and we were both 'jobbing' actors from the start, feet firmly on the ground. Corona did that.

So, at eleven years of age, there I was at an all-dancing, all-singing stage school, while all my other mates went off to their comprehensives. I took to it like a fish to water. What else would you expect, bearing in mind my name and the fact that I'm a Piscean?

I'm not sure that my sisters ever allowed me to have what might be called a cockney accent, but I was certainly from south London. From being an ordinary little toe-rag from 'the Ashburton' I was quickly transformed to a cap-doffing little toff. This didn't create any great problems for me back at Putney. I was still just one of the team. But later, when I was doing *Just William*, a little mob turned up from the estate round the corner to take the mick.

Where we did have the occasional problem was on the afternoons when we were having dance classes. To get to our theatre we had to cross the playground. The school was right at the entrance of Ravenscourt Park. Latymer Boys' School was on the opposite side of the main road, and a lot of the boys would pass our gates. Because we were prancing around in bottle-green tights, they thought we were a bunch of sissies. Every now and again we had to try and change their minds. I can assure you we were very, very normal boys. And there can't be many better ways to learn about girls than doing a pas de deux. Maybe it accelerated the process a little too fast, but it never put me off.

Even at this young age, drama school wasn't just a game or a hobby. You had to work. Learn whole dance routines in an afternoon, speeches, songs, and even if you couldn't get to class because you were working or had an audition you were still expected to have rehearsed on your own, and come back word-perfect. I have never had a great problem learning scripts or songs and dances. The Corona prepared me for being part of a company, whether it's rep or working with a film crew.

Throughout my time at school, I was also working. One day it might be a photo shoot for an advertising campaign. Once I was even the model for the silhouette for a health-food product called Vyrol. However, I was never aware of my career being planned by Corona. This may well be because my parents were not involved. That's not to say they were totally uninterested. It had more to do with the fact that they had no real knowledge of this side of life, and it was better to leave it to others who had. This variety of work probably stopped us from becoming too swollen-headed. And I was getting more and more work. Little bits in films and TV. Sometimes big bits in films and TV.

I did a film called *Snowball*. A little kid (me) spends his bus fare on some sweets or something and walks home. Because he is so late everyone is panicking. Rather than own up and be told off, he invents a story about the bus conductor throwing him off the bus. This understandably creates havoc and, if memory serves me correctly, the bus driver attempts suicide. How it finished I can't recollect. But Gordon Jackson played my father and Kenneth Griffiths the bus driver. Another movie I did at around this time was *Don't Take Sweets from a Stranger*. It starred Janina Faye and I was her little boyfriend. We were both at Corona and indeed had been sort of childhood sweethearts. She was later to be absolutely brilliant in the London production of *The Miracle Worker*. I spent a lot of time at her flat in Acton, which she shared with her brother and Polish father. We remained friends for many years, and along with Pat Wilson, the Sobell twins, Tanya, Pamela and a few others, she had no intention of letting me grow up too quickly.

The most fun was a film called *Pirates of Blood River*, for Hammer. I was the little villager who first sees the pirates land and rides off to warn the rest of the village before we are raped and pillaged. Christopher Lee was the captain of the blackguards and Oliver Reed was his chief nutter. Everybody was smashing to me, and a couple of the stuntmen taught me to ride.

The only person I didn't like was the director, John Guillermin. There was a sequence where I had to run to warn somebody or other that Oliver Reed and Co. were on the rampage. We rehearsed the scene for the camera, then the director told me to run around and get out of breath. So off I jogged, came back and said, 'Ready.'

'No you're not,' he insisted. 'Do it again.' This carried on for what seemed to me like hours. I was so aware of the whole crew having to sit around, waiting for me to get knackered. The problem was I was as fit as a fiddle, and could run for weeks. But this prick had made his statement and everybody had to wait until I'd convinced him that I was exhausted. I was acting, which I thought was the whole point.

Maybe one of the problems that child actors experience when bridging the dreaded age gap from minor to major is this: when you're a child, and the director tells you to laugh or cry, you do it. It doesn't matter that you might not know the reason why, or don't understand the script, you just do it. When you get older, you have to (or should) understand the reason for these emotions. This could be why the fall-out rate is so high. So many kids were never taught how to actually read a script. Sure, they were beautiful and could break your heart with a bat of their eye, but they never knew why. Now I'm about as far removed from an intellectual actor as you can get. My method is mostly based on heart and bollocks. I've also had amazing luck. Firstly I had been rehearsed from a very young age by Joy. She wasn't interested in a pretty little kid making the audience go 'Aah.' She wanted me to know what I was talking about, or at least to look like it, which isn't always easy with Shakespeare. And professionally, I was fortunate to be in quite challenging work from the start.

At age eleven, I played John Henry in the British television version of Carson McCullers' *A Member of the Wedding*, with Frances Cuka as Frankie. Between her and the director it was made clear to me what the book was all about, and why the characters reacted the way they did. Obviously the interpretation was fairly simplistic, but it made the part more interesting for me.

Shortly afterwards I did a live TV play (strangely enough playing another American) called *All Summer Long*. I had the part of Barry Foster's kid brother. This was directed by the highly acclaimed Peter Wood. Peter, I'm sure would acknowledge that he did have a reputation as a bit of a bully. But he explained almost everything in detail and didn't treat me any differently from the grown-up actors, which gave me enough confidence to make the occasional suggestion. So without appearing unbelievably conceited, I think I started to read scripts with a slightly, albeit ever so slightly, more adult approach. Part of a child's way of appearing twenty-one when only eleven, is always to listen to older actors gossiping and moaning. You retain it and repeat it as if it's your own opinion.

PETER WOOD: I directed Dennis on four different occasions.

With *All Summer Long*, I was an up-and-coming young TV drama director with a fat contract from H.M. Tennant. Dennis was eleven. A year later, in 1960, I directed him at Stratford in *The Winter's Tale* in the role of Mamillius. When we did *Carving a Statue* he must have been about eighteen. By the time we did *Windy City*, he was a grown man and a star. So in a way I worked with three different Dennises, and in a sense with three different personae. There was virtually no resemblance between the pubescent boy and the star of thirty-something. In a funny way, by the time he was an adult he'd found the family tradition of aggression rather handy, whereas as a boy, it seemed to me he'd rather run away from it. As a child he was quivering with sensibility, which was why I cast him in *All Summer Long*.

He'd already appeared in *Member of the Wedding*. A young Frances Cuka played the central character, a sort of boy/girl in khaki trousers, whose sister was getting married and who was feeling very left out because she was not a member of the wedding. Dennis played the little boy with glasses who was her confidant. His performance was so sensitive, it was almost surreal. Both he and Cuka gave extraordinary performances, he about childhood and she about adolescence. The piece was full of gentle humour, tender jokes drawn from what they think they know and don't. Delightful, amazing scenes with the young girl in voluminous shorts and the little boy in glasses who talk of life very seriously.

He was the same sensitive figure in *All Summer Long*, a play about a house that is falling down and the family who live in it. The play climaxes as the house disintegrates and the family splits. Dennis gave the most perceptive performance. Remarkable how he conveyed a child's contained imagination, a child totally happy within himself, where there is no need to share with anyone else. Also he never seemed to have 'learned' the lines, he was just saying them, 'being' the character. A talent which he has retained as an adult actor.

It was his ability to portray that strange, secret, introverted quality that was the reason for the play's success. It seems to me that as his career progressed, he sacrificed that wonderfully sensitive quality, which is obviously still there inside him, to play the more stereotype working-class side, whereas it would have been interesting if the sensitive paradoxical side had developed.

Much of my phobia about a lack of education is down to the long periods of work I did. The deal was that minors, working in any show, must have four hours of schooling a day. Sometimes a tutor would be employed, and they would do their level best to see that the rules were adhered to, but – and it's a big but – the producer is God, and time is money. And please don't think of me as a prissy little swot pleading to be educated. I've always been bone idle and was thrilled to bunk off class, but this has had an effect on me.

In 1960, I had the most concentrated year of education anyone could get. I auditioned for, and was accepted into, the Royal Shakespeare Company. This meant spending about nine months in Stratford-upon-Avon, and that was a very big deal.

On the day I was leaving I went to say goodbye to my father, who, for whatever reason, was in bed. 'I'm going now, Dad,' I said.

'Well ta-ta, Tarz' – sometimes he called me that, short for Tarzan, due I think to my minuscule frame – 'look after yourself. Oh, and here you are, take this.' And he gave me a sixpenny piece, a tanner, which in today's money is two and a half pence. Just enough to buy a chocolate bar. Now I know I was only eleven, but I have to say I was deeply unimpressed. Mum packed for me (something I've remained pathetic at all my life) and off we went to meet James Langley, another Corona kid, and our chaperone (one of several over the season) to take the train to the home of the Bard.

We were to stay in a small hotel run by the Probert family, where traditionally the Stratford child actors lived for the season. The Proberts had a daughter, Elizabeth (I think), and a beautiful Lassie-type collie. They were smashing, although they did have an unhealthy interest in the supernatural, but we'll get to that later. I barely knew James Langley at school, but we got on handsomely and he had a great family who would come and visit quite often.

For the duration of our stay we had a private tutor. I can't recollect our teacher's name, but we were the only two pupils in his house, and there was no way of shirking. It was organised that we would go to class every morning from nine till one, have lunch, then go on to rehearsals. Part of the season included the summer holidays, but when we were being taught, there was no escape, and I enjoyed it immensely.

This particular season at the Memorial Theatre was an historic one, although I can't honestly say that James and I were aware of that when we arrived. It was the beginning of a new era. The theatre had attained royal status. Instead of being called 'The Stratford Memorial Theatre', it was renamed 'The Royal Stratford Company'. It was also the first season for a new artistic director, a young man called Peter Hall.

The company was amazing: Dame Peggy Ashcroft, Eric Porter, Denholm Elliot, Patrick Wymark, Jack McGowran, Dorothy Tutin, and, in most of the lead roles, Peter O'Toole. The slightly smaller parts were played by Ian Holm, Ian Richardson, Dinsdale Landen and Roy Dotrice. There was also a beautiful actress, playing various wenches, called Diana Rigg, plus Mandy Miller, who had been a huge child film star. Not a bad group to pick up a few tricks from. I was (coincidentally) cast again as Mamillius in *The Winter's Tale* and as Biondello in *The Taming of the Shrew*. *The Winter's Tale* went without a hitch, as far as I was concerned. My family all came to see me and were, of course, terribly proud. My father, strangely enough, was very moved. He told me he had never been so proud, and that included seeing my brother become a champion. 'You came on stage in your beautiful golden costume and spoke in a proper accent and everybody in that huge, famous theatre could hear every word you said.' I was seriously chuffed.

STELLA: 'My God,' Father said to me, 'to think of him working with Peggy Ashcroft.' He actually admitted that, not to Dennis but to me.

In *The Taming of the Shrew*, Biondello is the servant of Petruchio (Peter O'Toole), and it is an important part. John Barton was directing and he had decided that, as in the original Shakespearean productions, this character should be played by a child. Me.

Opening night was approaching, the dress rehearsal was in progress and I was sitting in the auditorium waiting for my next entrance to be called. The scene in rehearsal was set in a tavern, and on stage, direct from a very liquid lunch at the Dirty Duck (the pub across the road from the theatre), were McGowran, Wymark and O'Toole, and not one of them could stand up. I was aware of these three gentlemen's penchant for strong liquor. I was even offered a Guinness by O'Toole, who had definitely had one or two himself during the interval of *The Merchant of Venice*, in which he was playing Shylock. He would then return to the stage after the interval and be absolutely faultless. That was not the case in this particular scene, but all three were hilarious. However, I think it was probably this episode that prompted Peter Hall to take over, or, maybe, assist John Barton. The opening night was put back. More rehearsals were called, and I suddenly learned I wasn't as good as I had believed I was. Peter came to see me in the dressing room and very gently explained to me that one so young should never have been cast in such an important part in such a big theatre. Basically, at the age of twelve, long before most people even had a job, I was sacked! He said I was wonderful as Mamillius and would I please help the new Biondello (Dinsdale Landen) and take the much smaller part of a boy player in the *Shrew*. I could hardly say 'Up yours' – not that it even crossed my mind – but I was devastated. I had failed. But everybody in the cast was super to me and John Barton gave me my first Waterman pen as a first-night present. Mind you, it meant I was even busier during the *Shrew*. Not only was I doing my own little part, I was haring around telling Dinsdale where to enter and exit, what scene came next and where he had to change his costume. To Peter's credit, he hadn't planned the change, and poor Dinsdale had to learn this quite large role virtually overnight.

James and I had a great time. With the exception of a couple of duff chaperones, one of whom gave me a terrible telling-off after reading a letter I had written home, where I described her as an old bag. Anyway, I got my own back when I barged into her room one night, before going to the theatre, to find her putting her wig on. She was as bald as a coot. I took great pleasure in passing on that information!

The Proberts were really nice to us, and as their daughter was about the same age, we had a ready-made little friend who had local knowledge. They also wound us up something chronic about the hotel being haunted. On one occasion we were going to play in a loft above the garage. It was pitch black, so we needed a torch. Elizabeth went first, followed by me, then James. When we got to the top there was this grotesque old man sitting looking at us. James screamed and shot back down the ladder. By the time he hit the deck, Elizabeth was laughing like a drain, so I realised it wasn't real. Don't get me wrong, I was as terrified as he was, but the laughter made me realise that it was a wind-up. It was just a dummy but it scared the shit out of us.

One evening, a little while later, I came out of my room on the way to dinner and saw an old-fashioned-looking woman turning the corner at the top of the staircase. In the dining room I asked who she was. I was met with completely blank stares. 'There's no little old lady staying here.'

'Well, who was it then?'

'No one.' I must have seen a ghost. Strangely enough, this had no effect on me whatsoever. I wasn't particularly frightened and when, in later life, incidents like these are discussed, I tell the story, but at the same time insist that I don't believe in ghosts . . .

We did manage to make friends with other kids in Stratford. We used to play football with Stephen, whose father was the leader of the orchestra at the theatre. Steve was particularly helpful in pointing out the male members of the cast who were liable to invite you to go 'swimming', people you should avoid at all costs. I know in this day and age it is considered politically incorrect, but I'm afraid that when you've been a child actor, especially from an ordinary straight family, it is very difficult not to be a bit homophobic. Consenting adults are one thing, but we weren't. Luckily, I was never greatly bothered until I was in my teens, and by then there was no way I was going to switch from girls.

James and I were very happy at Stratford – in fact he ended up eventually back at the RSC, working on the technical side. We went to the Mop Fair, on boat trips down the Avon, we played softball at an American air base, we were taken to teas and cinemas. One time, I had a serious problem with a tooth and was rushed to the dentist to have my first extraction. Ian and Marroussia Richardson were particularly concerned, and as a get-well-soon gift, I was given the complete works of Shakespeare signed by the entire cast. Still one of my great treasures. It is fair to say we were spoilt rotten, but our best fun was being in the theatre and hanging around with the cast and crew. The old cliché about the smell of the greasepaint is not a cliché at all. The smell of that particular theatre will live with me forever – the props, costumes, wigs, hessian, glue and paint and indeed greasepaint. I loved it.

It was a jolt having to go back to regular school again. I returned just in time for end-of-term exams. After my private tuition, I sailed through. This was both good news and bad news. Good news because it showed how brilliant I was. Bad news because I was so far ahead of the rest they put me straight into the top class. This meant that I remained in the same class for about three years. So at the beginning of the new school year, when the younger kids came up, I'd start the same lessons all over again.

Then it was back to work. After a long series of auditions, I landed the part of Winthrop Paroo in the big American hit musical *The Music Man*.

Bright and brash, sweet and sentimental, Broadway's *The Music Man* (Adelphi) has at last rollicked into London.

(Harold Conway 19 March 1961)

Meredith Willson's musical featured a travelling salesman hero who sells music to small communities. His powers of persuasion are such that he whips up the enthusiasm of key local personages into believing that music in their lives is a necessity. Before they know it they have subscribed to buy instruments and uniforms for a boys' band. Unfortunately the hero knows not a note of music, which makes him the vulnerable target of a jealous fellow travelling salesman. There is even talk of tarring and feathering this Pied Piper who has organised a boys' band without the faintest notion of how they are to be taught to play their instruments . . .

The prim, but pretty and cultured librarian suspects as much. It becomes necessary for the Music Man to woo her in the course of business. It is his good fortune that she has a younger brother who because he lisps will hardly bother to speak at all. But the excitement of owning a trombone gives the lad an interest in life. He not only begins to speak but to sing, and Mr Dennis Waterman sings 'Gary Indiana' most takingly, and his sister gratefully falls for the salesman.

(Anthony Cookman on plays, 5 April 1961)

Van Johnson came over from Hollywood to take the lead. I was the little brother of his love interest, played by Patricia Lawrence. I had one big solo number, a couple of features in some of the ensemble stuff and learnt to play the 'Minuet in G'. on the cornet. It was all exciting stuff. We rehearsed for about six weeks and previewed the show in Bristol for a few weeks before going to the Adelphi in London. And the first night fell on my thirteenth birthday.

MYRNA: Dennis was suddenly very successful. But there was really not much reaction from any of us because Peter had already done so well. He was the star performer in the family. Even when he'd finished boxing he had his own television show. He was the one everyone wanted to know. He was so good-looking all my friends were in love with him.

Dennis used to come by my office after a matinée, and no one took any notice. He didn't think anything of his sudden stardom either. It was just a job. He was just a normal little kid. He didn't think he was anyone special or wonderful. Shame, there were times in his life when a forceful ego would have served him well!

I had the biggest part, but there were three other kids in the show – Stephen Ashton, who was also my understudy, another bloke, whose name was Roger something, and Gillian Martindale. Stephen was from the north and had been dancing since he could walk. His make-up was always perfect and he spent a lot of time with the grown-up male dancers. I think he later became a ladies' hairdresser. Gillian was a plumpish, very nice girl from Croydon, with a sister I really fancied. Stephen was the leader in the dressing room, much more sophisticated than us and well into sexual innuendo. He also talked quite openly about masturbation, which shocked us. By now, I didn't have to wear my school uniform any more to go to the theatre, so I was buying 'proper' clothes and feeling more grown up by the minute. Gillian's sister and I didn't 'do' anything, but there was a lot of touching and flirting.

The show opened with lots of razzmatazz. This was real Showbiz and loads of my family came. Everyone thought I was wonderful, but then they would. Once again the cast were great to us kids. I remember having a crush on one of the girl dancers called Carole Naylor, and I was thrilled when we met years later that she remembered me. She is now happily married to Hank Marvin.

Van Johnson had been a big star in the thirties and forties; I knew him from black-and-white television films on Sunday afternoons. He was a handsome man, obviously from Scandinavian stock, big, blond and blue-eyed – the colour of his eyes highlighted by the application of heavy mascara on his eyelashes, on and off the stage. I thought this rather strange, but assumed that that was what Hollywood stars did. He dressed elegantly, and more often than not, a long black overcoat hung from his shoulders like a cloak. Invariably he wore bright red socks and embroidered black pumps. Because he was accompanied in London by his wife and daughter, I accepted this as his preferred style of dressing rather than an indication of his sexuality.

Van was very showbizzy. In fact I thought him rather hammy on stage, but he was a charming man, not at all starry or big-time, and very generous with all the kids. Every now and again he would take us to posh restaurants with his daughter, Schuyler, who was at school in Switzerland. We wrote to each other for a while. I think Van thought it was cute being with young people who said please and thank you. Years later, when I took my own daughters to Los Angeles, I found we received amazing service because, as opposed to most Californian children, my daughters displayed good manners.

Thanks to Van a lot of celebrities came to the show. One night we were all asked to stay on stage after the final curtain. Van wanted to introduce us all to a friend of his. Everyone was terribly excited and nervous, especially some of the male dancers. This bird-like little lady walked up from the auditorium, and rushed around telling everyone how wonderful they were. Finally she engulfed me in her fur coat and went on about how good I was too. I was gobsmacked. It was Judy Garland.

During this period there were two other shows in the West End with kids in the cast – *Oliver!* and *The Sound of Music*. We all used to meet up and compare notes. I honestly can't remember any animosity or jealousy. We were just big grown-up West End performers meeting each other for a coffee. But, of course, there was a downside. I was in the show for nearly a year. Except for the school holidays, including travel, I was doing a fifteen-hour day. Mostly I took it in my stride, and I don't recall ever being tired but I do remember being frightened.

In those days travelling by tube was not at all dangerous. Every night after the show I would go to Charing Cross, catch a District Line train to Putney Bridge and then a bus to the top of Putney Hill. Then the test of nerve. Some nights it didn't bother me at all, but at other times, for some reason, I was petrified. The road from the bus stop to the flats was long and dark, with some very large houses which, at this time of night, were mostly unlit, including the Haunted House where the police had once caught a group of us. Sometimes I would sprint down the road, but on other evenings I would try and be brave and just stroll, or do a mixture of both. I knew I was scared, but I didn't want to run, so I would walk down the middle of the road and whistle the hit of the day very, very loudly. My sister Myrna says she always knew what state I was in by the volume of my whistling.

MYRNA: It's extraordinary, looking back, just how casual we were in those days. All of us. Dennis was only a little skinny guy of twelve or thirteen but he used to travel up to London, do the show and come back late at night all on his own. You'd never allow that now. Our house was at the end of a big long avenue lined with trees which met overhead, very pretty in daylight but at night it was like walking down a long dark tunnel. We all knew he was alone and scared. We did nothing about it, though, just took it for granted. Isn't that wicked?

NORMA: Sure, he was frightened about coming home in the dark, but it built up his resilience. Besides, he loved acting too much to let it get in the way. He was too focused. We all led very independent lives and thought nothing of it. I'd just left Paris where all my fellow male dancers were gay and I loved them, but then I'd go backstage at the Adelphi and there was my beautiful little brother Dennis with a whole cast of gay people. That scared me.

During the long run, my friends on the estate and my family treated me as though nothing unusual was going on. I still had to make the tea, go to the shops and generally do what I was told. The only problem of mixing with other showbiz kids was that we were slightly more forward sexually. All talk of course. But when, as often happened, I was given a note by one of my sisters and told to give it to the chemist, I knew exactly what I was collecting, and found it acutely embarrassing.

Saturdays were great days. In the morning it was down to Putney Bridge for Saturday-morning pictures. I never liked Buck Rogers and sci-fi stuff but I loved the cowboy films. The great thing about having a sister who was travelling the world was the presents she would bring back for me. My pride and joy was a buckskin jacket and a pair of real cowboy boots. I was definitely the best-dressed cowboy in the whole of England. So when we were fed up with being thrown off the grass, I would always suggest we played cowboys. I even got my mum to get me some bits of leather from work and made my own holster, so I could be the fastest draw in Putney. The one drawback to Saturday was that my mum was a terrible cook. Every week she cooked the same really repulsive lamb stew. I'd look at the thick film of fat floating on the top and gently enquire if there was something else I could have. 'Why?' she'd say. 'You like this.' Every week the same ritual. Every week I'd scrape the fat to one side, avoid the bones and leave as much as I was allowed. Afternoons was football. On alternate Saturdays my brother Kenny would take me to Fulham and Chelsea. In those days they were in the same league, and Fulham was probably the better team – Johnny Haynes, Bobby Robson, Graham Leggat, Tony Macedo, Tosh Chamberlain, Jimmy Langley, even Jimmy Hill, with whom I now play golf.

Next I was chosen to play 'Just William'. There was a huge amount of publicity about this 'new William'. I didn't know what the hell was going on. I'd never heard of *Just William*. Well, I suppose I had, but I certainly hadn't read any of the books. They were for kids.

We did six episodes and people still tell me they remember me in it. It was great fun to do, but it seems to have left a much bigger impression on everyone else than it did on me. I'm still asked questions about the William books and I have no answers whatsoever. This may seem a little blasé or rude, even, but to us on the estate, William was a posh twit. We didn't want to have a gang and a camp and do dopey plays about pirates, we wanted to win the FA Cup. Nevertheless, I had a great time doing it and it must have helped me get an audition with Desilu Productions, who were in England to cast a typically English family to star in a Hollywood television series.

I had to go to the Dorchester Hotel to meet Cy Howard, the producer, and someone called Artie, who was the writer. The series was called *Fair Exchange*. An American and an Englishman who had met in the war decide to swap daughters for a year. So the English girl will live with the American family in New York and the American girl with the English family in London. Each family consisted of mum, dad, daughter and son, and it would all be shot in Hollywood.

The auditions were a slow process of elimination. Could this daughter match that father? Would this boy look like that actress's son? Eventually the son's part was short-listed to two: a kid called Dennis Gilmore and me. I was on tenterhooks. Hollywood was where everybody wanted to go. It was where you became a star. Eventually I was called back to the Dorchester. Cy and Artie told me that they thought I was absolutely marvellous, that I had a great future in front of me, but that the other Dennis was a little shorter than me, and therefore more like the American kid they had already cast, and they really liked that similarity. I was sitting there listening to all this, trying not to cry and thinking, the midget can't even act, he hasn't been to Stratford or in the West End or played 'Just William'. It was one of the few times in my life I've been truly jealous of another actor. In fact the other Dennis had done plenty of work and was particularly cute-looking with bright red hair and a funny little upturned nose.

So that was that. No Hollywood for me. Back to school and the estate and reality. But as it turned out, poor old Dennis Gilmore had signed a contract for another job and whoever they were wouldn't release him. Desilu came back for me. I had no problems at all with being second choice. I was off to Hollywood after all. Victor Maddern was Dad; Diana Chesney was Mum and my sister was Judy Carne. Hazel Malone's assistant, Al Mitchell, came round to explain the contract to my mum and dad. There we were in our council flat, and he was talking in terms of thousands and thousands of pounds to be earned by a fourteen-year-old. A bit like young footballers today. One newspaper quoted that I would be earning £52 an hour, a serious fortune. This was based on the fact that the contract was for five years, if the show was a success.

Patiently Al went through the contract. I can't imagine that my parents really understood much of it and signed without question. I had to get a passport, visa and inoculations. That proves how long ago it was – inoculations for America! I was to go to Hollywood for a month to make a pilot episode, then come home and wait to see if the show had been accepted by the networks.

FOUR

HOLLYWOOD

One of my first and most enduring memories of Los Angeles was waking up in the middle of the night and, for a nano-moment, believing I was dead. A bright white cross blazed through my window. It was midnight on 31 December, and everyone on Hollywood Boulevard was blasting their car horns while the huge illuminated cross that overlooks the City of the Angels was perfectly framed in my hotel window.

My chaperone, Rhona, the principal of Corona, and I had been booked into the Hollywood Roosevelt Hotel, right opposite Grauman's Chinese Theatre. In those days Hollywood Boulevard was a slightly tatty tourist attraction. People came from all over the world to look at the stars' names on the sidewalk and their hand- and footprints in the concrete in front of Grauman's. Rhona and I would wander down to the Capitol Building on the crossroad with Vine Street, shopping and reading the pavement, with absolute impunity. Sadly, these days the only people who walk the street are street-walkers, pimps and drug-dealers.

To me, the Hollywood Roosevelt was the height of luxury. Rhona and I spent many hours lounging round the swimming pool ordering Cokes and being wished 'Good day' by everybody. Rhona was always trying to stop me diving, insisting that it would affect my sinuses and ruin my singing voice. I had recently been knocked head over heels by *West Side Story*. Rhona said I'd never be able to sing 'Somewhere' if I kept bashing my head on the water; I argued that I'd just stick to 'Officer Krupky'.

We were picked up every day by a Lincoln Continental, the biggest, most luxurious car I'd ever seen in my life, and driven to Desilu Studios. The English and American families got on instantly. Victor Maddern, who played the English dad, was a veteran of hundreds of black-and-white movies, usually as the bloke who was the lowest rank in any one of the services in those countless post-war war films. The American dad was Eddy Foye Jnr, one of the 'Seven

Little Foyes' (a massively well-known vaudeville family in the US). He was a really lovely, gentle, funny man. The English mother, Diana Chesney, was an extremely eccentric out-of-work middle-aged actress who suddenly found herself starring in a TV series in Hollywood. She even shipped out her 1922 Rolls Royce. The American mum, Audrey Christie, was known mostly as a straight actress with a load of very fine credits. Judy Carne, the English daughter, was an extremely attractive dancer with loads of personality and energy. She took to 'Tinsel Town' like a fish to water, and treated me like my own sisters did. A smashing bird. The US daughter, Lyn Loring, I found strangely attractive, with a mother who was always hovering around the set. The American son was a ginger-haired kid called Flip Mark. Even for a fourteen-year-old he was extremely short. He had already done a number of really quite big movies. He also had an archetypal stage mother, who was even shorter than him. Flip taught me the intricacies of American football, baseball and basketball, but I quite quickly gave up trying to convert any American to soccer. They just couldn't get it.

To me Desilu Studios was the most exciting place in the world. Lucille Ball was not only our boss, but was still filming *I Love Lucy*. *Ben Casey* was being made on the same lot, as was *My Three Sons*, starring Fred McMurray. But by far the most interesting to me was the TV series *The Untouchables*, with Robert Stack. Although we occasionally played ball with *The Three Sons*, there was no real contact between the various companies, but the commissary (American for canteen) was always full of familiar faces, usually dressed in Prohibition garb, and the whole studio lot was littered with Al Capone-type automobiles. Next door was even more exciting to one who had been the fastest draw in Putney. It was where they filmed *Bonanza*.

The pilot of *Fair Exchange* was to take a month to make. A month is a long time in the making of a television show, but more time and care is taken when making a pilot because it then has to be sold to one of the networks. The other reason that our show took such a long time to make was the fact that *Fair Exchange* was the first hour-long comedy ever made for television. That's an awful lot of jokes!

Because of my school term back in England, I arrived a little later than everybody else. Robert Douglas was directing the first show. He had been a film star, generally playing the baddie in numerous swashbuckling epics. They had been rehearsing with a stand-in doing my part and I had the definite feeling that Douglas preferred the other kid to me, even though he had a distinctly American English accent.

We used two sound stages. One was the New York set for the American side of the story and the other was for London. Douglas had no sense of humour at all, but he must have done something right because Desi Arnaz used to pop on to the set and wreck many a take by roaring with laughter.

The pilot was a success. The show was taken by a network. For the actual series I went back to America with my Mum, leaving Myrna and Dad to rattle around the flat in Putney. We were installed in a ground-floor apartment on Rossmore Avenue, right opposite a huge hotel which Mae West apparently owned and lived in. We never saw her. Our apartment block was owned and run by a tiny bird-like woman called Eileen who doted on a repulsive chihuahua. She did her best to teach me to play the piano, but I gave up when it was evident that I wasn't going to learn to play *Take Five* after two months. What a dope.

It was just a short stroll from the flat to the studio. Unlike the pilot, the series involved using two directors working simultaneously on different sets, one filming the London side of the story, the other the New York version. This separation also meant Flip and I had different tutors too. But if we hardly met at work, we did see a lot of each other in our free time, and although totally different, our real-life mothers got on really well. If, for instance, there was a photo session involving us both, his mum would bustle round, making sure he was smiling, that he had loads of different costumes and his hair was perfect. My mum let the photographer and publicity people do whatever they wanted and carried on with her knitting. But that was what endeared us to the crew. No showbiz shit and hand-knitted sweaters for everyone. Although it must be said that we were paid nowhere near as much as the American cast, we were far better off than we would ever have been back home.

The English side of *Fair Exchange* featured what was supposed to be an ordinary London family. However, the producers, writers and set designers had a slightly different view of 'ordinary' family life from ours. This family lived in a mews house overlooking Hyde Park, we had a 1930 Daimler and every time we opened the curtains or went out, it was either pissing with rain or thick with fog. Victor's character was the owner of a sports shop. The only things he was ever seen to sell were croquet sticks, and the occasional cricket bat and ball. His customers were also fairly bizarre. Obviously Hollywood wasn't brimming with Brits in those days. The ones who were there had been there since the thirties and treated it a bit like the new Raj. Every customer Victor served spoke like a pre-war BBC newsreader and either had a handlebar moustache or a full James Robertson Justice with some kind of nautical headwear, but most strangely, a Chinese man in full city gear (with bowler) would often pop in to buy polo sticks. We were always telling them this wasn't exactly typical, if not totally wrong, but they insisted it was always just like that when they had been in England during the war. They thought it was hilarious. It may be the reason that *Fair Exchange* was only ever shown on Anglia Television in Britain. They too probably thought London was just like that.

The English cast socialised together a great deal, and my family and the Madderns, Victor, his wife Joan, and their three daughters, became very close. So too did Judy Carne.

Judy had no end of admirers. There were legends of her entertaining one beau, while another would be hiding in the bathroom, as someone else was knocking at the front door. Eventually, during a publicity junket, she met and fell for an actor whom she would later marry. The actor was called Burt Reynolds. At this phase of his career he was co-starring in a series called *Gunsmoke*. Now, this was, without any question of doubt, my favourite television show bar none. Because Judy and Burt were so nice to me, I used to visit the set quite often. It really was a dream come true. All the 'cowboys' in Dodge City really were cowboys, and they let me play with their guns (props) and taught me how to ride Western style. For a publicity shot, the star of the show, James Arness, let me put on his Stetson and gun belt. Now, James Arness was six foot seven, and I was not the largest fourteen-year-old in the world. The only way I could wear his gun was to hang his gun belt across my shoulder, and his hat virtually covered my whole head. I'd chat with 'Doc' and 'Miss Kitty' and have lunch with the cowboys. A wonderful experience for the 'Clapham Kid'.

Although Judy Carne was out of my league, I was beginning to develop quite an interest in girls. One in particular, called Diane, was very, very pretty although extremely prim and proper. Not so much as a peck on the cheek was allowed, but we had some lovely times. I used to go horseback riding quite a lot in Griffith Park. I had the use of one particular horse called Chester, and I would take him out for a day at a time, chasing coyotes and deer, pretending I was Davy Crockett in my real cowboy boots and hat. All over the park were huts that sold hamburgers and hot-dogs. I'd tie my horse to the hitching rail and imagine I was riding into town and going into the bar. One day Diane came with me. We were enjoying a pleasant hack when suddenly her horse's ears went back and he bolted.

MYRNA: I remember that incident and dangerous it was too. Dennis and Diane were out bareback riding when a lorry driving through the underpass blew its horn. This startled Diane's horse, which took off like the wind. Dennis hurtled after her, caught the reins and pulled her up. He was very big on riding then, really believed he was a cowboy!

After several months, it was decided to fly Myrna out to join us. I never knew how my father reacted to this, but he had always lived somewhat separately from the rest of the household and I guess that no one asked him. Also, at this time, Norma was dancing in Las Vegas, so we saw more of her than we had for years. It was great. Myrna is six years older than me (she'll kill me for that), and we have never, ever had a problem with each other. She was proud of me, because she thought I was rather talented, and I was proud of her, because she was very beautiful and had a great voice. She had been working at Chappell's Music in Bond Street for a legendary song-plugger called Syd Green. They had a magical relationship. It's no secret that if Myrna doesn't get enough sleep at night or can't get into the bathroom exactly when she wants in the morning, she is absolute murder to live with. Poor old Syd might be having quite an important meeting or something and, not surprisingly, would expect his secretary to make the tea or coffee. Not Myrna: 'If you want some tea, you know where the kettle is.' How she didn't get the sack no one knows, but he thought it was hilarious and was heartbroken when she finally left. He promised to keep her job for her when she returned, but she never did.

MYRNA: The Hollywood years were unbelievably exciting. I went over for what was meant to be a three-month holiday with Mummy and Dennis and to see Norma dance at the World Fair in Seattle and never went back.

So there we were, in our little apartment in Hollywood. I suppose it must have taken a bit of pressure off Mum. There was someone else to look after me or cook or do the shopping. It worked a treat. Also, it is virtually impossible to live in LA without a car. Because of everybody's generosity Mum and I had got away with it. There was no way she was going to learn to drive at her age, but Myrna could. I wanted a great big car but I had to settle for the smallest Chevrolet on the market, a Corsair, I think. This made us feel very Californian, but people were amazed that we still walked to the studio.

Mum, Myrna and I were having dinner one night when Eileen came to see us, in a state of great excitement. She had just rented out the apartment upstairs. 'He's just perfect for you, Myrna,' she enthused.

'I bet,' Myrna retorted with her well-known sneer.

'No, no, no, listen. He's tall, dark and handsome and he's got a Corvette.' My ears pricked up. A Corvette was the car that the guys drove in the series *Route 66*. A beautiful machine. 'He's from Indiana where his family have a farm, and, he's from German stock.'

This was supposed to prove that he was a hard worker and very reliable. Myrna wasn't convinced.

JIM STAUBLIN: I was in my early twenties and had not long moved from Indiana to Los Angeles and was living in this apartment on Fossmore near Vine when Dennis came and knocked on my door and invited me down to his place for dinner. My landlady had already mentioned that he had a sister about my age, so I thought, why not?

As soon as I saw Myrna I thought, 'Oh boy, I really wanna date this girl!'

Now, whatever Dennis suggests, I thought Rosie was a very good cook, and for that first dinner she'd made some special potato dish. For weeks I'd been living on McDonald's, with the result that I was having to watch my weight, so regretfully I refused them, but Rosie insisted. 'Come on, have some,' she said. 'They'll keep your pecker up!'

Dennis was already familiar with American slang, and tried to correct her. 'Hey, Mum, you can't say that over here.'

'Why? All I said was keep your pecker up.'

I noticed then, despite his seemingly happy-go-lucky attitude, that he was a very sensitive kid. It really worried him his mother making that mistake, he felt anxious for her. And later, when Myrna gave me a rough time, he'd tell her off: 'Hey, don't be hard on Jim. Give the guy a break. He's a nice guy.' I couldn't get over a little kid showing that much concern. Same today, he's got a really soft side. Comes out in rashes from worrying . . .

The landlady had mentioned that Dennis was doing a series at the studios. I'd never seen the show. It was aired at a time when I was working at the art studio. He was just a very nice young guy and over the year or more he spent out here we became very close. I had an open-top sports car which he loved, and which Rosie and

Myrna enjoyed too. We had a good time. Every weekend we'd go places together, climb the hills, visit the Observatory, Palm Springs, have picnics, or go riding in Griffith Park.

MYRNA: We all enjoyed the freedom over here. Mother especially being away from Father. After all that suppression, she suddenly blossomed.

JIM: Everybody loved Rosie. She was a sweet person, definitely not your average stage mother. She was a mum, a chaperone, she didn't bother anyone and she was a good cook. She reminded me of that character from *The Darling Buds of May*, always ready with something to eat. Everyone used to visit their apartment. Cast and crew, strangers visiting California, people from other shows, all used to gather there for a good English meal, lots of fun.

MYRNA: Burt Reynolds taught us how to play charades. He and Judy Carne were together then. Burt loved Dennis. We'd go over to his place for dinner often. Dennis was very popular, not just because he was a normal, unspoilt kid but because he was very funny, very witty, he really made people laugh. Even at that age he was good company.

JIM: There was a day I suddenly knew Dennis was going to be a star. I'd taken him shopping in Beverly Hills to buy some clothes. I'd parked the car on Rodeo Drive and I was putting money in the meter when I suddenly noticed Jane Powell walking towards us. There she was, this little doll-like figure, so blonde and beautiful . . . just as she was in *Seven Brides for Seven Brothers* when she was swept away by Howard Keel . . . Within minutes there were kids streaming around us, screaming and pointing – not at Jane Powell but at Dennis! Twenty-five or more teenage girls all crowded round him begging for autographs! Jane Powell just opened those huge blue eyes and smiled as she walked by as if to say, here's the next generation taking over.

Despite all the fame and success, Dennis never became flash or pretentious, never put himself on a pedestal. It was a job and a job he did well. The cameramen, grips, everyone would take time to tell him things, to teach him about the technical side of filming. He took a great interest in everything, he was curious and eager to learn. He was the complete professional even then.

Because I was always surrounded by older people, I developed a passable knowledge of current events. I was a fan of JFK, but I hadn't been in America long enough to share their fear and loathing of Communism. Fidel Castro and Che Guevera were to me romantic revolutionaries, freeing Cuba of a corrupt despot, Batista. Khrushchev seemed to me quite human and would probably transform the Stalinist Russia that so terrified most of America. I believed that shared wealth was akin to the Christianity that a large proportion of America espoused so loudly, and I was never able to come to terms with the fact that while quoting the Bible, some people could condone segregation and worse. Having grown up with Britain's welfare state I was amazed to learn that in the richest country in the world, if you couldn't afford medical insurance, you couldn't afford to be sick.

For a while, Flip and I shared the same teacher, named Marjory. She made me aware of how insular Americans can be. Our first history lesson was most interesting. According to her, nothing really happened in the world until 1775, the American War of Independence. When she referred to it as the 'first revolution', I felt obliged to point out to her that in fact, Wat Tyler and John Ball had led something called the Peasants' Revolt about four hundred years earlier. We chatted about revolutions in general, where she sort of glided round that little upheaval in France in 1789. After this conversation, she was insistent that I would waltz into university. All it actually showed was that European education was much broader-based. Similarly, while the *Los Angeles Times* has got to be the biggest paper in the world, packed with adverts, there's no chance of finding any world news in it. I remember trying to find out what was going on at Wimbledon. In those days the Australians were winning everything, so there were about two lines. And it was impossible not to be irritated by America's continuing insistence, not only on screen, that they had won both world wars, all on their own.

For a moment it looked as though they were going to start World War III. Kennedy had made an abortive attempt to invade Cuba at the Bay of Pigs, Khrushchev bashed his shoe on the table at NATO, and Macmillan asked for a translation, but it was no joke to know that Russian ships, presumably with nuclear weapons, were sailing towards the US coast. At first, we (the Watermans) comforted ourselves with the fact that the flotilla was heading for Florida and Florida was the other side of this huge country. However, every fifteen minutes on television a different senator would tell you what was really going on. The Hawks wanted to blow the Russians out of the water; the Doves believed there was still a diplomatic alternative.

What was even more unnerving was that we were unable to buy anything at the local shops. They had been stripped bare by people filling their bomb shelters. They had even bought up all the guns, to stop anyone stealing their supplies. My mother thought the 'Yanks' were just being stupid. She had come through the Blitz unscathed and wasn't afraid of anything. Even so I did not like the idea of that great big mushroom cloud. But Kennedy's brinkmanship prevailed, Khrushchev backed down, the Russian armada turned back to Cuba, and we finished filming *Fair Exchange*. The plan was to hang around in Hollywood to see if there would be another series. This was no big problem. We had a nice apartment, Myrna was engaged to James Staublin, we had money in the bank. I'm not totally certain we were ever planning to go home. It was probably the best holiday I've ever had.

Then one day the phone rang. It was the British Consulate, telling Mum that our visas were out of date, and if we stayed any longer we would be arrested as illegal aliens. So, in a matter of a very few days, we were on our way to LA airport. It was February and raining hard. Myrna was left to go to Indiana to get married, sadly with none of her family around her, and we were flying out of the glamour capital of the world back to a council maisonette in Putney.

FIVE

BACK HOME

My suntan soon wore off. It was actually never much more than hundreds of freckles joined up. I picked up with my old mates, who seemed to have barely noticed that I'd been away. But the place had changed. England had become cool, the place to be. New bands like the Beatles and the Searchers made my Beach Boys and Jan and Dean records sound old-fashioned. It was the era of protest music, I discovered Bob Dylan and began my lifelong love of guitar music.

Going back to Corona as a fifteen-year-old student, especially a student who had been to Hollywood, was a little different from going back to the estate. I still had to do all the training, be on time, but the little kids looked up to me and suddenly the big boys treated me like a big boy. So did the girls.

We ran our own football team and organised games against anybody who could raise eleven players. Our time was taken up with productions, directed either by Rhona or one of the ex-students. I especially remember a very good *Merchant of Venice*. Sadly, very few of the cast, some of whom were terrific, are still in the business. The fall-out rate of aspiring actors is huge. If you fail early enough, at least you have enough time to decide what you are going to do with the rest of your life. In my case, you are totally unprepared for any other sort of career. Presumably I would have had to have found some way of earning a living, but it certainly wouldn't have been in high finance, law or medicine.

Now that we were bigger and tougher, along with our regular theatrical training we were also being taught swordplay and stage fighting, which has probably been more useful to my career than any of the more theatrical skills. Having said that, I have earned a couple of quid with my singing, and people have been amazed at my twinkle toes.

By now, I was hanging out with a group that included Richard O'Sullivan. He had been a star since he was about two months old. He even had a sports car, so, naturally, he had first choice of any of the young ladies. Given all his advantages, there was never once even a hint of any kind of conceit or flashiness. He and Jeremy Bulloch were without doubt the 'Kings of Corona'. Between them, they were just the best at everything. Richard was already almost concert standard on the piano. They could both act, sing and dance the rest of us off the stage, and they both seemed to be able to play any sport they decided (to a seriously high standard). As regards the girls, it was like watching *Take your Pick*. And, to boot, they were both Chelsea supporters.

By now we were going to coffee bars to listen to the latest hits on the jukebox. I had abandoned my old record library of musicals (apart from *West Side Story*) and dived head first into pop, jazz and folk. Basically, anything that parents hated. Actually, apart from the music, I was fairly conservative. My real rebellion was to come a little later in the sixties, like everyone else in the world. I didn't drive my folks crazy with modern music because I could still remember my old man coming home one evening and ripping the plug off the record player while my sisters were jiving to some rock 'n' roll. I couldn't be bothered with the aggravation. Strangely enough he didn't seem to mind my mournful early Dylan imitations. Maybe he liked the idea that at least I was trying to play the little steel string guitar that Norma had bought me.

We were also now occasionally popping into a pub not far from the school, which was run by the parents of the very beautiful Pamela, who I got quite close to, but never quite close enough. Most of our gang were old enough to drink. I definitely wasn't, but nobody ever questioned me, and I took to it like a duck to water. A group of us were in there one evening after one of our shows and we decided that it was about time that Frazer Hines bought a drink, a very rare occurrence. Several of the students used to board at his house, and there were some alarming legends about boarders hunting for food and eventually finding some hidden in the washing machine. I'm sure it has nothing to do with Frazer's family being Scottish; nevertheless, no one in the pub could recall him ever putting his hand in his pocket and we weren't going to be disappointed that night. After some serious piss-taking we were astounded when he took off a shoe and sock and produced a handful of cash. His excuse was that he didn't want it stolen from the dressing room in the theatre. A fair point, but it must have been bloody uncomfortable walking.

We were also getting seriously into parties. Every weekend, if someone's parents were away, that was the cue for a 'Moriarty'. One of these was the location for 'the first time', 'it', 'all the way', 'enlightenment'; it was to become a new and absorbing hobby.

Monica was an ex-student who was teaching a class of the tiny kids. We didn't know each other particularly well, but before a party in Chiswick we came to an arrangement. If I would help her write some school reports, there would be a very fair chance of us ending up in bed together. It seemed a good deal to me. We went along in a big mob. I don't think anybody thought Monica and I were together, probably because we weren't really We were just at the same place at the same time. We danced and drank and fooled around until late into the night. One of the most difficult things to obtain at these do's was any kind of sleeping space. There was a serious pecking order and actual bedrooms were at a premium. Somehow Monica had secured one, and eventually, we retired. A deal is a deal, and out came the report slips. I'm sure we didn't get through all of them. There were over twenty to a class, for God's sake. She was twenty-one, and I was fifteen and a halfish. I can't say whether she knew how young I was, or that it was my first time. She wasn't a virgin and was rather sweet and shy.

Apart from my pride in 'coming of age', I experienced the wonder of waking up with a woman. In future, I would experience sex in a number of different locations at various times of the day, but no matter how much the testosterone was churning around, the thought of the morning after was always just as important to me. This is why I have always tended to prefer living with someone. Perhaps it's because I had five sisters and was a mummy's boy, or maybe I'm just more romantic than I want to admit.

Anyway, I was off and running. All over the place. And I wasn't alone in this quest. Don't get me wrong, we weren't like some rampaging horde of Vikings. We didn't have to be. Although I also met a load of girls who said no. I wouldn't put any money on the fact that this was because they didn't do 'it'. They just didn't want to do it with me.

NORMA: Dennis had girls in his room when he was fifteen! I was at home once on a flying visit. Vera came rushing in to see me, saying, 'Mummy caught Dennis in bed with a girl yesterday.' She was very shocked. Girls found him very attractive, they always have.

I had become friendly at school with a bloke called Rod Goodhall, who was also heavily into guitar playing and really quite good. By that I mean miles better than me. One summer we decided to go on the road. For some reason we wanted to go to Sweden. I think it had something to do with blondes. We started to hitchhike north with the idea of getting a boat to Gothenburg (working our passage, because we certainly didn't have any money). It was freezing cold and nobody was offering any lifts. Change of plan. Back to the south coast. We wandered around Kent and Sussex with our sleeping bags and guitars, busking in the occasional pub or club. It didn't take long to discover that just carrying a guitar was enough to be picked up by women. We didn't even have to take them out of their cases, and more often than not, we didn't have to unroll our sleeping bags either.

In the midst of all this partying I did manage to fit in some work. I did a film for the Film Foundation, who made movies for Saturday-morning shows. I played Jimpy, the leader of the 'good' gang, who were making their own mechanised soapbox in *Go Kart Go*. Frazer Hines was the baddie, and Rod Goodhall played my mate. It was a nightmare. Six o'clock every morning, we would all meet and drive out to Hoddesden in Frazer's sports car (after giving him the petrol money), which he insisted on driving with the hood down. He had all the gear – leather flying jacket and dopey hat; the rest of us froze our bollocks off. We'd get to the location, and the director would try to kill us. I had to drive this mock-up of a go-kart against real go-karts. The steering wheel had to come off in mid-race, so they took out the brake pedal and replaced it with a sort of steering device. I was supposed to manoeuvre the thing with one foot and once I had taken my other foot off the throttle it was supposed to stop. Good theory. Nobody had asked me if I could drive. I couldn't, but if they had, I would have lied. I might have been young, but I was still an actor.

Then there was the falling-in-the-pond joke. A rotten, icy, filthy pond covered with thick green slime. 'This is the scene where you fall backwards into the lake, Dennis,' said Jan Darnley Smith, the director. 'Is it safe?' I enquired. 'Absolutely.'

I was almost impaled on the sharp branch of a submerged tree, and it was a struggle to get back to the stagnant surface. There was nowhere to dry off and warm up. There was even an argument between props and wardrobe about whose towels I could use. So they boiled some water and poured that over me. It has constantly amazed me that the less you earn in this business, the more you have to do. But I was cheered up considerably when Rod wrote off two of the more expensive go-karts.

Less dangerous, and a great deal more enjoyable, was a children's TV serial called *The Barnstormers*. This was about a group of young people who wanted to start their own theatre. A couple of Coronites – Pat Wilson and Peter Hempson – were also in the cast. Pat and I had had a soft spot for each other for several years, but I think she was basically too nice for me at that time. Peter and I became great mates. He had been a very successful child actor. He was extraordinarily intelligent and went on to do very well indeed, but not in showbusiness. He was making more money out of antiques than acting even back when I knew him, and he continued to get more knowledgeable and probably a great deal richer than the rest of us put together. He also had a wicked sense of humour. We used to travel to and from rehearsals in Holborn on the train. He lived in Fulham, which is on the same line as Putney Bridge. One evening, deep into the rush hour, he got out at his stop, and just as the doors were closing shouted back into this mobile sardine tin, 'Dennis?' 'Yeah?' I answered, so of course everyone knew who he was talking to. 'I love you.'

I tried to laugh it off in as butch a manner as I could muster. And I suddenly had acres of space for the rest of my journey.

Peter had a Robin Reliant in which we travelled the country, going from bona fide antique shops and auctions to second-hand stores and jumble sales. We stayed in some very cheap and dubious bed-and-breakfast establishments. There was one place where the food was so disgusting and the owner so weird, we figured it was pointless to complain, so we would stuff our greasy sausages and fatty bacon anywhere we could – in vases, plant pots, even holes in the walls, of which there were plenty. It became a test of our ingenuity. I was going out with a girl called Theresa Clarke at the time – until she suddenly announced I was too young for her. A little while later she took up with Peter. And the three of us would often go out together. None of us had a problem with this. We even went back to her family's place in Esher, where I met her older sister, Lorraine. She wasn't worried about how old I was. She was terrific. We made love all over that nice suburban Surrey house, and in the garden too.

Through Peter I met a bloke called Albert Lampart. He was from the Midlands but retained his parents' Swiss nationality and was in a continual panic about having to go back to do his National Service. Al was always moaning about getting no work, and never having any money. Peter and I would often bankroll him for food, drink or whatever. Some time later I ended up sharing a couple of flats with Al, and was amazed to discover that all the time he was at Corona, his folks were sending him food parcels. He never gave us as much as a teabag.

Another mate, who inadvertently became a catalyst in my life, was Tony Villaroy. We hung around together, had some laughs, pulled a few birds, and had a couple of drinks now and then. I took him back to Putney once, only to have my father suggest that I didn't bring him home again. 'Why not?' I asked. 'Because he's a nigger,' he said.

Mum wasn't around to make the peace, so I packed a few odds and sods, got my guitar, and left. I ended up at Al's truly repulsive flat in Turnham Green. In fairness, it wasn't all his fault. I was the fourth bloke in this large flatshare. Al, Ray, Edwin and me. The other two guys were recent divorcees. The flat belonged to Edwin, whose father, strangely enough, had been my brother Peter's neurologist. I don't think I ever knew what Edwin did for a living, but according to Al, he had been so thick at school, he had to take English classes for foreigners. I had my own, very large bedroom, and we shared a kitchen, bathroom and living room. I am famous for my lack of domesticity, but this place was unbelievable. True Grit! Everywhere.

My mum turned up unexpectedly at the flat one night. Not surprisingly she was appalled at the squalor. Not real squalor, just four blokes living in a very dirty flat. I don't think we ever touched on the subject of why I had left home. There was no need. She knew. I was ashamed I'd left without warning or explanation, but then we weren't the sort of family who talked about anything.

She asked how long I intended to be away and tried to persuade me to come back there and then. I refused. I wanted to stay where I was for a while, although I did promise to visit her. She stayed for tea, then left, but it was obvious just how let down she felt. As much as anything, I think it had to do with that old working-class shame, where fifteen-year-olds don't leave home unless it's for some dreadful reason. Although she'd railed against Stella when she'd left at eighteen, I thought my reason was just. It didn't cross my mind that I was her last baby. I was certain I was old enough to live on my own. After all, I'd been earning money since the age of eleven, I was an actor – and horribly selfish as only teenagers can be.

After saying goodbye to her at Turnham Green station, I felt fairly weepy. And I kept my promise, I did go and see her, and in the long run it didn't do any great damage to our relationship.

Very soon I embarked on my first real love affair. Lesley Dudley was a stunning blonde a couple of years older than me. She had been a Corona babe (babe didn't mean what it does today; it referred strictly to age) and had starred in a very successful film, *John and Julie*. By this time, she had pretty well retired from acting, although for a while she was one of the presenters of *Crackerjack*. She lived with her family in a large house in Chiswick. Her father had a haulage company, and sometimes, when things were tough, I used to work for him delivering stuff all over the country with one of his sons.

Lesley bought me my first grown-up guitar. She also taught me a great deal about what men and women can do together. She was an inexhaustible teacher and I was a fit, avid and attentive student. Somewhere along the way, I had bought myself a bubble car, and we even had some lessons in that. When one day she announced that she was going to America to be an au pair for a while, I was heartbroken – I even wrote a song about her, 'Fly Away Little Bird', which was to be very successful for me. For a while we wrote to each other, but eventually we just sort of drifted out of each other's lives. She had left me well prepared for the future, though.

Now, for the first time, I was having to pay rent. People weren't exactly queuing up to employ me as an actor so I had to do something to get some money. Most actors go through patches like this at one time or another, and it's bloody horrible. I had gone to sign on the dole, which I was entitled to, but I just couldn't stand those repulsive halls filled with desperate people, who I figured were a lot worse off than me. And those idiots behind the windows who couldn't understand that actors had to have the kind of job that would permit them to take time off, at any given time, to go to auditions. 'Oh yes, sir, and what's an audition?' They did get me one good job, however. I was to do a time-and-motion study on the dustmen in and around Chiswick. I had to record how long it took to collect the rubbish from each address on the rota, note travelling time and how long and how many breaks they had.

I turned up with my clipboard and stopwatch. You can imagine how thrilled the dustmen were to see me. Here I was, a long-haired gink sent to spy on them. For a couple of days we did everything by the book. Then we started chatting about various things, like football and women and beer, and and they realised that I wasn't a council quisling, just a bloke who was earning a couple of quid for a couple of weeks. They explained that they could do all the work they needed to, and be in a pub in Brentford by lunchtime. We changed my checklist system considerably. I wrote down whatever they told me to. They still picked up all the garbage, they just did it a lot quicker than the council thought was possible. Brilliant. Nobody suffered, we had a nice long drink, and took the rest of the afternoon off.

The oldest standby for out-of-work actors is cleaning houses. I wouldn't have earned a bean if anyone had seen my flat. But I didn't have any choice. There was one place I really hated doing. An Irish doctor's house in Earls Court. The whole place was covered in lino, which I had to polish. The actual polishing didn't worry me particularly, but what did drive me crackers was the fact that when I had finished, this woman would cover the whole house with newspaper, so nobody would walk on her wonderfully polished floor. What was the point?

Another rotten job was a hand-wash car wash, deep into winter. For some reason we only ever had cold water. After a few minutes you couldn't feel your hands; you also couldn't feel if you'd cut them, which you often did on the bumpers. I didn't last too long there, but it took me weeks to get my hands clean again.

One day I was called for an audition at the Comedy Theatre, where I was surprised to see loads of kids milling about. I was given a script and eventually called on stage. As soon as I started reading, from the blackness of the auditorium a voice shouted out, 'Excuse me, what did you say your name was?' I told them.

'But you're a man!'

'Thank you very much,' I replied.

'But weren't you "Just William"?'

'Well, yeah. A few years ago.'

'Sorry, you're much too old.'

Funnily enough, I felt quite chuffed.

I was even more chuffed at an audition a little later in 1964. It was at the Theatre Royal, Haymarket. The director was Peter Wood; the play was *Carving a Statue*, the writer was Graham Greene and the star was Sir Ralph Richardson. It was a huge part, virtually a duologue with Sir Ralph. All the bright young actors were there, and over a few weeks there was a process of elimination. Because of the size and importance of the role, all sorts of ages were being interviewed, just in case they decided it would be safer to get a slightly older, more experienced guy to act young. Anyway, they chose me.

Ask any actor what is the worst moment on any job, and they will tell you it's the first day. It's not so bad if you're filming, because invariably you get straight to work. Inevitably you feel a bit nervous, but you get to know everybody fairly swiftly and just get on with it.

The first day of rehearsal for a stage play is truly frightening. You know you've got the job, but this feels like yet another audition. Generally, a great deal of coffee and cigarettes are consumed (this was in the days when smoking was allowed). A few people will know each other and chat. If you don't know anybody you just hang around and hope that they know why you're there. The real terror starts when the director's assistant suggests that everyone sits around a large table and you have a read-through. 'Everyone' includes producer, director, set designer (with a beautifully made model of the set), lighting designer, wardrobe master or mistress (sometimes you can't tell the difference), the cast and, most frightening of all, the writer.

So, there I was, sixteen years old, sitting next to Sir Ralph Richardson, opposite Roland Culver, about to start reading one of the biggest parts I'd ever seen. I was petrified. But I was also professional. I got through it. It was the same for everyone; you could feel the tension dissipate. 'Blocking' the piece is where the real rehearsal starts. This means working out with the director where to stand, your exits and entrances, and any problems you may have with the dialogue.

Peter Wood told me years later that there was some sort of conspiracy between Sir Ralph and Graham Greene. They had decided that they didn't want any changes to the script, so whenever Peter suggested even a slight cut, a huge discussion would ensue. Often a huge theological discussion.

PETER WOOD: This was because the star and the writer had completely different ideas.

Graham Greene had written a play about a failed sculptor with the incredible task of trying to create a statue of God of such an enormous size that on stage you could only see up to the knees; the rest vanished into the sky. The sculptor would disappear into the heavens to sculpt while family life continued below. Dennis played the sculptor's motherless son, isolated without love – left to look after himself.

What Graham Greene was trying to do was to write a play about failure. What Ralph Richardson was trying to do was enact a play about a great genius, the greatest genius since Leonardo da Vinci.

There was bound to come a time when the two of them would quarrel.

Ralph always referred to Graham Greene as 'the Poet', with a heavy emphasis on the last syllable. 'What does the Po*et* think? What does the Po*et* mean? I don't understand this play.'

I foolishly tried to solve the prolepsis by saying, 'This is not a complete play. Where is the third act? Where is it? Has the writer written it?' Both the star and the writer went white with terror. One because he didn't want to write it and the other because he didn't want to learn it.

There was a frightful scene late in rehearsals.

In those days the Star would always phone me late at night round about midnight. I had had dinner, done the *Times* crossword when Ralph called. 'Have you by any chance had a copy of the letter the Poet sent to me?'

It ended, 'I had hitherto supposed that the vices of the English theatre lay at the doorstep of the Lord Chamberlain, but I come sadly to the conclusion that they lie at the doorstep of the vanity and stupidity of aged actors like yourself.'

Ralph said to me: 'You do realise I suppose that if the Poet should try to come through the stage door I will have only one recourse.'

'What is that?' I asked.

'To knock him down.'

That's how rehearsals went on, with Ralph still playing genius and Graham saying, 'You must stop him.' It's very hard to stop someone playing genius.

Graham was famously a Catholic convert, and perhaps this was a play about God and Jesus. I can't honestly say I knew one way or the other, I just played the script. But I was surrounded by great intellectual conversations. Needless to say, I just did what I was told. People who have worked with me will testify that I do like input during rehearsals. But during these rehearsals, I don't think I spoke for the first three weeks unless it was in the script. I was out of my depth.

PETER WOOD: Dennis was easy to direct. You couldn't ask for anyone more willing to go along with the director. He was very good like that. Any actor is always at liberty to say 'May I try it another way?' And the director should always allow it and say 'Sorry' if it doesn't work. Dennis was always one of those people who would do that. He'd always have ideas.

Barbara Ferris was also in the cast, along with Jane Birkin, in her first professional job, so I did have some younger people I could relate to. But basically my work was with Sir Ralph. He insisted on calling me 'Quink' (another manufacturer of ink, like Waterman). One day, during rehearsals, he said, 'Quink, I'm taking Peter to my club for lunch. Would you like to join us, old boy?'

'Yes, thank you, sir,' I replied.

His club was White's in Piccadilly. Seriously posh. As we were working, I was dressed in slacks and a round-necked sweater. We were shown to our table by an incredibly fawning maître d'. I excused myself and went to the loo. I was washing my hands when an exceedingly flustered waiter came up to me and asked. 'Are you sitting in the window room?'

'I don't know,' I said, 'but there is a window there.'

'You can't sit in there,' he stuttered 'Not without a tie.'

'A tie?' I said. 'I haven't even got a bleeding shirt on.'

'Then I'm very sorry, sir, you can't dine with us, I'm afraid.'

'But I'm a guest of Sir Ralph.'

'Oh my God,' he groaned. 'Well, would you mind wearing a jacket?'

'Not at all. You get me one, I'll wear it.'

At one time the Incredible Hulk must have been a waiter at White's because this jacket nearly reached the floor when I was standing up. The only way I could eat was to roll the sleeves up several times. Doing this meant that all the striped lining was visible and looked absolutely ridiculous, but it made the maître d' happy and dear old Sir Ralph didn't appear to notice.

After four weeks of very heavy rehearsing we opened in Brighton. This was where the fun really started. On the first night, very high on the actor's fear factor, things went wrong quite quickly. Ralph was making a speech about how he had wanted to keep me small as a child, because he had wanted to do a sculpture of a Madonna and child. The line was 'I wanted to put gin in your milk, but she said gin would give you colic.' He was downstage, and I was behind, also facing the audience. Sir Ralph actually said: 'I wanted to put gin in your milk, but she said gin would give you tonic.' At which point he walked purposefully up to me, and said very audibly, 'I'll never understand this bloody play.'

'Yes, Father,' I said. 'Or do I mean no, Father.' I didn't know what was going on or what I was supposed to do. We ad-libbed for a bit and eventually got back to the script.

Quite hairy for a sixteen-year-old's first night.

The point of opening a play outside London is to fine-tune and make various little changes. Despite the fact that Richardson and Greene had decided there should be no such changes, Peter wanted to tweak a few scenes. He would come into my dressing room before the show and make the odd suggestion – like, don't sit on the beer crate during such and such a line, walk across the stage and sit on the statue's foot. This was no big problem for me, and every couple of nights we'd try a few more changes. No problem at all, except that Sir Ralph would say, in the middle of a scene, 'No, no, old boy, you're supposed to be over there.'

PETER WOOD: Ralph had a terrible tendency to undermine young actors. Was he jealous of them? Of their youth? Did he resent their young manhood when he'd lost his? It was something like that. He certainly didn't fancy them, because that wasn't who he was. With Dennis Ralph was naughty, very badly behaved. He wanted to add the role of genius to his star gallery. He'd never played a great artist, and even if this wasn't the chance, he'd make bloody sure it was. He was himself a very talented artist and drew most beautifully. He was also a man of epic vanity.

He refused to adhere to any of the changes I'd make with Dennis. Instead he kept saying to me, 'What about the boy? What are you going to do about the boy?' Indeed, after we opened at the Haymarket Ralph made it his business to rehearse Dennis behind my back. It must have been extremely unnerving for Dennis as a young actor, when the leading player calls a rehearsal in the absence of the director 'to put the scene right'. By which he doesn't mean 'put the scene right' but 'make it easier for him to play it'.

One slight cock-up, for which I could have got into trouble, happened before our very first matinée. Barbara and I decided to go the cinema, in the certain knowledge that the show was at five. It wasn't. It was four thirty. Strolling over to the stage door at four twenty-five ('the half'), we found RR in full costume and make-up pacing up and down the street. 'Come on, Quink, you're a little late, old boy.'

My understudy was already in my gear and waiting to go on. But after an incredibly quick change, we were off and running, with me somewhat shaky and very embarrassed.

I apologised to everybody and afterwards got a gentle chiding. Then I went to RR's dressing room to explain. 'No problem, old boy,' he said. I was extremely relieved and about to make a quick exit when he said, 'You only drink ale, don't you, Quink?'

'No, sir,' I replied, 'I try most things.'

'Oh good,' he chortled. 'Let's have a gin and tonic.'

Richardson was famous for driving a very powerful motorbike, and it was during this show that his family took out a court order to stop him riding it. He was not a happy knight. But what an extraordinary man. I was leaving the theatre one night, and was intrigued to hear one of the very first, newly invented, car alarms ringing out repeatedly. Outside the stage door, a fascinated Sir Ralph excitedly called out, 'Quick, Quink, come and look!' Whereupon he began bouncing up and down on the parked car, until the alarm was set off once more.

After three weeks in Brighton, we opened at the Theatre Royal in the Haymarket, London. It was big news. Sir Ralph Richardson starring in a new Graham Greene play. But the critics were confused. (They weren't totally alone!) It turned out to be the last thing Greene ever wrote for the theatre. I came out of it OK, but it certainly didn't leapfrog me to stardom.

In the olden days, we used to have one-off plays on TV. It was largely due to these that Britain got the reputation of having the best television in the world. Play of the Week, Play of the Month, Armchair Theatre, wonderful entertainment, covering an infinite amount of subjects and written and directed by some of the most talented people in their field. I had the great good fortune to do many of these during my career. Nowadays when I look through the TV listings it's hard to find anything I want to see. More and more channels and less and less to watch, dreary game shows, chat shows, shows that humiliate the public. Thank God for sport!

But back then, in the good old days of TV, I was offered a part in a play called *I Can Walk Where I Like, Can't I?* It had an amazing cast. Edward Woodward, Yootha Joyce, Judy Geeson and a twenty-two-year-old called John Thaw. It was about a young man (me) leaving the family nest and getting his first job in the building trade. I think today it would be called 'rites of passage'. John played a flash tough guy who was already established in the firm. Even though there was a significant difference in our ages – I was still only sixteen – John was extraordinarily kind to me. We'd often have a drink together; a couple of times we even went boating on the Serpentine, just to kill some time. Now and again we went back to his house, where I met his first wife. For a young actor who was on the verge of cracking it to be bothered with a dopey teenager really is quite unusual, and tells you a great deal about a great man. Just after this, he was to star in his first major TV series, *Red Cap*.

JOHN THAW: I have fond memories of that time. It was a play for H.M. Tennant, the theatre management started by Binkie Beaumont, who were contracted by Lew Grade in the days when they used to do so-called quality drama.

I liked Dennis on sight. He was a cheeky little lad with a great sense of humour. I actually wasn't that much older, but then, as someone said, I was born old. Which is probably why I refer to him as a lad.

Another future star who I worked with around this time was Hywel Bennett. Curiously, he had gone to the same school as my brothers, some years after them, but he told me what a huge hero my brother Peter had been to them all. We played the two major bullies in a TV play, set in a public school. (Yes, I could be posh when I had to.) It was called *Unman, Wittering and Zigo*, by Giles Cooper, and was directed by Donald McWhinney. This was the first time that I was to work with a director who enjoyed the pub more than the cast. The play was a great success and was shown all around the world, winning lots of prizes.

SIX

THE ROYAL COURT

My theatrical education took a dramatic upswing. I was accepted into what was suddenly to become one of the most exciting companies in the country. The Royal Court Theatre in Sloane Square was already famous for its groundbreaking productions under George Devine. Now, William Gaskill was running it as a repertory company, the first in London. Repertory theatres used to be dotted all over the country. They were like finishing schools for actors. Sometimes they did a different play every week (and bloody hard work it was too); sometimes two- or three-weekly. You would get the opportunity to play a whole gamut of parts and characters, different ages, social backgrounds, accents, etc. You might start in stage management, which meant putting up and painting the sets, making the props and of course the tea, also understudying any number of parts. With luck, you would graduate to bigger and better parts. These were the places where a great many of our finer actors and actresses learnt their trade.

With the Royal Court there was no star system, no such thing as a number one dressing room. It was about as democratic as you could get.

Mr Gaskill has a reputation for unusual rehearsal methods. During a spell with the National Theatre he startled Laurence Olivier by making him improvise during rehearsals for *The Recruiting Officer*.

He is keen on limbering people up and getting them to – as he puts it – 'relate to one another's imaginations'. He asks them questions like 'How much do you earn?' – which they have to answer in character. He challenges them to act scenes with chairs.

. . . He uses humour to control the cast.

'How do I get back to the table?' asks one actor, marooned, cup in hand, after a change in movement. 'Take a bus,' says Gaskill.

Mind you, he probably wouldn't have said that to Sir Laurence Olivier.

Charles Greville, *Daily Mail*, 20 October 1965

Being the youngest member of the company, I was surrounded by people who seemed to want to help me. They suggested what I should read, who and what I should watch and, just as important in this particular company, where I should drink. The cast was made up of some of the brightest young talent in the country, and maybe because of the historically leftist leanings of the Royal Court, a greater number of working-class actors than you would normally find in a company at that time. I was cast specifically for the first play, with the knowledge that I would 'play as cast' thereafter.

This first play was going to have a huge effect on British theatre. It would effectively end the Lord Chamberlain's right of censorship. The play was called *Saved*, by Edward Bond.

JILL ARLON: *Saved* was the second play staged by the Royal Court to be refused a licence by the Lord Chamberlain's office. In June of that year, the insistence that three scenes should be cut from John Osborne's *A Patriot for Me* had led to the decision to turn the Court into a club theatre. To see the play you had to pay five shillings for membership to the English Stage Society. Although very tame by today's standards, *A Patriot for Me* was considered extremely controversial.

TIM CARLTON: *A Patriot for Me* by John Osborne was my first play at the Court. It was about the collapse of the Habsburg Empire and homosexuality. The offending scene was the drag ball. As the lights came up and the dialogue began, you realised that what had at first seemed like a romantic masked ball was actually a stage full of men in drag. Ten or twelve of us all in full slap and drag, nothing salacious or obscene going on, simply men in drag.

There were two other scenes that aroused the anger of the Lord Chamberlain, where a character played by Maximillian Schell went to bed with the odd soldier, with their clothes on, all very innocuous. Even so we had the CID sitting out front every night watching for us to make the wrong move. George Devine issued strict instructions that we were not to speak a word to the press, otherwise we would be in danger of being closed down or even thrown into prison. It was great notoriety, we had permanent queues outside waiting for returns, the houses were jam–packed. It was a huge success.

Such was the stupidity writers were up against at that time that during the production of Osborne's *Luther* (the Court, 1961), starring Albert Finney, they famously altered Finney's line 'I swear by the Medici balls that I'll . . .' to 'I swear by the Medici testicles'! The Medici balls of course referred to the balls on the Medici coat of arms, but the Lord Chamberlain's office farcically insisted on 'testicles', which is far more revolting, as well as inaccurate.'

Saved was set in south London and dealt with the desperation and violence that can be found amongst some of the younger members of this sort of community. Barbara Ferris and John Castle headed the cast, as a young couple with a baby, living with her parents. It was a tough and abrasive piece of work, beautifully written, but sometimes brutally realistic. I played one of a group of young guys who were friends of Len (John Castle). They would hang around the park kicking a ball around, talking about girls and football, and the problems of finding a job. We were involved in the scene which was to cause one of the biggest furores in theatrical history. The boys start to take a crude interest in the child in the pram, which has been abandoned for some reason by Barbara and John. They take off the nappy, make jokes about the baby's genitalia, and then someone lobs a stone into the pram which results in the child being stoned to death. Understandably, this outraged many members of the audience. We were heckled, booed and people stormed out of the auditorium shouting about not having fought in the last war to have this sort of thing on an English stage.

JILL ARLON: Such was the uproar, the critics themselves held a public discussion at the Court in which the author and William Gaskill faced a panel of friendly and hostile critics under the chairmanship of Kenneth Tynan, who himself had breached all conventional proprieties by using a four-letter word on Radio 3 the previous evening, the first time ever such an utterance had been heard on public broadcasting.

The Lord Chamberlain's office demanded so many cuts, it was decided with the agreement of the Arts Council and the Court's lessee, Alfred Esdaile, that the only way left to stage it was as a club production, for members of the English Stage Company. However, this was revoked and summons were issued when a member of the Lord Chamberlain's office claimed he had visited the play without being asked for proof of his club membership.

Despite the magistrate finding against the Court, the ESC was fined only £50, and its secretary, Greville Poke, Gaskill and Esdaile were conditionally discharged. It was a moral victory and accelerated the end of the Lord Chamberlain's power over the theatre. Two years later another Bond play, *Early Morning*, with its irreverent appraisal of Queen Victoria, incited the Lord Chamberlain to order a total ban on its performance. This time the Arts Council did not favour a club performance. They did not want to lose what was already in sight, the abolition of censorship. Gaskill was persistent and mounted two Sunday-night performances. The police were a high-profile presence at the first, although no action was taken. Esdaile cancelled the second, and instead, a matinée, in the guise of a critics' dress rehearsal, was performed before a non-paying invited audience. *Early Morning* was the last play banned by the Lord Chamberlain. His authority over the drama ended with the Theatres Act on 28 September 1968.

A huge court case had ensued over *Saved* with the great and the good giving their opinions for both sides. One of our great defenders was Sir Laurence Olivier. The case turned out to be not so much about *Saved* but the protection of all writers from government censorship.

During the legal proceedings, we continued with the repertoire, and over the course of the three years that I was there did such plays as *Shelley*, *The Voysey Inheritance*, *Chaste Maid in Cheapside*, *Sergeant Musgrave's Dance*, *Johnsons Performing Giants*, *Their Very Own and Golden City*, *Ubu Roi*, *Twelfth Night* and *Early Morning*. Marianne Faithful played Queen Victoria, and part of the play was about her relationship with John Brown, suggesting that it was more than servant and mistress. I was very thrilled to learn from Edward that the character I played (Len) had been written specifically for me, a great honour.

Obviously, working together over such a long period, strong friendships were founded. There were no cliques as such, and I don't recall a single row or feud between any of the cast members. Over the years I've always been thrilled to bump into any of them. The quite extraordinary thing about the original company (apart from most of the directors, one actress and Ian McKellen, who joined us quite a bit later) was that it was one hundred per cent heterosexual.

One person to whom I was instantly drawn was Victor Henry, not long out of RADA but considered one of the most mercurial, talented actors of his generation. Before the first season started, we were all called to a meeting, where Gaskill outlined the philosophies and aims of the English Stage Society (our official name). He said at one point, 'I don't care who's fucking who, as long as it doesn't get in the way of the work.' Mentally, I agreed to do my best. He then asked if there were any questions. A long silence ensued. Then Victor put up his hand and enquired if there was any chance of getting a moving pavement between the stage door and the King's Head (the pub next door) as the fifty-yard walk was making him tired. We retired to said public house and the 'dynamic duo' was off and running. We would soon become 'the terrible trio' with the arrival of Timothy Carlton.

TIM CARLTON: I remember vividly seeing Dennis for the first time. No one had introduced us and I hadn't the faintest idea who he was, but I remember seeing him at rehearsals and thinking, 'What is this very young, terribly good-looking guy doing here?' He had a guitar case seemingly glued to his side and was sitting there looking decidedly unimpressed by our efforts as we rehearsed.

It took me some time to get to know him because we were involved in different projects. Dennis had taken up with wonderful, fiery, mad Victor Henry. They shared the same wit and certainly the same appetite for alcohol. Dennis may have been only sixteen, but he was always ahead of his time.

I was doing *Saved*, Victor, *When Did You Last See Your Father?* and Tim, who was seriously posh, was in *The Voysey Inheritance*, so the three of us didn't actually work together until much later. Victor and I just assumed that Tim was a stuck-up poof, until we noticed that whenever he was in the pub he was generally in the company of a very good-looking woman. Then we noticed that there were loads of them, hanging on his every word. On one of the few occasions that he was drinking solo we thought we'd better make ourselves known to him.

Tragically, our relationship with Victor wasn't to last. Sometime after the original company dispersed, he was involved in an extraordinary traffic accident. A vehicle out of control hit a lamppost which in turn fell on Victor. He was in a coma for something like eight years before he died. I would hazard a guess that no one who knew Victor would be surprised by him dying prematurely. I would also suggest that he himself would have put money on it, given his propensity for self-destruction. But to lose him in such a mundane, stupid manner was heartbreaking. The British theatre lost one of its brightest prospects, and Tim and I lost one of the greatest friends we would ever have.

We were an odd trio: Tim, a typical handsome product of public school – tall, willowy, suave and sophisticated; Victor – a short, thickly bespectacled, aggressively working-class Yorkshireman; and me – a long-haired, mid-teenage, guitar-playing ex child star from Clapham. We must have been a complete pain in the arse for some of the more upright members of the company, but in compliance with Gaskill's wishes, our endless endeavour for a good time didn't ever get in the way of our work.

The three of us once were having a quiet post-show beer in the King's Head, causing no trouble whatsoever. A group of fit-looking, twenty-something guys were leaving the pub, and as they passed us, one of them came over to me and called me 'a long-haired cunt'. None of us knew what had provoked this insult and we weren't too bothered either. When we left and were saying goodnight, I was standing on the kerb with my back to the road. A car drove by, and as it did, a hand snaked out of one of the windows, grabbed my arm and I was dragged halfway round Sloane Square. Luckily, I was unhurt but rather shaken. Somebody in our group had the sense to get the number of the car. The theatre said they would investigate, and got in touch with the police. It turned out that the car was registered to the MOD and there was nothing anyone could do. Revolutionary theatre isn't necessarily popular in a democracy.

Having moved from Chiswick, I ended up sharing a flat in the Brompton Road. This was very handy, insofar as it was just round the corner from the Webber Douglas Drama School. Which meant we were always in grabbing distance of a multitude of aspiring young actresses. Apparently one of these was called Rula Lenska, but we were not to meet until sometime later . . .

I was only earning about eight quid a week at the Royal Court. My outgoings at the pub were twice that. I could not keep my head above water. I moved back to the family nest in Putney. But I often ended up in a small flat off the Fulham Road, belonging to Victor and his wife Rosemary. Tim had a much better set-up. He shared a place with an old school friend from Sherbourne, whose family owned the *News of the World*. The house was just off the King's Road, very handy and rather grand with a very comfortable bedroom to crash in.

This was the beginning of the swinging sixties. The King's Road was basically the centre of the fashionable and permissive universe. I started working there at sixteen and a half, which coincided with the invention of the mini-skirt and the Pill. It was heaven.

Being able to play the guitar (however badly) was also a bit of a bonus, for women and for earning an extra couple of quid. The Court was very good to us. In the shows that we weren't actually in, we were required to understudy. In most companies, it was normal practice to keep you at the theatre until the final curtain. With us, as soon as the full cast was assembled and the curtain was up, we were allowed to go, which was very handy for me. One of the other 'gang members' in *Saved* was Johnny Ball, who also played guitar. On his nights off, Johnny played in a restaurant in Beauchamp Place called Borsht and Tears, and he suggested I go down with him and see if there was any chance of me getting a slot. We played together and separately down there for several years. Not only did they pay quite well, but there was free food and drink, tips and waitresses.

In 1966, the Royal Court did a production of *Ubu Roi*. I wasn't in the play but it had a huge cast which brought in a large injection of new actors, including Nigel Hawthorne, Jean Boht and someone who would become and remain a 'best' friend. Robert Powell had been to Manchester Grammar School, where he had studied, among other things, ancient Greek and law. On the face of it, these academic skills didn't make him a natural playmate for me. Robert had just come down from a great repertory company in Stoke. He had a small part in *Ubu* and was also understudying something like fifty-three parts. It was a very strange play. I met him when he was wandering round the theatre, not quite knowing who was who or where he should go. I suggested that the best way to meet everybody was to come with me to the pub. We've been doing that ever since.

ROBERT POWELL: I was twenty-two and understudying, he was eighteen and a pukka member of the company. Lunch was a pint of beer in the King's Arms and that was where our paths crossed. We became instant mates. An odd combination – me, the northern Salford lad, he, the south London boy – with ostensibly little in common, except we both adored football and it was the year of the World Cup!

Bob had a flat on Highgate Fields and our joint football career started by my going over there every few days for a kickabout. I'm not sure if he ever realised it, but from Putney to Highgate by bus took bleeding hours, added to the fact that I hate north London. (As do most south Londoners).

ROBERT POWELL: Den would arrive on the number 9 bus, we'd drop into the pub for a drink before football, then stagger out on to the fields frequently to get beaten by the local kids. Dennis was quite worldly-wise at the time; I was more strait-laced, which is not to say he led me astray, I'd just led a quieter life. But the lost weekends started with Den. We couldn't remember where we had been on Saturday night when we finally reached Sunday evening. There again, it was the sixties.

This was an extraordinary period for British theatre, with people like Richard Harris, Peter O'Toole, Richard Burton, Nicol Williamson and Anthony Hopkins. All of them considered brilliant at their craft, and also in the very top echelon when it came to raising hell. Huge drinkers to a man. In those halcyon days, alcohol was part and parcel of being an actor. I am that old cliché, a social drinker, although admittedly on occasion I have been a little too social. I have never been a solitary drinker and find it impossible to go into a pub or any drinking establishment if I'm not absolutely certain that there is someone there I know. For many years it didn't occur to me to even have a drink at home. Just for the record, before every film or TV series one has to have a medical for insurance, also for various mortgages and personal life policies. I've had very extensive examinations, which have only confirmed a sound constitution. The defence rests!

The play at the Court which was to have the biggest effect on my career was *Twelfth Night*, directed by Jane Howell. Patrick Proctor designed it and the costumes were made by Michael Fish. It was very King's Road. Both Proctor and Fish were very groovy at that time, the former being a very successful artist and the latter one of the most innovative bespoke tailors in town. Because of those two, we got a great deal of free publicity. The cast included Malcolm McDowell, Patrick Mower, Nerys Hughes and Jack Shepherd. I played one of the most thankless parts Shakespeare ever wrote, Fabian, a very unfunny apprentice to Feste. I played it like an Elizabethan gun-slinger. Whenever Aguecheek or Belch insulted me, I'd draw my sword and threaten them. I have to say, in all conceit, that it was one of the rare Fabians ever to get a mention, let alone a good review. But it wasn't the performance which furthered my career. It was Jane Howell. She came in one day and told me to phone a friend of hers who was casting a TV play that he had written. I duly phoned a Mr Douglas Livingstone. He told me that ATV were doing this ninety-minute play, which had a very big part for a young man of my age, and Jane had suggested we meet. 'Yeah, why not?' I said. 'It's a job, isn't it?' Doug told me later that he nearly hung up there and then.

It was a huge part; probably the biggest part ever written for a seventeen-year-old on television. I went to read for Doug and Alistair Reid, the director, and got the job. It was to be shot a few months later. In the mean time, I was to finish *Twelfth Night* and do another TV play for ATV. It was called *The Decorator* (me), with a very young and extremely sexy Georgina Hale, and James Beck, who went on to find fame and fortune in *Dad's Army*. It was an early piece by Richard Harris (the writer, not the actor), who was to become very successful with such plays as *Outside Edge* and *Stepping Out*.

It was a nice little sixty-minuter about a decorator working in a house with only the teenage daughter of the owner in charge, and the foreman getting in their way. On the face of it, not a very extraordinary piece, but it was the manner in which it was made that sticks in my mind.

We rehearsed for about four weeks and went into the studios to tape the play for two days. After about ten or twelve days of rehearsals, the director dropped out, and Dennis Vance was brought in to finish it. Dennis was legendary in television, first as a major innovator and secondly as probably the biggest drinker in England. We were rehearsing in the DeWalden Rooms in St John's Wood, a few yards away from the Star Tavern. The play was very near to being set, which is to say, the actors' moves, entrances and exits had all been worked out, so the hard director's work largely had been done. The first few days with Dennis were fairly normal, while he found his feet. Then the lunch hour started to get earlier and earlier and longer and longer. Eventually he started to get his mates to join us for 'a bevvy'. Now these weren't just any old mates. We're talking about the likes of Patrick Wymark and John Gregson, famous for their alcohol consumption; Jimmy Beck too wasn't backwards when it came to buying a large one. Georgina was not impressed. She'd been brought up in a pub and seen enough drunks from a very tender age. She was even less impressed when we started to come back after a liquid lunch and Dennis would suggest that his guests should try their hand at directing. It was bizarre. Every afternoon someone else would be telling us what we should be doing. In one scene, Jimmy had to pour us some tea and I was amazed to discover that the teapot was full of whisky.

Then it was on almost immediately to *Cry Baby Bunting*, Doug Livingstone's play. Set mostly in a prison cell, with my character (whose name I can't remember) talking himself through his life, with flashbacks to illustrate what had happened. The flashbacks were shorter than the cell scenes, so basically I was talking for the entire ninety minutes. The man was in the cell because he had killed his own baby. He had been seduced by his girlfriend, she became pregnant and they were forced to get married. He was blissfully happy with this, a caring, albeit too young husband, doting father, but he had to work all hours to pay for everything. He became a totally responsible, reliable young husband. This eventually made him boring to his young wife, who wanted more fun in her life, started going out and inevitably met someone. He was quite content for her to have a good time if it made her happy, but when she said she was leaving, he snapped. And in a last desperate attempt to keep her, he smothered his beloved child, in the deluded dream that this was what she wanted so they could spend more time together. The chance of playing such a complex and emotional role at the age of eighteen is very rare. It was a highlight of my burgeoning career.

It was about this time that I met Barry Krost, a hot young agent. He let it be known, having seen me on stage, that he would like to represent me. Hazel Malone, who had looked after my career since I was eleven, was probably best known for representing child actors. I decided I needed an agent who knew what was happening in the adult world of theatre and the new wave of films, including the ones that were being made in Swinging London. I girded my loins, and went to see Hazel, to tell her I thought it was time for me to move on. She wasn't best pleased. But I went to Krost Associates anyway, and instantly stopped being considered a child actor.

TIM CARLTON: Dennis had played relatively small roles at the Royal Court and I hadn't realised just how good he was as an actor. Seeing him in *Cry Baby Bunting* was a revelation to me. The different perspective of the small screen opened my eyes as to just what a great talent he had.

I remember one day around this time dropping in with Dennis to see his parents in Putney. Work at that time had not been too forthcoming and I expect we'd been moaning about it as usual. His father, who had been listening behind his paper, huffed a bit, then said to Dennis, 'Well there you are, see, Dennis, if you learned to speak proper like Tim, you'd get on in the acting job better.' A week later Dennis signed a contract for *Up the Junction* something for which I was hardly a contender.

Obviously I don't think his father realised what Dennis had got.

It was the era of the working-class kitchen-sink drama, the sudden starring of the anti-hero, and Dennis was perfect casting.

The successful screening of *Cry Baby Bunting* led to my being invited to do a screen test for the male lead in *Up the Junction*. I remember doing the scenes with a young lady, but I don't remember if she was testing as well or just employed to act with whoever was being tested. Peter Collinson was the director and Arthur Lavis was the head of photography. Both made me as relaxed as I could be under the circumstances. I did two or three scenes from various angles. After what was a very nerve-racking day, I was told that was it, followed by the inevitable 'We'll let you know.' As I was leaving, Arthur said, 'You've got it as far as I'm concerned.'

This was great for my ego at the time, but a nightmare for the endless waiting period. Every phone call was make or break from then on. Barry Krost eventually called me with the news that negotiations were in progress, the contract would be on its way shortly and filming would start on such-and-such a date. I'd cracked it. My first starring role in a big, grown-up movie. I was nineteen.

Sometime around this period I met Michael Bill. He was the assistant lighting designer at the Court. He had a large flat in Hammersmith and invited me to share it with him. He had been to a drama college called Rose Bruford and knew several ex-students who were sharing a flat down the road. One of them was Penny Dixon. She was a lovely, very straight, un-theatrical woman, who, according to my father, bore a strong resemblance to Dorothy Lamour. We kind of just drifted into a relationship because we got on so easily, and eventually we ended up living together, with Mike, at Hammersmith Grove.

PENNY: It was 1967. We met at the BBC club. Dennis had just finished the 'live' performance of a television play called *The Gun* and along with the rest of the cast was soothing his shattered nerves with a few large ones at the bar. Mike introduced us. *Cry Baby Bunting* had recently been shown and caused quite a stir. However I'd been away in rep in Chesterfield and missed it. Consequently I had no idea who Dennis was, but there was instant rapport, so much so that two or three weeks later I moved in with him. It wasn't his looks that attracted me, although he was good-looking. Dennis was just great fun, with a great sense of humour. He made me laugh and he was kind, very kind, most of the time . . .

It was while I was doing *The Gun* that I met a Scottish actor called Paul Young who played one of the squaddies. We got on immediately during rehearsals, and, when I found out he was staying in a dodgy hotel in Earls Court, I invited him to come and stay with Penny and me. This was the start of a lifelong friendship. Whenever he worked in London he was our guest, and whenever I was anywhere near Glasgow, I would do my best to finish his very fine wine collection. He had been a child actor (starring hilariously as 'the young Geordie' in the film *Geordie*). His mother, Freddie, was a successful agent in Glasgow, his father John was a well-known actor, and all Paul really cared about was fishing. Which he turned to his professional advantage, making films and documentaries about his hobby, all round the world. Paul is still a very fine and busy actor, but the greasepaint often gets in the way of the lure of the rod. I remember saying to him, 'Why don't you get an agent down here? You can stay with us until you get yourself sorted out.' And he would say, 'Are there any salmon in the Thames?'

> PAUL YOUNG: I was there the night Dennis met his first wife, Penny. He once commented that I've been to more of his weddings then he has.
> I was a real 'country cousin'. I only came down from Scotland when I had a job. I slept behind the couch in the front room. I'd put on my pyjamas, say, 'Goodnight lads' and drift off. There'd be Richard O'Sullivan, Tim Carlton, Geoff Hughes, Bob Powell, etc. Den would play guitar, they'd sing, carouse, have fights and I'd sleep through it all.

I had been working a great deal and decided it was time to buy a car. I found the one I wanted and went to the bank to get the money for it. I was told that I didn't have enough. That can't be right, I insisted, and asked to see the cheque stubs. About £500 worth of cheques had been signed by someone other than me. In those days that was a lot of money. I claimed that the bank should reimburse me, because they were at fault. The signature was nothing like mine. They said they could do nothing without a criminal conviction. Life at the flat had been particularly relaxed; we left money and chequebooks and stuff all over the kitchen table.

> TIM CARLTON: I'd started finding that my wage packet that I'd only had the day before was light!
> And I couldn't remember spending a penny. It happened

several times. More seriously, someone had emptied Den's bank account. It caused us a lot of heart-searching; we knew we would have to shop whoever it was. I knew I'd never get anything back, it was cash that had disappeared and there was no proof. Luckily I had no financial problems, but whoever it was had drained Den dry.

The police were called in, and it became apparent that it was Michael. What was doubly hurtful, shortly before this happened, Paul and I had spent a lot of money buying him a watch for his birthday. Mike went missing and eventually was arrested in Ireland and I did get my money back. But it wasn't the money. We were friends, we trusted one another. If Mike had financial problems we would definitely have helped him, but just to steal it upset me a great deal. What was also upsetting was that several people at the Royal Court seemed to think that I had done something wrong by bringing in the police. What else could I do? I was virtually skint.

PENNY: It destroyed Dennis having to go to the police but he had to do it. Mike had not only forged cheques, he'd written to the bank in Dennis's name which was why the bank honoured them.

   Dennis was absolutely broken, a friend had let him down. He'd never had that. Friends don't do that to Dennis. If you're friends with Den you're friends because you love him. And for Mike to do that . . . It wasn't the money, the financial thing, it was the act of disloyalty. He couldn't cope with that. I can still remember him crying his eyes out over it.

Before we started filming Nell Dunn's *Up the Junction* we rehearsed for a few days in a house in Barnes. We didn't exactly rehearse, but we did get to know each other a bit, which helped alleviate the nerves and shyness which occur during the first few days of any shoot. So I met Adrienne Posta, Maureen Lipman and the delicious Suzy Kendall, who was my leading lady.

   Ada (Adrienne) and I had met on various occasions. Like me, she had started acting at a very young age, and had also made a couple of records. Maureen was fresh from RADA and even then incredibly funny and talented too. The two of them were cast as cockney sisters who befriend a girl from Chelsea who they meet while working in the same factory. Suzy was the Chelsea girl, with whom my character has an affair. She was exquisite. For some absurd reason it always astonishes me when beautiful women are nice. Suzy was astonishingly nice.

I didn't know much about her, although I had been told she was a top model. Her eyes were the first thing I noticed. They were extraordinarily gentle, smiling eyes. During one of the coffee breaks she came up to me and said, 'Dennis, I haven't done much acting. You will help me, won't you?' Are you kidding? I would have helped her rob the Bank of England. It was instant attraction.

Up the Junction had been a huge success as a TV play. It was a tough, gritty piece of social comment about a community in Battersea. Because of the transfer to the big screen, and probably because of the American backing, the writing seemed to have softened. There again, Nell Dunn hadn't written this screenplay. I suggested to Peter that perhaps it would 'harden up', be more realistic, if it was shot in black and white, but it was considered that would have a detrimental affect on sales. Also, this was big, brash, colourful, swinging London. Not quite the spirit of the original.

Peter Collinson got me to have my hair lightened a little and cut in a more trendy fashion, somewhat like his. In the end I looked like his baby brother. He had been brought up in a Dr Barnardos' home in Brixton, one of whose patrons was Noël Coward, who, apparently, had been an inspirational figure to Peter. Having said that, I must point out that Peter loved women.

According to Arthur Lavis, Peter saw in me a working-class actor from just down the road in Clapham, a kindred spirit. It also didn't hurt that my father was a ticket collector at Clapham Junction. I hope he thought I could act a little too.

During rehearsals, Peter would take us both out to lunch in his Roller, and we felt like real film stars. It was exciting, romantic, and an affair was inevitable.

Suzy was, without doubt, the most attractive woman I had ever met. Unfortunately, she was going out with Dudley Moore at the time, and I was quite happy with Penny, but we were playing lovers in the movie, and it was a case of life imitating art. We met up all over the place, sometimes even risking the flat she shared with Dudley. We never misbehaved at their home, but we did drop in after a night shoot sometimes, or rendezvoused there, ready to be picked up for work.

I recall one afternoon I had the effrontery to be playing Dudley's piano when he walked in. I was so shocked, I leapt up and smashed a wineglass. We'd hardly been caught in flagrante, but the surprise of meeting the famous man face to face, and the guilt at being caught at his piano, was almost as bad. I don't think Dudley suspected anything was going on between us. At that time, he was the hottest thing in London, hugely talented and attractive. Why should he fear a callow youth who just happened to be working with his bird?

Now I find it incomprehensible that Suzy and I didn't stay together. Neither of us was married, and we both agreed it was possible, but I think I was a little out of my depth.

The post-production of *Up the Junction* was done at Twickenham Studios. Shortly after I finished the movie, Penny and I moved into a flat just around the corner from the studios. Guaranteeing that I would never work there again. Which, until *Minder on the Orient Express*, hundreds of years later, I didn't.

PENNY: *Junction* was the beginning of the ladies. I think! And Den's life has always been ladies, and his downfall.

I was aware of his affair with Suzy Kendall from the start. What is strange and hard for people to understand is that I put up with it. Maybe it was because I was young or because I knew Dennis never thought of it as serious, whatever, he always came home and back to me. I remember him phoning me from Worthing, and I said, 'What's happening? Are you with Suzy?' He always admitted he was, because he knew I'd always accept it.

Some affairs were more serious, like the girl in Argentina and Romy Schneider. Suzy flattered his ego. He was nineteen, and she was a sixties icon living with Dudley Moore. Plus he was egged on by that awful man who directed the film. I never liked Peter Collinson.

Tim Carlton once said to me that Dennis was totally amoral. That these affairs simply didn't signify. It mattered of course when he was older and had children, but with us, it just depended who he was working with. He was a hopeless romantic. I hope he still is. He wanted everything to be lovely, calm, no waves. I was ideal, I'd say 'OK, darling, as long as you come home.' And there I'd be, always there, waiting, ready to forgive.

I didn't work. Dennis didn't want me to work. We were fine financially, although for my own salvation I did do some part-time teaching at Webber Douglas. But Dennis wanted me home for no other reason than he got lonely when he was out of work and he did not like being at home alone, particularly during the day when all his mates were working and there was no one to go with him to the pub or to play football. I knew nothing about football, so to compensate I had to have football tests. Dennis would sit me down and question me: 'Who plays centre for Chelsea?' 'When did Osgood last score?' 'Who plays left back for Tottenham?'

I became very knowledgeable.

Most of an actor's life is spent waiting. Waiting for a job, waiting for a decision about a job, waiting for details when you've got the job, waiting around on the set when you're doing the job and waiting for your money. At this stage in my career the worst wait was for *Up the Junction* to be released. It took several months. It is murder to be, for instance, a guest in an episode of a TV series during this kind of period. Everybody is swanning around the star and you're thinking, 'This is dopey. I've just finished a huge international movie and they're all worried about that pillock getting a warmer cup of tea.' Then you let it drop quietly that you've just done the film version of *Up the Junction*. 'Oh, really, were you in the television version?' 'No.' 'What a shame, that was so good. And wasn't everybody in *that* marvellous?'

In those days, television, except for high-profile, heavy drama, was just something you did to earn a few bob. You actually worried about good actors who accepted a series, because it was possible to ruin a career. 'My God, what's he doing in that? Times must be very hard.' Soaps were out of the question. They were always filled with unknowns, not necessarily bad actors, but there was a strong possibility that if they had the courage to eventually leave, the chances of them getting anything decent were slim. A lot of careers were lost because of this rather élitist attitude. Theatre and film were acceptable, no matter how bad. How times have changed!! Now the big stars are in the soaps, also no matter how bad, and, luckily for me, having a series of your own is considered a success.

Eventually I got an invitation to the premiere. A lot of movies are just released, but you know it's serious if there's a premiere. I had visions of a big black-tie event in Leicester Square, the heart of film- and theatreland. I was a little shaken to find it was to be held at the Granada, Clapham Junction. It was perfectly logical and very good publicity, because this was the Junction of the title, but this had been one of my local cinemas, and was not at all special to me. As things turned out, it was a very glittering event. When the lights went down, the curtains opened to reveal a huge screen, Manfred Mann's soundtrack started, and in massive letters it said: 'Starring Dennis Waterman and Suzy Kendall.' I was gobsmacked. I'm a star! I'm a star!

In the run-up to the premiere, the publicity department had

arranged all sorts of competitions and promotions in the local papers, so that people from 'the Junction' would have the first chance of seeing the film. Most of the stalls were filled with locals, a lot of whom were young men. One of my big scenes was when Suzy and I finally get together. I take her to my old house, which has been partly demolished. There are bits and pieces of furniture still around, including a bed. This was the big romantic moment. The scene finishes with a big close-up of me saying, 'Do me a favour, seduce me.' I'd been told it was a wonderfully sensitive moment. The blokes downstairs didn't agree. That last line was greeted with howls of 'You wanker!'

The venue chosen for the premiere party was the Thomas à Becket pub in the Old Kent Road. I knew the pub well, because my brother Peter had trained in the upstairs gym. Again, I'd been looking forward to a flash West End do, but at least it was a star-studded event and not everyone agreed with the local critics. However, the atmosphere was a bit hampered by one of the celebrity guests. Lyndon Johnson was then the President of the United States, and for whatever reason, his daughter, Lindabird Johnson, was one of the guests of honour. This was all very prestigious, but it meant the place was bristling with very big men with very short hair and big bulges under their left armpit. Every time you so much as went to the loo, you were accosted by one of them, officiously demanding to know who you were and where you were going.

As luck would have it, the American money that had financed most of the swinging London films suddenly dried up. The producers and money men decided they couldn't work with our unions or taxman any more, upped sticks, went back to Hollywood and effectively shut down the British film industry.

It was at this point that I was invited back to the Royal Court to do Edward Bond's controversial *Early Morning* in the role of Len, the character, I was thrilled to learn, he had written specifically for me, but which consisted largely of being beaten and kicked around the stage by 'Mad' Jack Shepherd. Now the essence of stage violence is that you must be in control of yourself and be certain of what you're both doing. This was not Jack's natural way of working. But we rehearsed and rehearsed and I taught him everything that I had learnt about stage fighting and we finished up with a frighteningly realistic and vicious scene, without either of us suffering any injury in the process.

During the first week of rehearsal, Paramount Pictures got on to my agent, and told him that they wanted me to go with them to

Argentina, where *Up the Junction* had been entered in the Mar del Plata Film Festival. Amazingly, because we had something like five weeks' rehearsals, Bill Gaskill agreed to release me for a week. Everyone who was going had to attend meetings about protocol. A few years earlier Britain had blamed the Argentinians for an epidemic of sickness allegedly caused by Fray Bentos corned beef. Then in 1966, Rattin, the captain of the Argentinian football team, had been sent off to cries of 'Animal!' from the English press. We were told that although we had very close links with Argentina, and a lot of the larger landowners had British names and acted more English than the English, we should watch our step. I was even more concerned when George Brown (one of the producers of *Up the Junction*, who had a very beautiful Argentinian wife) suggested extreme care should be taken when approaching unaccompanied young women, as stabbings were not unusual. Charming, I thought.

We flew from Heathrow on Aerolinias Argentina. I was with Peter Collinson and Mr and Mrs Brown. As soon as we arrived, Peter changed into a kaftan, which was still quite fashionable in London. We were instantly surrounded by photographers and got lots of press. Peter looked almost Biblical, with his long blond hair and beard, but his 'frock' confused some people, and in every picture I was right by his side.

Mar del Plata is a resort, built by Perón, which boasts the biggest casino in the world. Although the weather was roasting, the Atlantic Ocean was freezing. However, I wasn't there for the swimming. It was an endless round of God knows how many cocktail parties, and the women were fantastic. But I followed protocol. For a while. After a couple of days of partying, I was invited out by the Brazilian delegation and was sort of adopted. Because Bob Dylan had been banned in most of South America, they kept asking me to play guitar for them and sing some of his songs, so I did my best nasal imitations and in return they played me the bossa nova. They were a great crowd and I found myself very drawn to an actress called Joanna Fomm, a tiny mulatto lady from Rio. Delicious. She said at one point that when she had seen pictures of our arrival in the papers, she'd assumed I was Peter's boyfriend. She soon knew better. It wasn't until we were getting rather heated one night in bed that I realised her long black hair was a wig. Anyway, with or without her wig, she was stunning.

The Browns took us one afternoon for a barbecue at this very posh ranch owned by old friends of theirs called Phillips, who looked terribly pukka until you heard their very un-British Spanish accents.

We were lounging around the pool when their very smooth son and heir turned up astride a snorting, highly strung black thoroughbred. He gracefully dismounted and made a beeline for Joanna. After a few g and t's and canapés, he asked her if she would like a ride on Black Beauty. She was a good rider and soon had the horse gently trotting and cantering around the pool area. She then suggested that I have a go. I declined but she insisted, 'Go on, Whitey' – her nickname for me – 'he's wonderful.' And everyone else joined in with 'Go on, Whitey!' On the whole, I preferred old hacks that would rather eat than run. I had a deep suspicion of any horse that was well bred.

We got on quite well for a couple of minutes, but the more confident I became the more fed up Dobbin got. I saw his ears start to flatten until they were hidden under his mane. 'Oh oh,' I thought, and he was off, with me hanging on for dear life. The pool area disappeared in seconds and I was doing one of the quickest tours of the pampas on record. The ranch extended for thousands of acres, and we were galloping towards a fence when a thought struck me: 'Time to go back for another drink.' So I bailed out. Because of my stage fighting and tumbling training I just jumped off, rolled and got up totally unharmed, except for a gaping wound to my pride. It was a long walk back to the party, and sheepishly I explained what had happened. Joanna thought it was hilarious, the Browns were quite worried about me and our hosts were deeply upset and concerned. About the horse! Perhaps they really were British after all.

The festival wasn't exactly overloaded with big names, but I did have the pleasure of meeting Jacques Tati. Jacques was as charming as he was funny. Tall and elegant, he had the air of a slightly bemused diplomat. Gracious but perplexed. I had the pleasure of sharing a table with him at various functions, and although he spoke little English and I almost no French, I enjoyed his company.

Alexander (Sandy) Mackendrick was there, as a judge, and I also had several cocktails with Troy Donahue, one of the first male sex symbols of film and television. Although at that time Troy was a bit past his brief peak, the blue-eyed hunk of former years was still very much in evidence, and ready to enjoy himself to the hilt. The women flocked round him in adoration, and I got the impression he was going to make as many as possible very glad they'd met him . . . He had been invited because he was still being watched on TV in Argentina. The Paramount publicity guy was an old friend of his, and always tried to get him on these jaunts. He told me, with a huge guffaw, that on Troy's publicity blurb, he was claiming to be twelve years younger than he had been at a festival four years earlier. He looked super and had a great time. Good on yer.

My time off from rehearsals was quickly running out when a rumour started to circulate that I was one of the front-runners for the Best Actor award. Paramount didn't have to go down on their knees to get me to stay on for an extra week. The other guy in the running was Tony Mussante, a New York actor who was there with his wife. They often stayed with Penny and me, back in London. He was one of the leads in a low-budget American movie called *Subway* or *Underground* or something, set in a train carriage, where he terrified a young soldier played by Beau Bridges. He must also have terrified the judges, because they gave him the award and I just got the air ticket home.

Joanna and I didn't even consider exchanging addresses. We knew what had happened and who we were. She lived in Rio, I lived in Twickenham. We had had a fantastic time, but we both had another life. I arrived back at Heathrow with two bob in my pocket. Somehow I had got away with it. My job was still there, and so was Penny.

Early Morning at the Court was only scheduled for a limited season. I always prefer that. It takes the stress away. You open and you close. The reviews are good or bad. Obviously I want everything I'm connected with to be a hit, but I never fancy a long run. I prefer touring with a play. When you are in a hit show in the West End, after about three months you might as well have an office job, except that you are always going to work when everybody else is coming home. Nevertheless, it's that same old drudgery of worrying about the traffic (contrary to public opinion, actors are hardly ever late), where to park, have we got an audience, have I got a cold, have I got any enthusiasm left, and eight times a week you spout the same bloody words. Some actors say they hate first nights, that it's all adrenaline-based and not an accurate performance until several weeks into the run. That may be true, but the only time that I really love the theatre is the first night. It's *your* night. You must be good. It's your turn to show off. In a way, it's like training for a fight. Rehearsing is your 'work-out', planning your strategy – when to rest and when to come on strong and go for the throat. Unlike a fight, however, you have to repeat it night after night. The dream is that you get wonderful reviews, win loads of awards and nobody comes to see it. The drawback of this, of course, is that you also don't earn any money. Ah well, you can't have it all.

PENNY: But he did have his music. Dennis spent a fortune on sound equipment, records and guitars. He played guitar all the time, either the Gibson or the Martin. The Martin had been bought at a time when we were particularly flush, but in hard times it would be taken back to a particular music shop in Richmond and traded in for a cheaper one. The guy there was particularly obliging and would keep the Martin in the back of the store until our fortunes improved once more.

Music, song-writing and singing were his solace. It seemed to be the one way he could pour out his feelings, express whatever angst was bottled inside him, and he had a wonderful voice.

After *Up the Junction*, if I wasn't exactly a star, I no longer had to audition as often. I would be invited to meet the director and producer without having to go through those dreary preliminary meetings with casting directors. It didn't guarantee that you got the job, but it was another rung up the ladder. Fortunately my hit rate was reasonable and I became a rather successful jobbing actor, going from television to films and back to TV.

I did another film, called *A Smashing Bird I Used to Know*. This must be in the running as the worst film ever made, period. The cast was quite impressive. Patrick Mower, Derek Fowlds, Joanna David, Maureen Lipman and me. The 'smashing bird' of the title was a newcomer called Madeleine Hinde, who had the unfortunate disability of not being able to walk and talk at the same time. But she was very pretty. The director boasted, 'I auditioned seventy-five birds for this movie and screwed at least half of them.' He also said one day, while directing a scene, 'Hold on, something's wrong, you've lost your *spontinuity*.' We all knew we were in deep doggie-do.

Towards the end of shooting there was a big discussion in the producer's office about the ending of the script. The girl and I just appeared to drive into the sunset. Very limp. I suggested half jokingly, 'Why don't they drive off a cliff?' 'Fucking good idea,' they chorused, and that's how the movie ends. But at least the pay was good and I bought my first brand-new car. There wasn't a glitzy premiere, thank God, but I thought I'd drag Penny, along with Paul and Tim, to the ABC cinema in the Fulham Road just for a laugh. As we were buying our tickets, yes, buying, I turned round and saw Pat Mower sidling out of the cinema in the hope that nobody would recognise him. No one did!

MGM were making a filmed TV series in England called *Out of the*

Unknown and I was invited to star in the first episode with the very beautiful and very cool Carol Linley. I played a troubled young man who falls in love with a mannequin in a shop window, and when she comes to life in my imagination, it turns out to be Carol. It was directed by an American called Robert Stevenson and gave me another chance to work with my old mate the lighting cameraman Arthur Lavis. Because it was the pilot for the whole series we were given a lot more time to shoot than normal – which meant a great deal more money for all of us. There was a sequence in the film where I steal the doll from a large department store in the middle of London. We had about a week of night shoots around Soho, which involved me lugging a life-sized model of Carol around the seedier spots of the red-light district. At this time, the ladies of night were still plying their trade on the streets. Some of the comments I got from them were priceless and unprintable. I also had to get on and off regular London Transport buses with a naked life-sized model under my arm. Contrary to what most people think, actors do get embarrassed.

I was soon to do *The Scars of Dracula* for Hammer Films. I wasn't embarrassed about doing a horror film but I was mortified by one particular scene, in which, just as I was about to thrust a stake through Christopher Lee's heart, his blood-red eyes would open suddenly and I had to faint with horror. I had never fainted in my life and I was useless at it.

The best thing about *The Scars of Dracula* was that it was my first experience of being directed by Roy Ward Baker. He has a list of credits as long as anybody's arm, including *A Night to Remember*, the definitive *Titanic* film. I asked him why he was doing a Dracula. 'Education,' he replied. It wasn't until I had my own children that I really understood what he meant. I'll never forget him running along the touchline when we were playing a friendly football match against another movie crew, shouting, 'Don't you hurt him, he's filming in the morning.'

ROY WARD BAKER: *The Scars of Dracula*, of its type, was a very good but very cruel picture. And the fans loved it.

It was about two young brothers. Dennis played the rather staid older one; the other one was the rascal, always after the girls. Thinking back, it was exactly the wrong casting which didn't occur to me at the time and wouldn't have worked, as the younger brother was killed quite early on, and Dennis, as the star, had to play right through the picture and settle the villain.

We got on very well but I think Dennis was a little bewildered by the period style of playing and I'm not sure he enjoyed it, although we did enjoy working together.

Roy also played one of the oldest film jokes on me. We were shooting a sequence of me walking through a forest. The camera was set up for the shot and Roy said, 'Just carry on until you hear me shout "cut!"' I walked and walked until I realised what was going on. I hid behind a tree and looked back. Nothing. By the time I got back, everybody had almost finished their lunch. Ha, ha, ha! I was later to get to know Roy better when he directed several episodes of *Minder*.

I had a lot more fun on *The Belstone Fox*. This was a story about a fox that is adopted by one of the hounds that has been trained to hunt and kill foxes. It sounds very Disney and sentimental, but it did raise serious questions about the whole foxhunting issue. Eric Porter was the huntsman, Jeremy Kemp was the master of the hunt and I was the 'whipper-in' – that's the horseman who is responsible for the hounds! Eric and I went down to Somerset two weeks before shooting started to get to know our horses and learn a little about handling the hounds. We met at the Castle Hotel in Taunton for dinner and Eric told me to meet him at seven the next morning. 'Seven?' I said. 'Just to meet some horses and dogs?'

'That's when they start working,' he replied.

We went out to the real whipper-in's cottage at seven thirty on Sunday morning, and were greeted by a very bleary-eyed Alec. 'You're up bloody early for actors, aren't you?' he said, and led us inside. He'd given a party the night before and there were bodies all over the place. Gingerly we stepped over his sleeping guests and were given a huge breakfast with big mugs of strong tea, then were introduced to the hounds. Every morning for the next two weeks we worked with the hounds, and every afternoon we rode. It was a great fortnight and Alec and I became great mates. I said to him one day, 'I think the hounds' – never dogs, I discovered – 'are really getting used to me, and a couple of them even seem to like me.' 'Of course they do,' he retorted. 'They love rotten meat.'

Eventually the rest of the cast and the crew joined us in Taunton. I was in the Castle Hotel with Eric, Jeremy, Rachel Roberts, Bill Travis, James Hill (director) and various heads of department. The crew were all in the County Hotel. After a week or so, so was I. We were to be on location for about two months and a large band of the crew were really looking forward to it. Well, we were the chaps all the way from Swinging London; we couldn't fail to pull down here, with only yokels for competition. How wrong I was. We worked very closely with a farmers' hunt and got to know the people pretty well. I'd mention to Alec, 'That blonde' – or brunette – 'she's a bit tasty.'

'You've got no chance,' he'd smirk. Then he would tell me who was involved with who, and that so-and-so was sleeping with him or her, and their husband or wife was having it off with somebody else, while their daughter was doing it with somebody else's fiancé. Even if the women had fancied any of us, they didn't have the time.

The director, although he had done some work with animals, just couldn't understand why some of the horses wouldn't hit their marks. With the exception of the young leading lady, who owned her own nag, the horses that we actors rode had been brought down from Pinewood Studios. They weren't trained to do anything specific but they were accustomed to cameras and lights. They were definitely not used to being at the head of a charge, with forty or so other horses bringing up the rear. My grey, whom I'd named Charlton, after Bobby, found the first day's filming very offputting. We did a short scene passing the stirrup cup, and he was fine. Then we trotted into a field and the hunt started with a gallop up a hill. Hearing the thundering of hooves behind us, down went the ears and he wasn't paying attention to anybody shouting 'Cut!' After a week or so of ploughing, head first, into prickly bushes, it occurred to him that it might be a lot less painful, for both of us, if he did what I asked him to do. We got on famously from then on.

Eric's horse was a wonderful big chestnut that he had named Flashman. We had to do this two-shot of us galloping together down a bridle path that ran parallel with a road for several hundred yards, which meant the camera car could be driven beside us. The plan was that when the road veered away from the path, that was effectively the end of the shot, and we should stop. Typically of Eric, he had worked very hard to get a good 'seat' so nobody could tell he hadn't been born in the saddle. We got our cue and kicked on. The whipper-in must never overtake the huntsman, so Charlton and I were just back off Flashman's flank. Eventually I noticed that the camera car had turned off and I shouted to Eric that we could stop. He seemed not to be slowing down. I wasn't that worried, it was a lovely day, and by now I was very comfortable with my mount. The wind was blowing in my hair and all felt right with the world. From the ramrod-straight back in front of me I heard Eric cry, 'Whoa, Flashman! Whoa ! Down boy, easy lad!' The horse did not check his stride. Then the most beautiful Shakespearean basso profundo echoed across the Quantocks: 'Flashman, for FUCK'S SAKE

Dennis, aged 3

(*Above left*) RSC Period. Stratford Mop Fair. James Langley and Dennis

(*Above right*) Myrna

(*Left*) Norma

(*Below*) Dennis

(*Below left*) Myrna, Dennis and Mother, Rose, in Hastings

Saved (SNOWDON)

Dennis with Father, Harry. A promotional still for *Up the Junction* (DAILY MIRROR)

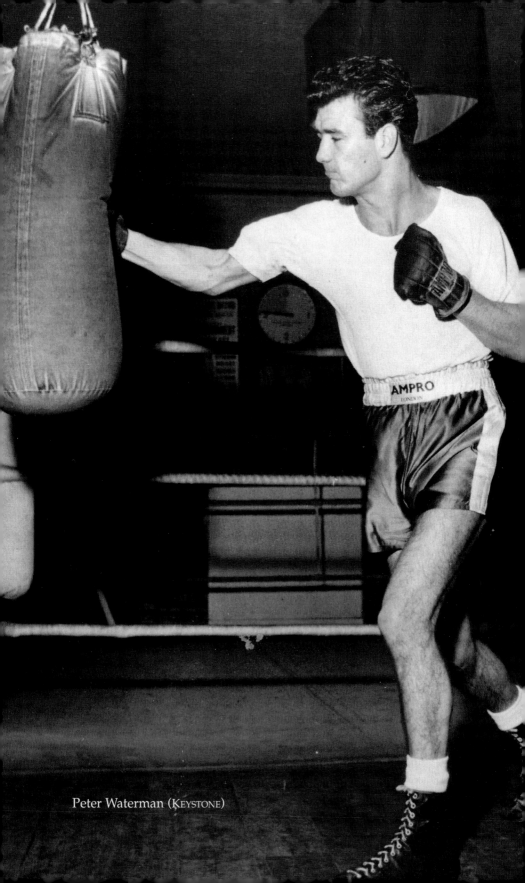

Peter Waterman (KEYSTONE)

My Lover, My Son with Romy Schneider

A Man in the Wilderness with Richard Harris

Gold Disc Time.
From left to right: Gerard Kenny, Nick Lesson, Peter Vale, Sheena Easton,
Deke Arlon, Chris Neil, Dennis Waterman

(*Above*) Wedding Day, with Pat and Hannah.
(*Below*) From left to right:
Jim and Myrna Staublin, Dan and Norma Randi, Dennis and Pat Waterman

The Sweeney with John Thaw (JOHN PAUL © SCOPE FEATURES)

STOP!' We didn't race as far as Bristol, although the horse did try. But for me those hills will forever reverberate with Eric's golden tones.

The next thing I did was a thriller for TV with Alan Armstrong and Colin McCormack, called *The Eyes Have It*. It was set in a school for the blind. There were seven or eight of us, young blind people who have to thwart some men who have taken over the building as a base for some sort of political assassination. The wonderfully 'bad' Peter Vaughan was the leader of the baddies.

Sinead Cusack played the only female part. She was very excited about this new man in her life, who apparently was quite a good actor and guitarist. His name was Jeremy Irons. I wonder what happened to him?

We spent several days at a real school for the blind and a few of them came out one day with us for a drink. We were in the Star Tavern, and one of the pupils asked the barman if he happened to have a collection box for the blind. 'Certainly, sir,' he said, and pushed the box over to the young man. To the barman's amazement he put it in his bag. 'What do you think you're doing?' the barman asked.

'Well, I'm blind,' the chap replied. 'I thought I'd cut out the middleman.'

It was difficult to tell if some of these kids had any impairment at all. They used to hare around their school at breakneck speed. They weren't allowed sticks or dogs within the building. I spent several days talking to one of the teachers, quizzing him about how difficult it was to teach these kids. I had absolutely no idea that he was blind himself. It was a humbling experience.

One evening Colin mentioned that he was seeing Richard O'Sullivan for a drink after work. 'I'll come with you,' I said. We all met at the Carpenter's Arms in Chiswick, and that became our local for quite a while. More memorably, it was my first encounter with the great Warren Clarke and the beginning of a life-long friendship. Richard and I started writing some music together and we all spent a lot of time in each other's company, including playing football for the Showbiz XI.

RICHARD: Dennis and I would spend hours together playing and singing and writing songs, with me on keyboards and Dennis on guitar. He wrote the lyrics, I did the music and some of the songs were really good. At least that's how they sounded at home. Performing in a recording studio in Denmark Street, centre of the music business was another matter. I was terrified. I made mistake after mistake, so much so that even one of our best songs, a real raucous rock number called 'Night at the Opera', came out on the demo sounding really, really rough.

My music career was put on hold while my acting career progressed with a TV play, one of a series called *The Root of All Evil*. In it, Michael Pennington, a fine actor and good friend, and I were both vying for the affections of a young actress called Susan George. In real life we weren't. She had just learned she had been cast as Dustin Hoffman's co-star in the film *Straw Dogs*, an exciting break for her, which was to make her an international star. We were all very thrilled for Susan, of course, but it didn't help her concentrate on our play.

Susan and I worked together on another occasion after *Straw Dogs*. I had received a phone call from Peter Collinson offering me a part in a film he was doing called *Fright*. 'It's not a very big part,' he said, 'but I can get you quite a lot of money.'

'No problem,' I said.

He was right. I did get a good few quid and it wasn't a very large part. I played the boyfriend of Susan, who was baby-sitting for someone. I turned up at the house for a bit of hanky-panky and was bludgeoned to death by an intruder. Smashing, I thought, a few days' work and loads of money. I hadn't taken into account that I died in the hall, and that whenever anyone was creeping, running or screaming around the house, they had to go through the hall – which meant I had to be lying there. Soaked in blood. I couldn't even go to lunch.

Early on in the shooting of *Minder*, George Cole and I were in a car together and I mentioned *Fright*.

'I was in that,' said George.

'No you weren't,' said I.

'Yes I was, and I don't remember you.'

GEORGE COLE: I guess he must have been that body lying face down in the hall that I'd been stepping over for the last three weeks.

It was about this time that I went to see Wilbur Stark, an American film producer (and Koo's daddy), and director John Newland about a film called *Hushabye Murder*. It was about a young man who kills his father because of the abuse his mother is subject to. The mother was to be played by Romy Schneider.

Romy, at that time, was not very well known over here, but on the continent she was a huge film star and used to star treatment wherever she went. She was incredibly elegant, beautiful and successful. She also had her own assistant, called Edith. I had never before come across an actor having his or her own assistant, and I was even more impressed.

The schedule was about twelve weeks. On set, Romy was efficient and professional, if a little confused by our informal attitude to her. We treated her like everyone else. Maybe because of this she was quite demanding, which exasperated some of the crew. With her fellow actors, she was fine, if at first a little distant.

With me she was delightful. Because we were the two lead characters, we worked together most of the time. I have never been pushy, and my natural shyness doesn't make for instant friendship, but the longer we worked together, the more relaxed we both became. I don't know if there are great barriers between actors and technicians on the continent, but here she was very surprised by my closeness with the crew, many of whom I'd worked with previously. It didn't take long before she too was joining in with the jokes. She would later refer to this as my 'freedom', saying how much she loved, envied even, my relaxed attitude.

It was my stand-in who first made me aware that her interest in me was not totally professional, when about a week and a half into the shoot he whispered, 'She really fancies you.'

'Don't be stupid,' I sneered.

He raised his eyebrows. 'Trust me,' he said.

There was no blinding revelation of falling in love, but her beautiful smile lit on me more and more, until it seemed the most natural thing in the world to spend all our time together. I was swept off my feet. I had no idea what she saw in me and I didn't care. She was fantastic. Of course she was older, she was playing my mother, but for us, the age gap didn't exist. Neither did our other lives. I knew she was married and had a small son; she knew I was living with Penny. It didn't matter, but then neither of us believed our romance would become as important as it did.

Our first assistant, David Alexander, and his wife had become great friends of ours, and their flat was our refuge. Romy's relative anonymity allowed us all to visit pubs and restaurants together, with no problems at all. The continental paparazzi snapped a few shots, but it was assumed that if she was seeing anyone, it was David – I suppose because he was closer to her in age. More often than not, we would stay in Romy's rented flat in Hampstead, where Edith also lived. And Edith was both loyal and discreet.

What her husband thought or believed was never mentioned. Maybe he accepted such situations. By then too, I had learned about her earlier affair with Alain Delon and the rumours of a *ménage à trois* with his wife. Frankly, I didn't care. It was one of the most romantic and passionate times of my life. While she was with me she was mine, and nothing else mattered.

The end of filming was not the end of the affair. Romy came back to London to finish the movie with some dubbing. This time she stayed at the Connaught Hotel – and so did I.

I have to admit, it made me a little uneasy. I wasn't sure how I was expected to dress, and I was convinced everyone was looking at me very knowingly. Nevertheless, it was extremely romantic. I bought her hundreds of records of my favourite music – Dylan, Crosby, Stills and Nash, and the Beatles. I wrote songs for her, and taught her 'My Old Man's a Dustman', which sung by her, with her Austrian accent, was wonderfully funny. Then the movie was over, and desperately we promised to keep in touch.

Whenever I am asked if I know the Connaught, I always reply, 'Oh yes, very well.' Which I did. One bedroom at least.

RICHARD O'SULLIVAN: Despite everyone being very fond of Penny, we were all terribly envious, and very impressed with Dennis' affair with Romy. He got ten out of ten for that one!

TIM CARLTON: This was one time he really fell in love. He was besotted by her. Normally he would talk about his conquests, but not this one.

PAUL YOUNG: I was on one of my visits to Hammersmith Grove and had come in early from work in the middle of the afternoon when I heard a voice: 'That you, Jock?'

'Yeah,' I called back.

'Great! Usual tea for me, and one with milk and one sugar.'

I took it up and there in bed was Dennis with Romy. I gave them the tea and left.

During the filming of this movie I had been asked to go and meet Ronald Eyre and Robin Maugham, director and writer of a play called *Enemy*, which was to be produced in the near future by Doris Abrahams. We met in her extremely expensive flat in Kensington.

The play was about an English and a German soldier, who are both lost in the Western Desert during World War II. They come across one another by the wreck of a Sherman tank, which has been left with its supplies intact. At first they sort of capture each other, but during the course of the play they find that they can't treat each other as enemies and decide the best thing to do is try and survive together. I was asked if I would consider playing the Londoner. I said I would, but was it possible for me to read for the German?

They looked at each other as if to say 'Is there time for this, and/or any point?' They had already talked about a German actor to be brought over to play that role. 'OK,' they said somewhat wearily.

There was a huge speech where the German soldier, Paul Seidler, tells of his life in Berlin and owns up to being homosexual. I read the speech in this incredibly smart lounge, and it was met with total silence. Ronald, Robin and Doris looked at each other. Eventually Ron exhaled very slowly and said, 'Oh well, somebody else will have to play the Englishman.'

It was probably the proudest moment of my professional life. I had gone in to be offered a part that I could play standing on my head and had acted myself into a part that nobody would have offered me in a thousand years. A German poof. Romy came to see the show in Guildford, during the pre-London tour. For a while over dinner she was quite reserved, but then she poured out a stream of compliments. She had had no idea how well I worked on stage, but best of all, after a couple of scenes she forgot that she knew me and firmly believed that I was actually a German. We didn't discuss how successful I was as a poof.

We had toured *Enemy* for twelve weeks or so and were waiting to go into the West End. Tony Selby ended up playing the English soldier and Neil Stacy played the English officer who comes on at the end of Act II and shoots me. It was like two tours in one. Tony was an old mate from the Court and one of the chaps. Neil had got a first at Oxford in history. During the day as we travelled from one show to the next, he acted as our tour guide and brought alive the history of Britain. Tony was our after-show night-time guide to the country pubs, clubs and hostelries. Both pursuits proved equally pleasurable.

Apart from one matinée in Hull, we had a very successful tour and got some great reviews.

Les Dawson once said to me, 'If God ever wanted to give the world an enema, he'd do it in Hull.' The New Theatre is a huge barn of a place, totally unsuited to an intimate three-hander.

There is an unwritten rule in the theatre – if the cast outnumbers the audience, you can cancel the show. This isn't very likely when there are only three of you. The audience for this particular matinée struggled to make double figures, but we had to go on. I absolutely hate matinées, and unless there is a good house, the only way I can make them bearable is to treat them like a race. I like to see just how quickly I can get through the play and how often I can corpse (make laugh) my fellow artists. This was a gold-medal matinée!

The set of *Enemy* was a tank bedded down in sand, in the desert. Tony Selby was in position, lying on his stomach in the sand, listening to my long speech about Berlin and my lover, Rolf, whom I'd left behind. This particular afternoon I decided to play it like a cross between Julian Clary, John Inman and Marlene Dietrich. I must have excelled at it; Tony couldn't look at me. His body quivered violently, he groaned, and every now and then, unheard by the audience, he gasped, 'Shut up, give us a break.'

This speech was at least four pages long. By the third, I'd progressed to playing it like Lily Savage – with a German accent. I was really going for it. I knew I had succeeded when I looked down and saw the sand around Tony's shorts getting discernibly darker. I'd cracked it, the ultimate corpse. I'd made my co-star piss himself with laughter. Fantastic.

We had to wait some time before a West End theatre became available, but eventually we were told we were going to open at the Saville.

It might have had something to do with touring for so long, or the wait between the tour and going to London, but there wasn't the usual buzz on that first night. We all felt kind of flat. Even so the event itself was a very glittering affair. I'll never forget my parents' faces. They were both dressed up. My mum, who was just about five foot tall, was wearing this huge fur coat which virtually reached the floor. I think one of the girls had given it to her and she had taken a bit off the hem and made a matching hat. She looked like Khrushchev's mother.

> PENNY: It was a glittering first night. I was standing in the foyer with Rose, and it being a Robin Maugham play, everyone was there, including, of course, Noël Coward. Rose was in total awe. She looked round, eyes wide, turned to me and said, 'All these people, and they've all come to see my Den!' She was so proud!

Robin Maugham came into the dressing room after the show and said how wonderful I was, and could a few old friends of his pop in? 'Sure,' I said – I think I was still only half dressed. First in was Noël Coward with one of those amazingly beautiful women from the early black-and-white films, closely followed by Trevor Howard and his lovely wife Helen Cherry. They all said how much they had enjoyed it and left. My parents couldn't really take it in. 'Those were real stars and they came in to see you?'

'Yeah, good, innit!'

The Saville Theatre was in a strange no-man's-land at the top of Shaftesbury Avenue, with hardly any passing trade. This might be the reason why we were the last play to appear there. It closed down after our run and is now a cinema. *Enemy* wasn't a total failure, but it didn't live up to expectations.

The same could be said of another performance I gave during that run. I was asked to play Rodolfo in the radio version of *View from the Bridge*. Rodolfo was a young Italian, an illegal immigrant in America who wants to be a crooner. In the late forties and early fifties, the era in which the play is set, the pop stars of the day were mostly light tenors, whilst I was still heavily influenced by Dylan and Rod Stewart! We were on stage doing *Enemy* when *View from the Bridge*, was aired. During the interval, I raced upstairs to my dressing room to catch some of it. It was the moment when Rodolfo was singing the Mills brothers' hit 'Paper Doll'. Imagine my shame when I realised that it wasn't me singing. The rest of the play was fine, but somebody must have felt that I was just a little too bluesy for the time and re-voiced me with a proper tenor. It has to be the apex of failure when you're dubbed on the radio!

There was another highlight during the run of *Enemy*, when someone informed me there was a very nice picture of me in *Gay News*.

'Do what?' I gasped.

Further down the Avenue, one of the big hits that year was the first overtly homosexual play produced in the West End. It was called *Boys in the Band*. Because of my character in the play, and the fact that it was set in the desert, *Gay News* had dubbed Tony, Neil and me 'Boys in the Sand'!

To protect child actors in America, twenty per cent of their earnings is put in a trust, which cannot be touched until they become of age. I was now twenty-one and decided to go to California to claim the money due to me from *Fair Exchange*.

I didn't tell either of my sisters that I was coming, I thought I'd surprise them. At LA International Airport I jumped into a cab and arrived at Myrna and Jim's address to find no one home. I asked a neighbour if she knew where they might be, she suggested I try our sister Norma. The taxi driver must have thought it was Christmas. We travelled miles and miles and for hours and hours, and got to know each other quite well. He was, would you believe it, a scriptwriter waiting to be discovered! In the same way that pubs in London could never operate without Australians or Kiwis behind the bar, Los Angeles cabs would come to a standstill without aspiring scriptwriters to drive them.

After a tour of the Fernando Valley, we hit the Hollywood Hills and Norma and Don's house. Lights were on, shadows crossed the window. I paid the driver (a small mortgage would have covered it), who asked if he could come in and see their reaction to my surprise arrival. As always, the front door was open. Norma, Myrna and Jim were playing cards. The driver and I walked in and Jim, without catching a breath, looked up and said, 'Hi, Den, shall I deal you in?'

I had been there for a month or so when I received a call from Romy. Myrna was far from thrilled with this. 'Find someone of your own age for a change. What does she want with you?' etc., etc. I had no real answers, apart from the fact that she was beautiful and I might be in love with her. 'Hmph,' came the reply – not an unusual reaction from big sister.

> MYRNA: I think he was out of his depth and came here to escape. I don't think Dennis really knew how to handle it, but Romy kept phoning and sending telegrams begging him to come back. Then again, he always has been one for the girls . . .

I received a cable suggesting we met in Paris, where Romy was making a movie. Edith would pick me up at Orly Airport. It is with considerable embarrassment that I have to admit I got a.m. and p.m. mixed up, and arrived in Paris twelve hours late. I telephoned the only number I had, and attempted, in my very bad French, to make myself understood by a foreign maid, who spoke equally bad French but with a South-East Asian accent. We did not get very far. Bitterly disappointed, I flew back to Heathrow.

I decided on one more call. This time Edith answered. Sternly she pointed out the cycle of the twenty-four-hour clock, and instructed me to fly back to Paris immediately.

I stayed with Romy for a few days in her wonderfully luxurious apartment. And there we remained as much as possible. It was my first visit to Paris, but because we had to be discreet in her home town and because we wanted to be alone, we didn't go out to eat, and my sightseeing was limited to taxi journeys. However, she did take me once to the set and introduced me to everyone. I was in my early hippy stage, at this point, and the reaction of her colleagues was rather quizzical, whether at my garb or our relationship, I'm not sure. Again there was no mention of her husband. Romy was just wonderfully relaxed and happy to see me again, as I was to see her.

We drove to Deauville and stayed in a beautiful hotel, but after a few days, my lack of French began to tell. It was terrific when we were alone, but we couldn't be alone all the time, and sadly our different worlds began to pull us apart. She was married with a young son and I was still living with the ever-patient Penny. Unless we were prepared to make a really life-changing commitment, we were going to end up making a lot of people very unhappy. We made love and cried and said goodbye.

It was with a heavy heart that I read some time ago now that she had died in her apartment in Paris. She had had an unbelievably sad few years. Her only child, her beloved son, had fallen from a window and died, her husband had committed suicide, and eventually she herself had died, apparently from a broken heart. Sad, sad, sad.

SEVEN

THE FIRST MORTGAGE

Slowly life got back to normal. I can't honestly say how much Penny knew. I had tried to be discreet, not to hurt her or embarrass her too much. Inevitably she did get hurt and angry, but when it was all over, she was there, as ever.

> PENNY: Ever-patient Penny nearly wasn't either there or patient. For me the Romy Schneider episode was the worst. It was inevitable, I suppose, that the two of them would have an affair. It was serious but hopeless. I resented and blamed her for pursuing him; she even phoned him at home – using her maid to pass on messages.
>
> Dennis never moved out, he still came home. In the end, I was the one who left. I was so angry, I ran away to Glasgow to see Paul and Sheila Young, then hired a car and drove all round Scotland. I went back to Dennis, of course. We never rowed about his philandering, but then we never did have rows, and I still loved him enough to put up with it. He came home and life went on more or less as normal, with Dennis being just as warm and loving with me as ever. He did like to have his cake and eat it, though!

With the money I had recovered from America, Penny and I decided to put a deposit on a house. My first mortgage at the age of twenty-one. We bought a lovely little artisan's cottage in Eleanor Road, Barnes, a bit on the wrong side of the track, but very pretty. When we were together, Penny and I had a great time. The area had a lovely villagey feel about it, with the butcher, baker, newsagent and a couple of pubs all within a short walk. We got two dogs, English setters called Greaves and Bremner – football fans will understand the names. Over the years we had cats as well. What did we call them? Pelé, Riva, Charlton, Chelsea, Hollins, to name but a few. We held open house most Sundays. Bob Powell would come over, we would play football in the morning, go to the Halfway House (my local), come back, watch the football on telly, have lunch, sometimes play Subbuteo, watch *The Clangers*, and go back to the boozer for a Sunday-night game of darts. What sportsmen we were!

The Halfway House was a focal point of the village. By now, Tim Carlton was also living in Barnes, so he was often to be found in the public bar, darts in hand. It was an old family pub, run by the Sutcliffes, to whom we became very close, especially their son, Mike, and his wife Monica. Many years later, Mike would be my driver in the early *Minder* days.

It was here that I started playing quite good Sunday league football. Mike's brother-in-law, Barry Carter, helped run a team called Robin Hood Gate, and I played with them for several seasons. Barry was also responsible for my getting a season ticket for Chelsea. It was a great period of my life. I was sort of successful and getting to be slightly well known, but there was no pressure, and I was very happy, with one notable exception.

It was 1970, the year of the World Cup, and several of the mates had devised a rota of where we would watch the games. Penny and I opted to host the England v. West Germany match.

Penny had prepared some wonderful food, we had a barrel of real beer from the pub, the television picture was brilliant and we were in very high spirits. We had beaten Romania and Czechoslovakia, we'd only lost to Brazil by one goal and now we were facing the Germans. There were rumours that Gordon Banks had been poisoned, but our Chelsea keeper, Bonetti, was in goal. 'The Cat' would save us.

The final whistle blew. We were in total despair. It was 3–2 to the Germans. We sat in front of the TV, numb. Sighs became consolations – we had played well . . . but that third goal? Whose fault was that?

I thought Penny was getting the food together, so I went into the kitchen to see if I could help. I knew she didn't mind watching football, and her favourite man was Bobby Charlton, but – and this really shook me – she was in floods of tears. What a girl.

PENNY: This was perhaps our happiest time. Work was prolific, we had cars and a lovely house! And so many friends around: Bob Powell, Tim, Richard O'Sullivan, Robin Askwith and all the girls that went with them. Everyone was successful, with money to spend. Robin was outrageously funny, starring in *Doctor in the House*, while Richard was having huge success with *Man About the House*. We'd often go to watch the shows being recorded, followed by endless pub parties.

RICHARD O'SULLIVAN: They were seriously wonderful times and it wasn't just a question of being laddish. We were a close group of friends, including wives and girlfriends. Sunday was our big day. We'd play football in the morning, then rush home to huge roasts which we all took turns in cooking. And then again, there were lots of parties . . . we were just normal red-blooded young men. And always there was Chelsea . . . Den and I were and are still big supporters.

We were very happy in Barnes, but after a while we decided to move to the country. I'm not certain why.

PENNY: I've no idea either. The cottage we found was near Andover, miles away from London and all our friends, and we didn't know anyone.

We bought the lodge to a large house in a hamlet called Smannel in Hampshire. It was not exactly the idyllic little cottage we had planned, but it had 'potential', which meant it should have been bought by a do-it-yourself enthusiast. I did try odds and sods, here and there, but I'm totally useless. After a couple of hours of fruitless labour I was ready to kill myself and any helper or critic, burn the project, and even the house.

It must have been a lean period for work, because I actually tried signing on again. I went to the dole office in Andover and joined the queue. I was halfway to the counter when the lady behind it looked up, saw me, and said, 'Oh, look, we've got a famous actor in today.' Everybody turned and stared. There were mutterings of 'I've never seen him,' and 'What's a rich actor doing in a place like this?' and 'He can't be much cop if he's signing on.' Needless to say, I never returned. It's strange, people firmly believe that all actors are millionaires, even if they've never seen or heard of them.

Between finishing the movie with Romy and its release, several Swedish films hit our screens and for the first time neo-pornography was being shown in the major cinemas. This was obviously noted by the distributors. I was driving past a cinema when I noticed a film starring Romy Schneider and Dennis Waterman. It was called *My Lover My Son*. I was shocked. Not at the change of title but at what they had done to the film itself, especially a particularly long scene in which Romy and I were seen dancing together. Somehow they had turned each frame in that sequence of the film on its side, so that it appeared we were making love, even though our clothes kept coming into shot. It was bizarre. They had transformed quite a good murder mystery into a rather sordid and unbelievable little story about incest. Luckily I've never met anyone who has seen it.

Meanwhile, Penny and I fitted in surprisingly well in Hampshire. We found a smashing little pub where we joined the darts teams. But whenever I mentioned its name to anyone in Andover, they would raise their eyes and mutter things like 'Oo-er.' The estate agent from whom we had bought the house, Peter Cranham, who became a friend, explained this mysterious reaction. 'You know the young bloke who works behind the bar, the son of the landlord?' he said.

'Yeah,' I answered.

'Well,' he continued, 'he was found in bed with a local landowner, a man.' I thought I'd left all that behind in London.

We had thought that moving to the country would at least be better for the animals. (Not that we were one of those couples so obsessed with their pets that they treat them like children. We just liked them.) Unfortunately we had moved near to an estate which bred pheasants. These dopey birds (and I know quite a bit about dopey birds) were so well fed and domesticated that I never saw one of them fly. You'd have to throw them into the air before you could shoot them. Even so, despite the fact that they were bred to be killed, the gamekeepers would shoot anything that might harm them. It's possible our cats were hit by cars, but I doubt it.

Apart from this, we were fairly content down there. Major motorways did not exist at that time but lots of our mates made the long excursion from London and came to stay. We were doing OK. I drove a Morris Minor estate car, not only essential for the dogs, but it could do nearly sixty miles an hour. Downhill with a following wind!

I got a job in an episode of *Churchill's People*, which was a televised version of Sir Winston Churchill's *History of Britain*. I played King Harold and had to age from mid-twenties to early fifties. This was done with the aid of prosthetics and I had false bags stuck on under my eyes. I had to perform one very quick change during shooting. My dresser was frantically fastening my cloak when one of the leather ties flicked my eye. My eye started to water, which in turn activated the glue holding the false bags. The pain was excruciating. Before long I couldn't open my eyes at all. I was rushed to the BBC nurse and filming was held up for two hours whilst my eyes were treated – not a great drama in itself, but it has always amused me that the Battle of Hastings was the scene of a similar event when King Harold got something in his eye.

Penny and I had been together for about five years. The time had come to get married. It would make things more settled, I thought. Penny was not so sure, but she agreed. The plans for our wedding were underway when I got a fantastic job.

PENNY: Actually, Dennis got the contract for _Sextet_ just after we'd signed the contract on the house and before we'd even moved to Hampshire, when I was already beginning to think it was all a mistake. The next eight months with Dennis travelling back and forth to London leaving me on my own, knowing no one, proved a very bleak and lonely time for me, saved only by our friendship with the Cranhams, especially Leslie, Peter's wife, who became a lifelong friend and whose daughter is now my beloved god-daughter.

And we did plan the wedding. Don't know why! Marriage was never high on my list. But Dennis wanted it. There again, he never took anything in life that seriously, except his work.

Roderick Graham had invited me to join a BBC television repertory company. There were to be three actors and three actresses, to play different roles in seven ninety-minute plays. It was an extremely challenging and exciting idea. Michelle Dotrice and I were cast for the younger characters, Ruth Dunning and Richard Vernon the older ones, with Billie Whitelaw and Denholm Elliot in the middle-aged roles. I said yes immediately.

I had met Michelle with her father, Roy, when I was at Stratford. Ruth was a household name from her work on early TV drama. Richard I didn't know too well, but I became a fan over the next nine months. Billie was one of the best actresses in Britain and Denholm was Denholm, an original, and one of our great, great actors. What a privilege. Not only did we have a dream cast; the list of writers was phenomenal: Dennis Potter, David Mercer, Hugh Whitemore, Peter Tinniswood, Peter Terson, to name but a few. It was a dream job and we all jumped at it. Seven different plays, playing totally differing characters, meant the chance to test and show your acting range to a mass audience, of viewers and potential employers.

I played characters ranging from the head of MI5, to a truly eccentric modern artist, to a neurotic who never travelled on the same bus twice, to a psychiatrist.

It was fantastic. Thank you, Roddy. Not only were we doing wonderful work, we were having a ball. Never slow to laugh, we were a very close cast, although the men, possibly, socialised together rather more than the women. Richard was a stunning actor with a viciously dry sense of humour, and Denholm and I became great mates and would often have a beer after work.

For me the work on each play was defined in three sections. If there was any exterior filming to be done, that would be shot first. A month of rehearsal would ensue, followed by four days' video-taping (very little film was used in TV then) in the studio.

We rehearsed in a huge eight-storey concrete block, with three rehearsal rooms on each floor, affectionately known as the Acton Hilton. With limited channels to watch at that time, any TV exposure ensured your face would be known to people. Total strangers would say, 'Hello, mate, how are you?' in the firm belief that you were personally acquainted. This was not just limited to viewers. In those days the Beeb was churning out thousands of shows and we all rehearsed at Acton. The amount of quizzical smiles I got from people after having long conversations with them in a corridor before realising, usually as I got into the lift, that I'd never met them in my life. I'd only ever seen them on telly.

There was also a 'green room' on each floor where you could relax and meet artists, actors and actresses from other shows as well as your own. I was in there one day when a shove-ha'penny tournament was going on. A beautiful, elegant woman seemed to be doing rather well. Eventually she looked up and said, 'Are you Dennis Waterman?' She went on to tell me that she knew my sisters from school, and we had a chat, then we had to go back to work. Later I asked one of her cast, 'Who was that seriously tasty bird I was talking to earlier on.' He said, 'Patricia Maynard.'

PAT MAYNARD: Weeks later I walked into a rehearsal room when someone announced that Dennis Waterman had got married the previous Saturday. I remember thinking, 'Oh, what a shame.' But then I was involved too.

Rehearsal days, for me, meant driving for an hour and a half each way, for a month, to and from Hampshire in that bloody Morris Minor. Studio days, I would stay in London. For a month I would hardly have a drink because I had three hours' driving a day, and then, at the important time of taping, I would be in town, surrounded by any number of scallywags trying to give me a good time.

At this time, Robert Powell was going out with the delicious Nicola Pagett, who had become a friend of Penny's and mine. She had a lovely little house in Mortlake and every now and then would put me up for the weekend. On occasions, things could be more dangerous. One of our assistant stage managers was a young man called Graham Benson, who is now an extremely successful producer with a large country home and even larger cigars, but back then was just one rung up from a gopher. One weekend he invited me to stay at his place in north London. Now, not only did he make me sleep under a poster of Arsenal, but every night on the way home he insisted we pop into the West End – this meant that for four nights on the trot, we were legless. Not the best way for an actor to prepare. Having said that, it did him more harm than me.

Part of an assistant stage manager's job is to act as go-between the director, who is in the control box, and the actors on the studio floor. He would pass on the director's notes, be it about a change of position or a technical problem. It was also his duty to cue the actors. I'll never forget seeing Graham's arm waving to cue me, from behind the set, while he buried his head and threw up. Good old days.

Norman Boyack had been acting for me at Barry Krost Associates. Eventually he branched out on his own and asked me to sign up with him. He was a terrific agent and would frequently visit the *Sextet* set.

One of the plays was called *Blur and Blank via Cleakheaton*, in which I played a bespectacled nerd with black hair, dressed in an ill-fitting suit and a raincoat, carrying a briefcase. I was pretty pleased with the effect. I was standing at the side of the set waiting to go on during one of the dress rehearsals when Norman arrived. He sidled up to me and whispered, 'Any idea where I can find Dennis Waterman? I was told he was down here.'

I was thrilled. Even my own agent didn't recognise me.

Later in my career he really impressed me. I was being wooed by a film producer and director into doing a series of movies, which they described as bawdy comedies in the 'Carry On' vein. I was flattered but worried, foreseeing a quick descent into a tasteless genre of tits and bums and worse.

I was working on a Play of the Month at the Beeb when Norman came to my dressing room. 'I think we should talk about this film deal,' he said.

'Are they talking good money?' I asked.

'Yes,' he said. 'But I don't want you to do it. Look at this play you're doing – wonderful writer, great director, a wonderful cast and you've got one of the biggest parts. Why risk all the credibility you've built up over the years for a handful of dosh, doing something that could be sneered at by the rest of the business?'

He risked losing a lot of money too with this advice, but it proved what a good agent he was, guiding and building my career rather than simply increasing the bank balance. So with untold gratitude to Norman Boyack, and with commiserations to my old mate Robin Askwith, I said no to the 'Confessions' films.

The Play of the Month, which I mentioned earlier was written by Peter Nichols, and called *The Common*. It starred Peter Jeffries and Gwen Taylor, in one of her first television appearances. The story called for my character to have an on-screen affair with Vivian Merchant. She had been married to Harold Pinter, and having starred in several of his plays had a reputation of being one of the sexiest women in the theatre. By the time we did this play, they had divorced and Vivien had taken it very badly. We rehearsed for about a month. Most of the cast got on well, but Vivian would complete a scene then retire, alone, to a corner, where she would sit sipping iced water from a cooling flask.

I was having quite a hard time working with her, especially in our romantic scenes. Eventually I talked to our director, Chris Moraghan. 'I know it's a satire,' I explained, 'and I know it's somewhat stylised. And of course she might not be able to bear me, but unless she at least pretends to fancy me, the story is out of the window.'

'Yes,' he conceded. 'It is a little strange; she seems to be playing it like a distracted sparrow.'

We tried various things and different ways of rehearsing, but we just couldn't get through to her. And that's how she finally played it – strangely distracted. We learned later that her cooling flask contained neat vodka. On the other hand, who am I to criticise anyone for having a drink?

One nice little American producer, called Philip, who used to laugh like a drain, cast me in a movie called *Wedding Night*, and took me on my first visit to Dublin.

The first day's filming was a funeral scene, located just outside the city. The funeral party stood around the coffin, mumbling something in Latin. Jim Bartley, who was standing next to me, leaned over and whispered, 'Do you know Dublin at all?'

'No,' I said. 'I've only been here a day.'

'Right,' he replied, 'I'll show you round.'

We finished work quite early. 'OK, let's go,' I suggested.

'Not yet,' grinned Jim. 'We're in Wicklow here, there's no "holy hour" in Wicklow.' While the pubs in Dublin closed for their compulsory hour, we had a drink in the local. Then we hit town. Actually, it was more like the town hitting me!

The next morning the car arrived at the hotel to take me to work not long after I had retired for the night. The sympathetic hotel staff were insistent. 'He's only just gone to bed,' they informed the driver.

I was woken up by the producer hitting me round the head with a cold flannel, shouting, 'Get up, you asshole, you gotta go to work.' Jim Bartley had failed to tell me he was not working that morning.

I got up on time from then on. But if Jim ever offered me any hospitality, I checked the schedule to make sure he too was on call the next morning. The film wasn't up to much, but what a town, and what great people I met.

We were working at Bray Studios, which has a fantastic view of the Wicklow Mountains – surely one of the most beautiful settings for a film studio. It was also very busy. *Ryan's Daughter* was being shot by David Lean in Dingle, which is way over on the other side of Ireland, but the two casts met up frequently in Dublin. *Ryan's Daughter* was going further and further over schedule, and everyone under contract found themselves working for months longer than planned. And paid, of course, very well indeed. I met some quite well-known actors in Dublin happy to be extras on that movie just because the money was too good to refuse.

They'd say, 'We can't be too late tonight, we're working in the morning.'

'Are you being picked up by a unit car?' I would enquire.

'No,' they'd shrug, 'We're not supposed to be here, we'll get a cab.' This had to cost two or three hundred quid at least, but they didn't give a monkey's; they fancied a drink in Dublin.

EIGHT

THE FIRST TIME

In 1972 Penny and I got married. Neither of us wanted a white or flash wedding, so it was a registry office job, and the reception was at Tim Carlton's house in Barnes. There were friends and family, of course, but it was a smallish do and very good fun. It has to be said that several friends and indeed some of my family wondered if it was a good idea. They all thought Penny was terrific and liked her a great deal, but just had a feeling that it might not be the right time for me to marry anyone. They were probably right, but we'd been together for five years, and apart from me misbehaving now and then, we got on very well and were happy.

TIM CARLTON: I never fully understood the relationship. Penny was a sweet person and we were all fond of her, but she was not just older than Dennis, she seemed more a mother figure than a sexual one. For once I did try to influence him by telling him not to get married. But he went ahead, and I was best man.

PENNY: It was a peculiar wedding. Den didn't want it to be big, which presented a problem for me because, of course, my parents wanted to give me a decent send-off. Den insisted it should be small, just brothers and sisters. Well, that was fine for him of course because he had lots, whereas I only had one brother, and my mum and dad!

I was also working quite a lot, so we decided that we had done the country bit, and moved back nearer London. We found a lovely little terraced house in St Margarets. This was a little strip of humanity between Twickenham and Richmond; lots of family-run shops, a railway station and a couple of pubs, where everyone knew everyone else. It was as close to being in a proper English village as you could get without travelling for an hour and a half. Probably the friendliest atmosphere I have ever lived in. At the top of our road was a place that would be my second home and base for many years to come.

The Turk's Head public house was one of the great meeting places. Warren Clarke had moved close by, Chris Lewis happened to live virtually opposite, Richard O'Sullivan was not far away in Kew, so unless work intervened, we all met there. Fred Brazier was the landlord, and 'Geordie' Jack Kell his left-hand man – a wonderful team. Fred was an avuncular, urbane man, who looked as though he had just stepped out of *Pickwick Papers*. He'd been in advertising, got fed up with all the bullshit and decided to take charge of his life and run his own pub. His customers were a diverse lot – they came from Twickenham Studios, which were just around the corner, from various big businesses in the area, and of course from the Rugby Football Union, whose headquarters were just down the road.

Fred's role was genial host. He would wander around the pub, meeting and greeting, while his excellent lieutenant, Jack Kell, ran the bar, and took the piss out of all the patrons Jack was trying so hard to impress.

Although the quality of the lunches at the Turk's was legendary, the restaurant never took over; it remained a pub, a local, and the public bar was exactly as it should be. One side could be full of film stars and businessmen, the other milling with working men and women who just wanted a pint and a sandwich at lunchtime. Fred knew how to mix princes and paupers perfectly.

The Turk's was the meeting place for at least two football teams, two darts teams, and even acted as my bank and office. It wasn't solely a male bastion either. Wives and girlfriends were equally comfortable there, either with us or alone. It was a great meeting place, a great local, and Penny and I quickly became a part of it. Wherever I've been in the world, from Disneyland to Portugal, Australia and even China, people have remarked, 'You're a long way from the Turk's, aren't you?'

Penny found herself a job teaching English and drama in a big comprehensive school, whilst I fulfilled a lifetime's ambition – to do a western. This wasn't the first time I had been offered a cowboy film, but it was the first one I did.

Years earlier, my agent had phoned me one morning to tell me that the producer of a Richard Widmark western, to be shot in Spain, was interested in casting me. I said, 'Great, get them to send me a script.' He explained it wasn't that simple. They really wanted another English actor for the part, but he was tied up in the theatre. Meanwhile time was pressing, so they wanted me to fly out to

Madrid for a costume fitting and then go out later to start filming. 'Sounds good to me,' I said, and waited for the call. Eventually it came. 'Sorry, Dennis,' my agent said. 'The first choice has managed to free himself from his show to do the movie.'

'Ah well,' I said, not a little disappointed. 'Just out of interest, who is the other bloke?' To say I was amazed at his answer would be an understatement. It was Derek Nimmo. Now I know the producer was American, so probably not very knowledgeable about English actors, but he must have had some British advisers. How the fuck could anybody have gone from Nimmo to me for the same part? Weird!

The western I did do was terrific. It was called *A Man in the Wilderness*, and starred Richard Harris.

Sandford (Sandy) Howard was producing the movie, and looked like a western star himself. He dressed cowboy style and was handsome, with jet-black hair and shoulders the size of a small buffalo. He was putting together a cast of good actors for what was to be a quite physically hard movie, in both the content and the making. It was based on a true incident in which a group of fur-trappers had to push their boat, full of pelts, through dangerous Indian country. In fact the character they wanted me to play was based on a true person who was instrumental in carving out the trail to the west. 'Oh yes,' I thought, 'I'll have some of that.' I could see myself in a suit of buckskin, a big hat, riding a beautiful white horse. Mine was an interesting part, not overly big, but important.

As with most westerns in those days it was to be shot in Spain. I arrived in Madrid for my costume fitting. The wardrobe designer looked exactly how I wanted to look. He wore a magnificent buckskin jacket, which was nearly as shaggy as his hair and beard, leather trousers, a truly memorable Stetson adorned with feathers, and a fantastic pair of boots. He also happened to be about seven foot tall. We met in the production office, and for the first and only time in my entire career I was excited about seeing my wardrobe. He took me into a large, elegant room and said, 'We're dressing this realistically.' He pointed to a pile of rags, and added, 'See if you can find anything there that fits.'

I rummaged around and eventually found some old woollen trousers and a jerkin, a rotten old hat and a pair of boots that must have been worn in every cowboy picture ever made in Spain. Not exactly my romantic idea of the west. Nor was the filming. We were all asked to grow our hair and beards. That was fine. We all thought that we looked rather groovy. Make-up was something else. First we were covered in fuller's earth, to make us look authentically dirty, then, for good measure, olive oil was poured over our heads, to make certain that no woman on the set would look at us once, let alone twice.

It was a good movie, by the writer who had achieved success with the film *A Man Called Horse*. Richard Sarrafian was the director; a short but huge man who must have weighed about twenty stone, a smashing bloke and good to work with. But the real treat, for us English actors, was that the leader of the expedition was played by the legendary director John Huston. The chief Indian was played by Francis X. Bushman who had been Masalla in the original *Ben Hur*. The other trappers, apart from myself, were Norman Rossington, Brian Marshall, Jim Doohan (the famous Scotty in *Star Trek*), Percy Herbert and John Bindon.

There was one other starring role, a grizzly bear named Stella. Norman, one of England's great character actors, and I were talking to her one day when, with lightning speed, she slashed at us through the bars of her cage and ripped Norman's scarf off his neck. Another half an inch and Norman would have been no more.

Percy was one of those English actors who had been around forever and, seemingly, had appeared in every black-and-white wartime film ever made. Sadly his own wartime experiences had left an indelible mark on him.

The storyline threw us both together, and separated us from the rest of the cast; because of this, we became good mates and hit upon the idea of sharing a flat together, to save some money, while we were shooting in Madrid. We weren't ideally suited, largely because of the age gap. He would listen intently to the BBC World Service and rarely socialise. Indeed, at times he could be quite unpleasant, and at night he suffered terrible nightmares. At first I just put it down to him being a bitter old actor who hadn't quite made it. One particular day he was tongue-lashing the Australians (probably due to a cricket score). I was quite used to him hating any nationality other than the English, but on this occasion I felt I should put up some resistance. He then proceeded to tell me about his experiences as a Japanese prisoner-of-war on the Changi railway. Horrific. I really didn't care what he said about anyone or anything after that.

John Bindon was a self-confessed thug who, somehow, had got into movies. A lovable and funny thug, it has to be said, but not what you could call an actor. John was a hard man and his stories of gangland exploits in London made your blood turn cold. He was a big, handsome fellow with extraordinarily perfect teeth. This never ceased to amaze me, considering his lifestyle. It has been quite widely documented, and endorsed by him, as to how successful he was with women, due, it was said, to his renowned 'manliness', shall we say. One of his party tricks was called the helicopter, which entailed him getting 'the rotor' out of his trousers and whirling it around like a helicopter blade. His other boast was that he could balance three pints of beer along its length . . .

Sadly, but typically, the main meeting place for us Brits in that beautiful old city of Madrid was the Red Lion English pub. In fact, our flat was right above it. This was located just off Fleming Street, named after the inventor of penicillin. Ironically the area was also known as 'Gonorrhea Gulch', in deference to the many prostitutes who plied their trade in the local bars. I must admit these were some of the most beautiful women I have ever seen; however, I did not indulge and never have.

The movie *Nicholas and Alexandra* was also being shot in Madrid, so the Red Lion was jam-packed with British actors and film technicians. A crowd of American servicemen had made it their haunt too, as well as a number of young American exiles escaping call-up service and the Vietnam War. Generally we got along fine, but – maybe because we had all grown long hair and beards for our roles – there was the odd occasion when one of the 'septics' (septic tank = Yank) would take exception to us. Trouble was usually avoided owing to the forbidding presence of Bindon – but not always. One particularly obnoxious Yank, well into his cups, went on and on about us looking like a bunch of women. Despite loud warnings to 'Piss off', 'Leave us alone', and 'Fuck off before you get a clump', he would not let go. Finally, with an air of resignation, John Bindon rose from his chair. 'OK. Outside. We'll sort this out.'

The septic started waving his hands around like a demented mime artist, claiming he was a black belt, a trained lethal weapon. 'We'll see,' sighed John.

We all trooped outside to the dirt square in front of the pub. The American pranced around like Nureyev. Bindon stood there watching and waiting until he skipped within range, then bam! One short right hook and it was back to the bar for a pint. A good man to have on your side.

Another incident at the Red Lion, which was potentially quite dangerous, happened one night when the police raided the place and arrested all the women on a charge of prostitution. This charge was absurd, as most of them were involved with one or other of the two films being shot. Nevertheless, the women were rounded up by a group of uniformed officers under the command of a little plain-clothes copper who looked not unlike Rory Bremner doing an impersonation of Peter Sellers in *The Pink Panther*. The actors in the bar took great exception to this, most notably Tom Baker, John McEnery and Michael Jayston, who were both vociferous and abusive, in English of course, which luckily few of the policemen understood. It was only as references to Berlin in the late thirties and the words 'fascist bastards' rent the air that the 'Pink Panther', in perfect English, warned them that any more insulting tirades and they'd be in bigger trouble than the girls. This was still Franco's Spain, remember.

The actors then took a different tack and threatened the detective with the mighty wrath of Sam Spiegel, the producer of *Nicholas and Alexandra*. Nothing worked, the girls were taken away and desperate phone calls were made. They were eventually released a couple of hours later after the personal intervention of Mr Spiegel. Rumour has it that he went straight to the General. That's power.

We filmed in the mountains in a place called Segovia, where, predictably, I bought a guitar. We went to bull fights, to Athletico and Real Madrid, and in the old part of the city listened to wonderful flamenco. Penny came over to help celebrate my birthday (she bought me a pair of football boots) and we were introduced to the delights of the Old Town by Richard Harris himself, with whom Penny instantly, and understandably, fell in love. He is a smashing man, if at times a little dangerous.

Richard had been impeccably behaved during the shooting of the movie. He and the director had made a pledge not to drink a drop until filming was over. And they didn't, but at the final 'Cut!' at the end of the last scene, they broke open a crate of wine and did the lot. However, this vow precluded Richard from socialising with the rest of us, although he was always eager to hear what had gone on the night before. Also because of the story line, once his character had been mauled by the grizzly bear, our paths diverged. His was a trial of survival alone, while we went on surviving as a group. The plots were in tandem but filmed separately, until the final scene when we were united again. So even in work we were divided.

Richard and I had met briefly during my Royal Court days, and he had recently made a film in Israel with Romy, who had told him of her high regard for me. Maybe that was why I was in the film. Apart from that, I was just one of a group of actors in his movie, until one day, when we were having a kick-about during one of our breaks and I scored two excellent goals with my head – his opinion of me rocketed after that.

It is always strange finishing work on location. Location is anywhere where you are working away from home. Wherever it may be, you adapt. You befriend certain people, you choose your favourite watering-holes and restaurants, you adopt the place and the people, and for a while it becomes your neighbourhood. Then someone shouts, 'Wrap!', you pack your gear, jump on a plane, train or car, head for home and forget all about it. After a day or so, it's as if you've never been away, and the old cry goes up again, 'Where's my next job?'

In this case it was a funny little half-hour play made by Harlech TV in Bristol. Other than Peter Vaughan being in it, there was nothing memorable about the piece, except that it was instrumental in changing my life.

Penny and I had lived together for about seven years and had been married for two of them. We had a nice little house, a couple of dogs, a few cats and a pleasant social life. Then I went to Bristol. And met Theophilla Littleton.

Theophilla was assistant to the producer. She was an incredibly stylish, cool and beautiful English woman. There is, or should I say was, a particular beauty about some well-bred Englishwomen. You would see them in places like Bond Street, wonderfully dressed, poised and confident. I've written that in the past tense because although the women are probably just as beautiful these days, they all seems to dress the same, in big, black, drab clothes.

Theophilla and I sparred with each other for ten days or so. With a name like that there is instant conversation. We were working together and getting on well, then there were drinks and then there were lunches and then there were dinners and then it was back to her little flat for coffee. And that was it. The beginning of the end of my first marriage. I'm sure that neither of us thought it would extend to anything more serious than a fling. We kept it as quiet as possible for as long as possible. But in the end I was spending more and more time in Bristol, and getting edgier and edgier with Penny, until, eventually, it was impossible to hide that I had met someone else.

There were no furious rows; there were unpleasant flare-ups, but it was mostly tears and pointless apologies. Penny and I never disliked each other for a moment, it was just that I had met someone else from whom I couldn't be apart. I moved out of the marital home into Chris Lewis's flat down the road, with only my clothes, my car, my guitar and my records. Penny sold the house and bought another little place. After two years' separation we divorced, amicably.

PENNY: 1974, seven years together, just two years married and it was over. Dennis had met another girl and it was time for a change. It was Dennis' decision that we should split. I was devastated. I'd changed my life and had to get it back on course. Dennis being Dennis was very generous. He gave me the house and paid the mortgage, in fact the only thing he took with him when he left was his 'music'. Straight away I got a teaching job in Hounslow, where I took over as head of drama and stayed for fourteen years in a super job.

Looking back I realise had we stayed together it would not have been a happy life. As it was, we met at the right time. We were young, it was the sixties, we were at the hub of it all, we had money, success, no responsibility. The music, Bob Dylan, the Beatles, London . . . it was all so good. It was more a boy-and-girl affair than a marriage, although sometimes I wonder if it wasn't a bit more mother and son! No, that's going too far, but there was certainly a lot of looking-after going on!

We kept in touch for a while, I even used to go the school where she worked, and instructed her drama students in stage fighting. Eventually she met a chap called Martyn, moved out of London and lived happily ever after. Ironically, I don't think Theophilla and I lasted the rough separation period. We were always working in different places and saw each other less and less until eventually we faded out of each other's lives.

Sharing a flat with Chris was my initiation into bachelorhood as an adult. I had lived with Penny from the age of nineteen. Now, at twenty-six, I was fancy-free and out on the town. Because Chris worked for the sports department at the BBC, I had access to all the big events; we played football every Sunday, went to the Turk's every night and pulled as often as possible. I had freedom, money to enjoy it, and I was working regularly in a profession I loved.

One job that stands out during that time was a TV play called *Joe's Ark*. It was written by the incomparable Dennis Potter and directed by Alan Bridges. I played an unfunny and unsuccessful Welsh stand-up comedian who is doing a gig on his way to see his sister (Angharad Rees), who was dying of cancer, at the home of their father, played by Freddie Jones. A fairly dark piece.

We were well into rehearsals at Acton and about to leave for location filming when I realised that, as yet, we had not rehearsed my 'comedy' routine. Alan, the director was nonplussed. 'Don't worry,' he answered nonchalantly, 'we'll do all that when we film in the

Avonmouth Dockers' club on the way to Wales.' I thought this was fine – until we got there. As usual, the company had hired the club for filming and filled it with a selected audience of extras. My 'act' as the comedian being so bad, Potter had written various terms of abuse for the planted hecklers to shout out. We rehearsed all morning, carefully timing the rude interruptions. The sequence was to be filmed in its entirety during the afternoon and evening. What nobody thought to inform me was that, owing to the constitution of the club, we could not prevent the members from joining the audience as well. Consequently on the night the audience was doubled by genuine dockers – none of whom had been instructed as to the pitiful nature of my performance. They came in roaring to be entertained, and when they weren't, you couldn't hear the well-rehearsed extras for the catcalls and streams of abuse issuing from the members.

Dennis had written an amazing stand-up routine with not one funny line in it. I pleaded with Alan to let me throw in a few funny gags, but he was loving it. He thought the dockers were brilliant. Personally, I was terrified they were going to haul me off the stage at any minute. I've never been so pleased to hear the words, 'It's a wrap!' in my entire life.

During the filming of *Joe's Ark* I met one of the prettiest women I have ever seen. Suzanne Broad was our make-up artist and seriously lovely. When you used to do old-time television you would meet everybody at the read-through, then, apart from the wardrobe personnel, you wouldn't see them again until you were in the studio taping the play, or on location filming all the exterior scenes. Location was where you all really got to know each other, and I desperately wanted to know Suzanne. Suzanne, just as desperately, didn't want to know me. There was lots of joking and flirting but never any closeness.

Make-up and wardrobe ladies, especially the good-looking ones, must dread location – surrounded by dopey actors and technicians, a long way from home, all thinking they are God's gift to every female on the crew. To combat such amorous advances, the women develop this brilliant technique whereby they become 'one of the boys' without losing any of their femininity. They also have a way of saying 'Piss off!' without upsetting anybody.

Like most people on a film crew, Suzanne loved her glass of wine after a day's work. Little groups would meet up in the hotel bar before going on to a local restaurant, and I always ensured that I was in her group, but to no avail.

Sometime later, when I was again doing something at the Beeb, we bumped into one another in the bar. We had a few jokes and quite a lot of drinks, during which she revealed how much she had actually liked me, and moreover, how much she still liked me. We had some catching-up to do.

RICHARD O'SULLIVAN: It must have been autumn! Dennis, the romantic, was always falling heavily in love, seemingly always in autumn. We used to tease him mercilessly. The standing joke became 'Is it autumn? It must be love!'

We lived together for some time over the next two years before realising we were driving each other crackers – in the nicest possible way. We bump into one another now and again and she quite often comes to see me when I am in the theatre. She is still absolutely gorgeous and as daffy as they come.

It was 1974 when my agent received a call from the director Tom Clegg, asking to meet me to talk about a part in an episode of *Special Branch*.

Tom is one of those blokes that everybody instantly likes. He also keeps a dossier of actors with whom he would like to work – luckily, I was on his list.

TOM CLEGG: *Special Branch* was my first venture into television drama and I wanted Waterman in it. I'd noted him at the Royal Court, seen him in *Sextet* and *Up the Junction*, and he was right, not for the main role, but a good part. The casting director more or less told me not to bother, that Dennis was too big a star to take anything less than the lead. With my lack of experience I listened. Sometime later I was contracted to do two more episodes; this time I called him.

We met at the Roebuck pub at the top of Richmond Hill. We never mentioned the script, we chatted more about football and boxing, but I knew he'd be excellent in the part and he agreed to do it.

I played a kid who has some sort of grievance against the world, and who sets out to put it right by stealing a military weapon. It was a challenging role and I enjoyed working with Tom, but more than that, although I didn't realise it at the time, it would prove to be a significant moment in my career.

NINE

SPORT

I first started playing serious football when I joined a team called Robin Hood Gate in the Sunday league. We trained a couple of times a week (work or laziness permitting) and there were some excellent players. Our captain, Barry Carter, was one of the most inoffensive blokes you could meet in the boozer, but a demon on the field with a pathological dislike of referees and linesmen, which meant we often finished our games with only ten men. I don't know what the Sunday league is like today, but for us, it got harder and harder every year. I don't mean physically harder in the playing, but harder in the way the studs were flying, and often fists and foreheads too. After two or three seasons I got frightened off, not of the fights necessarily, but of possible injuries that could seriously threaten my career. It's the old story of the actor getting beaten up, while his agent looks on, screaming, 'Not his face, don't hit his face!'

This retirement from competitive football coincided with my meeting John Foster, who was running the Showbiz XI at the time, and who invited me to play. This was in its heyday when even the substitutes were stars, and we had a great few years driving all over the country, every Sunday, raising many thousands of pounds for charity.

Eventually John retired from running the team, and although we still had the occasional appearance of Tommy Steele, Richard O'Sullivan and Kenny Lynch, a few good disc jockeys and the occasional ex-footballer, every week it seemed we were getting more and more policemen and friends of friends whose claim to fame was the odd appearance in *Z Cars* or as stuntmen.

CHRIS LEWIS: The crunch came one weekend when we were playing in Swindon. The posters, the publicity and the programme all credited the Showbiz XI with players like Sean Connery and Tommy Steele; fair enough, they had all put in an appearance on the field at one time or another – but that time had gone. On the day of the Swindon match only one star turned up, and that was Dennis.

It was also becoming more and more obvious that the charities involved were being short-changed. The players played for no money, but somewhere along the line, the organising bodies were using more and more money to organise and less and less was going to the charity. We decided to set up our own team and organise it ourselves. We both had great contacts and players to call on, Dennis with his list of celebrity showbusiness friends, and me with all my contacts at BBC Sport.

Within two weeks, the Dennis Waterman XI was formed and we went from Dennis being the only star at Swindon to a glittering line-up of 'lardys' (lah-di-dah = star). In fact I was the only one I didn't know, but being the manager and co-founder I was allowed to play in goal!

Because we didn't have the words 'Showbiz' or 'Entertainers' in our name, no one could complain that there weren't enough famous TV stars in the team. In fact there were – Warren Clarke, Richard O'Sullivan and Robert Powell turned out every week.

CHRIS LEWIS: Another regular was Robin Askwith, whose comic antics in the dressing room more than made up for his action on the pitch, and Jess Conrad, otherwise known as 'The Face' for his ridiculous good looks, the only player ever to put tan make-up on his legs and iron creases in his shorts!

ROBERT POWELL: Favourite moments? Those Sundays, off on the coach, Den and I sitting next to each other, playing cards with the lads. It was a hugely enjoyable experience, long days and nights of football, beer and mates!

I remember one Sunday coming out of the dressing room to be greeted by a whole bunch of kids all waving autograph books. Dennis and I were side by side signing when a cheeky little kid at the front called out to me, 'What's yer name, mister?'

I signed the book. Another kid at the back shouted back, 'Who is it?' And the one at the front yelled, 'Nobody!'

Dennis and I couldn't breathe for laughing.

Through Chris's connections, we had a fantastic array of sporting heroes in the team. John Taylor and Jan Webster, both rugby internationals; Martin Peters, Geoff Hurst and Phil Beal were all regulars, as were Neil Rioch (who we called Danny), his brother Bruce, and his other two brothers as well. Daley Thompson played for a season and scored an amazing number of great goals. We played all over the country, every Sunday. Our arrangement, with whatever charity we were playing for, was that we would receive absolutely nothing, but if the venue was over 150 miles from London then a coach should be provided for us, and whatever money we raised was all theirs. We had a fantastic decade or so. Wherever we were playing Chris would find out what footballers or ex-footballers lived nearby; sometimes we would have three or four ex-internationals playing for us. It didn't half help. We didn't lose too often. And we had some wonderful experiences. For example, we played at the old White City stadium against the 1966 World Cup team (we let them win, ha, ha). We also had the honour of playing at some of the great stadiums – Stamford Bridge, Upton Park, Highbury, White Hart Lane, Goodison Park, Craven Cottage. At Bramall Lane one day we lost, but the goalscorers for us were Allen Clarke, Georgie Best, Archie Gemmill and Dennis Waterman. Not too shabby! I have also led a team out at Wembley alongside the opposing captain, Bobby Moore.

RICHARD O'SULLIVAN: Dennis called me up one day. 'What are you up to?' he said.

I said I might be playing for the Showbiz XI.

He said, 'Well, I've got a game on Sunday at the Bridge!'

'What?'

'The Dennis Waterman XI at Stamford Bridge!'

'Count me in!'

I'll never forget the crowds, the floodlights . . . we stood there all of us hardly believing we were there, playing at the Bridge! That was such a thrill. God, that was fantastic!

We got to know some of the players very well – Peter Osgood, Alan Hudson, Johnny Hollins, Eddie McCready, Johnny Boyle. Like us they loved a party or three.

We spent quite a lot of time at the grounds. We'd meet up after the game, have tea then head off to the Ifield in Ifield Street, their local, for a few sherberts. Great days! Great nights!

CHRIS LEWIS: Playing at Fulham was the biggest day in the life of the Dennis Waterman XI.

It was in aid of the victims of the Harrods bombing and we'd been invited by Malcolm McDonald, the Fulham manager, to join the squads of two teams of international players who between them shared a total of 1,250 international caps. It was a massive turn-out, some eight to nine thousand people!

We'd asked Jimmy Hill, a very warm and charitable man, to referee it and invited David Coleman to do the commentary. David, being the ultimate professional, insisted on a preliminary site visit to check the position of the box and the equipment, etc. Johnny Walker came too, along with Barry Hawes, sound supervisor at BAFTA, who had brought along his own sound desk to plug into the PA system at the ground.

Coleman nodded approval, then suddenly said, 'Hill's refereeing, yes?'

'Yes.'

'Right, I want a radio mike on him but don't bring it up until I give you the nod!'

On the day, we equipped Jimmy with the mike and Coleman took up his position in the box and did all the introductions. About ten minutes into the game, there was a long pass between two of the players. Jimmy was racing along trying to keep up with the game. David watched and waited until Jimmy had done over a hundred yards, then announced, 'Right, you'll notice our man on the pitch today is Jimmy Hill. What are conditions like out there today, Jimmy?'

All you could hear ringing round Craven Cottage was the hoarse, laboured breathing of a knackered Jimmy Hill, too exhausted to speak!

That hugely talented, wonderfully nice and greatly missed man Dermot Morgan (who most recently played Father Ted) arranged for a game in Dublin. With typical Irish hospitality he welcomed us to our hotel, and invited us to a dinner with the opposing team, a great bunch of guys, eager to show us a good time. Dinner was followed by a tour of the nightclubs, where we were entertained royally with dancing, singing and gallons of alcohol – a typical Dublin night. I've never seen so many footballers fall over without being tackled.

We reeled to bed in the early hours, having agreed to meet the next morning for champagne and Bloody Marys followed by a light breakfast, again with the opposing team. The only trouble was, the following day, as we staggered into the dining room, the opposing team waving cheery good mornings was not the opposing team we had been out with the night before. We'd been stitched up. Dermot had arranged two opposing teams, one for drinking and one for football! We laughed our way on to the bus and got to the stadium, somewhat unsteadily it has to be said. We beat them 7–4, yours truly scoring four goals. This was particularly sweet for me, because Jim Bartley was in goal for them.

A favourite annual fixture was in Norfolk. Yet again, it was one where training was mostly based on lifting heavy glasses. As Martin Peters' very funny wife exclaimed at one après-game party, 'Isn't this wonderful, I'm drinking for charity!'

The weekend was organised by Chris's sister and brother-in-law, Aideen and David. For well over ten years, until age caught up with us, we spent several more happy years there, playing cricket.

It was made even more enjoyable by the fact that the opposition was made up of blokes from the local press, because nobody minded kicking them.

One particular year I was out on tour, and the night before the fixture was singing in a nightclub in Manchester. I came off stage at about three in the morning, had a few drinks with the band, then set out with Chris Lewis to drive the three or four hours, no motorways then, to Norfolk.

Chris drove for a while, but we were both wiped out, so we pulled over for a bit of a kip then I finished the journey. We hit Norwich at about eight on a Sunday morning. It was too early to go directly to Aideen and David's house, so we popped into the Nelson Hotel, run by a friend of mine, for a champagne breakfast or two, arriving at Aideen and David's some time later, looking and feeling like shit.

In desperation we turned to David (a doctor) for help. He said he had a couple of pills that might get us through the game. We took them with a pint of his home-made beer. He never told us what they were, but we played the best game of football of our lives. Chris saved a penalty and I scored another four goals. Brilliant. We won a lot more than we lost up there and our shield is still hanging up in our old headquarters, the Turk's Head.

PAUL YOUNG: Whenever I was down from Scotland I used to join the team. There was one occasion in Wales I will never forget, and neither has Dennis!

I'd picked up the ball well into our own half, run the length of the field and with a couple of interpasses faced an open goal. Unfortunately I was so knackered I could hardly lift my foot to kick . . . the ball limped past the outside of the post and I fell down. Dennis was stunned. 'How could you miss? I don't believe it.'

For someone who likes his beer and his fags and never really takes care of himself, Dennis was and is incredibly fit. I once saw him playing cricket at the Hurlingham Club with Dennis Lillee and David Gower. Dennis made one amazing catch, cracked a quick thirty or forty runs and hardly broke sweat.

CHRIS LEWIS: The Waterman XI, was one of the most successful charity sides as far as faces were concerned, although it did not run as long as the Showbiz XI which started way back in the fifties. Over all we averaged twenty-five games a season and raised an estimated £2,500,000, for the most part in aid of various children's charities or cancer research.

Although football was unquestionably my first love, I played cricket in the summer whenever I could, quite often for the Lord's Taverners and another charity team, usually with Bob Powell. I also had several smashing years playing for a village pub team, the Hit and Miss, when I moved to Buckinghamshire.

The most fun was when I played for the Eric Clapton XI, which eventually became the Travelling Bunburys. Both teams were run by David English, a well-known lunatic and very fine bat. I had opportunities to play with and against some of the great players at some of the great venues. I've played inside and outside at Lord's; I've bowled a red apple at Ian Botham; I've been laughed at by Courtney Walsh and Joel Garner and woken up Viv Richards when it was his turn to bat. Somehow I scored 36 off Dennis Lillee, and once, just once, was made Man of the Match.

I was invited to go to Portugal with David Gower and Allan Lamb, on what was called a cricket tour, although in seven days we only played once. We were sponsored and entertained royally by Dow, who make port. During the day we would drink cold white port, finishing at night, after dinner, with the red. I arrived home to a concerned Rula, who demanded to know if I had been in a fight. I was forced to admit there had been one memorable day and night, when the entertainment was at its most extravagant, and I had walked or fallen into an old Portuguese wall, several times. I had bruises all over my body.

As we played, so did we celebrate, hard and seriously. I liked squash, football, cricket and tennis, and continued well into my forties and, it has to be said, well past my play-by date. Celebrity sport gave me the advantage of playing with many of my heroes. I still get an extraordinary thrill when some of the greatest sportsmen in the world greet me like an old mate. It's the only name-dropping I ever do. Now, in my dotage, the only sport I'm fit enough to play is golf, but I still catch my breath when Botham, or, on a couple of occasions, Nick Faldo, says, 'How are you playing?'

WARREN CLARKE: Dennis and I finally gave up football in our early forties when we couldn't run any more. We found ourselves struggling against teams of young lads where our only recourse was to chop them down and take them out! Our play was getting so dirty Den decided we'd better stop, give it up and take up golf.

Golf I had always regarded as a stupid old man's sport. Now I am a stupid old man, one of the great regrets of my life is that I didn't accept the invitations to play when I was in my twenties. My thinking then also was that it was for posh old farts and I didn't want to mix with them. To a certain extent I was right; some clubs are still stiff with them.

I first took up golf when I was filming *Stay Lucky* in Yorkshire. I had been playing football for the writer Geoff McQueen's veteran team, and at the end of that season decided that I just didn't fancy it any more.

I had rented a cottage in Horsforth and from my bedroom window I could see the Horsforth Golf Club and a load of duffers spraying those little white balls all over the greens. I could do better than that, I thought. Geoff gave me a half-set of clubs and suggested I had some lessons. I phoned the pro and arranged to meet him on the practice ground, which for me was just over the little wall of my garden. I was hooked instantly.

WARREN CLARKE: One of the first games we ever played together was in Great Yarmouth. We'd stayed over after a football match, and were invited to play at a golf course which turned out to be set in the middle of a race course, surrounded by a holiday village of caravans. None of us could play at all. There we were, Richard O'Sullivan, Bob Powell, Den and I, hooking and slicing balls off the tees straight into the caravan windows where people were eating their breakfast. Helplessly we'd yell out, 'Fore!' while they tried to avoid the golf balls that kept plopping into their cornflakes.

RICHARD O'SULLIVAN: Dennis was as usual very eager to

play, even though he didn't know much about the game. We all thought there couldn't be that much to it. All you had to do was hit the ball in the hole! Dennis had a couple of swings, then Warren took a turn, and Dennis again. Thwack! He swung and hit Warren smack on the nose!

We all killed ourselves laughing but we carried on, Dennis getting more and more furious. He gave it up in the end, swearing it was not his game, he didn't have the patience for it. Now, of course, you can't get him off the golf course. He's there practically every day.

TIM HEALEY: Being a natural sportsman Dennis was very frustrated when he first started. He is extremely competitive in sport, strange because he is not at all competitive as an actor, quite the reverse. I'd already been playing for ten years when Dennis started; now he's the same handicap as me with his own annual tournament!

It is the only time (maybe with the exception of sex) that I have persisted at something that I couldn't do to begin with. Many of my mates on the unit of *Stay Lucky* played golf and encouraged me to persist. Eventually we formed SLAGS (Stay Lucky Amateur Golf Society). I got down to a 17 handicap, and now understand just how nice and patient those guys were when I was playing off 28. Once it was known that I was serious about the game, I began to receive invitations to charity do's, which again made it possible for me to play on world-class courses other good golfers would kill for. Not only some of the great courses in Britain, but those in Portugal, Ireland, France, South Africa and Mauritius. It is possible that this is the big love affair of my life – sorry, that's what this stupid game does to you. It has enabled me to make a whole new group of very good friends who helped me enormously through the break-up of my last marriage. The one place I could escape to and hide, when the news of our break-up hit the press, was my haven, the Lambourne Golf Club.

I had joined with Warren Clarke, after being invited to play there by our great mate Garry Carfoot. It is a young club, seven years old, so there are no traditional old fogies laying down the law, but it does have all the traditional values of golf, i.e. dress, behaviour and honesty. We use our beautiful clubhouse like a good pub. It is a major meeting place, groups of us have little away days, and we all join in the special nights that are laid on. When I say 'we all', I mean doctors, solicitors, judges, pilots, plumbers, builders, actors, sportsmen and even estate agents. You see, we put up with anybody.

TEN

REGAN

TOM CLEGG: When Euston Films decided to make *Regan*, they appointed Douglas Campfield as director, and my old mate Ted Childs as producer. I was still around editing *Special Branch*. Unfortunately for him but great for me, Douglas had a row with the writer, Troy Kennedy Martin, and Ted, and I was called in to direct.

John Thaw was already cast as part of the deal with Troy. John had starred in that very successful series *Red Cap*, also written by Troy, but in this instance the storyline called for a twosome. Dennis was top of my list. My experience working with him on *Special Branch* had been excellent, and Dennis by nature was very gregarious, always one of the boys who fitted in well with the crew, something I knew would be invaluable in creating a good working environment.

I felt the balance between the two of them would be right, that Dennis would bring an element of humour to the relationship, and add a true street quality to the show. I knew them both to be honest, generous actors, plus Dennis also had more experience working in film than John. However, I wasn't at all sure Dennis would want to do it. After all, he was used to playing leads and this, as originated, was role number two. He came in to see me, I explained how it was, and he agreed without even reading the script.

JOHN THAW: The producers knew that the part of Carter in *Regan* was going to be a running character and, if we were going to do a series, the chemistry between us had to be right. Consequently we saw a few guys for the role.

I'd read a scene with one or two of them that morning, then Dennis came along. I remembered him from the TV we'd done together years before, although we hadn't seen each other since.

He, of course, read the scene beautifully, and immediately

captured the character you got later on. He just had an instinct of how the bloke should be.

We broke for lunch and Tommy, Dennis and I went over to the the Red Cow, the pub which was to play such a large part in our lives over the next four years. Over a few drinks, we felt an instant rapport. That was it. On we went.

TOM: *Regan* was never intended just as a pilot. Lloyd Shirley, of Euston Films, had already commissioned the series from Troy and Ian Kennedy Martin on the strength of that one script, with the intention of developing the ideas and characters, but as he had a ninety-minute 'window' in his Armchair Theatre series, he slotted *Regan* into it.

My first day on *Regan* was potentially the most dangerous of my professional life. Not physically, you understand, but from a career point of view.

I was called for eight o'clock in the morning to the location base in Wapping. Usually there is a circus of caravans, action cars, make-up van, kitchen and catering buses; on this occasion everything was based in a pub called the British Ensign. Tom Clegg greeted me on my arrival, introduced me to the crew, to Lee Montague who was playing the chief baddie, and to the stuntmen who were playing his thugs. John Thaw and I had a brief chat, then I was dispatched to wardrobe and make-up.

I had some breakfast and sat back to await my call. I wasn't quite as nervous as I can be on the first day. I had already worked with both the director and the star and I knew a lot of the crew from my *Special Branch* days. The absence of nerves could also have had something to do with the fact that I was only in one scene, where I had one line. It centred around a confrontation between Regan and Lee Montague, who is forced into reeling off a list of names, at which point his thugs emerge from the shadows and threaten Regan. Then I appear from my hiding place, behind a car, gun in hand, and shout, 'Don't move!' Easy!

I sat back comfortably, as directed, and waited. At about one o'clock we broke for lunch. I hadn't done a stroke. We stopped for tea at four p.m., and roughly twelve hours after I had arrived that morning we broke for dinner and I still had not been called. By now I was being treated like a life-long regular by the landlord and his wife, who had been great fans of my brother Peter. I had resisted their hospitality for most of the day, but eventually, being stuck there in a pub while everyone else was out filming, I did succumb to a pint. I then gently drank and ate through the evening. At ten thirty p.m., fourteen and a half hours after I was first called, I received the words 'We're ready for you now.'

Because everything had gone over schedule, by now it was all kick, bollock and scramble. The scene and the camera was set, but owing to pressure of time, it was decided to shoot the scene without a proper rehearsal. 'Sure,' I agreed. After all, I only had one line.

I stayed behind my car, waiting for the litany of gangsters' names to cue my entrance. What I had forgotten was that Lee Montague reels off the list about four times before my intervention. Every time I heard the names I loomed from the shadows and shouted, 'Don't move!' The first time Tom said, 'Cut. Too early, Dennis. We'll go again.'

After a while, and a number of premature interruptions from me, Lee would say the line and all the actors would pause, pre-empting my shout. If I didn't come in, they would carry on with the scene until Lee repeated the names. Another pause of anticipation, and on they'd go. By the law of averages, eventually I got the line in the right place. I was certainly not drunk, I wasn't swaying or incoherent, but I had poured down enough beer to make me worried about being late for my cue. It wouldn't have been unheard of for an actor to be sacked after a sequence like that, or at least to get a severe bollocking. Luckily for me, everybody seemed to take into account that I had been called fourteen and a half hours too early, and apart from the occasional joke, it was never mentioned again. We went on to make one of the best and happiest shows anybody could remember.

One of the reasons Tom had been so keen to cast me was the fact that I came from a fighting family and he knew I had gone to boxing club. He had devised a scene where Regan finds me in a gym and asks me to join him as his partner in the Flying Squad. Tom wanted to see me sparring. Great. We shot it at the Thomas à Becket, scene of the premiere party for *Up the Junction*. Hundreds of champions had trained there, including Peter, and there were still billboard posters and pictures of him around the walls. Tom said that he had found an actor who had been a Scottish amateur lightweight champion and he would put three cameras in various places and just let us get on with it for a few rounds. 'Fine,' I said. I was only twenty-five or twenty-six at the time, playing squash, tennis and football non stop and in reasonable shape. The difference was that I hadn't done any boxing training since I was about twelve. I had forgotten just how fit those guys can be.

We were to do three three-minute rounds, shot from different angles. I started like a young champ, remembering all the old footwork, jabbing with a good fast straight left followed by the occasional right hook and upper-cut. First round, so far, so good. Second round, I was finding my arms were feeling rather heavy. Third round, I was finding my legs weren't actually doing what I was telling them. In three rounds I had gone from Cassius Clay to Sonny Liston, but without his ponderous speed. Then I heard the words all actors fear most: 'Hair in the gate!' This means that a piece of foreign matter has been found in the lens and there is a chance it may be on the negative itself. More importantly, it means that you have to shoot the sequence or at least part of the sequence again.

I was now well and truly knackered. We were both bleeding, although no real damage had been done, and just the act of lifting my arms up was a real test. But the show must go on, and we started again. Luckily, most of the earlier footage was usable and it turned out to be quite an impressive scene. But I beg you, the next time you are jeering at a boxer on the telly, just try it yourself. Those guys, even the lesser names, are seriously fit. Even we got a round of applause from the crew and bystanders.

And there can't be many boxers whose prize for a good (or in my case, adequate) performance is a large vodka and tonic given to them in the ring. That's showbiz!

TOM CLEGG: I don't think any of us realised when we were setting it up just how good it was going to be. We felt we'd never really got that first script right, but *Regan* had an immediate impact on the viewers.

The title *Regan* no longer seemed appropriate, and there was some debate as to what to call the series. The suggestion *Sweeney* aroused a lot of opposition. Too complicated! Too obscure! Audiences won't understand it! It's rhyming slang, Sweeney Todd = Flying Squad! Who cares, sounds good! The arguments raged. And finally we won the day.

Euston Films had been set up by Thames TV to make filmed programmes for television. Their first project was the 1972 series *Special Branch*, starring George Sewell and Patrick Mower, together with the series Armchair Cinema. There were six of these made, *Regan* being one of them.

Euston was headed by George Taylor and Lloyd Shirley, with Ted Childs brought in as producer of *Regan* and *The Sweeney*. Lloyd had an unbelievable track record. He'd been involved in most of Thames' great dramas, and he and George had worked together for many years, Lloyd on the artistic side and George on technical and organisation. And they had assembled a truly wonderful crew, who stayed with them for years. When I finished *Minder* in 1985, I was working with the same people with whom I'd done the very first episode of *Special Branch*. This was not because they were looking for a pension or security – they were all freelance – but with Euston they knew they would do good work; they cast good actors, commissioned brilliant writers and employed, mostly, terrific directors.

JOHN THAW: Because Ted Childs, the producer, and Tom Clegg, the director, had been cameramen, The Sweeney was shot in a 'cinéma vérité', hard-edged style. It was not set up and posed like some of the American counterparts, and was unlike any other TV police shows at that time.

TOM CLEGG: *The Sweeney* generated great excitement. We all felt we were pioneering and the scripts were good.

Euston Films was the first independent to film television drama out on the street. The early episodes of *Special Branch*, for example, were shot on video with all its restrictions – cumbersome cameras with miles of cable, which meant locations were usually limited to the studio. Once Euston Films took over, everything changed.

Z Cars was the first police series to take the action outside the studio, but in those days the technology and the action was restricted. With *The Sweeney* the world opened up. The Flying Squad couldn't be dramatised in a studio. Their whole life was based in cars out on the streets. Now for the first time we were shooting on 16mm film with small flexible cameras that could go anywhere; we could get the feel of real locations, go into real houses, follow car chases, do action sequences as never before, not on this scale and never for TV.

This became a new genre.

Mind you, by the law of averages, not everyone was top-notch. I came back one night straight from the set, still wearing my make-up. Suzanne, my make-up artist friend, looked at me quizzically and said, 'Aren't you supposed to be doing a police show?'

'Yes,' I answered.

'Then why are you made up to look like a Red Indian?'

I checked my appearance in the mirror. She was right. Our make-up guy had been in the business for decades, but he refused to change his methods or to come to grips with the fact that with modern equipment, thick 'paint' was no longer necessary.

Every morning this guy would plaster the stuff on, then, at our request, he'd carefully separate one two-ply tissue into two one-ply sheets, and watch, nonplussed, while we wiped our excess make-up off again.

He watched us doing it, and didn't give a monkey's.

ELEVEN

THE SWEENEY

We started shooting *The Sweeney,* in the spring of 1974. There were three regulars, John Thaw (Regan), me (Carter) and Garfield Morgan (our boss, Haskins).

John can be one of the shyest people you could ever meet, but being surrounded by this amazing group of technicians, he relaxed visibly by the hour. His desktop rendition of 'The Sun Has Got His Hat On' will live with most of us for the rest of our lives.

We were based at Colet Court in Hammersmith, a huge building which at one time was part of St Paul's School. It was a warren of strange-shaped rooms, perfect for Euston's purposes, and everything was there, from our permanent film set – squad office, which included several police cells – to all the offices for the producers, casting, wardrobe, make-up, etc. The location also gave us easy access to the whole of west and central London. This is a very important consideration. To move a whole film crew, with upwards of seventy people and all the gear involved, is like a military exercise every morning. The further you go, the more time it takes, and time is money.

The director of that first episode was Terry Green, who went on to do probably more shows than anybody else. He also loved the East End. You could guarantee that if he was in charge, sooner or later you would have to make the inevitable trek east. The first episode was called 'Ringer'. It was written by one of the two best writers that we had, Trevor Preston. The cast was quite impressive too: Brian Blessed, Ian Hendry and Alan Lake were the chief villains.

When a series of this size is being mounted, every eventuality has to be taken into account. Roads have to be cleared of traffic, city permissions sought, alternative indoor scenes have to be prepared, should the weather prove inclement, and stand-by equipment and crews have to be on alert.

The Flying Squad boasts that they are the only chauffeur-driven force in the world. The drivers are all highly trained, A1 police drivers, whose only job is to drive the squad car.

JOHN THAW : More than that, they are also not allowed out of the car to join or help in the action. They are not trained in combat like the squad, their role is to remain with the car and maintain radio contact at all times.

We were doing one of those scenes in which a call comes through to the office, we race out, and jump into the Granada, ready for the off. Except we jump in and nothing happens. The driver just sits there. 'Cut!' the director shouts. 'What's the problem?'

It turned out the driver couldn't drive. The actor, whom they had cast in the role not only couldn't drive, he didn't have a licence. We never found out if anyone had actually asked him if he could drive, or if, like a lot of actors, he had lied to get the job. In the end, the part of Bill, the driver, was given to Tony Allen, who was John's stand-in. It turned out he knew an awful lot about cars and was used to driving them very fast, but it has to be said, in his youth, generally in the opposite direction from the police. Tony stayed with us throughout *The Sweeney*, becoming one of our biggest friends, and in one capacity or another has worked with John ever since.

JOHN THAW: For the more dangerous chase sequences we had stunt drivers. This did not mean we could sit idly by and watch and marvel, we had to be seen in the car too. This could sometimes be quite hairy! Only once were we ordered out of the car and our places taken by two stunt stand-ins. Sure enough the car was pranged. It hit a pylon and was badly damaged on the passenger side, exactly where I would have been sitting.

There was nothing at the beginning to make you feel like a star. Everybody reads about actors and actresses lounging around in their luxurious mobile homes. Let me tell you, it took us two series to even get a chair! We hung around on the set or sat in the car or just hung around generally.

That first episode took place on a piece of wasteland in darkest Peckham, where we were to shoot an ambush and an arrest. It was also the day local elections were in progress. The schools were being used as polling stations and the pupils were let off to create havoc wheresoever they wished. Our location was bang in the middle of two housing estates, so all the young tearaways came sauntering around, making our lives hell. With nowhere to hide, John and I were left loitering in the gutter. Finally I was driven to say, 'Oh, sod this, let's go to the pub.' John looked at his watch. 'It's only half past eleven in the morning,' he said cautiously. 'Not to drink!' I exclaimed. 'Just to get away from all this crap. Just to have a half and a bit of comfort and quiet for a few minutes.'

We piled into the nearest pub, and lo and behold, Ian Hendry and Alan Lake had beaten us to it. They were sitting comfortably with their halves in their hands. I ordered two halves of bitter and asked if they'd like another themselves. 'Piss off,' said Lake. 'This isn't beer, it's brandy.'

This could turn out to be an interesting day, I thought. We were eventually called back on to the set to film the big arrest. A fight scene such as this demands detailed direction and careful physical and technical rehearsal. We were handed our weapons and slowly walked through our fight moves. Alan Lake had been given a cosh, which was made mostly from tape, wound round and round until it was thick and stubby. While he'd been hanging around, he'd amused himself by wandering about hitting anything and anybody with this thing. The more battered it looked, the more re-taping it needed and the harder it got, until in the end, in effect, it rivalled a real cosh – rock hard.

We finally got to the bit where there's a scuffle and John nicks Lakey. 'Cut!' was called, and I heard John mutter, 'Stupid bastard!'

'What's up, mate?' I asked.

'That fucking idiot just whacked me with his cosh. And it fucking hurt.'

John is the nicest, most gentle bloke around, but he had been hit by a hard instrument on the forehead by someone who was completely out of order, and he was ready to give Lake a sharp right-hander. In all the years we worked together, this was the only time I saw him as angry as this, and I have to say I wouldn't fancy getting a clump from John.

Peter Braham, our stunt co-ordinator, realised what had happened and calmed the situation. He had an equally skilled team of stuntmen working with him, half of whom were playing cops and half the villains.

He took John to one side. 'This time, when we do it again,' he suggested, 'stay back from Lake. Don't get to him quite so quickly.'

We re-shot it, only this time Peter and another stuntman got to Lake as soon as he got out of the van, as rehearsed, and didn't exactly pull their punches. By the time John moved in for the arrest, Alan wasn't in quite the same aggressive shape as in the previous take – the wind had been taken out of his sails. To his credit, though, he did carry on with his dialogue like a pro.

Everybody knows what a terrific actor John is, but he's also one of life's gentlemen. He has got a super sense of humour and is deeply sensitive; he is also a music buff, a great family man, and a loyal and true friend. He is the first to admit, he looks and behaves a little older than his years, but that is probably because his dad brought him and his brother up single-handedly, which made him very independent and self-assured at an early age.

He was one of the youngest people ever to get into RADA. To move from a working-class household in Manchester to the premier drama school in London, at the age of sixteen, takes gumption as well as talent. Although he is only six years older than me, I always feel that if I had any problems I could go to him and he would help me sort things out. And his generosity is huge. I know this because without that quality, *The Sweeney* would have been a very different show, especially for me.

The series was written specifically for John, as a vehicle to help propel him up the ladder of success, but it was he who encouraged the writers to make it a double act. Originally, my character was written very much as the second-in-command, always in the background. I'd stand by the door while Regan questioned someone, I'd pass on messages from the office, I'd wait in the car, or look on while he telephoned, until eventually John, of his own volition, started giving me lines of his to say. Finally he went to Ted Childs and pointed out that it was ridiculous to waste a good actor like me. It would be far more realistic, he suggested, if we interacted.

The writers noted how we threw lines at one another as if we'd been mates for years, and started writing more dialogue for the two of us. We had that one ingredient that cannot be manufactured – chemistry. We loved working together; we would improvise around the scripts and make the characters live, like real people. That sort of generosity from one actor to another is extremely rare. I trusted him so much, I even bought a car off him. Yeah, I can hear you all groaning – 'Luvvies.' Well, bollocks, I love the man.

TOM CLEGG: There's an exceptional feeling generated when you are working on something successful. Dennis and John, although very different personalities, bonded immediately. They also respected each other and each other's talents. As Regan and Carter they complemented one another and the audiences loved them. It gradually emerged that the real value was in the partnership. It gave them the opportunity to get away from strict police procedure, so that the dialogue between them rounded out their characters.

John's character, with a burnt-out marriage behind him, had sunk into a personal life which was bleak and empty. He could reflect this through Dennis, reveal the chip on his shoulder as well as his irritation with interfering officialdom. Dennis, coming from south London, had the natural humour and patois that could lighten the darkest situation.

They weren't heroes as such, more anti-heroes who broke the rules and enjoyed a drink. They were guys with problems and attitude who had a tough job to do, dealing with the seamier side of society. There was no glamour, no 'holier than thou' sanctimony. The audience liked this honesty. And for us, it was very exciting creating these three-dimensional characters, in the sort of action and ambience usually reserved for feature film.

It took eight five-day weeks to complete shooting one episode of *The Sweeney*. This included two weeks of pre-production – finding locations, casting, costume fittings, designing special set-ups, etc. – followed by two weeks shooting, then four weeks editing the pictures and two weeks editing the sound.

In all, for us actors, this meant the whole series took six months. People outside the business are amazed that it took us ten days to film a single episode that was finally only fifty-two minutes long. In fact it was a very tight schedule. In a cinema film, you'd be thrilled if you got two minutes a day in the can. With us, we were in dead trouble if we didn't shoot at least five. This meant that we had some very long days, but with the crew and cast we had, every day was a joy.

Word spread about the show, and the finest actors were eager to enlist: Dudley Sutton, Nicola Pagett, Billy Murray, Warren Mitchell, Stuart Wilson, June Brown, Tony Selby, Julian Glover, Tony Caunter, Christopher Ellison, Sheila Gish, Prunella Gee and my two old mates Tim Carlton and Warren Clarke, to name but a few.

JOHN THAW: Generally in television at that time the unions were strong and invasive, but with Euston we had the luxury of working with wonderful freelance crews. It was also the era when the barriers finally came down, the start of the breakdown of the rule book, set hours, overtime, etc. Our guys worked under the freelance rule of so much per week for so many hours. It was a different mentality. Obviously they didn't have the security of the studio boys, so it was important they did the job and did it well, and they were well paid for the hours they worked.

Sheila [Hancock] and I had not long been married when I started *The Sweeney,* and I know she did not believe we really were working such long hours. She was an experienced television actress and had never worked beyond five or six o'clock in the evening, yet we were not finishing until nine, nine thirty. Not only that, I would come home smelling of beer; my genuine excuse being that we often ended up filming in a pub, which we did a lot, and drinking real beer . . . She never actually called me a liar, but my account was received with a great deal of scepticism.

One day we were filming at Sandown racetrack, a private event, so I invited Sheila down with the baby to see the horses. When it got to past nine o'clock at night and we were still filming, I advised her, gently, that maybe it would be better if she took the baby home to bed. She never said a word after that.

We knew we were doing good work and had great confidence in the scripts and most of the directors, but I had never even considered TV ratings before *The Sweeney,* and I think I'm right in saying that they weren't such a powerful force as they are now. *Regan* had reached number three, but that had been a one-off. To maintain that standard over thirteen episodes was very different. We simply concentrated on doing the best job we could.

I wouldn't call it a treadmill, but the hours we worked were very demanding and our scripts were never far from our sides. Both John and I were lucky, in that we learned lines very quickly. My method was to work through the script and the schedule, marking the days where I had a little or a lot to learn. Days of stunts and action with only the odd line, such as 'He's over there. Get round the back' I knew I could learn in the car on the way to location. Heavier dialogue days meant getting home earlier and doing work on the script in the evening. However, a couple of bad-weather days and the shooting schedule could catch you out. A call sheet is handed out every evening, giving you all the information you need for the following day's work, including 'weather cover', which means an alternative indoor scene, usually for us in the squad office. We all tended to be somewhat lax in preparing for this. It was only after trying to film in a downpour, and hearing the desperate shout from a drenched first assistant, 'It's a wrap here, back to the squad office', that panic set in. Fortunately, John and I travelled to and from location in the same car, so we would go through all the new scenes together, on the move. Where it got really difficult was if you had a long list of suspects' names and addresses to give. Actors hate lists.

JOHN THAW: Looking back, it must have been hell for newcomers to the show. You had to be such a quick study. If you did more than two takes you could feel the atmosphere grow tense. Ideal, and expected, was one take, which, dare I say it, Den and I did more often than not. More than three and it was 'My God, they've gone to pieces!'

The Sweeney hit the nation's screens like a bomb. It was without question an overnight success. Euston Films had cracked it. *We* had cracked it. The reviews the next morning were fantastic!

On the other hand, the police were far from happy. *Z Cars* had been a groundbreaking series in its time. There had also been an offshoot called *Softly, Softly*, but by 1973, both were well past their sell-by dates. Scotland Yard was very critical of the way we portrayed them as hard-drinking, hard-living hard men. They didn't like the fact that we showed how often the police carried guns and that they collaborated with known villains in the search for information. We had two police advisers, one official, one unofficial. The official adviser would tell us that to get a gun you had to go to the armourer, explain why you needed it and sign copious bits of paper. The unofficial adviser told us that if you felt it might be prudent to carry a weapon, you got one out of the office safe and that was it. Both were correct, but one version was the way it should be done and the other was the way it was actually done.

The famous 'Get your trousers on, you're nicked' was a direct quote. We had asked if were correct in using, as an official caution, 'Whatever you say will be taken down and used in evidence.'

After some laughter, our unofficial adviser, Dave, said it depended who you were arresting. If the suspect wasn't being too aggressive, it would be 'Come on, son, you're nicked.' If there was too much lip, it would be 'Shut your mouth, you're nicked.' And if the villain was a real handful and determined not to go down without a fight, it would be a swift kick in the bollocks and 'You're fucking nicked.'

We preferred the unofficial approach.

TOM CLEGG: Obviously there was violence in the series and of course we faced a great deal of opposition and criticism from the likes of Mrs Whitehouse. Violence had to be an integral part of the series, although our aim was that it should never be gratuitous. But if it was there, we were determined not to dilute it. We felt strongly that the effects of violence should be shown, that if you stab or shoot someone it hurts and it kills!

The Sweeney was transmitted after the nine o'clock watershed, but we still had a responsibility to the ITA and clear directives – no bad language, no four-letter words, no sex words, no blaspheming, and any nudity had to be only ever a glimpse.

One has to remember that we were dramatising events, that investigations which took months were reduced to an hour. Everything therefore was intensified. We couldn't show the tedium of police work but we caught the flavour of the period.

JOHN: Playing the roles of hard-case Squad officers was not without its difficulties. People were sometimes never sure how much was acting.

I also remember Dennis telling me he'd been in a pub, while they were filming, where he was accosted by a very angry man who verbally attacked him because *The Sweeney* had 'too much fucking swearing!'

The man continued, 'That fucking programme of yours. I've got a little kid at home and I don't want him sitting in front of the fucking television, listening to that fucking language every fucking night. He's only fucking eleven!'

Shortly after the successful transmission of the first show, it was decided there would be a second series.

Once again we had the same great crew and writers, Trevor Preston, Troy Kennedy Martin and a few newcomers writing great scripts, with Tom Clegg, Terry Green and a few talented additions directing.

One of those additions was a Canadian called Bill Brayne, a smashing man, if somewhat proper and correct. It confused him, not surprisingly, when he heard John and me adding lines which were not in the script. He hadn't been told that we were allowed to tinker with our dialogue, and for all our explanations and assurances, he insisted that we keep to the official words. Finally, but in light-hearted vein, we sent the offending pages with our additions to Ted Childs, our producer, who duly signed his authority for their use. Bill didn't object after that.

It wasn't that we were rewriting the scripts – they were about as good as you could get – but we did embellish them. We would improvise lines in quiet moments, walking to the office, waiting in the car, usually about something outside the normal realms of police work. It could be about football, women, personal problems, anything that proved our characters had a life outside their jobs.

When the series started, Carter, for instance, was married. It was thought that this would be a good counterpoint to the male, buddy-buddy feel of the squad office. In a couple of earlier shows my wife, played by Stephanie Turner, shows her disdain for the Flying Squad in general and Regan in particular. In the second series she dies, after being in a hit-and-run incident. This gave me the chance to show the vulnerable side of Carter's character and Regan's reaction to it.

This was not a carefully considered storyline. Ted Childs liked the idea of Carter having a wife, but because the scripts were being written only weeks ahead of filming, it was impossible to assess, or guarantee, in what episodes the wife character would actually appear, if at all. Quite correctly, her agent was fighting for Stephanie to be put on a retainer for all thirteen, just in case. This wasn't financially acceptable to Euston Films, so after much arguing, Ted's solution was quite simple: 'Kill her!'

TOM CLEGG: Humour was an integral part of *The Sweeney*, as it has to be with members of the real Flying Squad. They have to make humour out of a black situation otherwise they couldn't survive. It's an escape valve that releases them from some of the awful things they see and feel. So the humour we brought to *The Sweeney* was real and truthful, not side-splitting, but moments of lightness. Dennis could lift a scene by adding a laugh, and John always had that lovely droll quality.

Humour was also part of the chemistry that bound John and Dennis together.

JOHN THAW: Den and I share a similar sense of humour, except he is much quicker and wittier than me.

There was a scene where we had a few seconds to fill in with an ad-lib or two. We'd just nicked a couple of villains after some raid. Den and I were leaning against the side of a big lorry, so to fill in, I took out a packet of cigarettes. Den said, 'Can I have a cigarette?'

I said, 'I've only got one.'

'I only want one,' he replied.

It was a gag we then used all time.

Things that made us laugh we put in where we could. The writers too understood our characters and personalities, and whereas they'd started writing for Carter and Regan, as the four years evolved they wrote more and more for John and Dennis, and our sense of humour crept in.

Troy Kennedy Martin, as a writer, has a knack of seeing things from a quirky angle and can find humour in the most serious situation. Trevor Preston, a great admirer of Troy's, took the humour a bit further in his scripts, and so it snowballed, with Dennis and me looking for a joke even if it wasn't there on the page.

There was involvement and interaction from everyone concerned in the production, and though it's a cliché to say it, over the years we became like a family of writers, directors, actors and crew. It was a fact that we spent more time together working than we did with our own families and wives.

There were roughly seventy people on the unit, so it would take another book to mention them all, but they know in what esteem the actors and the directors held them. The sparks, chippies, painters, props, grips, drivers, caterers, the lot. Magic.

Anybody and everybody could make a suggestion. There were times when we did a really good show in spite of the director!

By now, even the police accepted us. I think they came round to the view that it wasn't a bad idea to let the country see that our cops were as hard and as ruthless as the villains were. But their acceptance did have its drawbacks for John, Garfield and me. To keep in their good books and to guarantee at least some co-operation, we had to attend hundreds of police do's. During which, it has to be said we did meet some very good blokes. I thought actors and musicians could drink until I met a few of the Old Bill.

One little mob in Shooters Hill sort of adopted us. They even called themselves 'The Teeny Sweeney'.

TOM CLEGG: Despite *The Sweeney* becoming a cult show, and the boys enjoying enormous popularity, there was no special treatment reserved for them as with some star actors making films today. They were regarded much the same as the crew and other members of the production team, and working conditions were far from luxurious. They were out on the street. If they were lucky, they found respite in a nearby house, a shop, or a pub. Usually it was in the back of a van or car.

Eventually it did dawn on us that we'd have to do something. The guys couldn't work properly any more. The word would spread like wildfire when we were filming in a certain location and the crowds would gather. Frequently Dennis and John would be barricaded in the car with people, particularly women and girls, banging on the windows, screaming for autographs.

It was surprising in some ways. There was no glamour attached to the series. It was very macho, with very little sympathy for any women characters. Neither Regan nor Carter were successful in their relationships with their girlfriends or wives. They tended to be abrasive, dismissive and chauvinistic, reflecting police attitudes at that time.

Yet they were treated like pop stars. Young girls and women especially would crowd around Dennis. As John once remarked, rather gloomily, they treated Dennis like the boyfriend and him like the father.

We did another two series that were shown with great success in 1976 and 1978. In all we did fifty-three episodes. It was sold to fifty-one countries and is regarded by some as the best and most successful series ever made for British television.

JOHN THAW: And finally, on the very last episode . . .

Dennis and I had previously appeared on _The Morecambe and Wise Christmas Show_. We were enjoying a drink with them after the recording, and as a joke I said, 'Right, we've done your show. You should do ours!'

Ernie, a big fan of _The Sweeney_, pricked up his ears. 'Do you mean it?'

I hadn't expected this response and was a bit taken aback, but I said, 'Yeah, why not?' thinking it would never happen. But the next day, when I mentioned it to Ted Childs, he lit up. 'We'll do it. The last episode!'

Now throughout the entire four years, despite all the crowds, the fans, the difficulties and the promises, Den and I had never been given even the smallest, most basic caravan in which to relax, go to the loo, learn our lines or change. But we arrived for the very last programme and there were two identical, long, luxurious, gleaming Winnebagoes.

'Terrific!' I said. 'There's one for Eric and one for Ernie and we'll be in the back of the van again!'

At that point one of the directors called us over. 'John and

Dennis, this Winnebago is yours and that one's Eric and Ernie's!'

When the duo turned up we said, 'We can't believe this. Fifty-two episodes and now we get a Winne!'

'Down to us, boys!' Eric said.

'How come?' we asked.

Eric smiled. 'Our agent asked for a Winne. Euston said, "Fine, OK." So he said, "Right, same size, style, everything as John and Dennis!" They said, "John and Dennis don't have a Winne." "What do they have then?" "Nothing." Well, you can't expect Eric and Ernie to be in a bloody big Winnebago when the two stars of the show don't have anything! You'd better make sure they have the same Winnebago as Eric and Ernie, otherwise it will look bad!"'

Filming with Eric and Ernie was riotous.

In the storyline they played themselves, forced to call in the police after a series of threatening phone calls. Regan and Carter are sent to interview them at the club where they are supposedly performing and discover that unbeknownst to the two boys, they have been implicated by a fellow artist in a drugs scam. It all ends in a Keystone cops style chase. All quite straightforward on paper, except with Eric's genius inventive humour and the banter between the two brilliant comedians, the script was enhanced with breathtaking ad-libs that had the entire company aching with laughter.

Eric's main concern was that his wife, Joan, would find out he was indulging in a little drink now and then, something strictly limited since his recent heart attack scare.

We shot the episode at the Lakeside Club in Frimley, near Guildford. The morning after the episode had been aired, we read in the paper that that same night, the club had been burned down. Hopefully it was nothing to do with our performances!

We also did two *Sweeney* movies.

The first one I didn't like much. It had a great cast – Ian Bannen, Barry Foster, Colin Welland, Brian Glover, Diane Keen and Lynda Bellingham – but it just didn't work for me. It was all done in a rush, John and I didn't really see the script until we were about to start shooting and we weren't consulted about any part of the making of the film. If I had had anything to do with it, it would have been written by either Trevor or Troy and directed by Tom Clegg. For whatever reasons, they got Ranald Graham and David Wickes. Ranald had written a couple of scripts in the second series and they were very good, but he certainly wasn't one of the guys who was responsible for the show's success. And personally, I didn't have a great deal of time for Wickes, either as a man or as a director.

It seemed to me a great opportunity totally wasted. We had a huge fan base and turned out a very ordinary and very 'English' little film. *Sweeney 2* was a different matter. Clegg directed it and it was exactly what the show had been about. Not just a longer episode, but a really good cop film. We had an excellent script by Troy, and apart from Denholm Elliott and Ken Hutchinson, a cast of not terribly famous but brilliant actors. Sadly, because of the let-down experienced by so many after the first film, this one didn't get the audiences it deserved.

Halfway through the making of the fourth series, the question of a fifth arose. In the car park at Colet Court, John and I decided not to do any more. I think John had already made up his mind, but, being the gentleman he is, we had a chat about it anyway. The conclusion was that we might have run out of good storylines. After all, how many different ways were there to rob a bank or murder somebody?

We decided to quit while we were on top.

JOHN THAW: The very last day of that very last episode, Dennis, me and the crew all went to the pub for a farewell drink and a game of darts. My very first game of darts with Dennis. Normally they would not let me play because I was so bad. But on this occasion they agreed *even* John could have a game – even John. And he might hit the board because he's had a few drinks!

And I beat Dennis! I beat him and I've dined out on it ever since!

DEKE ARLON: With *The Sweeney* at an end, Dennis and I felt we needed to look to America to expand his career.

A very dear friend of mine and my family was the number one agent of ICM [International Creative Management], Dennis Selinger. He died, sadly for all of us, a few years ago.

Back then this dapper, white-haired gentleman was affection-ately nick named 'the Silver Fox'. He had overseen the film careers of Michael Caine, Roger Moore, Telly Savalas, Sean Connery, Peter Sellers and many more. I thought he was just the right man for us.

At first, I reckoned that ICM would be too big for me and I would be lost among the hundreds of names on their books, but the reason Dennis Selinger had such a good reputation in the business was that he was accessible. He was always in the office and he always returned calls. Very rare in my experience.

He knew the what, where and when of all the movies being made. He was also a lovely bloke to be around. He would even phone me if he had just heard a good new joke. Well, I heard a lot of jokes but didn't do a single movie. He kept saying, 'I can't get you a film, you're always working,' which I suppose was true.

TWELVE

DOMESTICS

A series can take over your life, partly because of the hours you work and partly because you want it to. In fact this is true of nearly every job an actor does. A few of us try to look terribly blasé by pretending it is just a job, but basically this is a lie. Your life is ruled by two bits of paper: your script and your schedule.

Nevertheless, real life does go on around your call sheet. And it was while we were filming in the squad office that I met Patricia Maynard again.

PAT MAYNARD: Since Dennis had first challenged me to a game of shove-ha'penny, it was extraordinary how often we had met. We'd cross in the corridors of various studios, wave at opening nights or chat in various bars, especially in Twickenham where we both happened to live. Although we never worked together as such, there was a time when we were both based out at Elstree. I was in *General Hospital*, Dennis was in a different production altogether, but casts and crew would all meet up in the local pub. It was during this period that my car was written off in an accident. Dennis heard about it and offered to give me a lift to and from work until my new car arrived. We got to know each other quite well over those two weeks, became good friends. And that was it, we didn't see each other again until much later, when he was just starting *The Sweeney*.

I was in the fourth and last production of the Armchair Theatre series; *Regan* had been the third. This particular film starred Edward Woodward, Rosie Leach and myself, and during rehearsals we all went over to the Red Cow for a drink. There leaning on the bar were Dennis and John Thaw.

We chatted, I asked after Penny and he told me they'd split up.

Three or four months later I received a phone call inviting me to an 'end of production' party of a new series called *The Sweeney*. The production assistant went on to explain it had originally been part of the Armchair Theatre series, and the producers thought it would be a nice idea to invite the casts from all the other productions.

I had just returned from holiday and was looking very tanned and rather good, I thought. And I was in need of a job. So I went.

The wrap had been called, and Colet Court was packed with non-*Sweeney* people, including Pat. This final episode also happened to be one in which Warren Clarke had been guest-starring. He and Pat had worked together in the theatre and were old mates. She was looking stunning, and we both zoomed in.

WARREN CLARKE: Pat and I had been in a production of *The Anniversary* at the University Theatre in Manchester; Pat was playing my fiancée.

One afternoon I was invited by the chairman of Haig's whisky to sample a few of their special reserves, and returned a bit merry but not too bad. However, during the evening performance, we came to the scene where Pat and I were kissing and cuddling on the sofa. I'm afraid I went a bit too far and put my tongue in her mouth. And she bit it! Her anger only relented when she watched me struggling to get through the rest of the play with a painfully swollen tongue!

PAT: Dennis didn't speak a word to me. Warren monopolised me totally until the end of the evening, when he went to get me a drink, and Dennis took his seat next to me and refused to give it up when Warren returned. Dinner had been arranged at a local restaurant, and Dennis asked if I'd join him. What I hadn't realised, and didn't learn until later, was that it was Dennis who had arranged my party invitation through Leslie Petit, the *Sweeney* casting director!

I got lost driving to the restaurant, so arrived late. The long table was packed. There were only two spare seats, one next to Dennis and one next to Warren. I thought, 'Oh, crumbs!' I sat next to Dennis. For the next two years relations were somewhat strained between him and Warren.

Pat was (and still is) seriously tasty, and before long it was very evident that we weren't going to leave on our own that night. We went back to her tiny flat in Chiswick.

The next morning Pat was going to Chichester to visit Peter

Gilmore and Jan Walters, whom I had already met through Richard O'Sullivan, and she invited me along. I remember McCartney's *Band on the Run* had just been released and I had the tape in the car. We gave it a terrible hammering on the way down to Sussex. We had a super weekend and I don't really think we were apart, except for work, from then on. In a very short time I had moved out of Chris Lewis's place and that was it. I now lived in Chiswick.

> PAT: I realised things were getting serious when his music, guitar and ratty old dressing gown arrived. That was all he had. He'd left everything else with Penny. We started from scratch.
>
> It was the element of danger about Dennis that attracted me. He was good-looking, well-read and intelligent, although he constantly puts himself down. We were both south Londoners, shared the same kind of history, came from council flats with families that had no money. We were comfortable with one another. And he made me laugh.
>
> John Thaw tells the story of one *Sweeney* episode during which the new director was particularly ineffectual, so much so that his direction was constantly being ignored, until finally he complained, 'I don't know, sometimes I feel like the invisible man!'
>
> Dennis turned round, quick as a flash, and quipped, 'Who said that?'

Pat was beautiful, funny and gregarious, a talented actress who was highly rated in the business. She was also very sexy. And single, only because for several years she had been involved with a married man. Shortly after we met she knocked that affair sharply into touch and we were a couple.

The summer of 1974 was brilliant. I had a wonderful woman and a fantastic job. Heaven.

We moved out of her little flat in Chiswick and bought a lovely house in Arragon Road, Twickenham. Very adjacent to the Turk's Head!

> PAT: It also overlooked the cemetery. I remember a taxi driver came to pick Dennis up one night. He looked at our little house and said rather disparagingly, 'Dennis Waterman lives here?' Dennis was a bit stung. 'I've got to live somewhere!' But it was an indication of just how successful the series was becoming. It was also beginning to change our lives.

JOHN THAW: They certainly started charging us more for vodka and tonic.

PAT: We had been together for only three months when Hannah was conceived. Looking back, I suppose it was rather irresponsible. We certainly did not intend to start a family at that time but we were in love, happy and I wanted her desperately. I wasn't sorry when it happened. I was also secure in myself, I had my own car plus a successful career, and if the worst came to the worst I could always support her. Luckily I never had to.

On one of my very few days off, Patricia presented me with an absolutely beautiful little girl, Hannah Elizabeth Waterman, born on 22 July 1975. As we would learn to expect with Hannah, this was not without a little drama. We got to the hospital around six in the morning. My plan was to be there for the birth, and everything seemed fine, apart from my feeling decidedly wobbly when they administered the epidural. It was when all the colour drained from my face that they suggested I step outside for a while. I did not resist.

The waiting room had just stopped spinning when the door was flung open and the doctor pronounced, very gently, that it now appeared the baby was breech and would I give permission for a Caesarean section. 'Of course,' I quivered. 'Fine,' he said. 'In half an hour or so, say around seven thirty, you'll be a daddy.'

Seven thirty came and went, expectant fathers came and went and my fears grew and grew. I'm embarrassed to admit that I was actually too scared to ask anybody what was going on. I figured they knew I was there and if anything was to go wrong, they'd tell me. Being a hospital that specialised in births, they would know how to treat a first-time expectant father, suffering a particularly acute attack of anxiety.

At about ten o'clock and a hundred cigarettes later, having watched the jubilation of a lot of other new fathers and having paced (yes, you actually do pace) about a hundred miles or so, I finally summoned up the courage to ask what was going on. I found a nurse and with great trepidation explained what had happened. She frowned and looked through a lot of files.

'But your wife had a little girl at seven thirty this morning. Didn't anyone tell you?'

'No,' I growled. 'Where are they?'

I was hurried to the ward, accompanied by a babble of apologies. Maybe, somehow or other, I'd fallen between shifts. Oh well, these things can happen, I suppose. I'm calmer about it now.

Pat was sort of translucent and in considerable pain. I don't think she had even noticed I wasn't there. She was just insistent that she would never go through this again. At that moment, I can't say I was terribly sorry.

Eventually her pain abated and was totally forgotten when we held our little girl. Because of the Caesarean delivery Hannah hadn't suffered the trauma of a normal birth and was just perfect.

There was one very slight problem. It hadn't occurred to me that Pat would possibly give me a daughter. Every stitch of clothing that we had prepared was Chelsea blue. On the other hand, she did look good in blue. I had had this dopey macho image of twin season tickets at Stamford Bridge and eventually of watching my boy play various sports for his country!

PAT: I remember coming round from the Caesarean, hearing a voice say, 'You've got a lovely little girl' and my voice answering, 'No, I'm having a boy.'

When Dennis came in I was crying, saying how sorry I was. But he was over the moon. 'Don't be silly,' he said. 'I've seen her. She's beautiful!'

It was also amazing that her birth coincided with a scheduled day off and with the rest of the unit filming in Chiswick, just round the corner from the hospital. Wet the baby's head? We soaked it that lunchtime.

Pat's ward in the hospital was awash with flowers and cards, not to mention champagne. Which we discovered, when mixed with Guinness, can clean out a baby's digestive system in seconds, even when it is second hand! The nurses weren't over-impressed, but it hasn't done Hannah any harm. Actually, thinking about it now, Guinness is about the only thing she doesn't drink.

PAT: This was a very happy period, Dennis adored Hannah. He was very affectionate with her and even changed her nappies once or twice!

Babies were something of a mystery to me but I did think I was slowly becoming more knowledgeable about baby things and more proficient at handling Hannah, so when one day Pat sent me off on an errand to buy some Baby Bio, I confidently searched the shelves of the local chemist, and when that drew a blank, trailed around the area to look in another four. My final exasperated enquiry drew yet another strange look and a rather waspish comment about trying a garden centre.

'Why would I look for baby stuff among gardening things?' I snarled back.

'Because Baby Bio is for plants. It's plant food!'

My confidence was totally sapped!

PAT: The Waterman family were delighted with the new addition. I'd been at school with Norma and Myrna. They, together with my brother and me, had been very much involved in various school drama productions. Now, with the birth of Hannah, we, and all the other brothers and sisters, drew together as a family. With the sad death of my own mother only three months after Hannah was born, Rose became especially close and supportive.

Harry never did. He was a terrible man, whose racism and general vile behaviour aroused nothing but loathing in his own children, who had witnessed their father's compulsive gambling plunge them at times into abject poverty. In an unusual moment of candour, Rose told me of the death of her baby son. Times had been particularly hard, there had been no money to pay for the funeral so the neighbours had raised enough to cover the costs. Rose had paid for the coffin and left the change at home while she went to the funeral. She returned only to find Harry had got there first, and put the money on a horse. She never forgave him for that.

It was an extraordinary love–hate relationship, exactly mirrored in the sitcom *Till Death Us Do Part*. She would never leave him but bore all the hardships for the sake of her children. She was particularly wonderful with Hannah.

When Hannah was eleven months old, I was offered a part in a television series about Yorkshire hill farmers called *This Year, Next Year*. Obviously it was set in Yorkshire, which meant I would be away on location for about a year. At that time, Dennis and I weren't married, although we were living together. Being an independent woman, I felt very strongly that I should earn my own living and bear my share of the responsibility for Hannah. So I took the job.

I hated it. Dennis hated it. Hannah hated it. For eleven months I saw them only at weekends. On a couple of occasions Rose came up with me to help look after Hannah but it was not practical and didn't really work.

Then Dennis asked me to marry him, and I decided to put my career on hold, to enjoy my child and husband and maybe have another baby.

I believe I joked that we should get married on April Fool's Day. Pat's response was 'No, that's a Friday. We'll get married on the second.' Hannah was two years old and a bridesmaid!

The reception was held in the Winchester Hall, attached to the Turk's Head. It was a noble gathering of wonderful friends.

CHRIS LEWIS: Some of us almost never to return! Dennis held the record, set at 2 mins 38.4 secs., for the quickest time from a sitting position in the lounge of my flat to the bar of the Turk's Head. I hold the record for the longest time back. The night of the wedding, I finally dragged myself away from the festivities in the Winchester Hall at about four a.m., and decided in my inebriated wisdom to take a short cut home across the St Margaret's roundabout. Somehow I got lost in the bushes, sat down to ponder the meaning of life and woke up some five and a half hours later with the rush-hour traffic roaring round me.

So there we were – a lovely family, a super house and a smash-hit series. What else could anyone want? A bigger house, another baby and another series. It was all to come. What a lucky little sod I was. Nothing could possibly go wrong.

Then my mother was diagnosed with cancer. It was so advanced it was beyond treatment. She had fallen foul of the renowned Waterman ethic of not believing or letting on that you're unwell. She must have suffered the most agonising pain, for how long none of us knew. The doctor could only wonder at her stoicism and courage. My mother had been forty-five when I was born and had always seemed old to me. I suppose I must have been preparing myself from a very young age that she might die. But it didn't alleviate the feeling of shock when that death was imminent.

She was taken to Putney Hospital. It was almost impossible to comprehend that the backbone of our family, who had worked all her life, could actually be ill, let alone terminally. My sisters came over from California and I knew it was close to the end.

She was allowed out of hospital for Christmas, and came and stayed with Pat and me. The great joy for Mum was Hannah. She was a sunny, smiling little blonde tot, and my mum adored her.

She returned to hospital after Christmas. They saturated her with morphine and we never saw her in a normal state again. Did she know us? We never really knew if she was even aware we visited. In her agony she became very violent and lashed out at anyone close by. It was a traumatic time. Then she was gone.

I didn't know how to react. Obviously I was terribly sad, but because the end was evident, it must have seemed I took it in my stride. Which, in a way, I did. The funeral was even arranged for midday, lunchtime, to accommodate my working schedule. A pathetic case of 'the show must go on'.

I was in my mid-twenties; I had been working since I was eleven years old, and the thought of holding up filming for whatever reason was unthinkable to me. Not so now, but then – then, I don't think I even asked for time off, which I am sure Euston would have granted and understood. I just bottled up my emotions and got on with life. Until one night, on a shoot, I fell apart. I started crying and could not stop. My driver Alan took control. Everyone knew what was happening. He drove me home.

The next time all the siblings were together was when I was the subject of *This Is Your Life*. We had a wonderful, very long night but the overwhelming feeling was of sadness that Mum had missed it. Not only because it was a sort of honour for me, but because she had definitely been Eamonn Andrews' biggest fan.

Looking back on *This Is Your Life*, I realise now you have got to be absolutely stupid not to figure out what's going on. What am I? Absolutely stupid! Suddenly there are loads of phone calls for your partner and nobody wants to leave a message. I must have been in a remarkably placid state of mind because nothing seemed untoward to me. I do have a tendency to jealousy, and quite often just a slightly strange phone call can get my insecurities buzzing. However it does give you a clue as to how sneaky your partner can be.

I was caught by the man with the red book on the set of *The Sweeney* and whisked off to the studio, where I was not allowed out of the dressing room unaccompanied (not even to go to the loo) just in case I saw who was going to be on the show.

It was a memorable night. All my mates from *The Sweeney* were there, of course, together with friends and family, including my three sisters secretly flown over from LA.

Emotion, and nerves too, play havoc with your head. You hear voices over the speakers that you know so well, and your mind goes blank. I feel shamefaced even now that I didn't recognise the voice of my sister Vera. And when my two brothers came on, I was so thrilled, I had this urge to hug them! I didn't, of course. It was not done in our family. We had a terrific night which finally finished at five in the morning. I think!

PAT: Thanks to *The Sweeney* we moved to a lovely house in Richmond.

Dennis was so proud. I remember standing there, looking round at our beautiful new home, and Dennis saying, 'By golly, Pat, haven't we done well?' And we had. For the first time in our lives we had real money, but more than that, it was something we'd achieved together. And I was pregnant again. We were happy. Of course, success also brought changes and problems. Taking Hannah to a funfair, our visit lasted all of ten minutes before Dennis was besieged by fans. Our privacy had gone. Even Harry was quick to jump on the bandwagon.

Despite everything, ever since Rose's death, we had invited Dennis' father over to the house as much as we could. It was not enough. He threatened that unless we invited him more often, he would go to the press and tell them that Dennis was a terrible son. Dennis was appalled and angry, and refused to be blackmailed by his own father. Harry went ahead anyway and sold his 'story' to the *News of the World*, condemning Dennis as the unfeeling, awful son and me for being as cold as a block of ice.

The family were incensed. Myrna wrote to the press exonerating Dennis by revealing what a violent and heartless monster their father had been to them all, throughout their lives. For Dennis it was the end of a miserable relationship. We cut ourselves off from Harry totally after that.

Apart from that very upsetting episode, our early years were incredibly happy. We were not just lovers, we were great friends. We shared a passionate love of music and a group of wonderful friends. Dennis was always a 'man's man', but women loved his company too. He was fun to be with. He loved that warm feeling of fellowship, being with mates, in the convivial setting of a pub like the Turk's or the Red Cow.

And he was generous to a fault. He was always trying to buy me jewellery, which unfortunately didn't interest me greatly.

The price for our new lifestyle was high. It rewarded us well, but the demands were great and the hours extremely long. It meant Dennis getting up at the crack of dawn, and not getting home until very late at night, by which time, inevitably, the exacting pressures of looking after two small children had often left me exhausted, too tired to keep up with Dennis' boundless energy.

THIRTEEN

MUSIC

My first brush with Tin Pan Alley had not been a success. The demos I made with Richard O'Sullivan still lay hidden in some drawer. But I played guitar, wrote songs and sang whenever I could. The high profile of *The Sweeney* opened up the possibility of a recording career yet again. Through a friend of mine, John Foster, I was introduced to one of the world's great drummers, Brian Bennett of the Shadows. The band, originally famed as the musical line-up backing Cliff Richard, had gone on independently to enjoy huge success around the world. They toured until they dropped, then disbanded whilst they were still at the top. Brian, a fine musician, had continued doing session work as a drummer, extending his range to include jazz and classical music as well as playing in the pit for West End musicals. At the same time he was writing, arranging and producing while he pursued his ambitions as a composer of film and television music.

BRIAN BENNETT: John Foster suggested I meet up with Dennis to listen to his songs, advise him on material for an album, and maybe collaborate with him on writing and recording some tracks to present to a record company.

I liked Dennis immediately.

His lyrics had an honesty about them. They were not the usual flowery odes penned by most actors aspiring to be songwriters. But it was his voice which hooked me and made me want to get involved. It had a bluesie edge to it, and below the surface the resonance of deeper emotions wanting to get out.

A deal was struck with Tony Palmer, the then head of A&R at DJM Records, for two albums. I was to arrange and produce, the songs to be mutually agreed.

Brian's studio, the headquarters of Shed Music, was indeed a shed, a very small shed, in his back garden in north London, but he has come up with some super music in there. There we wrote five songs for the album and routined a song that he had written. It became the title track, 'Down Wind of Angels'.

BRIAN BENNETT: The first sessions were booked at Abbey Road. I wanted the album to have the feel of a working band rather than a mixed bag of session players, so I played drums and we surrounded ourselves with the best both musically and socially. And it worked. There was a terrific atmosphere in the studio which extended into evenings at the Alma pub round the corner. So convivial was the set-up friends would often drop by, including John Thaw, who came for lunch on the first day to wish the boy well.

As a producer working within a given budget to a strict timetable, the flow of Dennis' friends occasionally created something of a problem. Studio guests not only want to hear a playback of what you have recorded but are inclined to make helpful comments like 'I think he can do better than that.' So, apart from musical considerations and getting the best from your artist, a producer has to be a diplomat – hear people out and clear them out as tactfully as possible.

I had decided to use a boys' choir on one of the tracks, 'I will Glide', written by Philip Goodhand Tate. I will never forget the sight of those twenty excited young choristers filing across the famous zebra crossing into Abbey Road Studios and down the stairs into Studio Two, world-renowned recording 'home' of the Beatles.

'Down Wind of Angels' was released in 1976.

We went back into the shed.

Despite my being deep into the next series of *The Sweeney*, working with Brian was such a pleasurable experience, we managed to find time to meet up on odd evenings or at weekends to write another six songs, songs which could be performed with a band. My enthusiasm was fired up, I was hungry to perform live, rock, blues . . .

BRIAN BENNETT: The record company had other ideas. David Soul, star of the American cop TV series *Starsky and Hutch*, had just had a big hit with a soft middle-of-the-road ballad. The record company leapt at the formula. 'Waterman's an actor. Let him sing ballads!'

Dennis was having none of it. Though I agreed with him and fought to do something different, I was employed by DJM and forced to take the brief from them. So back to diplomacy and compromise. I found a song at ATV Music in Los Angeles, 'If Ever I Say Goodbye to You'. We recorded it at CTS Studios, Wembley, with a large orchestra. Dennis hated it.

My second album, with the inspired title of *Waterman*, was released in 1977. It didn't sell a whole lot better than the first one.

Even today there are rigid boundaries that define the spectrum of the music business. Music is 'bagged' as rock, alternative, retro, rap, garage, hip hop, MOR (middle of the road), etc. It is an endlessly evolving scene, bound by mindless whims and rules.

It was hard back then for an actor to cross over into the music world. Admittedly David Soul had slipped through the net, but he was American and that seemed to make him acceptable. I experienced enormous prejudice, particularly among the disc jockeys, who would damn you as being 'another bloody actor who wants to be a pop star', without even listening to a single track. Even worse, because I was, at that time, a 'commercial television' actor it was almost impossible to get airplay on the BBC. All I'd like to say now is that there are a great many more actors who can sing than pop stars who can act!

During the late seventies, John found a band that would act as my backing group. I can't remember what they really called themselves, but whenever we did gigs they decided that they would appear as 'The Sprinklers'.

We did weekend gigs all over the country when I was filming and more when I wasn't. John Foster had done all this largely as a friend, just taking a percentage whenever we worked together. We did personal appearances, shop openings, record signings and laughed our way all round the country.

BRIAN BENNETT: I was moving more and more towards my first passion, writing music for film, some of which was even being used for *The Sweeney*. I decided what Dennis needed was a third party to inject some magic into his embryonic music career, someone to shape the next move, a strong music man. Some years earlier I had had the good fortune to work with Deke Arlon and I knew he would be ideal for Dennis.

Without being disloyal to John, I knew that if I wanted to continue with the music side of my life, I would have to have a more professional form of management. Brian introduced me to Deke.

Deke had been discovered by Lionel Bart and recorded by the famous Joe Meek in the late fifties/early sixties, when rock-and-roll singers, apparently, had to have a strange name. Now, nearly twenty-five years after we first met, it doesn't seem like a strange name at all. Outside my family, my relationship with Deke is the longest and most constant one in my life. We've been through ups and downs, highs and lows, hell and high water, and we're still playing golf together. He is still nicking all my cigarettes and I'm still nicking all his good wine.

He was primarily into music, but knew all about other aspects of the business, theatre and television, and soon was negotiating nearly all my deals.

DEKE ARLON: I had never actually 'managed' a performer. Primarily, I was a song man, a music publisher. I worked with people like James Taylor, Gilbert O'Sullivan, Chicago, Blood Sweat and Tears, Chinn and Chapman, and Kenny Young. Together with Kenny Young, our production company had produced a number of top ten hits with Clodagh Rogers and a group called Fox. I had also produced musical shows in the West End for my other clients, Ned Sherrin and Caryl Brahms, all of whom I'd advised and helped in their careers in various ways without actually calling myself a manager.

The prospect of developing a wider career for Dennis seemed to me a challenge to be relished. I took my music seriously and he was a truly serious singer. I saw him play a gig in Croydon with The Sprinklers and was instantly impressed with his vocal performance, even though he himself seemed to lack a certain confidence in the physicality of his role as a singer. A simple matter of making him believe in himself and his talent.

I decided to put together a TV special featuring Dennis and one or two other musical stars with a London background, and approached Yorkshire Television, with whom I had a close association. Together with Vernon Lawrence, then head of light entertainment, we co-produced *Dennis Waterman – With a Little Help From My Friends*.

Brian Bennett, as musical director, put together a great band. Joe Brown sang and played wonderful guitar, his wife Vicky (who sadly died at a very young age) joined three backing vocalists, Linda Lewis sang, and Willie Rushton, swathed in a tent-like gown, performed a wonderful spoof of Demis Rousos.

I remember we were relaxing late one night after rehearsals in the hotel bar, all standing singing round the piano, when suddenly Linda noticed her handbag being plucked from its perch on the top of the piano. By the time she realised it was being stolen, the thief had hightailed it out of the room. Linda's husband Jimmy Creggan (lead guitar player in Rod Stewart's band), Dennis and I hared after him down the hotel corridors and stairs and out on to the street, where we finally caught up with him. The poor guy was so shaken at being nicked by the star of *The Sweeney* himself, he meekly handed over the bag. We let him off lightly with a good reprimand and a warning to behave himself in future.

There was a comedy sketch in the show during which Joe Brown, in a parody of *The Sweeney*, came on as a policeman wearing a helmet with a flashing blue light on top. At one point, bored with waiting around during rehearsals, he left the studios and started directing the traffic on the Kirkstall Road. Amazingly, everyone obeyed him, but it's a wonder he wasn't arrested.

BRIAN BENNETT: I produced an instrumental version of 'Don't Cry For Me Argentina' with the Shadows. It became a top ten hit, and with a new record deal in our pockets, Hank and the rest of us felt the urge to go back on the road. Dennis and I drifted apart, although we still remain friends. Last time we all were together was in Australia. I was recording Hank Marvin, and Dennis was touring in *Jeffrey Bernard is Unwell*. We played some enjoyable golf together, or rather, spent time looking for balls in the outback.

DEKE ARLON: Dennis asked if I would get involved in all of his career, not just the music side. At that time he was represented as an actor by Boyack and Conway, an excellent agency. I had already had conversations with both men pointing out that my position as a manager need not get in the way of theirs as agents. There was a place for both in Dennis' career, and although there would be an initial cost factor to the artist, the enhanced financial gains would be considerable.

Agents frequently have a roster of thirty to forty or more actors on their books. A manager, on the other hand, because of the comprehensive nature of the work, has a very limited client list, and consequently, when the one actor you represent is highly sought after, you have enormous leverage.

I believe fervently that anyone who brings a great deal of creative input to a project deserves more than a set fee. In the same way that a songwriter should own a piece of his publishing, or his own publishing company, so an actor should retain certain overseas or domestic rights for his performance.

Dennis understood this. And I think he realised that at last he had someone in his corner willing to go into battle for him.

Negotiations were about to begin for the second *Sweeney* film. His fee was £5,000, a high fee even then. Until I discovered John Thaw was being paid considerably more. I understood the logic of this. It was his series, he was the leading player and the weight of responsibility lay on his shoulders. But in terms of popularity and audience appeal, the two men were equal.

I had a real tussle, but we got there in the end. And Dennis was paid a great deal more than £5,000. We also held on to some of the rights to *Sweeney* and later to *Minder*. They got a first run on terrestrial TV but other rights and usages we did not give away. Something which, with the advent of cable and satellite television, has proved extremely lucrative.

Despite the high profile of the TV Special, and Dennis' popularity, the BBC would not give the records air time.

So, under the musical direction of ex-guardsman, superb sax player, professional drinker and colourful eccentric Neil Lancaster, Dennis went on tour, aided and abetted by some fine and convivial musicians. Too convivial sometimes.

NEIL LANCASTER: Twelve noon on day one of the tour, the coach arrived at the appointed pub car park to find the motley band of maestros and artists already in the Turk's Head, warming up for the journey to our first gig that evening in Manchester. Within the space of one and a half hours, the pub takings were the equivalent of an entire day's trading. The door burst open. Silhouetted within its frame was the Emperor, Dennis' personal manager, Deke Arlon, an imposing-looking man, and snappy dresser, although it soon became clear that what we had taken to be a handkerchief in his top pocket was in fact Bill Tansley, an assistant to Deke who was learning managerial skills.

Deke was a man who knew what he wanted, and how to get it. He enforced only two rules:

Rule 1: Deke is always right.

Rule 2: If Deke is wrong, Rule 1 applies.

He bought the last round to send us on our way. We left as we intended to go on, at least three drinks ahead of the rest of the world.

I seem to recall our two-hour journey stretched to something like six and a half as we refreshed ourselves at the various hostelries en route. Our late arrival meant we had to dump our bags in the hotel foyer, grab our instruments and run to catch our sound check. This brought home rather forcefully the fact that on this particular tour, we did not have 'roadies' to carry our bags. Something which Ray Flacke, our leading guitarist and most experienced tourer, could not get to grips with. For some reason I ended up carrying his gear.

NEIL: Sustaining those initial high spirits when on the road, living in each others' pockets, performing the same show nightly in a different town, is neither easy and never glamorous. Tempers fray, moods swing. At the untimely switch of an amp switch or the waft of stale air from the turning page of a horn player's porn magazine, a level-headed keyboard player or even a celebrated singer can suddenly turn into a red-eyed monster.

To counteract these negative and dangerous moments I devised an on-the-spot system of fines for anyone who erred. The ground rules were set and agreed. By the end of the tour we had built up a slush fund of £462, which was spent in one glorious end-of-tour bash.

The system worked like this:

Tripping over any word, or step: £1.

Losing the thread of any story, sentence, statement or thought process during the course of any normal conversation: £1.

Hesitation when speaking: £1.

Having crumb on lip: £1.

Having crumb on lip while speaking to lardie (lah-di-da = star): £2.

Farting on bus: £2.

Farting loudly on bus: £3.

Farting on bus, not owning up but being found out: £4.

You name it and I would fine for it. Of course it was also means-tested, in that lardies would, of course, pay five times more than anyone else, while management was on a flat rate of £10 and multiples thereof for any misdemeanour. It goes without saying that should I be caught out, it was very expensive indeed.

There is a tenor sax player who will doubtless recall a top fine of £10 imposed upon him for bringing the previous night's conquest to the breakfast table, still dressed in her party dress, her nose streaked with mascara, lipstick smudged up to her left ear, a somewhat unsightly shadow of hair on her top lip, and with the name of Sharon! To be caught even standing anywhere near a dodgy bird was instantly fineable. To bring one to the breakfast table in close proximity with those of us in a state of near sobriety was considered strictly out of order.

Out-starring the star was another punishable offence, one for which Ray Flacke paid dearly. His nightly solo guitar spot had earned him much praise from audience and fellow artists alike, until we noticed it was getting longer and longer and longer and longer and longer.

Finally, we could bear it no more. As his solo stretched into overtime the entire band surrounded him waving white flags of surrender!

DEKE ARLON: The imbibing of alcohol was an integral part of what was in essence a very successful tour. However, Dennis' attempts to keep up with Neil were not totally successful. I went down to breakfast one morning at around nine to find Dennis and Neil still at the bar. They nodded solemnly and unseeing at my greeting, and slid carefully from their stools. Dennis somehow managed to avoid hitting the floor and very unsteadily made his way towards the lift. Neil, on the other hand, ever the professional ex-guardsman, marched off ramrod-backed with never a waver.

NEIL LANCASTER: This was the night of 7-14-21. A drinking game for true devotees. Once players had joined, the only way they could leave was by disqualification, that is, if they passed out or threw up. Faking or pleading was no excuse. Participants took it in turns to throw a single dice. When the accumulated numbers resulted in seven, that person chose the drink. There was no restriction on the concoction, although extremes, like a pint of whisky, were deemed stupid. If it was drinkable it was on. So 7 made the choice, 14 paid and 21 drank it. Down in one! Of course it was not unheard of for some smartarse who had selected a killer drink to end up not only paying for it but drinking it as well!

We were in Manchester concluding a game when the bar closed. Not to be defeated, we advanced on the huge wall-mounted cabinet bar in reception, and agreed to the money for each drink being added on to our respective hotel bills by the all-night female receptionist, who resembled an all-in wrestler, but who grew lovelier and lovelier by the glass. As dawn broke, the game was down to Dennis, Chris Lewis and myself, at which point, too drunk to add up, we declared a draw, threw away the dice and continued to consume whatever alcohol we could lay our hands on. We were still going strong when the postman arrived to join us in a bottle of champagne. Chris crawled to his room, while Dennis and I drank the bar dry.

Our hotel bills were exceedingly sobering.

In February 1978 I was thirty, and so was Ray Flacke. By this time my lead guitarist, who is now a very big name in Nashville, was playing with a band called Meal Ticket.

We decided to have a joint birthday party and were invited to throw it at Anne-Marie Ward's house in Chiswick. She was an old mate of Pat's, had been to school with Deke's wife, Jill, and worked as head of make-up at ATV during the *Crossroads* years, where as young actors Deke and Jill first met. She was also a fan and a friend of Ray's and together we used to go to all the Meal Ticket gigs.

The band had not long returned from playing in the south of France, where Ray had met a little American guy singing and playing piano in a bar in St Tropez and invited him to the party.

There were musicians everywhere that night at the do, but inevitably, as we would learn, the piano was commandeered by the diminutive American. Deke and I and a few hundred others were, as normal, in the kitchen, happily partying, when Jill came in and insisted Deke should go immediately and listen. Deke, somewhat in his cups, said something along the lines that he was off duty at a party, not at an audition. Jill was adamant. It wasn't just that he could play piano or that he had a great voice, she enthused, but the songs he was singing were his own compositions and they were very special indeed.

In we trooped, and that is basically where Gerard Kenny was discovered and started his career in England. He was brilliant.

Deke steamed in and asked him straight out if he had a record deal. Gerard had been round the block a few times and had heard this kind of dialogue before. 'Sure,' he sighed cynically. 'Show me your Rolls Royce and we'll start talking.' Deke took him to the window and pointed. 'Sorry,' Deke said, 'it's only a Bentley.' Two days later Gerard had a record deal with RCA.

DEKE ARLON: 'I Could Be So Good For You' at last put Dennis at the top of the charts. When I negotiated the terms of Dennis' deal for *Minder*, I made sure that the theme music and the title music, its publishing and the making of it, was controlled by us.

Chris Neil, a highly successful producer client of mine, was in the studio with Gerard Kenny making his first album. It seemed a good idea for Dennis and Gerard to get together to write one or two 'B' sides, one of which was 'I Could Be So Good For You'.

PAT: Gerard arrived at our house in Richmond and started playing around on my old piano, which never stayed in tune. Dennis already had a few ideas for songs, so I left them to it and went off to make some coffee. I was only gone for about twenty minutes, but when I came back I could sense they were quite excited. 'How does this sound?' they asked too nonchalantly. And there it was, that tune.

DEKE ARLON: Chris Neil produced it, Dennis sang it, and with the repeated success of *Minder,* it went on to reach number three in the British charts, number one in New Zealand and number one, three times, in the Australian charts. That and the wonderful album that subsequently followed went on to win gold discs, while the song itself achieved one of the highest accolades awarded by the British Academy of Songwriters, Composers and Authors when in the summer of 1981 it won an Ivor Novello award for 'The Best Theme from TV and Radio in 1980'.

It was even used as a theme song by one of the political parties in an election in Oz!

Finally the BBC relented, and I was invited on to *Top of the Pops,* where I amazed the people at the Beeb by insisting I sing live, when everybody else was miming to backing tracks. This was only because I had written it and could never be certain of singing the right lyrics. Even now, other people remember the words better than I do. This is interesting in that I can remember lyrics that I used to sing as a child, but not a big hit that I actually wrote. Weird.

DEKE ARLON: This was an extraordinary period. Not only was Dennis in the charts, but so too were some of my other clients. Gerard Kenny with 'New York, New York', and a young singer called Sheena Easton. Sheena had taken part in a TV programme called *The Big Time,* which had enhanced her ambition to become a pop star by filming her being recorded by top producer Chris Neil. Chris was so impressed he insisted I manage her. The exposure immediately pushed her first single into the top fifty.

It was such a great package of names, I decided to put together a tour. The show opened with two young, extremely talented singer-songwriters called Leeson and Vale, who went on to write numerous hits, including the theme to the Bond movie, 'For Your Eyes Only', which was written by Mick Leeson and sung by Sheena Easton. Sheena closed the first half, Gerard opened the second half, with Dennis headlining as the star.

It was the biggest and most organised gig I ever did and was called 'Friends on Tour', which indeed we were, all being Deke's clients. With amazing timing, we were on the road when all our records were climbing the charts. Sheena even had two records at one time, 'Modern Girl' and '9 to 5', which hurtled up to number three!

She really was an overnight success, her records were on the radio all the time and her picture was everywhere, and very good she looked too.

I was running through some of my numbers when this little bird strolled in. We assumed she was one of the backing singers until Deke arrived and introduced her to us as his new protégée.

'That's Sheena Easton?' we all gasped. And I suddenly realised why Deke was constantly singing the praises of photographer Brian Aris. All his pictures of Sheena had portrayed her as unbelievably glamorous, whereas I was confronted by a fairly pretty but ordinary girl. She was a nice bird too and she certainly sang like one, but, sadly, in my opinion success did seem to go to her head rather quickly. By the time we were on the road, she was almost a different person.

I thought that because she had been to drama college and was training for the theatre she would be able to handle it, enjoy it and be grateful. We were called 'Friends on Tour', which for the rest of us was true, but she was really not mixing with anyone.

Neil Lancaster was once more our musical director. And once more his cod tour contract of fineable offences was in force, only this time it was extended. I ended up even more out of pocket. If I turned round too quickly in a bar I was fined for dancing in public; I was fined for being too theatrical, singing like an actor and even for singing too well for an actor.

The extent of my victimisation is best illustrated by the occasion when, quite innocently, I asked the tour bus to stop so I could buy some cigarettes. The driver pulled up by a regular bus stop, where a very pretty girl was waiting. Naturally I asked her if she would like a lift and she accepted. By the time she had got out of the bus a couple of miles down the road, I was nearly skint. I was fined for interrupting the tour, for stopping the bus, for being flash by pulling a bird, for pulling a bird in the shortest time, and then for losing her almost immediately. Thirty quid in about fifteen minutes!

All used to good effect, I have to say, when at the end of the tour we had a huge farewell party.

DEKE ARLON: The tour had been the hottest ticket on the road.

They played the length and breadth of the British Isles, and to crown it all, every one of their albums won a gold disc.

Some weeks afterwards I received a call from a promoter, Stephen Komlosy, who wanted to book the show with the same line-up for a theatre in Glasgow. Sheena, being Scottish and from Bellshill, near Glasgow, helped make it a sell-out.

This was the first time Sheena had played her home town. But on the day of the opening night, she lost her voice and was confined to bed, locked in her hotel bedroom with a throat infection.

It was decided I would double the time I usually did on stage, using material from my previous solo shows, while Gerard would add a number of new songs. That way the audience would not be cheated, and the show would run for the same length of time, although without Sheena.

A voice specialist was flown up from London with the unusual name of Punt, which of course raised the question 'If your throat doctor's called Punt, what the hell's the name of your gynaecologist?'

Sheena did not perform or appear on stage until the very last night.

There was a huge row with the promoter, and I don't know what happened with the rest of the cast, but I suffered a personal loss of £7,500. I found this particularly galling, as I had doubled my workload, no one had asked for their money back and everybody had enjoyed the show.

While *Minder* was still so hot, I decided to write a novelty song for Christmas. George Cole agreed to record it with me. It was called 'What Are We Gonna Get 'Er indoors?' and went to number twenty-one in the charts. Once again we were invited to perform on *Top of the Pops*. Being the professional that he is, George said, 'Of course.'

Rarely could anybody have been so out of place. It was hilarious. There he was in his suit and trilby, surrounded by rock and punk bands, all of whom loved him. But he swanned through the song knowing how much kudos it would give him in the eyes of his children.

FOURTEEN

THEATRE

Sometime around 1978, I received a call from Ronald Eyre, who had directed me in *Enemy*, inviting me back to the Royal Shakespeare Company, where he was directing a play called *Saratoga*. This was a frothy neo-farce, set in turn-of-the-century America. I was to play a likeable man-about-town who happened to be engaged to six different women at the same time. The play was set during 'the season' in Saratoga, where, just by chance and unbeknownst to each other, all my fiancées are taking the waters at the same time.

DEKE ARLON: *Saratoga* was an important choice for Dennis. When an actor enjoys a high profile in a long-running popular television series, it is essential to ensure that some of the work chosen is not merely financially rewarding but takes the artist back to the roots of his talent. In this case, it meant going back to the theatre, playing a character away from the hard-hitting London lad of recent roles. Dennis had done so much television that by this time people were beginning to forget his background as a fine theatrical actor.

Ron was very keen for me to do it. I was wined and dined by the casting people and invited to see one of their current productions, *Much Ado About Nothing*, starring Joyce Nettles and a very delicious young actress by the name of Cherie Lunghi. I was smitten the moment I saw her and insisted she should play one of my fiancées. Ron agreed. At least I was certain one of my prospective future wives would be seriously tasty. However, she found me profoundly resistible, I regret to say!

There were something like thirty-six characters in *Saratoga*, all played by members of the RSC. I walked into the rehearsal room in Floral Street and immediately felt seventy eyes wondering just why they had cast some TV cop in the lead role when the company was overflowing with talent. Had anybody actually asked me, I would have had absolutely no answer.

We had something like nine weeks' rehearsal for this show. Admittedly there was a large cast to organise and a few songs to rehearse and dances to choreograph, which required a little more work than your normal play, but nine weeks? I found this excessive! I had been used to learning fifty-minute scripts on a Sunday night. Even in the theatre the longest I had ever rehearsed was four weeks. But this was the RSC funded by your and my money. Commercial considerations did not exist; they could do whatever they wanted.

We did the introductions and the read-through, and listened to a little speech from Ron, in which he explained our schedule, which included rehearsals every Saturday. This came as something of a shock.

'Ron,' I muttered afterwards, 'I can't do every Saturday.'

'Why not?'

'My season ticket to Chelsea. I can do some, but I'll have to leave about noon if they're playing at home.'

Now this was in the days before the yuppies, bankers and wankers had discovered our national sport.

Ron was taken aback. 'But, we've got to rehearse,' he said.

'Of course,' I agreed, 'but even so, we've already got three times the time we need.'

Ron knew me quite well. He knew I wasn't lazy or throwing my weight about. 'We'll see,' he smiled. I didn't miss a single match.

Lunch break loomed. I asked whoever was next to me which pub they used. This provoked total incredulity. 'We normally get some food from the health-food shop round the corner and come back and talk about the play.'

'Jesus,' I thought, 'this is going to be fun.'

A Welsh actor called Allan David came to my rescue. 'Come on,' he said, 'I'll have a pint with you.' He was a smashing bloke; so was James Laurenson, but apart from them and a couple of my fiancées, that was it. Unusually for me, out of a cast of thirty-six, I actually liked and got on with about five of them. I think it must have been around this time that I first asked the question 'Doesn't anybody talk about football and fucking any more?'

Luckily, *Saratoga* was in repertory, so we only met up three or four times a week, and not every week at that. The play was well received and remains a favourite among several of my friends, but I can't honestly say I enjoyed the experience.

Although it did give me time to work on presenting a children's programme, called *Words at War*, devised and directed by the legendary Dennis Vance. Each week we would perform songs, poems and extracts from plays that had anything to do with war and attitudes to war. Because of Dennis Vance, we had amazing casts. Trevor Howard popped in to do a bit of George Bernard Shaw. Ronnie Frazer, Gareth Hunt and Robert Duncan acted scenes from *The Long and the Short and the Tall.* Apart from my acting in various extracts and presenting the show, every now and then I got to interview famous figures.

One I will never forget was Dame Vera Lynn. It was incredibly moving to witness the effect she had on those members of the crew old enough to have been around or involved in World War II. They treated her like the Queen; it was fascinating to watch. To us thirty-somethings she was just a singer who had been a bit of a star during the war. To those guys she was one of the reasons we won.

FIFTEEN

MINDER

After *The Sweeney*, Thames TV and Euston Films started looking for a new series for me. One or two ideas were quite interesting, including one in which Carter goes underground, a sort of British *Serpico*.

DEKE ARLON: A meeting was held over lunch at Thames with Brian (Ginger) Cowgill, Jeremy Isaacs, Verity Lambert, Dennis, myself, and Jill, my wife, who at that time worked as part of the creative side of our business, and Dennis Selinger, who was then new to the team.

The plan was to create a new series around Dennis, this time featuring him in the leading role. Their intention was to approach all the top writers for ideas, but in the mean time, his popularity was such, they were eager to hold him under contract, for fear he might be poached by the 'other side'. Dennis and I decided this was not necessary. We did not want to be bound by anything. He would go under contract only when a series had been developed with which we were happy.

Various fairly predictable plots and situations were suggested, all heavy-hitting and aggressive along the lines of *The Sweeney*. In contrast, Jill, knowing Dennis, proposed that a series should be developed which exploited Dennis' lighter side, whereby, although he was obviously physically capable of looking after himself, he escaped tight corners using wit, charm and humour rather than fists. Rather like the character played by James Garner in the old American TV series *The Rockford Files*.

We had such a character working for us at that time. Danny Francis, the son of George Francis the renowned boxing trainer, was employed as 'minder' to the young Sheena Easton and travelled the world with her on tour. He was a giant of a young man with blond curls and a baby face, and seemed as gentle as a lamb. He raised his voice to no one, and sorted out any dodgy situations with a smile and a joke, but if push came to shove, boy, could he sort things out.

Many tense moments on the road had been deflated by Danny's sense of humour. In fact we had begun to doubt his dad had taught him anything at all about using his fists, until one night in a hotel bar in Hong Kong, when a group of very drunken Scottish rugby players, mistaking the glossy tour jackets as belonging to Americans, decided to take on the boys in Sheena's band, who were enjoying a quiet drink after the show. Danny was sitting in a rather low chair with his back to them. They teased him about his golden locks, and the others too about the way they looked, until tempers began to fray. Danny calmed down the band and tried to finish his drink in peace. But the Scots wouldn't give up. One burly bloke, red in the face, lurched over and demanded a fight with one of the 'poofs' – why not Goldilocks? And he tugged Danny's hair. Wearily, Danny got up – and up and up and up. The Scot was aghast. Almost casually, Danny let rip with a short right and the Scotsman flew across the room as though he was on a wire. Not another peep was heard out of them.

George Taylor, of Euston Films, phoned up one day during Christmas and asked if he could drop round a couple of scripts and an idea for a new series. He also lived in Richmond, so within half an hour I found myself reading two finished scripts and three or four storylines of something called *Minder* by Leon Griffiths.

Leon had an amazing reputation and was correctly regarded as one of television's best writers.

Although beautifully written, those early scripts were far more gritty and vicious than the series eventually became. What I relished was the humour. And the characters – Arthur Daley and Terry McCann. They were real, they were three-dimensional, and as people commented later, there's a Terry and an Arthur in every walk of life, and we all know one.

I needed no second thoughts.

In those days, once a television company had decided on a production they got on with it. The power of casting, budget and scheduling, etc. was in the hands of the programme maker.

Now, within commercial television, everything has to be presented to a central committee. It and it alone has the ultimate power of selecting what programmes are to be made. The committee exercises enormous influence over budgeting and casting, and has total control over times of transmission. There have been instances, for example, where it has completely overridden the choice of actor by the writer and the creative team, and cast someone totally unsuitable for a role, purely on the grounds of their being 'flavour of the month'. I certainly know of one such show, where the leading part was written especially for a particular, excellent actor, by an extremely eminent theatre and TV writer. Fearing the actor was not commercial enough, the committee recast, and as a result, the show died on its feet.

Today's television hierarchy is totally obsessed with ratings. Had the Programme Centre been in situ in the late seventies it is questionable whether there would have been more than one series of *Minder*, because it certainly wasn't an overnight success.

However, in 1978 everything swung into action fairly quickly. George Taylor and Lloyd Shirley, the old *Sweeney* team, were to produce the series for Euston Films, which ensured the quality of production would be high. Verity Lambert was appointed executive producer, and Linda Agran script executive – a formidable and talented duo.

LINDA AGRAN: It was very different from anything we had done before, in that it was the first drama that employed a strong comedy line throughout. It says much about Dennis' good judgement that he recognised immediately just how much that would stretch him as an actor.

We shared some hilarious lunches, or 'meetings', during which we discussed choice of cast and crew. Of course the ultimate decisions were theirs, and I'm sure seeking my opinion was purely cosmetic, but it was lovely to be so involved at such an early stage.

Remembering his wonderfully seedy performance in the film *Alfie*, and how much I had enjoyed working with him, I suggested that maybe Denholm Elliott would be interesting as Arthur Daley. He was duly added to the list.

In a restaurant in Kew, I was told that George Cole would be my co-star. 'Oh,' I countered, 'isn't he a bit posh and maybe a bit too soft?'

'We think he'll be perfect.'

I knew he was a wonderful actor, I had been a huge fan since seeing him in a series, written by my old chum Doug Livingstone, called *A Man of Our Times*. Obviously, I also remembered him as Flash Harry in the St Trinian's' films, but this new series was set deep in the underbelly of current society. Fifties 'filmic' Londoners were a far cry from what we would be portraying.

LINDA AGRAN: Denholm Elliott was without doubt a fantastic actor. The problem was he had the look of an ex-minor public school man on the way down, debauched, slightly shifty – a man on the skids!

Our man Arthur was quite the opposite – a man on the make! A sort of Freddie Laker (without the success), no education, who left school early, and fought his way up. A man who never really does anything but always believes that the big time is just about to happen.

GEORGE COLE: I was in a very depressing Dennis Potter play about a young spastic girl who gets raped, at the Open Space, which at the time was just that – a very open space in what had been Warren Street post office. My agent phoned to say Lloyd Shirley and Linda Agran had called for a meeting about a possible show they'd like to talk about over a drink, maybe, before the theatre.

I thought for a moment. I live way out of London. It would mean coming up early and I was driving, besides which I never drink before or after the show.

'No,' I said. 'Besides, I've done Armchair Theatre; they know me and what I can do.'

Three days later they phoned again asking me at least to come and have a Coke with them.

Grudgingly, I agreed. I had no idea whether they were going to talk about a play or what. It turned out to be a series.

'Do you think you have enough stamina for that, Mr Cole?' Lloyd Shirley asked. Five hundred and seven episodes later and fifteen years further on, the answer is 'Yes.'

He showed me the format, and immediately I read the description of the character of Arthur Daley, I knew I wanted to do it. It said, 'He is the same age as some good-looking American film star. He's totally behind the Home Secretary as far as law and order is concerned. His favourite film is *The Godfather* and he dresses like a dodgy member of the Citizens' Advice Bureau.'

Next thing I knew we were shooting the titles and I hadn't even seen a script.

TOM CLEGG: When the directive came out that Thames was looking for a new idea for Dennis, I sat down with Troy Kennedy

Martin and Trevor Preston but we never came up with a successful format. Then Leon wrote *Minder* and I was asked to direct the first two episodes, except when I read it, I wasn't too sure what we were supposed to be aiming for. Was it a gritty street series or a comedy? I also didn't like the first episode, 'Gunfight at the OK Laundrette'. It began with Dennis imprisoned as a hostage with George on the outside. I thought, what a stupid way to start a series, with the two main characters separated. I turned it down.
LINDA AGRAN: At first, people did not know what to make of it. Because there was a strong element of comedy, there was even the thought of trying to make it more entertaining by adding a laughter track.

To perform comedy without audience reaction is very difficult for actors. They have to time their lines where they think there might be laughter, so that the speech that follows is not lost.

The fact that the crew may laugh at something is not always a true indicator. Dennis was always so popular with all the technicians, they laughed easily. The only thing that does work is an essential feel for timing, and a true understanding of both material and characters. Dennis and George were both masters of the art.

Roy Ward Baker directed several episodes, and he grasped the spirit of the piece immediately.

ROY WARD BAKER: You could not resist the innate essence of the thing. Leon was a man who, although a serious writer, never took anything too seriously. He'd written a number of films and a lot of television and was a man I respected and liked. There were no arguments with him, he just laughed. However, I did think the balance would be difficult to maintain and it would become much more an entertainment show.

For a reason I'll never fully understand, the first episode was given to Peter Sazdy to direct. He had quite a good reputation, but he was Hungarian and lived in Weybridge. I have absolutely nothing against either Hungary or Weybridge, but I don't think coming from either location gives you a great insight into the gutters and drinking dens of west London. He also used to arrive with a detailed storyboard illustrating how each scene would be shot before we actors had set eyes on the location, and without allowing us the chance to have any input at all.

And he talked me into having a perm. I initially agreed with the theory that it would get me away from the old *Sweeney* image, but it ended up looking really dopey. Should you happen to watch any *Minder* repeats you will notice that in the credit sequence at the beginning I've got a very strange 'barnet' indeed.

It was during this pre-production period, when you are called for various meetings about clothes and make-up, that George Cole and I first met.

Neither of us are the most outgoing types when it comes to first meetings, so it was all rather restrained. I was still worried he might be a little too urbane for Arthur. But we would be working together for the next six months, so we might as well get on. And we were getting on, albeit in a very polite manner.

Finally we started filming. Because of my history with Euston Films, it was like coming home. For George, it was a whole new ballgame, which must have made him feel like an outsider. For the first few days everything was terribly professional – on time, word perfect and very respectful. Then I started having a laugh with the crew and noticed George occasionally looking up from the *Times* crossword to see what was going on.

GEORGE COLE: Dennis and I circled each other for about three or four days. After that, you would have thought we'd been working together for years.

I've never had a job which I've looked forward to going to so much every single day.

Personally, Dennis and I are complete opposites. He is a social animal. I prefer being at home doing nothing, watching racing on TV, or doing a bit of gardening. To illustrate how differerent we are – Penny and I were driving home past our local village pub when we noticed a sign in the window advertising fresh eggs. We went in, bought some, and had a drink. The barman chatted away, then said, 'You thinking of moving down this way sir?'

'I've lived here for over twenty-two years,' I answered, 'just never been in the pub!'

When we first started the series we each had our own Winnebago. Half way through, we both agreed, 'This is silly. We've got so much work to do together, let's share one between us.' He had one end, where he could play cards, and I had the other, where I could smoke my cigar at lunchtime and do the crossword, although before long Dennis joined me in doing this too.

From 1978, on and off until 1987, through sixty-three episodes and one Christmas special, George Cole and Dennis Waterman laughed all day, every day of their working lives.

By the second episode we were brothers in arms, and woe betide any director who tried to get either of us to do anything we didn't agree with. I don't mean us to sound like a couple of prima donnas, who refused direction, but we both had exactly the same instinct about what worked and what didn't.

GEORGE COLE: We used to meet up in make-up every morning at about seven a.m. and go through the script and the day's work. If either of us wanted to cut something or change the script, nine times out of ten the other would have marked it.

LINDA AGRAN: 'Gunfight at the OK Laundrette' really set up the characters. Leon knew and loved all these people. They were real, which is why he portrayed them so vividly. He used to frequent a drinking club in Hampstead known as Death in the afternoon. It was there that he first heard the phrase ''er indoors', from a character at the bar who had informed him, 'Gotta go back, 'er indoors wants to go shopping.'

The episode was based on a real event – the Spaghetti House siege in Knightsbridge. A group of fanatics had been cornered in an Italian restaurant, where they held hostage the very excitable Italian staff and demanded a plane to Ethiopia. Needless to say, it was a bungled operation and the siege failed. I'm sure those involved at the time were not amused, but Leon immediately saw the comic side and thought it would make a great *Minder*. Dave King, the comedian, gave a brilliant performance in one of his first straight roles as an actor.

As for Dennis and George, it was instant combustion on the screen. The chemistry was in their complete differences. Dennis had an extraordinary rapport with the crew. There was this feeling on the floor that they were *his* crew, and they were the ones he relaxed with, talked with of laddish things, drank with in the pub. Yet for all that Dennis is far more complicated than he either appears or pretends to be. For a man whose reputation lies in being gregarious, he gives off conflicting signals of being guarded, insecure, lonely, and even solitary. George, on the other hand, was quiet, shy, quite bluff but grounded, a man happy with his lot, always open and receptive, quite content to sit and do his crossword, then jump in his car and go home to his wife.

GEORGE COLE: It was during the first episode that I had my moment of inspiration. We were organising with wardrobe how we should dress as the characters. Our director, Peter Sazdy, decided Arthur should be smart, not grotty, but elegant and sharp. I was dispatched to Savile Row with instructions to buy two suits. The producers were not best pleased. It was not their idea of Arthur, and the bill was not within their budget. The suits cost £400 each!

We were shooting a scene in which Dennis was involved in a fight. Another character appears round the corner, I was supposed to grab him and he starts to fight with me. I stopped and called the director over. 'Just a minute,' I said. 'Do you know how much this suit costs?'

He said, 'Why?'

I said, 'Because if we so much as get a mark on it, the producers are going to kill us.'

He blanched. 'What are we going to do?'

'Tell you what,' I said, 'as soon as I see him coming, at the least whiff of a scrap, I'll duck out, whisk away round the other corner, and leave Terry to handle it.'

From then on, whenever there was any aggro, Arthur always slipped away. I never did like fight scenes.

TOM CLEGG: Dennis was incredibly lucky to go from one successful series to another, but even luckier to enjoy not one great partnership but two! It was incredible.

Very soon, we were asking directors not to give us close-ups (virtually unheard-of in television), because any scene in which we were both involved worked a hundred per cent better if the two of us were in shot. We were so in tune and our ad-libbing was so proficient that if the scene called for it, directors gave up saying 'Cut!' allowing us to carry on improvising our dialogue. I have to say, somewhat immodestly, that some of our lines have been quoted in the papers as illustrations of the strength of writing in the show!

GEORGE COLE: This was where Dennis and I were wise, we never laid claim to any words we might have added. We never said to the writers, 'You didn't write that. We did.' Never. And it worked, it was a team effort. If it was a good line and they were happy with it, they were quite content to believe they'd written it, and we left it like that. In fact when *It'll Be Alright on the Night* started, the show in which 'out cuts' from various shows were exposed to the public eye, we had very few to send in, simply because when Dennis and I were in a scene together and one of us delivered the wrong line, the other would respond to that line without a thought. There was that kind of instinctive rapport between us.

ROY WARD BAKER: There was hardly anything for a director to do, you could put in odd little touches, pump up a line here or there, play something funnier or darker, but apart from that they swanned through it. I was lucky in that I worked mostly with Leon's scripts, but occasionally we altered dialogue, sharpened it, moved it around a little, put in jokes as long as the humour was right and relevant. We liked to nudge the audience, to make them 'brisk up at the back there!'

The series was handled rather well, I thought, unlike some which are rushed on to our screens, ill conceived, pouring out episode after episode, ill written and ill directed. This one did not force the pace and the characters evolved rounded and three-dimensional.

It was also very much the Thatcher era, with Arthur Daley as a confirmed eighties Tory, although Arthur's character, the small-time wheeler-dealer always ready to turn a quick profit, even if it is on the shady side of the law, is as true now as it was then. Part of the very success of *Minder* was that it was apolitical and, to a certain extent, not politically correct. We introduced all types and nationalities; the only thing we could never do because it would have created too much fuss was to have a black person as the villain, or, equally, as the hero, which was all very boring. Apart from that we took the mickey out of everyone and it was fun.

LINDA AGRAN: Our research showed young people especially regarded Arthur as somewhat of a clown, naughty rather than nasty, whereas Terry they saw as the really good guy.

Athough it was subtle, the series had a strong moral thread running through it, an underbelly of significance, even though people didn't necessarily realise it or care. It was that added depth that in the end helped to bring it to cult status.

The eventual success of the show had a great deal to do with some of the fine actors who played our semi-regulars. Who could possibly imagine anybody else running the Winchester Club but Glynn Edwards as Dave? Or who else in the roles of the policemen, driven to despair by Arthur's machinations, but the sadly missed Peter Childs, who played Detective Sergeant Rycott, and Patrick Malahide, in his inspired performance as Chisholm, a character worthy of a series on his own? Even Warren Clarke had an episode trying to catch us; not, it has to be said, with much success.

We were at Fulham football club one Saturday after that particular episode had been transmitted. During half time, Warren visited the bog and found himself standing next to a little old Fulham fan, who stared hard at him, then said, ''Ere, ain't you off the telly?'

'Actually, yes,' said Warren.

'Weren't you in that *Minder*?'

'That's right.'

'I thought so,' said the man as he was leaving. 'Fucking useless!'

During the last of the first eleven episodes Pat, who was now my wife, chose another rare day off to present me with another beautiful blonde bombshell. On 15 January 1979, Julia Martha was delivered, once again at Queen Charlotte's Hospital. Thankfully, the birth was a lot less dramatic than the first, but it must have been quite dramatic for Pat. Julia weighed in at 9lbs 13oz. Once again we were certain it would be a boy but this time we had made contingency plans. If it turned out to be a girl, we had decided to name her Martha. But once I held this tiny golden-haired, blue-eyed bundle in my arms, there was no way I could call her Martha. It was just too mature for her! So it became Julia. Thinking about it, and the effect she now has on young men, maybe it should have been Juliet.

The original launch date for the series was a disaster. Thames TV was on strike. The show moved from September to January, directly after the strike at ITV – but during another strike, at the *TV Times*'. This scotched any chance of pre-publicity, apart from the odd line in the entertainment section of the national press. There had been no pilot, so the first awareness the audience had of *Minder* was the transmission of 'Gunfight at the OK Laundrette', which had been scheduled to go out at nine p.m. in the old *Sweeney* slot.

People didn't know what to make of it.

Looking back, I suppose it was really quite unusual for television. Films had been made about crooks getting away with crimes in a light-hearted way, like *Butch Cassidy and the Sundance Kid*, but TV had always been much more black and white. Heroes were goodies and baddies were bad. We were neither. Arthur was not quite a real crook and Terry had been to prison but was now trying to go straight and, with no qualifications at all, get a proper job. Terry also had a strong ethic of right and wrong, albeit more to do with cowboy films than most modern morals. He was also often stupidly loyal.

Series evolve with the addition of new writers, and over the years, the comedic side of our characters was utilised more and more, until, in my view, the programme eventually became far too soft. This loss of edge also coincided with developing concern about TV violence and, eventually, the dreaded political correctness.

Contrary to popular belief, we were contracted to do the first eleven episodes and nothing more. It was the same with *The Sweeney*. Whenever we finished a series, we would have a drink and say our farewells with absolutely no guarantee that we would ever be back for more.

I don't think I was that aware of how low the viewing figures were for that first series, but it did attract a small cult following, which encouraged George and me to have private chats about the possibility of a second season. I had just moved to a bigger house in Richmond and I remember saying I wouldn't be averse to another year's guaranteed money and neither would my mortgage company.

George smiled and said, 'You've got a mortgage, have you?'

'Yeah, hasn't everybody?'

'I haven't had one since the late fifties,' he said, with not a little smugness.

At the end of a television awards dinner at the Dorchester, I found myself sharing an elevator with Brian (Ginger) Cowgill, Programme Controller at Thames Television.

'I really enjoyed that *Minder*,' he said as we descended to the lobby. 'Would you fancy doing some more.'

'I wouldn't mind," I responded. 'I thought the scripts were terrific.'

'Hmm,' he mused. 'Let's have a go, shall we?'

I can't tell you whether they had already planned another season or whether seeing me had jogged Brian's memory, but things moved pretty quickly after that, and we started the new series of thirteen shows in early 1980.

The only black spot was that, sadly, since finishing the first series, old Leon Griffiths had had a stroke. However, although undergoing treatment, he was sufficiently well to oversee and consult with some of the new writers commissioned by Linda Agran.

The first day's filming was more like a happy reunion of old friends than the start of six months' hard graft. Once again I had Barry

Summerford standing in for me, and my old friend Mike Sutcliffe driving. George was equally at home with everyone. It was as if we'd never been away. We shared a dressing room and a caravan, did the crossword together, and occasionally lost some money on a horse. We even agreed to wait for each other when called for a scene together, so that neither one nor the other could ever be accused of being late on set.

There was only one bone of contention. George would not join the crew and me in the pub at lunch time or after work. Since he refused to have a studio driver, he had to drive himself, which meant that not only did he not drink, but neither did he buy anyone else a drink either, which duly gave rise to my calling him 'a mean sod'!

Eventually, we came to an arrangement whereby he would come to the pub on the last Friday of every month and whenever there was a birthday. With a crew in excess of sixty, there were several birthdays during the shoot. George would buy everyone a drink, have his Coke and go back to his lunch with the caterers.

GEORGE COLE: Every fifth Friday, Dennis made sure everyone, including total strangers, was told to be in the pub at lunch time because George was actually going to buy the drinks!

I don't know how they did it. They'd down two or three large vodkas and then be back on set. The only time I saw it affect Dennis' work was after lunch on his birthday. That wasn't a very good afternoon, simply because we'd started shooting early that morning and the landlord, who'd worshipped him in *The Sweeney*, had been plying him with drinks at eight a.m.

There was also the occasion when a director new to the show tried to sack the entire unit for coming back from lunch the worse for wear and a little late. He's now a sheep farmer in Sussex.

The routine was too well established from the *Sweeney* days for anyone or anything to change it. Because Dennis was almost never affected by these liquid lunches, and his work never suffered, it didn't disturb me. What I did find shattering, when I was drawn in for those fifth Fridays, was the amount of money that got spent. I'm sure some of those people couldn't possibly afford to buy such huge rounds of drinks every day.

I said to George one day, 'You could have one little whisky and still be all right to drive.'

'No I can't,' he replied. 'When I have whisky, it is never one and certainly never little.'

He proved this to me when he threw a party to celebrate forty years as an actor. I found myself saying 'when' to dissuade him from pouring quadruples every time I had a drink! He had a house full of guests and family who loved him, and the more he drank the more he smiled.

I would have said it was impossible to get on with another actor as well as I had with John Thaw, but with George it wasn't so much chemistry as magic.

The first episode of the second series was televised on 11 September 1980. Written by Willis Hall and directed by Martin Campbell, it was called 'National Pelmet' and centred on me guarding a racehorse. This meant sharing a stable with it. There was one scene where I'm trying to go to sleep but being severely put off by the horse's flatulence. I don't know where they got that horse, but believe me, it farted right on cue.

That first episode made the top twenty of the ratings and every week the show climbed higher. I can't explain why. As good as the new scripts were, they were certainly no more brilliant than the first series, but people were rushing home to watch our programme. My theme song rose to number three in the charts and suddenly we were an overnight success.

By the end of 1980, *Minder* was one of the biggest shows on TV. Now there was no need for a great deal of discussion about doing another series. Scripts were commissioned immediately.

GEORGE : One thing Dennis and I agreed on was that a lot of the swearing had to go. We also made a decision about directors. Neither of us knew enough about all the up-and-coming crowd, so 'director approval' was hard to justify. We solved it by coming up with the idea of 'director disapproval'! This epic piece of diplomacy was created whilst sitting in the car one day waiting for our cue. We started going through our list of 'don't wants' – when one of us said, 'Oh, and who's the one who directed that episode about such-and-such? What was his name?'

'Don't know but we definitely don't want him.'

'What *was* his name?'

'Christ, no!'

We looked at each other. 'It's the one who's directing this one!'

Linda Agran had been nurturing a writer called Tony Hoare, who had written one episode in the first series, four in the second and would go on to share the bulk of the work in the third series with Andrew Payne and Leon. Happily, Leon had recovered from his stroke and was well enough to come back to work with us.

Tony, it has to be said, above any other writer I have met, had a tremendous knowledge of how to deal, or rather not deal, with the law. I hope I'm not libelling my old mate by saying I believe he actually started writing while being entertained by Her Majesty's Prison Service. He may have been a great loss to the criminal fraternity, but he was a real bonus to us.

We had honed down the directors to Robert Young, Ian Sharp, Mike Vardy, Francis Megahy and my old buddies Tom Clegg, Terry Green, Roy Ward Baker and Ian Toynton. By now, too, with the acceleration of the show to cult class, people were begging to be in it. Wonderful artists like Suzi Quatro, Mike Reid, Richard Griffiths, Gareth Hunt, Alfie Bass, Nigel Davenport, Gary Olsen, Pete Postlethwaite, Billy Murray, Russell Hunter, Paul Eddington, Simon Cadell, Honor Blackman, Richard Briers, Simon Williams, Maurice Denham and Max Wall.

These last two fine performers played a couple of old lags who in their younger days had pulled off a big robbery. Max Wall's character had taken the rap and been sent to prison for a very long time, but their booty had been hidden and never recovered. It was called 'The Birdman of Wormwood Scrubs'. Max Wall, although a comic genius, at that time had limited acting experience. In one particular scene, Arthur and Terry have to pick him up from jail and drive him to his house.

Quite often when we were doing car sequences, we would rehearse the scene statically to make sure the camera angle was correct, the microphones were not in shot and the actors knew what they were doing. A camera would be rigged to the side of the car and the sound equipment would be set up on the floor together with the clapperboard, which, because of the confined space, we operated ourselves. Once all was in order we would drive the designated route until actors, director and crew were happy that everything was right.

In this particular instance, Max was in the back of the car and George and I were in the front, with me driving. The script was supposed to go like this:

Arthur: Come on, Terry, this place gives me the vapours.
Terry: (To Max) All right, son, where are we going?
Max: Take me to Primrose Hill . . .

We took up our positions and prepared to start. I turned on the camera, and George the tape machine: 'Twenty-seven, take one. Action.'

Arthur: Come on, Terry, this place gives me the vapours.
Terry: All right, son, where are we going?

Total silence.
'Cut.'
I turned round. 'Max,' I said, 'we've started the scene. Do it just like we rehearsed.'
Max nodded. 'Of course, carry on.'
We started again. 'Turn camera. Sound. Twenty-seven, take two. Action.'

Arthur: Come on, Terry, this place gives me the vapours.
Terry: All right, son, where are we going?

Once again, silence.
I repeated, 'Where are we going?'
Max looked puzzled. 'I don't know,' he said. 'Didn't the director tell you?'
We stopped the car, turned off the equipment and explained again. 'When Terry says, "Where are we going?", you say, 'Primrose Hill.' And we carry on with the scene, OK?'
Max's face cracked into that wolfish leer. 'Sorry, lads,' he said. 'You two are just like real people. I didn't realise you'd started acting.'
Also in this particular show was a woman called Rula Lenska. But I'll get to her later.

The hours we worked were sometimes extremely long and there was always a lot of dialogue to learn, but my overriding memory is of the good time we had. We still had most of our original crew, including Dusty Millar, Roy Pointer, John Maskall and Tony Dawe, who had all been there on the first day of *The Sweeney*. I can't tell you how comforting this is. There might be an instance, for example, when the director would be quite happy with a scene when we would not. John-John (Maskall) knew us so well he'd intuitively know. 'Didn't you like that?' he'd ask us quietly.
'Not as much as the rehearsal.' So rather than George or me requesting to go again, he'd claim he had a problem and we'd re-

shoot. There is an unwritten law that if a cameraman says he wants to re-shoot a scene, it is accepted without question, but if an actor makes the same request, the director invariably responds with something like 'It looked fine to me, and we're running out of time.'

Obviously by now we had a certain amount of power, but George and I believed the director was nearly always right (nearly), and was definitely the boss. Several of the crew, especially John-John, Dusty and Roy, were keen for me to direct a few episodes. I loved the idea too, but whether it was fear or just my usual laziness, I shied away from suggesting the idea. Besides, George and I were allowed so much input that quite often I felt I *was* directing the show!

Every now and then a new director would be discovered and allowed to work on the show. It must have been very strange for them. Normally they'd say, 'I want this, I want that, we'll shoot this there and then we'll etc., etc.' With us it was slightly different. George and I never threw our weight around. We would listen to whatever they had to say, and if we agreed, we would do whatever was asked of us. But if we thought there was a slightly better way, we would suggest it. We were very aware that new directors want to do their best work, in their own way, in their own time. We were also more than aware that they would only be around for two weeks at a time, whereas we and the crew were working five days a week for six months or so.

I really resented days when I was working and George wasn't. Not because he was having time off and I wasn't, but I knew that the day just wouldn't be as much fun. The first thing we always did when we received a new script and schedule was to check who had which days off. If he had more than I did I would say, 'Oh no, you're going to leave me to work with those strangers again.' It really was an extraordinary relationship considering how different we were, although both of us used to boast about coming from 'The Golden Triangle' – Brixton, Tooting and Clapham – and from working-class families. Maybe we had more in common than we thought.

Minder peaked with the third series, winning huge audiences around the world, except for America, where the language barrier and the accents baffled US executives and made it unacceptable. They even suggested sub-titles!

GEORGE COLE: Dennis and I began to realise just how much *Minder* had pierced people's consciousness when taxi drivers would shout out, 'How's 'er indoors?' or 'You should pay that boy more than you're paying him, you know.' We even received letters from people asking if they could buy something from Arthur's lock-up!

During one of the breaks from the series, Dennis was performing in the West End in the musical *Windy City* when there was a dust-up between him and his musical director. The press were immediately on to me. 'What do you think about your boy then, Arthur?'

I was appearing in *Pirates of Penzance* at the same time when my co-star Pamela Stephenson was reported for saying something obscene at a Savoy women's lunch. Again the press wanted to know what Arthur Daley had to say about it. I was also asked what Arthur would think about Fergie going off on holiday leaving her children behind!

TOM CLEGG: Although the series was originally written for Dennis, as it progressed it became more a shared thing. This is where Dennis was so generous. Quite legitimately he could have turned round and objected. After all, George was becoming quite the star. Most of the storylines inevitably centred on Arthur Daley's wheeling and dealing and the writers found it easier to write all that rhetorical non-abusive Alf Garnett stuff than they did to expand the sub-plots and dialogue for Dennis. However Dennis is not an actor obsessed with his own ego. He lives for his work, he loves his work, he is an extremely good actor, the ultimate professional, maybe sometimes too modest for his own good, but someone whose only interest is what is right for the project.

It became obvious fairly quickly that the strength of the series lay in the relationship between the two guys. You could be out on great locations, doing amazing car chases, yet some of the best scenes were just the two of them talking in the bar at the Winchester Club, with Dave interjecting his lovely dry comments. Wonderful stuff.

LINDA AGRAN: Those early series broke new ground. It was tough drama with comedy. It had a dark side and the comedy was not straight. If you got the jokes, great, but no one was stopping for it. But bit by bit a shift took place, the balance changed and they allowed it to become funny.

Leon and I were both concerned. Three series had been enough. The writers had used up the best ideas, the most exciting storylines, but Thames wouldn't have it. They were determined the show would go on. So it stopped being creatively led, the original writers had written themselves out and the new ones force-fed the programme with jokes.

Dennis became increasingly uncomfortable and quite rightly so. Terry was turning into a feed for Arthur. What a shame *Minder* was not killed off at its peak. Instead it was allowed to die slowly in front of the public.

SIXTEEN

THE WORLD CUP

In our downstairs loo, we kept various silly books, one of which was by some bloke who had become famous for being a sporting memory man. I often used to test myself – like trying to name the great Brazilian football team of the seventies and what position each man played.

It was while perusing this book one afternoon that an eight- or nine-line paragraph caught my eye. It was about a lowly team of miners from West Auckland in County Durham who in 1910 were selected to represent England in a competition called the Sir Thomas Lipton Trophy.

The competition, involving several European nations, was held in Italy. Not only had those miners never been out of England, they didn't have the money to make the trip. In order to pay their fares they were forced to sell what little they had. Amazingly, they beat both Stuttgart in the semi-final and Juventus in the final and returned home with the cup. The very first 'World Cup'. Nowadays they would have been treated like heroes. In those days they came home and went straight back down the pit.

The following year, having been given time off with no pay and again having raised their own expenses, the team won again, but, ridiculously this time, they had to sell the cup in order to raise the cash to get home again.

It occurred to me that the current World Cup was set to be played next year. So I phoned Tom Clegg and told him I'd got this idea for a film . . .

Chariots of Fire had recently been on release and had been a major international success. Why shouldn't we do the same thing for football? Deke was brought in to produce and do all the business, and Waterman/Arlon Films was born.

We discussed various writers, but one name stood out above the rest – Neville Smith, an old friend of mine, an actor/writer and what's more a football fanatic, a real fanatic. He has to be. He supports Everton. Neville had written a film script called *Charlie Bubbles* and a TV semi-documentary called *The Golden Vision* about Alec Young, one of his favourite team's great heroes.

While Deke and I tried to get the money together, Jill, Deke's wife, tracked down a reporter in West Auckland who had actually covered the original event and Neville started to research the story. It was fascinating stuff. The only thing we could never find out was why West Auckland were selected. They were fourth from bottom in the Northern Third Division, yet they went to Turin two years on the trot and won the Cup 'in perpetuity'.

TOM CLEGG: The imminence of the World Cup dominated our schedule. The script had to be delivered by September. Neville determined to go over to Turin to research Juventus' records and football library, although fear of flying forced him to take the lengthier route by ferry and train. Apart from watching Juventus, he found little information in the library and uncovered very few stories. But he assured us he'd got the elements in his head. Dennis and I talked to him about the story, what we envisaged, the important elements and the structure but left him with a relatively free hand.

'You've got a month,' I told him 'Put together the characters, an outline, and a first draft. No one will bother you for a month.'

In the mean time, Deke and I hit all the usual brick walls that first-time filmmakers always come up against. We decided that time was running out for a feature film so we concentrated our focus on television. Deke had been a major player at Yorkshire TV at one time, so through his contacts there, we were put in touch with their associate company, Tyne Tees Television, which had just been contracted to take over as the regional station covering the West Auckland area and were eager to prove their worth.

TOM CLEGG: By the middle of the third week there was not a peep out of Neville. I began to get a bit edgy, and gave him a ring.
'How's it going?' I asked.
'Fine. Great. No problem.'
'How many pages?'
'Six.'
'Six!'
'Yeah, but don't worry. I've got it all in my head.'
Another three weeks passed.

'How's it going, Neville? How many pages?'

'Seventeen.'

By now, things were tightening up with Tyne Tees. This was to be their major showpiece drama. Our contract had to be completed by 1 December, and that meant the script had to be seen and accepted not only by Tyne Tees but by the other independent companies before the agreement could be concluded.

Finally, six weeks late, the script was delivered. And what a script! We red-starred it up to Tyne Tees immediately. They loved it.

We didn't have to change anything but the sub-plot, which made the film too long.

The budget wasn't big but the cast was – starting with a football team of eleven, plus Richard Griffiths as the manager, a young reserve, Dai Bradley, and guest actors like Nigel Hawthorne. Everyone, no matter who, was on the same salary. It wouldn't make us millionaires, but *The World Cup, A Captain's Tale* would bring us a great deal of enjoyment and not a little pride. Sporting films are famously difficult to make, and it's even harder when you have to be accurate about period detail. We found craftsmen who could still make the boots and balls that would have been used in 1910, most of which we donated later to the West Auckland Football Club, who have a mini-museum at their clubhouse.

TOM CLEGG: To keep it as authentic as possible we held football trials. We did not want to cheat and rely on close-ups of the feet of professional footballer stand-ins. We wanted genuine players. It was like becoming chairman of the England selection committee. It was a bitter disappointment for those who didn't make it into our final squad. Neville Smith, who is a good actor, wanted to play. Unfortunately he had a bad ankle and wanted a stand-in. We refused. He started off in the trial then substituted himself. Dennis was in seventh heaven, of course – football, acting, mates and a team.

We narrowed the list to twenty-two. With Chris Lewis as referee, the final audition was a match on an all-weather pitch in north London on New Year's Eve 1981. Luckily for me, as a co-producer, I was definitely in the movie and would play the captain, even if I was from south London and scored an own goal.

The final selection was held in the club rooms after the game, when we tested the Geordie accents. Jimmy Yule had been selected for his sports skill. However he'd imbibed a little too freely of some vodka shared out by Chris Lewis after the game, and by the time he was called in he could hardly speak let alone tackle a Geordie accent.

In the end we put together a terrific team including Ken Hutchinson and – a new name to me – Tim Healey.

We had a fantastically diligent casting director called Marilyn Johnson who had scoured the north-east for acting footballers. She told us that she had found a bloke who was acting in some fringe theatre in Newcastle who she thought would be brilliant, although she wasn't certain of his fitness or general football prowess. He came along to the ball audition, and although he was a little out of condition (weren't we all?), Tom and I agreed that he was the only person who could play 'Dirty Hoggy', our right back. This was the first television job of a young man who would become one of my greatest mates.

TIM HEALEY: That part changed my life. Luckily I was quite raw, and had the right accent. I'd also played football in my early twenties for the local town and the factory where I'd worked as a welder before I'd gone into showbusiness. But I hadn't played competitively for years.

As Dirty Hoggy I had to really go for it, do slides, tackles, get stuck in, be a real dirty player. On my way home on the train my legs seized up. I could hardly get off at the other end, and went straight to bed before the midnight hour. A real hard man.

TOM CLEGG: We spent four weeks filming in and around Newcastle. The period of the film being 1910, the actors had been instructed to arrive with short back and sides. Dennis was the only one who had done it. He'd had a very short cut indeed, which encouraged the others. The spin-off from this came when we filmed in Turin. All being red-blooded young guys, they couldn't wait to have a good time after work in the local clubs. The Italian girls were quite happy to have a few drinks, but because the haircuts were so dreadful, no one wanted to be seen out on the dance floor with them. Saved a fortune on expenses.

By the time we'd finished filming in Newcastle we had done a certain amount of training and developed a real team feeling, which was to serve us well in our games against Juventus when we got to Turin.

Unfortunately the authentic footballs we had had made proved to be too light, they bounced too high. We opted for those of a later period.

> TIM HEALEY: These were so heavy, at least twice the weight of a modern ball, they nearly took your head off. The authentic boots too were very difficult to play in, all hand-made of course, but cut uncomfortably high and they had cork studs. As for the long shorts . . .

We flew to Turin for two weeks' filming of the final. The schedule being quite tight, it was arranged that we would start shooting the very evening of our arrival. We were picked up at the airport and taken straight to the hotel to change into our costumes for a short sequence in the old part of the city.

Dressed in the clothes of 1910 miners, with our correct, shorn hairstyles, we didn't look unlike English skinheads, who at that time had a very bad reputation all over Europe. To the elegant populace of Turin we must have appeared something of a threat, especially in mufti.

On this particular evening, we were milling around waiting to start filming. The shops were just closing, blinds were being drawn and awnings put up. Suddenly the air was rent with Italian abuse. We spun round to see Ken Hutchinson being clumped on the head. We immediately jumped on him and calmed the irate shopkeeper. Ken, it seemed, had not only boasted he was Scottish but let them know what he thought of their national football team and their chances in the forthcoming World Cup. 'Good friends you are,' he snarled at us. 'I nearly get knocked out, and you jump on me. Why the fuck didn't somebody hit him?'

> TIM HEALEY: It was all men in the production. No women. So perhaps we were a bit wilder than we would normally have been. We'd go to bed in the early hours then get up and play football with a thumping headache. Dennis was a diamond. He looked after everybody. None of us had much money but he'd take us all out for dinner, make sure everyone was all right. He and I may have been the last to bed, but when it came to work, he was first up, the ultimate professional.

I had been warned that Turin wasn't a classic Italian city, being mostly industrial. I thought it was smashing. And the food and wine were delicious. Juventus were unbelievably helpful. After Neville's failure to come up with anything much, we double-checked their archives looking for any record of the event. Not only was there no evidence of this match, there was no record of the club ever having been beaten!

The people who ran Juventus also owned Fiat and Ferrari, and they loaned us several wonderful vintage cars to use as set dressing, and, perhaps more importantly, a team to play against. No one from the real Juventus, but a selection of players from various clubs under their general umbrella.

Tom wanted us to play an ordinary game for forty-five minutes or so, enabling him to cut in some free-flowing football, after which we would choreograph some of the incidents from the script. As it was, we had some good players ourselves, including nine people who had actually had first division trials.

TOM CLEGG: Our team was totally fired up. All they wanted to do was win. I had to plead with them to give the Italians some possession, and insist that they be allowed to display their ball-dribbling skills, etc.

They agreed on five minutes, then they were going to play hard again.

At first the Italian side started taking the mickey, shouting at us. After ten minutes the cry had changed to '*Animalios!*' as we kicked the shit out of them. We went for everything. We were playing the World Cup. On screen and off, we won.

The World Cup, A Captain's Tale was shown the evening before the World Cup proper started, and was a huge success. We were nominated for an Emmy Award and won a special certificate of merit at the Pye Television Awards. Had it not been watched by anyone this film would still be amongst my personal favourites, and guess who scored the winning goal?

There is a rather sad postscript. In May 1993, the original Sir Thomas Lipton Trophy was stolen from the West Auckland clubhouse and never recovered. Obviously it can never be replaced, but I'm glad to say that I was there a couple of years ago to help present them with an identical replica made by a silversmith in Sheffield.

SEVENTEEN

RED ALERT

Rula Lenska was cast in *Minder* as the ex-model daughter of an old robber, played by Maurice Denham, determined to retrieve her father's lost booty. I had met her on a couple of occasions at charity events with her husband, Brian Deacon, and was quite impressed, especially with her apparent lack of vanity. I thought she was a nice bird with very long legs, great hair and a dopey name. She had become famous as one of the stars in a TV series called *Rock Follies*, which was about the trials and tribulations of a female singing trio. I remember being singularly unimpressed, as only one of the cast, Julie Covington, could actually sing.

It was reported in the *Sunday Mirror*, and thereafter quoted endlessly, that at my first meeting with Rula I felt I had been 'hit in the stomach by a bag of cement'. That is absolute bollocks. I even met the journalist responsible for writing it, who boasted about making it up. Rula was, without doubt, a very attractive woman, but I wasn't interested in getting involved with an actress, let alone an actress with a dodgy name who had been in a series I hadn't liked.

LINDA AGRAN: It was a very male-dominated set, and Rula was very flirtatious. Everyone fancied her but it was Dennis she was after.

PAT: Dennis' career had really taken off, and I was thrilled. What I didn't realise was the stress it was placing on our marriage. Dennis has always needed his partner's full attention. I had always met him after work, gone to the pub, become a pretty good darts player, joined in with everything. Now I had two little ones to look after, I had to divide my time more carefully.

Dennis had to be off at the crack of dawn and work till late at night. I was getting up at four in the morning for feeds, coping with the children during the day, yet was still expected to be there when he came home in the evening. Sometimes I was so tired that by the time he arrived I would have gone to bed. He could not comprehend why I wasn't back on my feet, whizzing around with him. My tiredness really upset him, especially as we had a nanny. However, I was insistent that I wanted to feed my baby myself during the night, and I was resentful that Dennis wasn't more tolerant and understanding.

It is a common problem, experienced by many couples whose lives are changed by the arrival of babies, but I thought we were coping. We still had great fun and laughs together, but during this period, as Dennis became gradually more resentful, I withdrew. Perhaps if he had been more patient, I would have come through it and we'd have been proper partners again, but by then, I think Rula had arrived on the scene.

Throughout that episode, Rula hung around more and more. The end came, and as usual a group of us decided to meet up in a Greek restaurant in Putney. I was committed to do a personal appearance at some event that night but agreed to get to the restaurant as soon as I could. I was extremely late, and was surprised to find Rula was still there. That night our affair began. It may not have been consummated, but that's where it started.

Both of us were married and well known. Privacy was essential but hard to find. However, Rula proved both determined and resourceful, and invited me to meet her at a friend's place. There followed a year of secret meetings in various 'safe houses' all over London. Rula, it seemed, had an endless supply of friends willing to allow us the use of their flats or houses. Friends, I might add, who were never seen before nor since, certainly not by me, and as far as I know in the time we were together, not by Rula either.

LINDA AGRAN: Usually when someone has a fling, both cast and crew tend to gather round and be protective. On this occasion there was a general sense that Dennis needed protection from Rula and from himself. There was a sense of general disapproval, a feeling that this was going to be damaging to everyone involved.

Rula was a glamorous, schuzzy, leggy redhead, but Pat was seriously smashing, and enormously respected. She was attractive and smart, a wife who gave Dennis all the support he needed and yet allowed him to be the man he was, to lead the boy's life.

George, being a happily married man, and very moral, did not approve at all.

PAT: The second time I did *Minder* I had a funny scene with George where I'd beaten him up with a handbag, and I remember no one laughed. It felt very uncomfortable. I couldn't understand why the crew were being so strange with me . . .

GEORGE COLE: Everyone had such a high regard for Pat, it was difficult to know how to react. When the story finally hit the press, our publicity lady at that time, Sally Croft, came up to me and said, 'George, I'm terribly sorry, I thought it was you.'

'What?' I said.

'Having the affair. Every time I came into your Winnebago, she was in there with you.'

Of course she was always in there waiting for Dennis. He'd go on set, I'd come off, and there she'd be and I'd be left sitting with her. I was always puzzled why Sally would come in and go, 'Oh, sorry.'

ROBERT POWELL: Rula and I happened to bump into each other at some function. She realised I knew Dennis as well as anyone, so asked if she could talk to me.

I gave her the only advice I think I've ever given to anybody who's asked me about Dennis – he is what he is. If you like what you see, then fine, but do not imagine for one second that he will change, because he will not. That's why we all love him, because he is constant. That's why all his mates are still with him after thirty years or more.

If you disapprove of any element that is Dennis – his enjoyment of pubs, of sport, his friends, his tendency to enjoy men's company more than women's (in which he is not unique by any means), then I suggest you look elsewhere.

It is amazing how few women have ever listened to that advice. Dennis has always suffered from being such an immensely charming and attractive man. Women are always convinced they can get that other twenty per cent – once they've got hold of him.

At home I tried to behave as normally as possible. I was fairly certain this was just another affair that would fizzle out and everything would return to being the way it was. But the longer it went on, the more emotionally involved I became, until one night in her car when she proclaimed, 'I love you,' I heard myself saying, 'I love you too.' From then on we found it almost impossible to be apart.

Had those words not been spoken, maybe the affair would have cooled. We could have returned to our spouses and our worlds would not have turned upside down, but we said them and our lives would never be the same again.

DEKE ARLON: It was sad for all of us who adored Pat and the family.

Dennis had enjoyed a number of passing fancies but they had meant nothing and hurt no one. As his personal manager, whether I approved or not, it was my job to shield him, and also to protect his family from any unnecessary pain or gossip. With Rula it was different.

Rula had focused on Dennis, and there was no escape. At first, I'm sure, he was incredibly flattered that such a beautiful and sophisticated woman would find him so appealing. Insecurities about his lack of education, the genuine modesty that refuses to recognise his own intellectual potential, left him in awe of her self-professed education, her Polish background, and her ability to speak several languages.

Our secret time together was a lot more difficult for Rula to arrange. She had a two-year-old daughter, but she was amazing at organising her life and finding baby-sitters. All I had to do was lie!

Whenever there was a legitimate reason for us to be away from our homes, especially on location, the other would be there. She came to Newcastle and to Italy where I was filming *The World Cup*.

I picked her up at Turin airport, and as she emerged through customs, I was surprised to see she looked visibly relieved.

'Is everything all right?' I asked.

She hesitated. 'I wasn't certain I would be let into Italy again,' she said.

'Why not?' I persisted.

It appeared that when she was nineteen, she had been singing in a club in Sardinia when there was a drugs raid by the police. She and some others had been arrested and imprisoned for eighteen months. This came as something of a shock from my elegant Polish countess. I knew that she often used marijuana, and on the odd occasion, I would join her, but the drugs scene was not for me. I preferred another poison. There was a time, later in our relationship, when our disagreement over this particular topic led to my walking out on her at a party because of the amount of dope that was going down.

Someone in the music industry whom she had met during the making of *Rock Follies* had invited us to a party in Chiswick which was being thrown by a very famous and recently retired ballerina. The ballerina had become involved with the young leader of a punk band, who was playing at the party. Everything was fine until the cocaine appeared on every available flat surface. This was definitely not my scene. Hypocrite I may be, considering my penchant for alcohol, but drugs really bother me. I did not want to hang around, so I left on my own. She came running after me, furious with me for being so boring. It was a very tense and silent journey home.

PAT: Dennis had sent my Auntie Connie and her husband with me and the kids and my dad to Lanzarote, the first holiday I'd had since my mother had died. We'd only just got back home when the phone rang and some journalist blurted out, 'What do you think of your husband and Rula Lenska?'

Dennis denied it, of course, but it soon became evident that something was going on.

I just hoped it would die a death.

DEKE ARLON: The press had a field day. 'The Cockney and the Countess' they were dubbed.

Even if Dennis had wanted to back out, by then they were both infected by the tabloid fever. Dennis was in turmoil. He believed he was in love with Rula, but he was distraught about leaving his family.

LINDA AGRAN: Dennis is the sort of person who can normally manage with very little sleep and a lot of vodka and still be perfect on set, but during this period, he was under enormous stress. You could see it in his eyes and occasionally he started to lose it. He was being hounded by the press. But no one was going to take him on one side, and advise him what to do. Dennis is not that sort of person.

PAT: The press set traps for me all the time, rephrased questions to trick me. I didn't want to say anything, especially in the emotional state I was in. They wanted me to talk about Rula. I wouldn't give them the pleasure. What good would that do anyone? Everything would have backfired on the children and my one priority was to protect them.

The bell rang one afternoon when I was in bed, not well. Hannah, aged only six, answered the door and I could hear her talking to someone, then the door closed and she came upstairs and said to me, 'Mummy what do journalists look like?' I think I'd probably given her the idea they had horns. 'Do they wear suits?' she asked.

'They can do.'

'Well, I've just shut the door on one,' she announced proudly. 'I got rid of him for you.'

One of them did half apologise. His shamefaced excuse was that he worked for *The Times*. I said, 'I don't care which bloody newspaper you work for, leave us alone.'

Christmas 1981, and Rula was invited to appear with my old mate Les Dawson in pantomime at the Theatre Royal, Richmond, just down the road from my marital home. It was the final straw.

Both Pat and I were totally miserable. I had become increasingly distant, unhelpful and sexually inactive. Pat had never been anything other than a wonderful wife and mother, but I found myself being 'faithful' to my mistress! After a very tense and unpleasant Christmas, I had to make a decision, and at the end of January, I left home. Happy New Year!

DEKE ARLON: Dennis was in an agony of guilt, self-loathing and grief at this decision. Despite his petty philandering, he is very Victorian in his attitude to marriage and the family, yet here he was breaking up the very thing he most respected and wanted.

He hadn't fallen out of love with Pat, but he had fallen passionately in love with Rula.

In these situations, the tabloid press can behave disgustingly. Because I wouldn't speak to any of them, one particularly odious columnist for the Mirror Group dispatched his own ten- or eleven-year-old son to our house with a message asking me to phone him. His own son!

PAT: The vultures would be hovering outside the house when we came home, or would try and catch us when we went shopping. I'll never forget one man holding up a photograph of Dennis with Rula, and talking about them quite explicitly in front of Hannah, as if she didn't exist.

It was horrible. They wanted to see me cry, to snap pictures of the embittered wife. But I refused to let them see me like that.

HANNAH: Sadly, some of my earliest memories are of the sound of Mum and Dad rowing – raised, angry voices downstairs or through closed doors and Mum saying, 'Hush, you'll wake the children.' Parents always hope you don't notice their distress, they try and put on a brave face, but it doesn't work.

After Dad left, Mum never once said anything against him. I walked in on her once in the bedroom. She was sobbing, and angry that I'd caught her. She didn't want me to see her so vulnerable, so desperate and hurt, but the separation was so public and there were pictures of Dad and Rula everywhere.

We had a pathetic dog called Seamus. Dad had bought him for Mum when he left, which was nice. Seamus was a poor excuse for a water spaniel, useless as a guard dog, neurotic and dead scared of men. When Mum threatened the press that if they didn't go away she would set the dog on them, poor Seamus was shoved outside, with a command to 'See 'em off!' He turned tail immediately.

PAT: The press manipulated and exacerbated the situation for all it was worth. The excuse is always that anyone in the public eye is fair game. But I believe that everyone, from a king to a pauper, has a fundamental right to privacy. Take that away and there is nothing left. The gutter press not only victimised the children, me and Dennis, it destroyed what little hope there might have been of our getting back together.

I made one last desperate attempt to retrieve our marriage. Dennis was in Bristol at the beginning of the tour of the musical *Windy City*. I drove down to see him. He looked drawn and ill. I begged him to come back. We were both in tears. It was hopeless. His final words were 'I'm sorry, Pat, I have to be with her.' I cried all the way home.

The worst thing was telling the children. I sat with my arms around both of them and explained that, although Daddy loved them, he would not be living at home again. They were desperately upset. 'You mean never?' Hannah gazed into my face. 'He's never going to live with us again?' She took it very hard.

For their sakes I tried to act in a dignified manner. There was nothing to be gained by being vitriolic. Besides, if you allow bitterness and envy to take over, you become poisoned yourself. Of course there were moments when such emotions threatened to consume me, but I had to abandon them, to try and distance myself. And I'm a fatalist too. Dennis had made his choice and there was nothing I could do.

Rula's daughter Lara was so affected by doorstepping photographers that for many years she was terrified whenever she saw a camera! If you ever threatened these big brave boys in their flak jackets, they would whinge, 'I'm only doing my job, don't hit me.' I did hit several. You are allowed no protection from these people. There was a time when they were virtually camped in the garden, with one of their cars parked across the gate stopping anyone getting in or out. I phoned the police, but all they could do was to tell them off for illegal parking. I said I was going to take my two dogs and a golf club out there and tell them to fuck off. The policeman said, 'If you do that and one of them gets hurt, they'll sue you to high heaven.' 'But they're on my land, they're trespassing,' I said. I was informed that there was no law of criminal trespass in this country. Terrific!

It would be a good idea to publish an underground paper, or whatever, to doorstep and photograph and print the way most reporters live. I wonder how they'd like that.

I had walked away from my home and given away another house. There was no question of my doing anything else. Nobody else was to blame for my leaving.

I had to find somewhere to live. I spent several months being put up by friends. Not close old friends, it has to be said. I assumed that I'd be able to take back my old bedroom in Chris Lewis's flat. Much to his credit, he told me that I couldn't. In his own words: 'I'm a Pat person.' This meant that I was estranged from one of my greatest mates for some time. Warren Clarke also said that, although he liked Rula, he didn't want to be seen to be taking sides.

WARREN CLARKE: If I said Dennis was a sensitive soul, he'd say, 'Bollocks', but over the twenty-odd years, we have always confided in each other.

If Dennis had asked my advice maybe I'd have given it, but he didn't. You can't stick your opinion on someone else. Life is life and although Michelle, my wife, and I were good friends with both Dennis and Pat, and we were understandably upset at their break-up, we did not interfere. Pat would come and see us, talk to us, come away on weekends with us and we were as supportive as we could be. But Dennis had made his decision and there was no going back. And Pat, like Penny before her, was exemplary in the way she behaved.

For a while I shared Chris Walford's house in Twickenham. The only bright light during this period was being again in the company of Les Dawson.

I had first met Les in the early seventies through a mutual old friend, John Foster. He walked in while we were playing snooker in the Eccentric Club, and joined us for a game. I believe I can claim it was friendship at first sight for both of us.

Les was, without doubt, one of the nicest and most naturally funny men I have ever met. Kind, compassionate and extremely intelligent, he was drawn to legitimate actors, in the belief that they had a deeper understanding of his passion for the eccentricities of our language. It was this as much as anything that drove his comic genius. Although he was never attention-seeking, unlike some performers, who are never 'off', he loved to try out on us some of his wonderfully lugubrious, brilliant monologues.

Like me, he was a pub man who enjoyed the company and the friendship as much as the drink. We spent many happy hours together in this way.

I remember, one evening, visiting his home in Lytham. Deke's assistant Bill Tansley and I were scheduled to fly to Dublin the next morning. Needless to say, we missed our flight. Les was most reassuring; he knew several blokes who owned small planes who would be pleased to whip us over the Irish Sea. No problem. We arrived in Dublin six hundred quid poorer. But we cared not a jot; that night with Les had been worth every penny.

He also claimed I was responsible for his shortest press interview ever. He had agreed to do his stuff in the Cobwebs, the pub local to the Richmond Theatre. A few of us were already there sharing our usual drink with Les when in walked this particularly odious journalist, who had written a foul article about my father and me and whom I'd sworn I would knock out if ever I had the chance.

Les stood up, greeted him and said, 'Hello.' At which point, the journalist locked eyes with me, colour drained from his face, and he beat a very hasty retreat.

Rula and I were both very fond of Les, and like everyone who knew him were devastated when he died so suddenly.

Eventually I left Twickenham and moved into a flat in West Hampstead owned by Sheena Easton, who by then was pursuing her career in Los Angeles. And I was back on the West End stage.

EIGHTEEN

WINDY CITY

In the midst of all this personal trauma, I was asked to audition for an important new musical that was going into the West End. This came as something of a surprise, as I hadn't auditioned for anything for years. However, the director was the much-acclaimed Bert Shevelove, whose credits included the Tony Award-winning production of *A Funny Thing Happened on the Way to the Forum* and *No, No, Nanette* at the Drury Lane Theatre. The audition was actually to assess my vocal range and ability for what was quite a difficult score.

The composer, Tony McCauley, had been a high-profile writer-producer in the world of pop music since the late sixties, and had had numerous chart successes both here and in the States with some of the brightest stars of that era. This was his first musical, commissioned by Stoll-Moss and enthusiastically endorsed by the theatre group's chief executive Louis Benjamin. McCauley was also involved with most of the major casting sessions.

I went along typically unprepared. 'What would you like to sing?' I was asked.

'I don't know,' I answered. 'I half know the lyrics of hundreds of songs. If you've got a songbook, I can certainly get through some of them.'

Tony sat at the piano and accompanied me while I sang a selection from Nat King Cole to Rogers and Hammerstein. Each new song he played in a higher key until he was satisfied that I had the necessary vocal range. I did.

Dick Vosburgh, a witty and creative writer, fresh from his success with his own smash hit in London and on Broadway, *A Day in Hollywood, A Night in the Ukraine*, had written both book and lyrics, and they were brilliant.

Windy City was an adaptation of the classic Hecht and MacArthur play *Front Page*. Written in 1928 by two journalists, it had already been much revived as a stage play and filmed three times. Set in a newspaper office in pre-war Chicago, it purported to reflect their own newspaper experiences and the callous and indifferent attitudes to people, life and death of those hell-bent on scoop and deadline. Rewritten as a musical it lost none of its gritty, satirical toughness.

I had absolutely loved the most recent film version, starring Jack Lemmon and Walter Matthau. I was signed to play Hilde Johnson, the Jack Lemmon part. The Walter Matthau character, apparently, was to be played by Telly Savalas. Carl Toms was the designer of what was to be a very imaginative multiple set, Diane Langton was cast as the tart with a heart, and a rising young actress, Amanda Redman, as my leading lady. Fellow courtroom reporters included, amongst others, Victor Spinetti and Benny Lee.

The pre-London tryout was to be in Bristol at the Hippodrome, followed by a London premiere at the Victoria Palace Theatre.

DEKE ARLON: *Windy City* came at a time when Dennis' career was at its zenith. Louis Benjamin, the producer and head of Stoll-Moss, and a major player in our industry, had sold the show to us, as a star vehicle for Dennis, with the charismatic and gifted American actor Telly Savalas as his co-star. It was to be a formidable pairing. Not only that, with America and Broadway definitely on the agenda, such a high-powered international casting was essential.

When it finally reached the stage the show was well reviewed, and even won a couple of awards, but tragedy struck less than three weeks before we went into rehearsal when Bert Shevelove, who had spent eighteen months working on the show with Vosburgh and McCauley, suddenly died of a heart attack. With him went all his ideas for the production. He was a dear man, wonderfully experienced in musical theatre, brimming with enthusiasm for the show, and he would have been wonderful to work with. Peter Wood, a very talented but different theatrical animal, was brought in to pick up the pieces.

Next came the devastating news that Telly Savalas had dropped out. McCauley had been to see him in Hollywood and had discovered that Telly did not believe he had the vocal range for the show. With Broadway on our agenda, we needed a big American star, and big American names were being bandied around when, suddenly, I was told the part had been given to Anton Rodgers.

DEKE ARLON: This left Dennis as the only star draw. Anton may have been a respected actor, but at that time in his career, he did not put bums on seats. Stars do that. That is why they are cast, to draw in people to the box office, to sell tickets. It is a big responsibility.

Disappointed though Dennis was at the turn of events, he did not want to withdraw from the show and let down Louis Benjamin and everyone else involved.

On the day of the big press announcement, Dennis and I, Louis Benjamin and one or two others were waiting in Dennis' number one star dressing room, ready to go down on to the stage for the press launch. Benjie suddenly disappeared into the adjoining anteroom and appeared with a poster for the show which none of us had seen or even discussed. Above the title, in the star billing position, was:

DENNIS WATERMAN – ANTON RODGERS

It gave equal billing to the two names, both in the same size lettering and colour. Admittedly Dennis' name was on the left, giving it a superior position, but it was a flagrant breach of theatrical etiquette, an insult to Dennis' status and all he'd been led to believe.

Dennis had remained true to Louis throughout all the problems; this showed neither loyalty to Dennis nor respect for his standing in the show.

In that moment I saw in Dennis' eyes the feeling of being used and let down. His position within the production had been usurped and it coloured his attitude throughout the entire show.

There had been no discussion and no forewarning. Had the poster been shown to us earlier, it would not have been allowed. But it was a fait accompli. We had no alternative but to go with it. The press were waiting.

Our contract had read 'star billing', and technically this was it, but it was not what we had been led to understand was the intention.

Rehearsals started, and so did the tension. You could feel it immediately.

Rehearsing a musical is much more compartmentalised than rehearsing a straight play. You have at least three bosses – the director, the musical director and the choreographer – not to mention the big boss, the producer. While you're working with each of these people they are in absolute charge. You can spend the morning being screamed at by the MD and the afternoon being shouted at by the director.

Our MD, Anthony Bowles, had a very waspish tongue, plus the ability to make you feel very inadequate. He petrified the singers. I actually liked him a lot and we got on very well. Under his tutelage, we learned the songs and followed his conducting as he led the orchestra and cast at each performance.

Ken Oldfield, the choreographer, had a more difficult task. There are rarely any directions in a script that describe the sort of dancing envisaged. It is up to the choreographer to interpret the score and select the appropriate style. *Windy City* had a large cast, thirty-six actors and singers, few of whom specialised in dance. He had also to satisfy the 'vision' and comply with the direction of the other bosses involved, ensuring a character would end the set dance piece on the correct side of the stage for his next entrance or exit. I don't know how much co-ordination had gone on with the bosses beforehand, but despite the producers being very much in evidence, there was a distinct feeling of the right hand not knowing what the left foot was doing. Ken's ideas did not suit everyone. He left halfway through and was replaced by David Toguri.

Then there is the company manager, whose job it is to make sure everything 'gels' – in other words, to schedule rehearsal calls, to ensure everybody gets their wages and to co-ordinate the timing and building of the sets and the completion of costumes. It's a difficult and demanding job, but I reckon it's a misnomer to call them 'company' managers. They don't really give a monkey's about the actual company. The company they regard as a bloody nuisance. Of course, not all company managers are like this, just nearly all of them. We had some Scottish bird who I thought was a serious pain in the arse. If she's not still in the theatre, I would take a guess that she's working as a traffic warden.

Despite the rocky start, the rehearsals turned out to be good fun and the cast generally good and nice people. Anton and I got on OK, and I adored Amanda Redman. And Victor Spinetti, as always, was fantastically entertaining on and off the stage. Diane Langton was a particular mate of mine, and has got to have as fine a voice as you will hear on the English stage. Even if she does forget to turn up every now and then, she's always worth it. My fellow reporters were without exception a smashing and talented group of blokes. No sign of a chorus line here; they all had very distinctive and definite characters of their own. Robert Longdon, excellent actor, but as nutty as a fruitcake, played the escaped convict. Very good casting.

Peter Wood, the director, had mellowed a great deal since the first few times we had worked together. Even so, every now and then you would see him starting to zone in on one of the cast. But he wasn't as fierce as he used to be.

Emotionally, I was a mess. My marriage to Pat was over, Rula was on tour in a play, and, somewhat inevitably, Amanda and I got together.

We were playing fiancés on stage, and behaving like it off stage. Peter Wood took the piss out of us mercilessly. I thought Amanda was truly terrific, and still do. She had a boyfriend at the time, and my current situation was well publicised, but we just couldn't help it. We had a duet called 'Perfect Partners', and we very nearly were.

By the end of the first week in Bristol I had got very close to the band. An orchestra, to a certain extent, is the theatre's equivalent of a film crew, full of truly talented nutters, and can they ever drink? Our particular pal was trumpeter John Huckridge. Amanda and I were the only non-musicians who were part of the highly exclusive sect known as 'Hucks Cuffers' – 'cuffer' being a drinker, derived from the cockney rhyming slang, 'cuff links' = 'drinks'.

The set was, at that time, the largest moving solid set in the history of the British theatre. The play and the costumes were great, but the changes and fine-tuning to the show rapidly meant that Dick Vosburgh was doing daily rewrites, which often resulted in a bewildered cast.

After four weeks in Bristol we moved back to London for three weeks of previews at the Victoria Palace. But by the time of the official first night, my enthusiasm had waned. I was bored to death.

I firmly believe that, had we not done Bristol or all those previews, I would have got really good reviews. I did get good reviews, but had I been in my 'let's show 'em' mood, I would have blown the critics away.

It's easier to sustain interest in a musical. You may feel down when you go into the theatre at night, but once you hear the orchestra strike up the overture, it's very difficult not to feel that buzz. For a while! It's not the actual work that I find so tedious, it's the fact that you are always leaving for work when everybody else is going home. You have all the mundane aggravations of finding somewhere to park, getting parking tickets, or, even more irritating, having your car broken into. I felt more like an office worker on nights.

I enjoyed friends coming in to see the show. It gave me a reason for performing, and they were unanimous in their praise. But on too many occasions my flagging interest often meant I switched to automatic pilot; I just could not ignite that crucial extra spark. All desperately unprofessional and regrettable. I heard members of the cast saying, 'It would be great if we could get two or three years out of this.' Are you fucking mad? I'd top myself!

Strangely enough, despite being old mates, there was no real company spirit. Most of the cast were used to doing musicals, they turned up on time, did their job and went straight home. Absolutely correct, that's what you're supposed to do. Join a singing bank!

Fortunately the musicians had a band room which was better equipped than many pubs. We had many a good session, some, it has to be said, between the matinée and the evening show, which was not good news. I was never out of control on stage but I could be slightly out of kilter. This made me want to laugh and make as many other people on stage laugh as well. I can see how some of this behaviour exasperated Anton.

Anton is one of those super-professionals who finds anything untoward worth a complaint. I thought he was a bit of an old woman. It might have been because of the way he was cast, but I didn't really have much time for him. He was also susceptible to any advice. You always knew when someone he knew had been in to see the show, because the very next night he'd be brimming with new ideas. 'So-and-so was in last night, and had a very good point about my entrance, maybe we should rehearse it?'

'Piss off! We had six weeks' rehearsals, a month in Bristol, three weeks' previews and we've been running now for two months. If you think I'm going to start rehearsing again, you've got another think coming.'

What was even stranger, and more annoying, was that he'd listen to anyone. It didn't have to be someone in the business, like Julia McKenzie (who it often was). If his dentist came up with an idea, he'd want to do it.

Having said that, he was exceedingly good in the part. It was just a shame that we were such different types. And I admit, he had a great deal more to complain about than I did. At times I was behaving about as badly as I have ever behaved in the theatre, or anywhere else, as it happens. The longer the show ran, the more I resented it.

Things came to a head one night when the deputy musical director took over in the pit and, in my opinion, accelerated the tempos. In one big drinking number with the reporters, the song finished with us all throwing our drinks in the air, and mine just happened to go over the MD. It was a joke. It was only water, but the dickhead abandoned his job and left the pit. Walked out. Of course it hit the press and I got all the flak. Nobody mentioned his conduct. Fortunately the keyboard player took over, who was much better.

A time came when I remember saying, with relief, to Deke, 'Well, I've only got four months left.'

'What are you talking about?' he asked, frowning.

I went through the litany. 'We rehearsed for six weeks, Bristol for a month, three weeks' previews, two months' London. That means I've only got four months left.'

'No, Diesel,' he said slowly. Diesel was his nickname for me. 'The nine months only starts from the official first night.'

'Are you telling me I've got another seven months of this?'

He nodded. It was like watching a judge putting on the black cap.

With hindsight, I regret that such a good show came to me at exactly the wrong time. It's true the production was fraught with problems, but I believe I was having a minor breakdown. I had left my family. The woman I'd left them for was away on tour somewhere, and I was involved with my leading lady. I was living in a new place every couple of months, and every time I turned round there were the paparazzi in my face. I was thirty-four years old, with no home of my own. Supposedly I was highly successful, but I didn't know what to do next. Eight shows a week, that's what I had to do next. Until I could get out of *Windy City*, I was a mess. Amanda, it has to be said, was putting no pressure on me whatsoever; I was doing it all to myself.

DEKE ARLON: Bristol was a brief escape from the dilemma. Amanda was fabulous. She made Dennis happy, she made him laugh, something he had not done for a long time. But delightful though she was, I admit I was surprised that he plunged into an affair with her. As if his life wasn't complicated enough!

I don't believe Dennis' need for women has ever been a particularly sexual one, although I'm sure he keeps his women happy. It has more to do with a craving for affection, for being wanted, and the dread of being alone. I'm sure it all stems back to his childhood, being starved of love and affection. It scarred him. It's probably why most of the women in his life are older than him. The recent death of his mother had also affected him far more than he would ever admit.

Eventually Rula finished her tour. Although she was the one who had committed adultery, somehow she had talked her husband into moving out of their house. And after a decent period of separation – I moved in.

Slowly, the relationship with both exes became less aggressive, and thanks to the children, we slipped into a surprisingly relaxed way of treating each other. Pat decided to move to Norfolk, an area she had grown to love, to be near her closest friend, Chris Lewis's sister Aideen and her husband. I agreed with her about the advantages of bringing the girls up in the country, but Norfolk is three and a half hours away from anywhere. Hannah and Julia would come and stay with us for weekends, and Julia and Lara, who were about nine months apart, became very close.

By now we were looking for a new house. I didn't want to live in Wimbledon, where Rula had her house, and Rula didn't want to live in Richmond, largely because of the Turk's Head.

CHRIS LEWIS: The Turk's Head featured very heavily in our social life, especially the Monday Club, when ten or twelve of us, whoever was free or not working, would meet up at noon and stay through until eight in the evening. It was a coming-together of friends, showbusiness or otherwise, but amongst them were some great wags and raconteurs. The jokes, the stories, the banter was superb. Pat had always joined in, as had the other girlfriends or wives, but I think Rula felt threatened, and was jealous of the close friendship we all enjoyed. My family were also emotionally and, by then, geographically close to Pat and the girls. At first Rula seemed to accept the situation and to behave like one of the boys, but it was the beginning of the end.

I remember she wanted to throw a surprise birthday party for Dennis but, being new to the scene, she did not know many of his closest friends or relatives, so she asked me to organise it for her. I booked a favourite restaurant, San Rocce in Mortlake, and invited a whole crowd, plus Joy and other family members including Myrna and Jim who flew in from America. It was a lot of work and the evening was a huge success, except that I was seated at the far end of the table and when the time came, Rula stood up and took all the glory for the evening with not a word of thanks to me.

The following year she arranged another birthday party, and the only old friend not invited was me. I heard about it the next day and told Dennis just how hurt I felt. He wasn't happy about what had happened but was too involved with Rula to realise what was going on below the surface. After being so close for so long, I felt totally cut out, and although I still managed the Waterman XI, I was effectively cut adrift.

TOM CLEGG: Rula made no attempt to fraternise with Dennis' friends. Chris Lewis, in particular, Rula considered part of Dennis' wicked Turk's Head past. She tolerated me because I was a director. I never felt comfortable with her at all.

We decided to look further afield for a house. Rula's mother lived in the Kilburn area, but I said, 'No way, I've kept away from north London for thirty-odd years, I'm not going to weaken now.' Deke suggested that we look around the Beaconsfield area in Buckinghamshire, where he lived. Rula was wary about living that far out of town, until one day when we were in Soho in the morning and had arranged to visit a house out there in the afternoon. It took less time to drive the twenty-five miles to Beaconsfield than it had to travel the twelve miles to London from Wimbledon.

After seeing many nice but ordinary houses, we finally found one we wanted. I had no grandiose ideas, and this house, set in acres of countryside, was large and comfortable. It also had a tennis court, a swimming pool and, very important, a snooker room.

The owner was a very clever salesman. He and his wife had shown us round in the normal way – 'This is the kitchen, this is a bedroom, etc.' We thought we had seen it all, when he invited us to have a drink before going back. 'That sounds nice,' I agreed. 'Then let's go through here,' he said, opening a door to reveal a full-sized snooker room. Oh yes, I thought.

Rula was impressed too. 'Could we put wheels on the table to roll it out of the way for parties?' It was necessary to point out to her that the table weighed at least three tons and this wasn't such a good idea.

Because I had left our family house with Pat, Rula, with her half-share from the sale of her family house, paid the deposit and I dived into a large mortgage. *Windy City* had finally come to end. Luckily this coincided with Euston Films asking me to do twenty more episodes of *Minder*. All were up to the usual standard. Great writing and directing and wonderful casts. Art Malik, Patrick Mower, Beryl Reid, Bill Maynard, Billy Murray, Brian Cox, Jan Francis, Ronald Frazer; even Rula did another episode. It was huge.

DEKE ARLON: Rula completely took over Dennis' life. She loved the publicity, the 'golden couple' image, the big house in the country, the attention and the excitement of being with Waterman.

With all the interest still focusing on them both, we were

inundated with offers for them to appear together. Rula was very keen, Dennis wanted to please Rula, and I was against it. I did not want him out on the 'personality' circuit unless we had something specific to promote, and even then we would be highly selective in our choice.

Understandably, Rula saw a opportunity to re-create her career. She was on the front of every newspaper, casting directors were calling, and her money had gone up accordingly.

Her ambition was for them both to work together, to create a 'couple' career like Michael Dennison and Dulcie Gray. She intimated strongly that I should manage them both in the work they could do together, as well as in their family affairs.

When it comes to work, Dennis is very single-minded. But he found it impossible to say anything to Rula, so it was left to me to dissuade her from pursuing this plan of campaign. For me to have managed both would have meant compromising my position with Dennis and all he had worked for. For Dennis, if the piece was right, he was agreeable.

An offer was made for a tour of *Same Time Next Year*. I remembered it as an excellent film starring Alan Alda. Paul Elliott, a successful theatrical producer and old colleague, approached me with the idea of Dennis and Rula taking it to Australia, and I didn't see any reason to say no.

Although she was unknown in Australia, Rula insisted on star billing. She also fought hard to get the same money as Dennis, but this I could not allow. Dennis was at the top of his career, able to command top money; Rula was in a lower league. Still, for the sake of peace in the home, we accommodated her.

NINETEEN

THE WIZARDS OF OZ

Rula and I had had a great time in Australia on a previous occasion, albeit briefly, when I was invited to present a Logie Award, their biggest night on television. In lieu of a fee, we were offered a two-week holiday anywhere we chose in Australasia. We plumped for Hayman Island off the Great Barrier Reef. It was stunning, and that was the start of a love affair with Oz.

Minder was very popular out there. Bob Hawke, the then Premier, apparently halted Parliamentary proceedings regularly, by calling a recess, in time for everyone to watch. 'I Could Be So Good For You', which had been number one, in the charts – twice! – was even used by the Opposition as a campaign song during one of their elections. It was also said that George and I were the only two people who could get into Australia without passports. It wasn't quite the same for Rula. Australian Actors' Equity objected to her taking away an Australian actress's job. This was ridiculous. I refused to do the play without her. It was only a two-hander, after all. The whole point of the tour was to do it together, plus it would have meant all the Australians booked to work on the show – stage management, wardrobe, light and sound, etc. – would be put out of work.

Apparently *Rock Follies* wasn't considered that big a deal over there. But after much debate, involving the Arts Minister of Western Australia, we were eventually allowed to continue with the show.

Perth is probably my favourite city. If ever I were to think of living outside England, this would be the place. Perth is very pretty, caught between the desert in the east, and in the west, with thousands of miles of white beach bordering it, the Indian Ocean, which never seems to be cold. Paradise.

We were flown out first class and installed in a beautiful apartment near the zoo. This could have been considered a drawback, as the gibbons can be exceedingly noisy, but we loved it. The apartment building, incidentally, was called Minderup. This is an aboriginal word, but the happy coincidence made us laugh.

We had an absolutely fantastic time. So did Hannah, Julia and Lara, who joined us for part of the time. We had left England as the winter was beginning and hit Oz as their summer was starting. Perfect timing. Perth was absolutely buzzing. It was the time when Alan Bond won the Americas Cup for Australia, which was all happening just down the road in Fremantle.

We were lucky enough to meet a marine vet who was preparing to put some Sea World dolphins back into the sea. He invited us to go and swim with these beautiful creatures. We would do this quite often. It was a great privilege and the start of another love affair. There again, everybody loves dolphins. How could you not? We cuddled koalas, fed kangaroos, watched the quokkas on Rottnest Island, rode Lipizzaner horses at a stud farm north of Perth and there were numerous boat trips. The only slight drawback was that we had to do a show every night. Even that was fun. We were sold out most nights and it was a great success.

After a wonderful couple of months in Perth we were to take the play to New Zealand for two months. We spent a few days in Sydney on the way, and our nanny, Jean, took the kids back to England in time for their school term.

New Zealand is an extraordinarily diverse, beautiful country, a wonderful place to look at, but not necessarily to take a play to. It was quite a shock, after the huge success in Australia, to be met with such indifference. And because of the long distances the audiences had to travel to see us, the curtain went up much later than normal, at eight or eight thirty. This meant that by the time the curtain came down, everywhere was closed for dinner. However, had the play started at seven we would have had the same problem. There still wouldn't have been anywhere to go. It is impossible to eat before a performance, so we had to bribe restaurateurs to stay open. They agreed, but only on condition there were enough of us to make it worth their while – difficult when we were a cast of two. Consequently, we had to take the rest of the crew with us just to get something to eat.

Being in a country the size of Britain with a population of only three million does have its advantages, though. I remember a fantastic drive from the top of the South Island, down the Kaikoura Coast, ending up in Christchurch. We stopped at a seal colony for some fresh crayfish and vodka, very romantic. In a journey of some six or seven hours, we saw only eight other cars.

I have been back since and New Zealand has grown up considerably, with lots of good, late restaurants and, of course, their own wonderful wines.

Although the play wasn't a wild success, the trip itself was a great adventure. If there was anything to see or do, we did it. And we met some fascinating people. There was one occasion when we were invited to help with the opening of a Maori kindergarten. It was quite an event, supported by a number of Maori chiefs, one of whom was a tall, handsome, white-haired gentleman who had been a big hero in the war. When we were introduced, he immediately welcomed Rula in perfect Polish, as did a heavily tattooed, muscular, distinctly Maori young man who was digging a large hole in which to cook some local dish. It was quite bizarre.

Back in Blighty, Paul Elliott, our producer, had asked Rula and me to do *Cinderella* together at the Beck Theatre in Hayes.

I had never liked pantomime as a kid, but they were offering lots of dosh, it was just down the road and we figured that the kids would love it. It was the first time that Rula realised the difference between us. I was offered about three times the money that she was.

'My part's as big as yours,' she complained. 'How come they're offering you so much more than me?'

I shrugged. 'Because I'm a big name on the telly.' She got her agent to complain, but the producers wouldn't budge. In the end I persuaded Deke to let her have some of my salary, just to keep the peace.

DEKE ARLON: Rula's vying for equal position and equal money was very offensive to Dennis. He had spent years building his career to a position where he could command top dollar. Other than her new-found partnership with Dennis, Rula had done nothing professionally to merit such rewards. Her attitude showed no respect for the star status he had achieved. But she was domineering and Dennis was non-confrontational, so the money was split and Dennis received only half the income he deserved. It would not be the last time.

To my surprise, *Cinderella* was great fun, even though I found it pretty stupid What did amaze me was that a pantomime is one of the most complicated shows to put on. It involves a cast of thousands, hundreds of different sets and costumes, loads of singing and dancing, magic tricks, slosh scenes, and that's not including the animals. To do a straight play with one set, two people and no costume changes, you have a minimum of three weeks' rehearsal. For this extravaganza you get ten days. And somehow, and God knows how, you do it. Twice daily. The longest run I've ever done in panto is six weeks, and that was five weeks too long. Once the kids have gone back to school, the whole thing is absolutely pointless. Three and a half to four weeks is more than enough. And Christmas jokes in February are not funny at all.

After having Christmas Day to ourselves, Rula and I went back to work on Boxing Day. Cinderella had achieved a certain amount of publicity as a harpist playing at the Ritz tea room. She was very pretty and not unpleasant, but for me, it was as if she came from a different planet. She was no baby, but she had a stage mother who watched her like a hawk, and the daughter did everything she was told. The two of them had even arranged privately for the well-known designers the Emmanuels to make her wedding dress for the finale. Anyway, on that Boxing Day, everyone started comparing notes – whether or not we had had a good time, if we had had loads of presents, and were we sober yet? Then Cinderella arrived, and someone asked if she'd had anything nice for Christmas. 'Yes,' she beamed. 'A racehorse.' A lot of the young dancers started to think very seriously about taking up the harp after that.

I got back to do some more *Minder*s, including a Christmas special called *Minder on the Orient Express*. We had a terrific cast: the late great Ralph Bates and his beautiful wife Virginia, Honor Blackman, Ronald Lacey and, for some reason, Adam Faith.

The script directions suggested that Terry should appear very nervous at the prospect of coming up against a particularly fearsome-looking character who was working for the villains. This was the role in which they'd cast Adam Faith.

'We're going to have to rethink this one,' I said to Francis Megahy, our director.

'Why?' he asked.

'I'm supposed to be frightened of him,' I retorted.

'And you don't think it's going to work?'

'Hardly,' I said. 'I've got two daughters who are bigger than him.'

Somehow, we made it work. The film was a big hit when it was shown on Christmas night. And we had a great time making it, especially during the ten days on location in Boulogne; it was dynamite.

In the autumn of 1985, Rula and I took *Same Time Next Year* on a twelve-week tour of Great Britain, culminating in an eight-week limited season at the Old Vic. What a fantastic theatre and a wonderful way to finish off a great run of a super play.

Rula and I had worked together for quite a long period and, for the

Minder with George Cole and miniature pony (WHITE AND REED)

The *Minder* caravan, with (from left to right), the late, lamented Peter Childs who played Inspector Rycott, Dennis, Ian Toynton (Director of *Rocky 8½* and Associate Producer) and George Cole (RICHARD REED)

Star players in the Waterman Celebrity Pro-Am team include here –
Bruce Grobelaar, Alan Wells, John Conteh, Garfield Morgan, Kenny Lynch,
Tim Brooke-Taylor, Dennis, Simon Bowman, Russ Abbott, Robert Powell
and Jasper Carrott

Julia, Lara and Hannah (BRIAN ARIS)

The World Cup: A Captain's Tale with Ken Hutchinson and John Bowler just behind Dennis, and Richard Griffiths in the lead (TYNE TEES TELEVISION)

Not a bad stroke   The Dennis Waterman XI (MIKE KENNY)

With the late, great Bobby Moore at Wembley

Panto – with Jan Leeming and Rula Lenska
(NIGEL NORRINGTON)

Circles of Deceit
(YORKSHIRE TELEVISION)

Stay Lucky with Jan Francis

Jeffrey Bernard is Unwell (JAMIE HANSON)

Julia, Dennis and Hannah

Pam Flint
(FUNCTION PHOTOGRAPHIC SERVICES)

most part, in a play where we were the only cast! A true test. But we were very much in love and the experience had been a pleasure. And apart from my sleeping with the leading lady and running through our lines together, we did not take work home. We also managed to avoid the danger of trying to influence each other's style and interpretation, leaving that to our director.

The only thing that marred our perfect life was that I hated getting to the theatre too early, but as we were always travelling together, I had to fit in with Rula's timetable, which meant getting there at least an hour earlier than normal.

The Life and Loves of a She-Devil, adapted from the novel by Fay Weldon was, perhaps, the most unusual piece of television I've ever done. Philip Saville was the director, and he really went out on a limb in casting me. I played Bobbo, a very successful upper-middle-class accountant, husband of the *she-devil* of the title. Not a character the British viewing public was used to seeing me portray. Julie T. Wallace played my wife, in what was virtually her first TV role. Apparently, when she heard that the BBC was making a TV version of Weldon's novel, she wrote to them telling them that she was a six foot, fifteen stone actress who could understand and identify with all of the characters and their emotions. Philip met her, got her to read a bit of the script, and to do a few improvisations. She passed with flying colours and went on to give a fantastic performance. I must say, though, that it was rather off-putting, in the make-up bus, sitting next to the woman who was playing my wife, while the make-up girls were putting false moustaches on both of us.

For a while I was one of the most envied men in Britain, due to the fairly steamy love scenes I had with the delicious Patricia Hodge.

Nineteen eighty-six was also memorable for a three-week classical tour of China. It started purely by accident. The *TV Times* magazine invited me and Rula and several other celebrities to an informal dinner, which was held in honour of some of their most important high-spending advertising clients. It was a nice evening, with easy, free-flowing conversation which touched at one stage on the benefits of sending some soap star to the Caribbean for a couple of weeks just to take a couple of dopey pictures of her in a bikini.

My ears perked up. China had recently opened up a lot more territories to tourists.

'Why not send us there?' I suggested. 'We could do a more in-depth travel piece.'

'We might think about that,' someone said. A few days later a representative from the *TV Times* phoned to ascertain if we were serious. We said, 'We'll organise our work diaries with our agents.'

They wanted a photographer and a journalist to join us, but we insisted we were quite capable of fulfilling the assignment ourselves. They finally agreed, once we'd assured them we'd take loads of film and would write up our individual daily diaries.

Some days later I received an anxious phone call from Deke. 'Dennis, you do realise there is some sort of Cup Final in June?'

'Come off it,' I sneered. 'The Cup Final's in May.'

I was so caught up in the spirit of adventure that for the first time in my life, I had forgotten the World Cup. Oh well!

We flew with China's own airline, CAAC, which we quickly renamed Cack Airlines. What surprised me was that it had first class, or their version of first class. The air hostesses were the largest Chinese women I'd ever seen, and they certainly didn't consider charm and helpfulness to be part of their job description. We decided it was easier to just eat and drink whatever they gave us and watch the movies. For the most part these proved to be nothing but revolutionary propaganda in very murky, scratchy black-and-white film, all in Chinese, until suddenly Clint Eastwood hit the screen in *Pale Rider*. Presumably the Chinese saw more in this allegorical western than either we or Clint ever noticed.

Having landed, we hung around waiting to see if any of our luggage would turn up. As one did in those days, while I watched the empty carousel revolve I lit a cigarette, then wandered around the big hall looking for an ashtray. There being none to be found, I assumed that people stubbed them out on the floor and did just that. Immediately, a tiny little bloke with a dustpan and brush appeared before me, shaking his finger at me. He then started rummaging in his trouser pocket, while a high-pitched stream of Chinese issued from his mouth. Finally he pulled out a book of what looked like raffle tickets, tore out a bit of paper and thrust it at me. It seemed I was being given the yellow card for foul play and fined for bad behaviour. I tried to indicate that I had no money and no idea what he wanted, and eventually he gave up.

Some time later, we retrieved our luggage, met our guide, and were put on a bus for what was to be a tortuously slow journey to our hotel. The guide apologised for the traffic and explained that there must have been an accident. Then he pointed out of the window. Right beside us was a burnt-out motorcycle and sidecar, with the charred remains of the owner still attached. This is good, I thought.

I've been here just over two hours and I've been fined for smoking and seen my first dead body.

We were on a regular package tour, which meant spending the whole trip with the same people, most of whom we got on with very well. The tour started in Beijing and criss-crossed the huge expanse of China by train, bus, boat and plane, ending up in Hong Kong three weeks later.

Our itinerary took us to all sorts of hotels, from country style, usually wooden and very basic with very thin pillows, to great echoing Russian monoliths with thousands of bleak rooms. The further south we went, the more luxurious and westernised the hotels became. What did amaze me was that no matter the quality of the hotel, each room had its own colour television set. What further amazed me, and really got up the nose of some of the ladies, especially Rula, was that there was live World Cup coverage every morning at eight o'clock and more at eight o'clock in the evening. There was one other bloke on the trip who shared my passion for football, and the two of us conspired to keep up with what was going on. We didn't let it get in the way of the tour, but if eight o'clock coincided with a dead period of the day, we dived for the nearest television. We became expert in recognising each country's team colours; we had to, all the commentaries were in Chinese.

So I had the best of both worlds – the World Cup every day and an extraordinary trip.

We saw about as much as you could see in three weeks – the famous Wall, the Ming tombs, the Forbidden City in Beijing, and the strange lunar landscape of Guilin. We saw dead bodies floating down the Yellow River, even as the boat's kitchen staff hauled up buckets of river water to wash our crockery; we marvelled at the Terracotta Warriors in Xian; we visited the markets of the mountain people, selling their meagre pickings and anything they could rustle up to please the tourists – wood carvings, clothing, bric-à-brac. We went to a meat market once. I'm not sure what the meat was, but it was big and it stank. Mao Tse-tung had directed that 'If every Chinese killed a fly a day, the country would be rid of them.' The extraordinary thing about this market was that despite the bloody hunks of meat and the putrid smell, there was not a fly to be seen.

After the cultural shock of ancient China, we entered the modern world of Shanghai, with its westernised society clad in blue jeans, its streets teeming with hookers and homosexuals, beggars and pedlars, all vying for your attention. And millions and millions of bicycles everywhere, many loaded with what looked like travelling kitchens.

One thing was certain: having been shown around one of their hospitals, Rula and I were determined never to be ill on that trip.

I recall an enchanting evening of entertainment at one of their Children's Palaces; disgust at one of their zoos, where the animals were kept in the most atrocious conditions; the look of joy on the faces of proud and protective parents when I presented them with a Polaroid picture of their beloved only child; and chatting about Liverpool and Manchester United to English-speaking teenagers. Then there was the truly horrible food in some of the hotels, and the amazed stares, in some of the more remote places, at Rula's luxuriant red hair and long legs. Finally, there was the awful culture shock as we flew into the gaudy lights, colours and noise of Hong Kong.

We had taken the pictures and kept our diaries and they ran it in the *TV Times* for three weeks. It had been an extraordinary adventure, and a time of great happiness for Rula and for me.

TWENTY

THE REAL THING?

Our friend and producer, Paul Elliott, suggested that we should take Tom Stoppard's play *The Real Thing* to Perth for the winter of 1986. We agreed immediately. Four Australian actors, two males and two females, were flown to England to rehearse and to play for one week in Guildford before we flew out to Australia.

The title of the play was apposite, and we decided that this would be a good time to pledge ourselves to each other for the rest of our lives. It would also avoid the necessity of a huge wedding, which would be inevitable if we got married in England. We flew to Australia with our three girls, our nanny and Rula's mother. We also arranged that Myrna and Norma would join us from Los Angeles. We were installed in a lovely house on City Beach and life was perfect.

In Australia, you were allowed to get married wherever you wanted. In Britain, at that time, the only choice was either a church or a registry office. We were invited by Pat and Mike Gibson, friends of the theatre, to hold our wedding in their beautiful house in Shenton Park, Perth. An interior designer was brought in to make the place even more beautiful. They erected a marquee lit by fairy lights and floated water lilies in the pool. An old mate of ours, photographer Brian Arris, came out to take the pictures, which, to my eternal shame, had been pre-sold to an English tabloid. Rula wore a long beaded kaftan and I was got up in a cream collarless shirt and cream trousers, while the girls were dressed in slightly more traditional bridesmaid's dresses. We all looked very beautiful indeed. The cast and several of our friends from Perth were there, along with Paul and Linda Elliott, and under a beautiful Western Australian sky, on 3 January, Rula and I got married. It was a super day, apart from Rula and Lara both bursting into tears during the ceremony. Maybe that was a sign . . .

HANNAH: Although Julia and I had visited Dad, Rula and Lara

frequently, and shared exotic holidays with them, this new 'family' set-up did not feel comfortable to any of us.

The wedding itself was yet another day of playing happy families for the camera, but for us little ones that was not so easy. I think when you're a child of a divorce, you always have this secret dream of your parents getting back together. Now, even though Mum was happily married to Jeremy, Dad and Rula getting married seemed so final.

The day of the wedding, we three girls burst into tears. Lara missed her dad and didn't want another one, and Julia and I were not mega-keen on having Rula as our stepmother, especially after Rula had confided to us that morning that she and Dennis were planning on having a baby boy. This snippet of news was too much for Lara. 'I don't want a baby brother, I don't want a baby brother,' she cried. This set Julia off: 'I don't want a new stepmother.' Which in turn got me going. There we were, three little bridesmaids in our pretty white smocked dresses, japonica in our hair, in tears. With five minutes to go before the ceremony, as the eldest I tried to pull myself together and take control of the other two, especially as there were photographers everywhere waiting to snap us.

To explain away our red eyes I concocted some story about our being very upset at having forgotten our wedding presents. And primed with this, we followed Rula down the aisle.

It was like a fairy tale. White doves with their fan tails dyed pink fluttered in cages waiting to be released with showers of sugared almonds. Everything was pink and white and very *Dynasty*. After the ceremony we changed into sarongs. Dad, in an extremely jovial mood, thought it hilarious to unroll me out of my sarong, in front of everybody. I was ten, in my knickers, and mortified. And even more embarrassed when he tried to make me swim in the lily pond – for a photo call! Julia and Lara were willing, but I was not, just in case anybody saw my boobs, which were not even there yet, but could have been. I was very self-conscious.

As we were still doing the play, we couldn't scoot away on honeymoon, so the family stayed on for a bit and we honeymooned on the idyllic South Sea island of Rarotonga,

The only downside on this trip to Perth was a phone call from my brother Ken, telling me that our father had died. I didn't know how to react to this news. I didn't really dislike him, I just didn't feel anything. I regretted that we had never had a proper father–son relationship, but we hadn't. I felt guilty that I wasn't filled with sadness, but I wasn't. There was a certain sorrow, but not a great sense of mourning, just a determination that my children wouldn't feel the same way about me.

The happy couple arrived back in Britain in the spring of 1987. While I was in Australia I had been asked by a well-known production company called Roadshow, Coote and Carol to appear in an Australian movie that was going to be shot mostly in England. It was called *The First Kangaroos* and was about the first Australian rugby league team to tour northern England, in the early 1900s. I pointed out to them that the only sport I'd never tried was rugby, but I wasn't averse to having a go. The attraction for me was that it had the same feel to it as *A Captain's Tale*, the film I had made about the first World Cup.

They wanted me to play Albert Goldthorpe, who had been the star player for Hunslet, and considered the best of his time. The action centred upon the final game, which was billed as a personal battle between him and the Australian star Dally Messenger, played by Dominic Sweeny.

We filmed the match at the London Scottish rugby ground at Richmond. Eight Aussie actors were brought over as the mainstay, the rest of the team being supplemented with local rugby players. The Hunslet side was all local players, except for me. We played for two or three days (not non-stop, you understand) so that they had enough footage to edit down to an exciting match. Certain sections of play were choreographed, but as much open play as possible was filmed.

I really enjoyed it. Like real Australian sportsmen, the Aussie actors were intent on showing just how much better they were than us. This, together with the basic nature of the game, resulted in some fairly robust tackling. After I'd been on the receiving end of one particularly hard tackle, my team mates checked to make sure I was all right, then assured me it would not go unpunished. It didn't.

At the end of the day's filming, most of us on the English side would jump into the big baths in the dressing rooms, get cleaned up and head for the bar. Every night we invited the Australian guys to join us. And every night they refused. They'd get straight on the bus back to town still sweating in their kit, covered in mud, blood and everything. This rather shocked me. Having spent a fair amount of time in Australia, I knew just how much a beer was appreciated.

I later learned they'd get cleaned up at their hotel and tear the arse out of Earls Court. One got nicked for whacking a policeman, and on another exuberant occasion, so rumour has it, a television set was seen flying out of one of their rooms, high over Kangaroo Valley.

The First Kangaroos turned out to be a really smashing film, beautifully directed by Frank Cvitanovich. I didn't know anything about the original events and simply played the role as the script was written. My character, Albert Goldthorpe, was determined to do anything to beat the upstarts from Down Under, and that included giving Dally Messenger a fairly hefty forearm smash when he thought there was a chance the other side might be winning.

After it was shown, I got some very irate letters from relations of Goldthorpe, complaining that he had been a wonderful sportsman who would never have resorted to such unseemly tactics. I wrote back apologising; my only excuse was the script had been written by an Australian.

In the mean time, Rula had been doing a play in the West End called *Double Double*. This was an intriguing little thriller written by the actor Roger Reece and his partner. It was a two-hander, with the male actor playing two parts, one a very successful London business-man, the other a Glaswegian tramp. They shared an uncanny resemblance; not really surprising, as they were both played by the same actor. Roger had written it purely to see if he could fool the audience into believing that both characters were on stage at the same time. He devised a scene in which the businessman is seen falling down the stairs, ending up on the stage at the same time as the other character enters stage left. It was very clever, and, depending on the sight lines of the theatre, really made the audience jump and squeal. Rula and I toured it, at a later date, all round the country, to great success. We rounded off the year with a humdinger of a panto at Wimbledon. She played Robinson Crusoe and I played her brother Billy. I bet not many of you knew that Robinson Crusoe had a brother, did you? Daniel Defoe must be spinning. It really is extraordinary, being in a show with your wife when in the end she gets the girl.

Then there was the final series of *Minder*. Again we had a great time and fine casts, notably Billy Connolly. A great compliment to George and myself was the fact that every now and again Billy wouldn't pick up his cues. His excuse was that he was having too much fun watching us. I have known Billy for many years now and can honestly say that after all the huge successes he has had, he seems not to have changed at all. He remains the same great bloke.

Although we were still able to pull in wonderful guest stars, it was evident that there were problems getting good new scripts, and I thought that some of the shows we did during this period were frankly stupid. Also, and I say this with absolutely no hint of jealousy, that it had become 'The Arthur Daley Comedy Hour'. Political correctness had curtailed a lot of our old sharp dialogue, and the fear of too much violence on television had stopped me actually being a minder. I had a chat to George Taylor, the producer of both *Sweeney* and *Minder,* and he told me that although he was sure they would probably want another series, he agreed with me about the scripts and wouldn't be doing any more.

GEORGE COLE: 'A new series, starting October, how about it?' they asked me. As usual I said, 'Check with Dennis.' The next thing I heard, the start had been brought forward to September but they still hadn't heard from Dennis; he was doing a film somewhere. Again I responded, 'Check with Dennis.'

Finally they called back to tell me he no longer wished to do the series. That was that, as far as I was concerned. We couldn't go ahead without him. I couldn't find out why or what had happened. I didn't know if they'd got through to the house in the country and Rula had said no or what. I didn't know who to ask. At that stage a lot of friends had lost touch with Dennis because of Rula.

Four days later they phoned back and asked if I was prepared to go ahead with a new minder. I said, 'If you're prepared to take a chance, I am. But I can't see it working without Dennis . . .'

Two things had happened in the interim that had confirmed my decision to say farewell to Euston Films. One was the initial discussions about a film, and the other was a lunch to discuss a new television series for Yorkshire Television. The working title was *Northern Lights*, but it turned out, very happily, as *Stay Lucky.*

At some point during the filming of one of those final *Minder* episodes, Terry Green, the director, invited his partner/producer in advertising, Ross Cameron, on to the set. They started telling me about their plans to make a feature film of a script which Terry had written. It sounded terrific.

There were two main characters in the film: Father Jim, a Catholic priest; and an ex-pro boxer who was reduced to fighting in non-licensed bouts. Having worked with me right from the first day of *The Sweeney* and filmed me in a million fights, Terry suggested I should play the fighter. I disagreed. I wanted to play the priest. After many meetings and many drinks, I was invited to join as the third director in their joint production company, called East End Films. It would eventually almost bankrupt me. More of that later.

DEKE: From a career point of view, it was time to break the husband-and-wife 'double casting' 'golden couple' mould, which threatened to bury Dennis' future in cement. Their theatre productions had toured successfully but he needed to get back into television. We had to find a new series, and without Rula.

I still enjoyed a very close working relationship with Vernon Lawrence, a friend from my old days at YTV. Vernon had been head of light entertainment for YTV, at the time he produced Dennis' show *With a Little Help From My Friends*. Now he was executive producer and director of drama.

He and I met for lunch, to talk about finding something for Waterman – a new series, a film, a play. He called me up not too long afterwards. 'I've got something here that might appeal to Dennis,' he said. 'Just a paragraph, by Geoff McQueen. I'll send it round.'

It read something like . . . 'Charming south London rogue, on the run from seriously hard East End gang, is picked up hitchhiking on the M1 by smart, forthright Yorkshire lass, in two-door Mercedes, returning north to take over her deceased husband's business. She hires southerner as help.'

You don't always need a huge script to feel instinctively that something is going to work.

DAVID REYNOLDS (Director, YTV): I wanted the opportunity to work with Geoff McQueen again. We had already done two series together, which he had written, *Give Us a Break*, with Robert Lindsey and Paul McCann, and *Big Deal*, with Ray Brookes.

I wanted him to write something about Yorkshire. I was the blunt northerner, Geoff the sassy southerner. I wanted to exploit those differences that we ourselves shared. The idea was that instead of two blokes, we'd have a London bloke and a northern girl. It had to work. We wanted to turn the tables, to make the woman tough and forthright and the guy more vulnerable, always on the run, ending up falling in love with the woman and staying in the north. The comedy lay in the fast-talking southerner realising that the guys who don't say much are just as likely to shaft him as he them. The premise gave us great scope for comedy, love and affection, a series people would want to watch.

Dennis Waterman was absolutely perfect for the part. People were genuinely fond of him, men as well as women. There was always a warmth about Dennis that came over on the screen, and he was not afraid to show he had a heart, that he was vulnerable.

Deke had bought one of our favourite pubs in the area, the Hit or Miss. It had its own cricket field and team, of which, I was a stalwart member. The pub also had a very good restaurant. Deke, who was very proud of this, talked David and Geoff into coming all the way out to Penn Street, in Buckinghamshire, for lunch. Quite clever really. If we came to an agreement about the series, he would get my commission, and if we didn't, at least Yorkshire TV would have to pay him for lunch.

DAVID REYNOLDS: I missed my train from Yorkshire, so by the time I met up with Geoff we were late arriving at Deke's farm, where we were meeting Dennis, for the first time. We got there around one o'clock and Deke took us to the pub. I'd already warned my driver to make sure he came to pick us up at two thirty p.m. in case it all went wrong and we hated each other on sight. At six thirty p.m. he was still waiting.

We hit it off immediately. David was an avuncular, pipe-smoking Yorkshire gent with a great sense of humour and an even greater fondness for food and drink. Geoff loved a pint, women and football and had even been on West Ham's books when he was a little younger. It was perfect casting. I loved the concept of the Londoner who has to leave home in a hurry and ends up in Leeds involved with a woman on a houseboat. It would take me away from the tough cop image and provide the added challenge of having a working partnership with a female co-star.

My experience working on television series had taught me to value the crews. It was an important issue for me. David assured me that most of them would be in-house technicians who had done a great many films for TV. Having worked with certain in-house crews I was not so sure, and suggested it might be better to get a good freelance crew. 'Trust me,' he said.

DAVID REYNOLDS: It was seven o'clock and the restaurant was about to open again when we offered Dennis a lift home.

It was dark when we arrived at his place. As the car drew up in the drive, the door opened and the longest shadow you have ever seen in your life loomed out of the shaft of light. The shadow was Rula. I remember Geoff McQueen calling out, 'Good evening.'

'It's certainly evening,' came the icy reply.

That was our first introduction to Mrs Waterman, and it probably influenced her opinion of Geoff and me for quite a long time. But it had been a brilliant meeting. We had all got very excited at the project. We'd got Dennis on board, and we knew he'd be perfect. I don't know what kind of evening Dennis had, but we continued celebrating the signing of Waterman well into the night.

DEKE ARLON: In many ways it was a tough call for Rula. With Dennis, her life had changed out of all recognition. She had the big country house, better roles, star billing and a much-improved financial status. Even so, with Dennis away and unavailable to star with her, she must have realised herself that a certain amount of work would no longer be forthcoming.

By this time, too, many of the old friends and associates whom she considered could influence Dennis had been ostracised, leaving the field clear for her to keep a very firm control over his life. Now, with the prospect of her husband going to Yorkshire for months at a time, he would be out of her sight. Knowing his weakness for women, she must have been worried.

I'm sure Rula was also aware that a conscious decision had been made not to cast her opposite Dennis in the series. Yorkshire were adamant that a husband-and-wife team, with their inevitable domestic affairs and crises, would bring added stress to an already pressurised situation, and this would not be conducive to a happy set.

Dennis and I had enjoyed a close personal friendship, as well as a professional one, for many years. During his time with Pat, our families were on holiday together in Los Angeles when, at the age of thirty-four, I collapsed with a heart attack and was rushed into intensive care. Myrna and Jim, with whom Dennis and Pat were staying, immediately moved Jill and our two young sons to their house, where Dennis and Pat could take care of the boys along with their two little ones while Jill was at the hospital with me. Sharing experiences like that bond people. We'd gone through thick and thin together. Now, very subtly, we were being moved aside. Suddenly parties and dinners were being thrown to which we were not invited.

The most hurtful and insulting was an occasion when Rula phoned to ask me as a favour, one Saturday, to deliver a case of wine to the house from the pub. I arrived to find a big barbecue party being prepared for all Dennis' friends, from which she had clearly excluded me and my family.

JOY WATERMAN: For the first time the Waterman family were not made welcome, and a gap was driven between us. Dennis, Myrna and I had been very close. Now we lost all contact. What was also upsetting was to see Dennis separated from the people who had guided his career, people he needed.

Dennis was in awe of Rula. I invited them round for dinner at one point. Rula dominated the conversation, while Dennis said hardly a word. He was a changed character, so subdued, and totally lacking in confidence.

Most of the rest of that year was spent trying to raise money for our movie, *Father Jim*. Ross and Terry had got some of their former film crew to design and build the interior of our office. It was basically a pub with a desk. Not totally conducive to working. Our timing was also less than perfect, as we were trying to raise money during probably the most damaging recession in years.

We had hundreds of meetings with various money men, all of which came to nothing, so much so that we joked we should write a book called AFT – Another Fucking Tuesday. It seemed that every time we had a positive meeting, 'the suit' would shake hands all round, with the promise that he would be recommending the project to his board and that he'd get back to us by the following Tuesday. And we would never see or hear from him again. We had a theory that these guys had to be seen to hold at least two meetings a week to justify their large salaries. They never appeared to do any actual business, just held meetings.

It may sound like a recipe for disaster having an actor and a director trying to raise money, especially considering that Terry had even less idea about business than me, but Ross, who had produced hundreds of very expensive and successful commercials, was our leader. We eventually made a deal with a distribution company, which took a lot of the pressure off us. They were confident that most of the money would be raised through pre-sales. We had also got on board a man called Paul Shakespeare, a seemingly very successful businessman, whom I had met in the south of France.

That trip to the south of France turned out to be a very expensive one.

Rula and I had been visiting friends, James and Nicole Mason, at their lovely house in Taradout, when James told us of an old dilapidated farmhouse which was for sale in Vidaubon. It was barely more than a roof and four walls, but it was set in three acres of beautiful hillside. We decided to buy it and renovate. We would avoid all those famous nightmare building stories, because we had friends on site. Besides which, not only was Nicole French, but James spoke the language fluently, albeit with a very strong Lancashire accent. They also had renovated their own house, and knew how to evade all the pitfalls . . .

Exploring the area, we had stopped for coffee at a little café on the front at St Raphael, when the waiter brought us two large brandies, with the compliments of an English couple sitting several tables away. This sort of thing was not unusual in England, but for us, the joy of going to France had been that nobody recognised us.

Naturally, I acknowledged the drinks and said thank you. They introduced themselves as the Shakespeares. Much to Rula's annoyance, I invited them to join us. We chatted away, and it came up in conversation that he was interested in putting money into the entertainment industry. At the time he was about to go to London to launch his own Formula One racing team. Now, one of the sports in which I have absolutely no knowledge or interest is motor racing. What I did know was that it cost untold money to run a team. I gave him the office number and we arranged to meet as soon as possible.

Back in London, he wined and dined us at great expense and invited us to the launch of his Formula One team. He appeared to have everything he said he had, and before long we invited him on to the board of East End Films.

It has to be said that both Rula and Ross's wife, Jacqui, felt uneasy about our involvement with this bloke, but it seemed to us that there was nothing to lose.

Looking back on the whole sorry episode, it wasn't that Mr Shakespeare made anything out of us – there was no theft or anything – but a year or so later, his broken promises and guarantees would eventually cost me very dear.

This all coincided with a period when I didn't have Deke's business acumen to protect me. I had decided (with Rula's prompting) that having a manager *and* an agent was too expensive. I was being percentaged out of the game. I opted to be represented exclusively by Dennis Selinger. Most actors only have an agent and I was persuaded that that was all I needed. I can honestly say that had that not been the case, I would never have been allowed to put a cent of my own money into any project. Eventually, I would have to turn to Deke to try and sort things out, but by then I had stupidly dug myself too deeply into the shit for him to be able to do anything other than damage limitation.

DEKE ARLON: Dennis' 'Dear Deke' letter came sometime after he had completed the first two series of *Stay Lucky,* and just as I had made the deal for him to do *On the Up.* With Dennis, it would be a matter of honour to continue paying my commissions for the duration of both those deals. So he paid the fees without the added bonus of guidance.

It was madness, Dennis needed guidance. He had always been far too generous for his own good and could easily be talked into things. I had had to be very tough on his behalf on many an occasion.

During the run of *Windy City* one of the musicians had cornered him in a pub and persuaded him to hand over a cheque for £10,000, as an investment in a coffee bar the chap wanted to open. Had I not walked into the bar at the precise moment that Dennis was about to sign the cheque, he would have handed it over with no paperwork, no guarantees, no protection whatsoever.

We were at a moment in history when the British film industry was at its absolute nadir. Even television was feeling the pinch. Historically, whenever the country had been in crisis, the entertainment industry flourished, as, for example, straight after the war, when the public needed and wanted to be cheered up. In 1988, with the slide into recession, nobody could afford to be cheered up. Stupidly, we carried on. Suddenly, our major distribution company went bust, with debts of hundreds of millions of pounds. We were assured the money could be replaced, but it was suggested we change the location of the film to America, so that, instead of my playing a Scottish priest in the East End of London, I would play an English priest who turns up in Chicago, thus ensuring help in distribution in the USA.

The title was changed to *Cold Justice* and everything seemed to be going swimmingly. We were so confident, we were even investing in future projects – it was all spend, spend, spend. We went out to Chicago to look for locations and to cast the picture.

What I didn't expect was such an architecturally beautiful city. Of course, I was aware of the importance of Chicago in the pantheon of music, but didn't realise how alive it was. It seemed there was a blues or jazz club on every corner, with fantastic performers in every one. The food and drink were a bit special too.

We also discovered one of the major differences in our respective film industries. There, we could not be helped enough. Sadly, not with the raising of money, but the Chicago and Illinois Film Institute was only too happy to promote and offer advice on movie-making in the city or the state. We were told the areas where it was and wasn't safe to film, and the number of police we could have to organise traffic, etc. We were advised of the availability of helicopters to gain an overall view of the city, of crews and facilities (such as editing suites), everything, that encouraged people to make movies in their city. How different from dear old England, where everything is a stumbling block.

We signed up the cast and crews, found most of our locations, decided on the schedule and returned to England to finalise the financial side, which we were told was close to being a hundred per cent sorted. Everything should go ahead with no problem. In early November, we went back to Chicago to start shooting.

I suppose, in the end, all of us at East End Films were responsible for our own downfall. My own particular stupidity was proven halfway through the shoot, when Paul Shakespeare and his brother came over to inform us that a lot of the promised money had fallen through. We either had to pull up sticks or find other sources of funding. The other option Shakespeare suggested was that I stood side by side with him, and that we personally put up the money. His plan was that I should put a mortgage over my house and he would guarantee the shortfall. In a bar in downtown Chicago witnessed by Russ Cameron and others, we shook hands on the deal. Dumb and dumber Waterman. I put up our house, believing in his promise that the guarantee would never ever be enforced. Rula, as co-owner, had to sign documents too. Quite rightly, she was far from happy, but, because she was under the impression (certainly not prompted by me) that the financial guarantee was only for seven days, she consented. With these new arrangements in place we could finish the movie and have a product to sell.

Terry Green had written a good script, but with the change of setting, it was too English. Prior to shooting, we had flown over one of our American cast to help 'Americanise' the dialogue. We'd worked hard and ended up happy with the piece. It was only when we started work that it became apparent that Terry was ignoring most of the rewrites.

Terry is a terrific director, but this protection of his script was benefiting no one. We ended up with a strange Anglo-American hybrid. And even more disconcerting for us was that he never checked the rushes of the previous day's work. When working for Euston Films, Terry had got used to letting the editor assemble the episodes in a rough way before working through it with him, but here that was not practical, and he was working for our money, on our budget. We had our own editor in Chicago, who was excellent, and who had worked with Terry and Ross on numerous occasions, but even he couldn't get Terry to look at the rushes on a daily basis. It's imperative to ascertain, as quickly as possible, if anything needs re-shooting before you leave a location or dismiss an actor. To recall an artist, or re-locate a production team for the sake of one shot, is cripplingly expensive.

Nevertheless, we finished the movie, and it must be said we had a fantastic time. We had taken over our own lighting cameraman, dear old Dusty Millar, Ross's assistant and my old mate Barry Summerford. Apart from Roger Daltrey, who played the boxer, and myself, all the actors were from the US, and they found our modus operandi a bit odd.

It started on the first day, when our first assistant director called lunch at around twelve thirty p.m. 'OK guys, we'll take thirty minutes.'

'No we won't,' was the instant response from the Brits. 'It'll be an hour and where's the nearest bar?' American eyebrows hit the ceiling with a thud. Over there you can use as much dope as you can roll or inject, take cocaine till your nose drops off, but have a couple of beers at lunchtime and they want to call in a therapist. However, it didn't take long before most of the crew accepted our invitation to join us.

Cold Justice was sold to satellite television, got a very limited distribution in England and I lost a cool £200,000. I paid fifty grand straight away and asked for some time to find the rest. After several writs asking for my house, I managed to cough up another fifty. At one point it was alleged I owed upward of half a million, as the sum escalated with unidentified interest.

DEKE: I was at my desk one day when there was a knock at the door and Dennis walked into my office. 'Hello, Captain,' he said. (That was the nick-name my clients called me). 'Can I come back?'

'As far as I'm concerned,' I replied, 'you've never been away.'

Of the producer, Shakespeare, the least said the better. On a handshake, witnessed by others, he had persuaded Dennis to stand with him as a fifty fifty partner in raising the money to finish the film. Dennis was to do it by re-mortgaging his house while he, Shakespeare, personally guaranteed his half of the shortfall. When the film failed and the money was called in, there being no written agreement in evidence, Shakespeare simply denied ever having been a party to the guarantee. Dennis was forced to take him to court and won. The court upheld that the guarantee did exist. It being a personal debt between them, Dennis sued Shakespeare for his half of the shortfall, only to discover all his so-called partner's assets and wealth had disappeared, his estate was valueless and Shakespeare was effectively bankrupt. Dennis recovered not a penny. And Shakespeare walked away, leaving Dennis to carry full responsibility for the loan.

He still owes Dennis a lot of money.

I remortgaged the house, paid off the rest of the debt and found I was able to sleep again at night.

Apart from the money, the really annoying thing about the whole exercise was that the film was crap. I haven't even got a copy. One hears about people taking big risks to make movies and losing their shirt, but at least they emerge with the compensation of artistic credibility. We just lost our money.

TWENTY-ONE

STAY LUCKY

I wish I could write about my early days with Rula in an objective and kind way. We truly did have some fantastic times together, but my opinion of the way our marriage ended, or perhaps her highly publicised opinion of the way it all came to an end, has made me very bitter about the whole thing.

We had done all the creeping about, the lying and scheming, just to see each other, and, in the process, had destroyed each other's marriages. The press had found us out and had a field day. But now we were a couple.

The early days at Sheepcote Grange were terrific. The kids were in the pool all the time and we were getting better and better at snooker (well the truth is, Rula was). I was still playing football and cricket and would often ask people back for a quick game of snooker. 'Quick' would often end up with 'Would you like to stay the night?'

Not unreasonably, Rula had gone off the idea of trailing round the country watching us play football and drink, but she did bring Lara up to the Hit or Miss to watch the cricket.

HANNAH: For Julia and me, the family home was with Mum. Then she married Jeremy, who had three children, and Dad went with Rula who had Lara. Suddenly Julia and I were part of two new families. Jeremy's kids, who for the most part lived with their mother, were all about my age; Lara was a little younger than my sister. I considered them both as babies.

It was harder at first for me to adapt to Jeremy. Dad was my hero, on a pedestal, and Jeremy, who is the most wonderful man in the world, had to put up with some horribly rude and resentful behaviour from me. With Rula, I was always very polite. I suppose, too, because I lived with Jeremy and Mum, it was hard to hide my hostility twenty-four hours a day. In Dad and Rula's house I could be more guarded; besides which I didn't want to upset my father.

Throughout the whole sorry break-up and divorce, Mum never

said a bad word against Rula, and we had as much access to Dad as possible. The first two years we all got on fairly well as a family. We stayed at Sheepcote in our school holidays and shared exotic vacations in Kenya and Australia. It seemed a super-luxurious lifestyle, removed from normal, domestic life.

JULIA: Dad had left home when I was two and half, before I had any real chance of establishing a real relationship. I had shadowy memories of him sitting in his leather chair in the house in Richmond, and of him getting up in the middle of the night to make me a drink when I couldn't sleep. And when he went away, I missed him. I remember being very upset on an occasion when he picked up Hannah from school. I saw his car pull up in the street, not the drive, Hannah and he get out, he kissed her goodbye and then drove off without coming into the house.

Mum was brilliant. She never ceased telling me how much he loved me and that, even if he wasn't around, he was still my dad and I should love him. We were never forced to make a choice, and unlike many of my friends who found themselves caught in the middle of divorce, neither Mum or Dad ever used us as a weapon.

Jeremy entered my life when I was four and a half, and was always there. He seemed more like my dad than Dennis, who began to seem more like a favourite uncle who you see every so often and to whom you are polite.

The situation wasn't eased when we stayed at Sheepcote because I was always left to play with Lara. I never did the usual things a six-year-old would do with a father. Because of his high profile, it was impossible for him to take us to funfairs or playgrounds. And Rula was always far more concerned with my building a friendship with Lara than a closeness with Dad. We were rarely alone together. I didn't resent it at first because he took us on some amazing holidays, but as I grew older, I became aware of a distance between us.

When I was upset, which I frequently was, it would be Hannah who looked after me, who told me not to cry, to be brave and not to let Mum down.

HANNAH: We didn't see Dennis and Rula for some time after their wedding, but then they came back, and Dad started doing *Stay Lucky*.

We shared some happy times as a new family but there were the inevitable childish squabbles. I had always assumed Dad would be on our side. I remember once we three girls were playing frisbee in the garden when, purely by accident, Julia's throw hit Lara. It was no big deal but Lara went in crying to her mother, who stormed out and slapped Julia. I was outraged. My sister and I were both upset and crying. I went and explained to Dad what had happened. I think it was the only time I tested him and pulled him on to my side against Rula.

I have always felt very sorry for Lara. There may be no reason why step-parents and step-children should ever get on with each other. I believe, however, that Lara and I did. We had absolutely nothing in common, if that can be said of a child and an adult, but there was genuine warmth and tolerance, I thought. When Rula and I first got together, Rula was quite forceful in her view that I should be the main male influence in Lara's life, and I was more than happy to be her surrogate dad. Her natural father, Brian, had total access, so there was never any fear of her losing touch with him, and indeed he is a brilliant parent, but I was to be her everyday contact with the male of the species. Maybe not the finest specimen, but I was there. My understanding was that, apart from when she was with Brian, I would be Dad. The only problem with that was that in the event, Rula did not allow that to happen. I could praise and comment on the good things Lara did, and there were plenty of those, but I was not permitted to correct her, disagree, criticise or tell her off.

HANNAH: From a very young age, although I shared some good times with Rula, when she'd teach me how to put on make-up, for example, I was aware that these occasions were very short-lived. There was a resentment underneath the surface, perhaps of anyone who came between her and Dennis.

Dad and she were still besotted with each other, but her many efforts to change him and his lifestyle were not always successful. Dad was a social animal, Rula was not. Warren and Michelle would come over for dinner, and her own family too, of course, but she did not entertain like Mum, who always had a full house. Dad still met up with friends and enjoyed a drink, and Rula was determined to stop this.

She had constantly stressed to me that I was Dennis' favourite. I was eleven when she decided to use me in her war on his drinking. She persuaded me to write to him saying I did not want an alcoholic as a father. Apparently he was so furious he ripped up the letter and threw it in the bin. I was distraught.

JULIA: I thought Hannah could cope with the constant subterfuge. She was older and more sure of herself and her position with Dad. I was forever being told by Rula what a shame it was that my father didn't love me, and how much she wanted to help, but sadly there was nothing she could do. He just couldn't accept me. The Waterman family were condemned as dreadful people to whom I didn't deserve to belong. So I found myself caught between what I believed was Dad's irritation with me and Rula's constant criticising. Year after year it wore me down. Much as I sympathised with Lara, I was always blamed for anything she did wrong. I was cast as the delinquent. I used to look at Dad and think, 'Can't you see what's going on? Why are you doing nothing about it?'

The constant emphasis on my father's alienation from me became a major problem for me as I grew up. I confided in no one, not even Mum, until this last year, when for the first time I broke down and confronted Dad.

Hannah had witnessed some of it. She would comfort me at night when I was crying and tell me that of course Dad loved me, and help me back to sleep.

By the age of twelve I found it painful even to meet him. I felt I'd failed. Hannah seemed such a success in his eyes, whereas he and I had nothing to say to each other.

Julia and I had always had a somewhat difficult relationship. I blamed it mostly on the fact that I had left when she was so young. I think because Hannah and I had already established a relationship, it didn't seem to affect her in quite the same way. I believed that as Julia grew up, she would learn to understand things a little more and we would gradually get closer and closer. It didn't happen. Maybe my easier bond with Hannah alienated Jules to a certain extent, although I certainly tried not to favour one more than the other.

On holiday in Portugal once, Rula's mother pointed out that I was trying so hard not to let Lara feel left out that I was giving my own kids too hard a time. And maybe I was guilty of that. However, it is only recently that I learned that Jules had been told that I didn't love her. Why, or to what end, anyone would wish to convey such a damaging allegation to a child, I cannot begin to comprehend.

Children and their upbringing became a major point of contention between Rula and me. She was obsessed with keeping children young; I vehemently disagreed. I was all for preserving the innocence of childhood, but then kids have to be allowed to grow up naturally. Rula believed in keeping them young at all costs. I hated to see Lara so overprotected, and unable to mix with her peers. I was very happy with the way my girls were allowed to mature into well-rounded teenagers. Rula was convinced they were heading for a fall. Bitter rows ensued over this fundamental divergence of opinion.

I guess we had reached the point where Rula had got fed up with the bloke she had fallen in love with, and felt it was time to change him. Sundays are family days, I was informed. That meant no more football. I could just about get away with cricket, as long as I was back at a reasonable time. I remember pointing out that she never consulted me about her day-to-day plans, yet mine had to be logged in the diary. Dates that had been there for weeks would have to be cancelled if her family was coming for Sunday lunch.

I should have realised what I was getting into when, early in our relationship, Rula said she was worried about how her mother would react to us being together. I said, somewhat flippantly, that I wasn't going to be living with her mother. Back then I didn't know that family, *her* family, meant everything to Rula, until she announced one day that Sheepcote was now her family home. I agreed heartily. 'Absolutely, you, me and the girls.'

'No,' she emphasised. '*My* family's home.'

Rula's parents were a count and countess, but once they were forced to leave Poland, those titles were left behind. When her father was invited to run Radio Free Europe, he had to become an American citizen and was informed that he could use 'Count', but as a first name only. Rula use to drive me mad by saying that she had no feeling of being English. Yet she was born in St Neots, and it wasn't until very late in our relationship that she actually went to Poland.

In a way, I was jealous of Rula's family. They were seriously close. That doesn't mean they all liked each other, but on high days and holidays they had to be together. And Polish Catholics had loads of high days and holidays! Each one had to be celebrated, and always at my house. Individually, most of her family were extremely nice, but there were hundreds of them. I grew to dread birthdays, Easter and Christmas.

Rula's mother was a wonderful woman who, along with her sisters, had endured a dreadful war in prisoner-of-war camps. She refused to talk about it. She was a charming lady, with not a bad word to say about anyone. I cared greatly for her. Her ex-husband (Rula's father) was a nightmare. He had been a hero in the war, and was one of the Polish government in exile. He used to come every Christmas and stay for about a month or so, eyes glued to the news in the hope of catching a war somewhere. When Poland at last had free elections, his whole reason for living had gone. He became a cabbage, a six foot five cabbage, and not easy to entertain at Christmas.

There were two nutty uncles. One was trying not to drink at all; the other was trying to drink as much as humanly possible. They were smashing. As was Rula's sister, Anna, half-brother, Andrew, a talented musician, and great-cousin Antek, whose real name was Antony, but that's too simple for the Poles.

Rula didn't get on with her sister Gabrielle (Gaba), but because blood is thicker than intelligence, every year they came to us for Christmas. Gaba had moved to America so her husband could get a better job, having failed somewhere along the line over here. They had two children who had become totally American. By that I mean they had totally forgotten the magic of 'please' and 'thank you'.

It was during this period that I realised the power of the panto. You only had Christmas Day off.

There were only two occasions that I recall when *my* family were involved. Once I was allowed to invite my brothers and sisters on Boxing Day, and once we went to my sister Vera's. In thirteen out of fifteen years, the Polish contingent swarmed over our house every Christmas. They made no attempt to speak English, and my main function was to pay for everything, be chief butler and wine waiter.

The most unnerving thing about Rula was that she could never be wrong. Never. If there was ever a problem at home, she would say we had better talk about it. This actually meant I had to listen and agree. I don't remember her ever saying sorry, to anybody. It must be wonderful to be so certain everybody else is wrong.

She was also a faddist to the nth degree. Whatever the fashion of the moment, she was into it. She always had a penchant for dope. And I should know; I was the dope for a while. In the seventies, she and her ex-husband went in for Est. You paid loads of money and joined a group in a room, where the person to whom you had paid all this money would tell you what arseholes you were. As if you needed telling? She had moronic and colonic irrigation. Anything that was recommended in the *Daily Mail*, she did.

David Reynolds rang me one day to ask how I would feel about Amanda Redman as my co-star in *Stay Lucky*. 'Wonderful,' I replied. 'But Rula would probably chop off my bollocks before I made it to Leeds.'

DAVID REYNOLDS: Several names had been put forward. Jan Francis was favourite. The moment she walked in, we knew she was it. She had recently finished *Just Good Friends,* so she was 'up there' with star profile as well.

For her to agree to the series was a big decision. She lived in Kent, and had a young family. Shooting away from home in Yorkshire meant an absence of some six to eight weeks with only one break. We also needed a commitment for two series.

Jan is possibly the nicest and most attractive woman in the whole universe. Every male I know agrees. She is a one-off, one of those rare women who can appear to be one of the boys without losing a jot of her grace or femininity.

Having worked for so many years with two male stars, I had been harbouring one or two secret fears at the prospect of working closely with a woman. Horror stories abounded of entire productions grinding to a halt because a certain actress was unhappy with her hair, her make-up, or her wardrobe.

With the casting of Jan, all fears dissolved. I don't think I have ever met a less vain actress. She would just run her fingers through her hair and say, 'That looks all right, doesn't it?' And get on with the scene.

JAN FRANCIS: Dennis and I had first worked together on an arty Alan Plater TV play called *Give Us a Kiss, Christobel,* when he was at the height of his *Minder* fame.

We were filming in Brick Lane in the East End, and our headquarters were in a derelict shop, next to the market. As soon as the word spread that Dennis Waterman was in there, the crowds gathered. It was mainly women and girls, but we were imprisoned with people banging on the windows, screaming and howling his name and hating me because I was some actress hussy who wanted to get her hands on their beloved Dennis.

Although I was cast as a northerner in *Stay Lucky,* I was actually born in Streatham. Being a south Londoner earned me a lot of brownie points with Dennis. I belonged to the same patch for a start – that triangle between Clapham, Streatham and Tooting Bec Common. We shared the same strong territorial feelings, knew the same places, and understood well that the divide between north and south London is as much in evidence as the divide between north and south England. What's more, my father was a lifelong Chelsea fan, who'd imbued me with his loyalty, and although I wasn't anywhere near as keen as Dennis, I still followed the team.

Early on in the series, the great divide theory was tested. Geoff, Barry (my old mate and stand-in) and I were challenged by the crew to a light-hearted drinking contest, North v. South. 'Sure,' we said, 'Barry will arrange the date. You choose the start venue.'

We ended up in the early hours of the morning at the Queen's Hotel in the centre of town, which was where we three southerners were staying. By five thirty a.m., there were five of us left standing (sort of) – the three from the south, plus Korky (our soundman) and Graham (our chippy) who had also wisely booked a room in the hotel. Around six a.m. Graham said, 'OK, we give in, at least let's get some sleep, it'll be time for work soon.' 'Not that soon,' Barry smirked. 'We're not called till after lunch.' It was their own fault. They shouldn't have let him arrange the date.

DAVID REYNOLDS: I didn't get involved, I knew someone would have to be there to pick up the pieces. I arrived on location at seven a.m. to watch the remnants of my crew arriving. I had never seen a more bleary-eyed, ragged lot in my life. They were shot all morning. But Dennis turned up, raring to go. We were doing a scene in the warehouse, where we'd built the boat set, and it was very warm in there. I could see some eyelids beginning to droop. I called the crew together and started ranting on about their disgraceful behaviour, how they only had themselves to blame, when I noticed the sound recordist had actually fallen asleep.

'And don't you fucking fall asleep whilst I'm bollocking you!' I shouted, at which Dennis and the whole crew collapsed with laughter.

Much of the story was centred around a houseboat and the Manchester Ship Canal. Geoff loved writing water gags for me. If it wasn't the canal, I was either soaked by a passing lorry on the A1 or he had me falling in a lake. All very funny, except this was Yorkshire, we were filming from November to February and it was bleedin' freezing.

As an actor, working with David was terrific. He knew what he wanted to see in a scene, but was still open to input from actors and crew, so there was a sense of contribution from everybody. And he believed that work should be fun.

The schedule was more flexible than at Euston Films. There we had worked on a ten-day turnaround; David insisted on twelve. To a layman that might not seem much difference, but to us it was invaluable. There was more time to work on individual scenes, instead of often compromising in the race to get things in the can.

David also insisted on a read-through before we started filming each episode. I don't necessarily think this is a great idea, in as much as things tend to change once you're on the set or location. But with David these were very relaxed affairs. He wasn't looking for a performance, it was more an opportunity to sort out script problems or questions of wardrobe and make-up.

It was also a social occasion where all the cast could meet up, be introduced to one another and relax over a drink. It took a lot of tension away from the first day's filming, which can be nerve-racking for newcomers, especially on a series with an established cast.

DAVID REYNOLDS: We had trouble one day. Something was not working on a low loader, shooting car shots. It was a shambles. I stopped filming, apologised to the actors, and told the crew to sort it out and we'd shoot again the following morning.

Dennis was amazed. I remember him telling me that an incident like that in London would have detonated twenty-one calls to head office and endless discussions.

That was the benefit of a small company, where everyone knew each other well and trusted each other's professionalism.

I don't think television's like that any more. It's all big business and money dominated. Then our sole concern was making programmes to the best of our ability. We had to keep to a budget, of course, and we knew ours was very limited, but I didn't concern myself too much. In those days the programme controller was more interested in quality work and good programmes, whereas today they worry about inbuilt profit margins and ratings.

With *Stay Lucky,* even if it had not taken off immediately, we still had time to develop a moderate success into a big one. As it was, that first series of three one-hour programmes, shot into the top ten. We'd thought it would do quite well, but the public loved it. They were fired by the on-screen chemistry between Dennis and Jan, and their teasing relationship. And by the fact there was no violence.

JAN FRANCIS: I wasn't at all sure that Dennis' fans would appreciate him in a romantic, softer light comedy role. But they did.

He is a remarkable actor but he fights shy of revealing the depth of his vulnerable side. We would be doing a scene, and he would be wonderful and I'd look in his eyes and see it all there, that deep sensitivity, but then something, some deep-rooted defence mechanism just would not allow it to surface fully.

I often wondered if he found it difficult to let go because all his mates, the crew, were standing around watching . . .

Anyway, we didn't make demands of each other, we did our lines and built up an easy, relaxed relationship which grew in trust and friendship.

As the stars of the show, Jan and I had a Winnebago each. But the budget was limited, and although there were one or two caravans in which visiting actors could change or relax, if a real name came into the series I would be asked to share with the male guests and Jan would share hers with the ladies. And Jan and I were not the sort of people to say no. However, on location, your caravan is the only place where you can enjoy a few moments of privacy and quiet, besides which, it's not always guaranteed that you and the visitors will have anything in common. Jan and I resolved the dilemma by using the same caravan, leaving the visitors a nice posh bus all to themselves.

I can't imagine that in the long history of film there have been many leading men and ladies sharing a caravan, not unless they were having an affair, and we definitely weren't.

JAN FRANCIS: There had been a sharp intake of breath when we'd made this suggestion originally, but we insisted we'd be happy, and if things didn't work out, we'd go back to the old system. It worked perfectly. We could get on with our lines and just relax. It was so much easier than being forced into making conversation with strangers and, lovely though they could be, trying to establish new relationships every week.

Rula was shocked at first, and a bit frosty towards me, but after a few days she realised that obviously nothing was going on and Dennis and I were just good mates.

I've worked with many a lead star who had very short arms. Dennis was the opposite. Each day Dennis and I were given money for our daily expenses in little brown envelopes. Dennis called them 'vodka vouchers' and used them solely for treating everyone.

It wasn't the drinking Dennis craved, it was the company. At the end of the day, the prospect of going home to an empty hotel room, with no one to talk to or share a meal with, was very daunting. You think you can cope at first, but I got very lonely and I missed my little girls.

But Dennis was beginning to dread going home. I drove back

once with him and Barry, who also lived in Kent. We dropped Dennis off first. As he went in the front door, we both cringed when we heard Rula scream, 'Dennis, why are you late?'

Rula and I were bickering a bit at this stage, but I figured that was what happened to married couples after a few years. I think her initial meeting with Geoff and David had made her suspicious about the whole venture. And me coming home half cut every Friday night didn't make her feel a whole lot better about Yorkshire.

It's an extraordinary thing, but when you're working on a good show, the adrenaline flows, you can rock and roll every night, grab a few hours' sleep a night, get up and go to work quite happily. But once there's no real reason to get up, you don't!

Weekends I could get up and go and play football or cricket, but once I was told we had guests for dinner, I became very weary. And then it was back up to Leeds on Sunday night. Not really conducive to nuptial bliss.

The original series of *Stay Lucky* had been quite hard-hitting, as well as amusing, with reasonably strong language, and consequently had gone out after the nine o'clock watershed. It was immediately recommissioned as ITV's weapon for an onslaught on the seven thirty p.m. slot.

JAN: Both Dennis and I recognised the style of the show would have to change, and to soften, which it did. It was still a great series but it lost its bite.

We also learned two more regular characters were to be introduced.

DAVID: They were Niall Tobim, who we cast as an old Irish reprobate, and Emma Wray, as a young northern girl in her early twenties, who would act as a sidekick to Dennis. Emma had come from nowhere, she was a Scouser, a tough little character, whom we had spotted on a comedy series for Granada. The minute we met her, we realised she would fit in perfectly. She was a strong, independent spirit. She didn't give a damn about authority, money or material possessions, and she certainly stood up to Dennis, until he was driven to say, 'Excuse me, this is my series!' She'd turn round and tell him to 'Bog off!'

I'm not sure just how well they got on, because they were too alike. But put the two of them together and sparks flew.

For the second series, Barry and I found a cottage to share several miles outside Leeds. It was behind a big house, and had been the stable block, now tastefully converted into three cottages. Gradually, other employees of *Stay Lucky* moved into the other two, with Korky frequently making use of our sofa.

We had a great time up there in Horsforth and were soon accepted as quasi-locals. All the restaurateurs got to know us well and the quiz nights in the Queen's Head were rarely missed. People often ask me, 'Is it difficult to go out without getting hassled?' It isn't if you act like a normal human being. Then you get treated like a normal human being. Soon we were being invited to parties and weddings, like regular members of the community.

Once again, Geoff's scripts were great, we were attracting some really good guest stars and life was made easier by a deal with British Midland, whereby for less than a train fare we could fly to and from Heathrow, cutting the journey home by more than half.

There was an added bonus – Fiona Black. She wasn't new to *Stay Lucky*, but she had gone from being a pretty little semi-punk to an extremely attractive woman. She had grown her blonde hair, replaced her quirky little glasses with contact lenses and now dressed in a totally different style. What had brought about this metamorphosis I don't know, but it had an enormous effect on me.

She was an assistant floor manager and one of David's favourite employees. When we met up for our first read-through I didn't recognise her at first. Maybe it was love at second sight?

I remember her suddenly being called away to the phone. She came back, ashen-faced. Her flat in Glasgow had burnt down. She was prepared to work the rest of the day, but we insisted she went home immediately. From that moment on, I wanted to be certain that she was OK.

At the end of one episode, Barry and I decided to have a unit party at our place. The director of this particular show was Graham (Harpo) Harper, and Warren Clarke was our guest star. Those two, alongside Geoff, were staying in the adjacent cottages.

Our location caterers provided the solids, while we arranged to get all the booze, including some proper kegs of beer, from the Queen's Head. We invited a few of the locals to join us. I had a couple of guitars and a fairly hefty sound system. And with amazing timing, this was the first truly beautiful day of the year.

We started mid-afternoon. Korky and his band had a gig that evening, but he set his drum kit up on the lawn just to get the party going. There were about four of us who could play guitar to varying degrees, Harpo never travelled without his saxophone and Warren would sing anywhere. It was like a Yorkshire Woodstock!

As always, a hard core of us, including quite a few of the girls, stayed the course. A few of the chaps went down to the pub, but I couldn't handle that, and a few of us, including Fiona, hung around gently winding down. Eventually I asked Fiona if she would stay the night and she quietly agreed. Not that it made a dramatic difference to our relationship, because, sadly, I was out for the count as soon as my head hit the pillow. Pathetic! I woke up to find myself alone, deservedly.

On Monday we all met up at work and everybody was congratulating us on a terrific party. Sheepishly I approached Fiona, apologised and suggested maybe we could try again sometime. She smiled and said, 'Maybe.'

A few nights later we found a way to be alone together. Obviously, she knew a lot more about me than I knew about her. I found out that she was married, although the marriage hadn't been particularly successful for several years. It also emerged that she was a born-again Christian. Fortunately, she did not try to convert me.

We didn't rush into an affair. We saw each other when it was easy and possible. At the end of the series we had lunch and said goodbye. Fiona returned to Scotland, and I headed off to Chicago to make the film that was about to ruin my life. She didn't want to give me her phone number but I insisted. Maybe that was a mistake . . .

After the *Cold Justice* disaster, I did sitcom in early 1991. It was called *On the Up*. I hadn't tried this genre since I'd played Hans Wassermann in *Man About the House* with Richard O'Sullivan back in the seventies.

We met up in a church hall in Kensington and our producer/ director, Gareth Gwenlan, told us what the schedule would be. We would work for three or four hours a day, for five days, then go into the studio on Sunday, where we would perform in front of a live audience. It was a terrifying prospect. I couldn't see how we'd manage to do it, but Gareth had done countless hugely successful sitcoms – *Rising Damp*, *Waiting For God*, *Porridge* – and knew exactly what he was talking about.

GARETH GWENLAN: The thing that attracted me to the scripts was that the comedy was grounded in reality. I'd seen Waterman in *Minder*, and knew he would be superb in the lead part. He had the right balance of naivety, credibility, humour, charm and toughness.

Sam Kelly had been superb in the original pilot. Joan Sims was a bonus and Judy Buxton was exactly right as the wife. No horror stories at all.

But Joan had never worked in front of a live audience and she was petrified. She was a brilliant actress, yet she'd sit quaking in the make-up room, convinced she was useless and that it would be better for everybody if she went home. Joan was without question the best thing in *On the Up*, but you could never convince her of that in a million years. Then she'd stroll into the studio and steal every scene. We are not talking about a lady looking for compliments and attention; she was genuinely frightened.

GARETH GWENLAN: Dennis himself proved to be an absolute natural, possessed of that innate, instinctive timing and rhythm of all good comedians and comedy actors. He had an immediate understanding of the script. He is also the quickest study I have ever known, although when he does it still baffles me.

On location days we'd finish filming at around six or seven in the evening. Enjoy a couple of stiff ones at the bar, shower, change, meet for dinner, enjoy a convivial evening until the early hours. Dennis would arrive on set, six o'clock the following morning, not only having learned his script, but with keen and interesting suggestions and questions, whereas I could just about keep my head up.

Technically, too, he is the best. He knows exactly where every camera is, the angle, the distance and the effect. He can anticipate direction, even though there isn't a monitor or screen in sight.

We worked to a very tight schedule. Frequently we'd have scenes with extras who would stray from their mark. Instantly Dennis would be aware of this and seamlessly move his position, find the angle and carry on, whereas any number of well-known professionals would stop the shooting and make a fuss.

Larby's scripts were a joy, but every now and again I would ask if there was any chance of me having a funny line. 'Don't worry about it,' they'd say. 'It's all super.' It was, and they were, and I was the dopey straight man.

GARETH GWENLAN: Dennis played the character who had made it to the top. He'd risen through the social strata, had married well and adapted effortlessly to a lifestyle of success. The humour lay in the fact that his two friends, as housekeeper and chauffeur, did not know how to react or behave, and made constant gaffes. They were the chaos, Dennis the rock. They had to have the jokes, to be the butt of the laughter; they were the clowns, while Dennis looked on with affectionate humour.

He carried his humour in the situation, they carried theirs in the gags. It would have been wrong for Dennis to crack jokes. He wasn't the straight man or the fall guy – but the rock against which they bounced.

During this period Fiona had moved to London, and we saw each other a couple of times. Rula had come in on a studio day and had been handed the key to my dressing room, where she found a rather romantic letter I was writing that was not addressed to her.

I attempted to reassure Rula that Fiona was not going back to Leeds for the next series of *Stay Lucky*. And decided, after all the rowing and bitterness over the film, to try again, to get our marriage back on an even keel.

If we had been brutally honest, we would have admitted then that our marriage was desperately in trouble before I even met Fiona. I was becoming more and more frustrated by Rula's overbearing unwillingness to listen to anyone's opinion but her own, unless it was someone she had only just met. She was fed up with my lack of domesticity. I had never been a 'new man,' a domestic creature, and although at one time she had me wearing trousers instead of jeans, and tweeds instead of suede and leather jackets, all her efforts to reform me had failed.

I was constantly informed what a good father and husband her ex-husband had been and just how attentive he had been in cooking for the family. I had never done that stuff and well she knew it.

There was a time when Rula was working in the theatre and dinner was left for me to organise and cook, ready for when she returned. I tried, but it was hopeless and I was useless. In the end, I resorted to buying the meals from the golf club and bunging them in the microwave just before she got home.

Then again, I would come home from Leeds only to be confronted by another Polish invasion. God help me if I wanted to watch football on telly. I would be berated for not playing music, then bullied for playing it and especially at the wrong time. But when else do you play Dylan except in the early hours? It was all petty, but the bickering went on and on.

And in the middle of it all, the horror story of *Cold Justice* had unfolded. This left me more stressed than I could have imagined possible. I was displaying all the classic symptoms – waking up in cold sweats, my skin not only breaking out but literally flaking off me.

There were interminable meetings and lawyers' letters. I still didn't realise how deeply I was in the shit, until one day there was a knock on my front door and I was handed a writ, saying the money was being called in and our house was about to be repossessed.

I had always believed that in such a nightmare situation my wife would be there supporting me. All I got was 'You'd better sort this out. I'm not leaving this house because you've fucked up with some crappy film.'

Happy families, eh?

While we were making *Cold Justice*, Rula had been granted power of attorney so that she could be called upon to sign whatever papers needed my signature while I was away filming in Chicago. She had taken legal advice on this, and insisted that her involvement and responsibility was for seven days only from signing. Which made me solely accountable for the debt. That would cost me dearly when it came to our divorce.

At the same time, we'd be forced to attend all these charity do's, saving elephants and tigers and whatever, and everybody would be thinking how selfless she was, always trying to help others less fortunate than herself.

One of the things that helped me keep my sanity during this traumatic period was playing golf and the support of my friends at the Lambourne club. Rula had alienated so many of my old mates, we could only go out as a couple with certain people. And I wasn't even safe at the club. We would go to a function, and not only would Rula ignore everybody, she'd make it very clear just how boring she found them.

The membership of Lambourne is made up of a vast cross-section of society: doctors, pilots, sportsmen, lawyers, builders, car sales-men, publicans, even the occasional actor. Rula's complaint that they only talked golf was nonsense. Of course there was a certain amount of discussion over a particular game, but start an interesting topic of conversation and everyone had an intelligent opinion to air. Admittedly, not everyone there was desperately interested in what *she* was doing, and as her manner became more and more offputting, people stopped bothering to ask.

Things were going from bad to worse. Everything was a drama. Things that had to be done had to be done immediately, and I was expected to jump to every order.

One thing I really hated was going to the supermarket. I don't have anything against men going shopping, it was simply a nightmare for me.

Rula refused to acknowledge why my being 'known', and easily recognised, should exempt me from this duty. The problem wasn't that I never had a clue where anything was stacked; it was the earache you have to endure while pushing a trolley around Tesco when you are known as a hard man 'off the telly'. It drove me crazy. But I did it.

Ironically, from a work point of view, I could not have been happier or busier. I had this totally enjoyable new series with the BBC, and *Stay Lucky* with Yorkshire, both of which, for the next few years, I was to continue dovetailing with various other bits and pieces, including the splendid *Jeffrey Bernard is Unwell*.

When the first series of *On the Up* finished, it was back up the motorway for another six months of *Stay Lucky*.

I have said sometimes that I would be happy to be on location forever, and in a way this is true, because it leaves you free to be totally involved in all aspects of the job, professionally and socially. I'd always thought it was easier if your partner was in the same game, that they would understand the ridiculous hours, the worries and the inevitable problems.

Rula knew she could come up to Yorkshire and stay whenever she wished, which she did quite often, and was welcomed warmly by everybody. What aggravated her intensely was that I was always keen to get back to work every Sunday. It's true that it did take me away from normal family life. But she'd known this had been the pattern of my life since I was eleven.

I have always boasted that I am about as normal as an actor can be, but where work is concerned, I have tunnel vision. Work is the most important thing in my life, the one constant.

Actors and musicians go where the work dictates. It's not a nine-to-five job, it's not a normal job. It is a selfish profession, and Rula was part of it, and equally prepared to sacrifice home and family life when the right job came along.

But Rula complained that my work was more important than my family. What she meant was that my work was more important than *her* family. And she was right.

I tried the argument that without my work, her lifestyle would be very different. The fact that she too did the odd tour for weeks at a time never came into the discussion. There was one set of rules for her and another for me.

One time we were visiting my sisters in Los Angeles and Rula used it as an opportunity to try and find an American agent. She had become a semi-icon some years earlier because of a series of shampoo commercials she had done. The commercial had promoted her as the flame-haired beauty with the exotic name. But she was a complete unknown in back-stabbing Hollywood, and much fun was had at her expense by a sudden explosion of T-shirts carrying the banner 'Who the Hell is Rula Lenska?'

Our visit came at a time when there were a number of Brits appearing in various high-profile soap operas. Through some agent or other, it was arranged that Rula should meet up with the producer of one of these soaps. She came back on a real high. Without even seeing a script (just about the most important item on the agenda) there had been all sorts of dialogue about, amongst other things, whether or not she would be prepared to have plastic surgery!

I would have left there and then. Rula said, 'If this does work out, I'll have to sign a contract which has a six-year option. So you will have to move over here, to look after Lara.'

I've been told recently that one of my problems is that I say 'yes' just to keep the peace, when I actually mean 'no'. At this particular point in time I obviously hadn't been beaten into submission, not quite. 'All my work is in England,' I said. 'I'm damned if I'm going to give up all that I've achieved to come over here on the off chance of getting a job, just to baby-sit.'

The outcome of that particular row was taken out of our hands. The job never materialised and Rula heard nothing more about it.

There are two sides to every break-up. For me it was the psychological warfare that wore me down. Nothing I ever did or achieved was right or good enough.

This was the era when I discovered golf. I had by now realised that I was getting too old for football. I used to turn out every now and then for Geoff McQueen's veteran team in Royston, but even playing against older players was getting to be hard work. And then one day I looked out of my window in the cottage in Leeds and realised I was looking at the practice ground of Horsforth Golf Club.

Together with the SLAGS (Stay Lucky Amateur Golf Society) I played some smashing Yorkshire courses, and where night filming in the summer had been a pain (hanging around, waiting for the light to fade, at around ten o'clock), now it was a godsend, because we could get a round in during daylight.

Rula hated it. I don't know why. It wasn't stolen time when we could have been together. I was away working and this was healthy exercise. I was walking five or six miles every time I went out, and I wasn't getting into any trouble. But it caused untold problems at home.

When Rula and I were first together, the telephone became crucial in our relationship. This was before the proliferation of mobiles. We had our own private landmarks all round London. At one time, romantically, we thought of putting one of the old red phone boxes in our garden, just for old times' sake.

Away on location, you feel duty-bound to phone home at least once a day. This is fine at first, but then it becomes a chore. The timing, for one thing, is never right. If I couldn't get through at a reasonable hour, I was forced to phone at night, often when I got back from a night out with the lads. I could never understand why it should upset someone in Buckinghamshire that I'd been drinking in Leeds. I'm not talking about being incoherent or legless (although on the odd occasion this was the case), which I would have understood.

The other bone of contention was my reluctance to talk about the day's work. Rula would always ask, 'How did it go today?' And I'd answer, 'Fine.' I never knew what to say. Obviously if something worthy of note had happened, I'd relate it, but usually it was a day's work like any other and what anecdotes there were would not have been funny to anyone not involved.

I used to go to work, have a good time and come home. There was actually little to report, but it grows in significance when you are away.

JAN FRANCIS: The third series was my last. The essence of the show had been diluted too much. There was a new producer, and new writers, although Geoff was still there to write a few episodes and Magic Reynolds still oversaw it all.

I read the latest scripts and was appalled. Both Dennis and I were great allies in this respect. We knew our characters, their speech patterns and behaviour and where we wanted them to go.

At our request, Geoff did some rewrites, but the programme had become light entertainment with smutty jokes instead of potent comedy drama. Everyone was forced to dance to the tune of the network centre. They dictated the format and their only concern was ratings.

We all felt betrayed and disappointed. Our two lead characters, Thomas and Sally, had tickled the public's imagination with their teasing on-off, off-on romance. The new hierarchy had us living together too soon, the tension evaporated, and *Stay Lucky* became domestic and tame.

Dennis came back, obviously stressed by the situation at home, his financial problems over *Cold Justice*, and the prospect of trying to keep a show going that was running out of steam. He was also riddled with guilt over Rula and his affair with Fiona.

When I got back to Yorkshire, David Reynolds warned me that they had a policy whereby people in a relationship were not allowed to work together, which meant taking Fiona off the show. 'Please don't do that, we'll be all right,' I promised.

Since the last series, Barry had taken a job working with John Thaw, which was nearer home and more convenient for him. This meant I was living in the cottage on my own. Fiona came to stay more often, and eventually she moved in.

DAVID REYNOLDS: I was unhappy with the situation because I'd known Fiona and her husband for a number of years, and, working in a small community, so had most of the crew. I had also been instrumental in her coming to work at YTV. It may be hypocritical, but if you have a fling or a secret affair, no one is affected except those concerned, but when there's a public show of affection and you are supposed to be a member of the production team, it undermines every bit of authority you might have. It also upset the crew. Dennis had been one of the mates and to see him cuddling up to this lady who was part of the unit broke one of the unwritten rules and the atmosphere changed totally.

I did think long and hard about sacking Fiona, but Dennis was in such a fragile state, I did not want to add to his problems. People did drift away from him, though, if only for a short time.

I had always felt Rula did not like the series, and did not think Dennis was doing good work. He was actually doing terrific work, but it is very difficult when a partner constantly undermines your confidence in what you are doing, and persists in thinking that you are only doing it to have a good time. Dennis took his job very seriously and professionally and Rula was not as supportive as she should have been. There was a lot of jealousy involved.

Another pressure, which none of us realised at the time, was that the film he'd done in Chicago had not worked and the money was being called in; consequently he was under tremendous financial strain as well as the additional emotional stress. His extreme unhappiness resulted in him drinking more. Looking back, I don't think anyone could have coped in any other way.

JAN: The funny thing was that Dennis and Fiona seemed to make each other so unhappy. We'd go out to dinner, and they'd have terrible arguments in front of everyone. Fiona, far from being serene, could be very volatile.

It stopped us working in the same way too. I couldn't get Dennis to do his lines, he was always with Fiona, And it made life difficult on the set. Dennis and I had to do a passionate kiss at one time. Throughout the scene, I was aware of Fiona glaring at us in the background. She couldn't bear to see it, she adored him so much.

We all felt desperately sorry, watching him sinking deeper and deeper into confusion. He lost so much weight, got thinner and thinner, we really feared for him.

I was living virtually parallel lives. Weekdays in Leeds with Fiona and home at the weekend. I was not a good enough actor to carry it off. I was becoming increasingly unpleasant at the weekends. And sexually I wasn't working normally either. I was in that stupid situation where I wanted to be faithful to Fiona.

Strangely enough Rula had always suspected that I was having an affair with Jan. I don't recall the final explosion, but I packed a few things and left. This was a foul time for everyone, but I was sure I had done the right thing.

DAVID REYNOLDS: Inevitably the press found out about the affair, but couldn't find any proof. But one day, despite the smokescreen we'd made, they got pictures of Dennis and Fiona together in Twickenham, sometime during a filming break before the show went on the air.

JAN FRANCIS: The *Sun* had picked up something about Dennis and Rula breaking up. Very deliberately they held off publishing the story until the day of our press launch for the series. That morning it was all over the paper.

The launch was held at BAFTA. The place was packed, not just with official TV journalists, but with the worst of the gutter press, who had crawled from under their stones.

Reynolds rushed over and warned me that I would have to do all the talking as Dennis had refused to speak.

The photo-call took place afterwards outside St James's Church in Piccadilly. It went on and on until finally we had to push our way out to escape. Next day the front page of the *Daily Mail* carried a picture of Dennis with his arm round me, to protect me from the crush of journalists. The headline read 'Rula leaves Dennis' and the photo caption ran 'Dennis seen with Jan Francis, yesterday in London.' There was no explanation of why we had been photographed together. My parents were hysterical. Everyone was appalled at what they'd done. Even Nigel Dempster of the *Daily Mail* phoned me to apologise, offering to make a public apology in his column. I decided it could only make things worse.

I was homeless again. While I was working in Leeds it was OK, because I still had the cottage, but then I had to go back to London. Initially I rented a flat in Montagu Mews owned by my agent Dennis Selinger's wife, Debbie. It was very pretty and I hadn't lived in central London since my early twenties. I used to walk to the office every day. Exercise was about the only thing I got out of East End Films.

Fiona and I lived in the mews, but I was in dire financial straits and there was no way we could stay. None of this was easy on Fiona, and at times our relationship was fairly combustible. She had a friend working in Scotland who had a little flat in Clapham, into which, Fiona informed me one day, she was moving on her own. After a few days and millions of phone calls later, she let me join her.

By now the press were buzzing around everywhere. It seemed that not a day went by without my telling some photographer or member of the fourth estate to 'Please go away!'

The flat was tiny and not terribly clean, and we retired to the ever-welcoming 'West Wing' of Chris Lewis's flat. However, our stay was not to be a long one, because by then I was preparing *Jeffrey Bernard is Unwell*.

Keith Waterhouse's play chronicling the life of his old friend, the columnist Jeffrey Bernard, had been a smash hit in London. Originally starring Peter O'Toole, it had since been interpreted by Tom Conti, then James Bolam. I saw Jim and he was terrific, but I think, for all of us who played the part, we knew that we were on a hiding to nothing following the great O'Toole. Except maybe Conti. Tom apparently has never been drunk or ever smoked a cigarette in his life. These are not the ideal qualifications to play Jeff. Bernard was a four-times-married, self-confessed alcoholic, diabetic, gambling, chain-smoking womaniser!

KEITH WATERHOUSE: I'd wanted to write something about Soho, but I didn't know what. But one night, sitting in the Coliseum, listening to some Italian piece by the ENO, I was sort of dozing off when, for some reason, I started thinking about John Murphy, a casting director from Granada, who'd got himself locked in Gerry's club one night. He'd fallen asleep, drunk no doubt, and woke at three in the morning to find himself alone. He'd phoned Gerry who'd responded, 'Don't move, I'll be there.' For some reason that and the opera came together and I got the whole theme for *Jeffrey Bernard is Unwell*.

I took some of the play from Jeff's own writing and some from other sources. The egg trick, for example, I'd seen demonstrated by the educational correspondent of the *Mirror*. He used to do it at conferences. He taught it to me and I taught it to Jeff. It worked wonderfully on stage.

Peter O'Toole was perfect casting. He'd known Jeff for years, from the old days, when Jeff had worked at the Old Vic as a fly man. Peter had been rehearsing the part for thirty years.

We thought it would be seen as a novelty turn and last twelve weeks, the run of O'Toole's commitment in the West End. It took off like a rocket, and inspired cartoons and controversy from the moment the play opened. It even hit the headlines on the front page of the *War Cry*: DOES MR WATERHOUSE THINK ALCOHOLISM IS FUNNY? ALCOHOLISM IS NOT FUNNY, MR WATERHOUSE.

The idea of Dennis Waterman as Jeffrey Bernard was very appealing. He seemed to reflect the same qualities and to have similar attitudes to life as my hero.

Some people think the play is about being drunk. It is not. It is about friendship, and Dennis has great qualities of friendship. He took on the character and did it wonderfully well.

NED SHERRIN: I'd always thought Dennis very underestimated as an actor. People think only of the wide-boy television image, whereas I had seen him over the years do all sorts of excellent things like *Saved* and *Saratoga*. I knew he had a far more extensive range and I knew too he would understand about having a hangover and all that.

The part is very demanding of an actor in that it requires a huge amount of theatrical experience and expertise. The character is on stage throughout the play. It is impossible for someone with no technique to sustain the part. Dennis is as thoroughly grounded in theatre as he is in front of the cameras.

The litmus test of *Jeffrey Bernard* is in the huge, page-long speeches where the actor has to pace his breathing to negotiate those almost Shavian paragraphs. It was these reams of exquisitely written words that attracted O'Toole to the part.

One had to believe that Dennis could exercise the same skill, and he certainly could. One man, on stage, talking directly to the audience, has to bring a lot of his own personality to the role, and Dennis did that too.

Some of the scapegrace episodes in Jeffrey's life were not too far removed from those that had happened in Mr Waterman's life, so again we were sure he would be perfectly able to believe and understand and realise what he was doing in the parallel situations.

Apart from the technical skills of delivering those tracts of long, almost philosophical passages, with all the innate demands of timing, rhythm and sense of comedy, the actor has to endow an impossible old bastard with charm, so that the audience can fully comprehend Jeff's effect on people in his good moods and still empathise with him when he is exposed in his bad and rude moods. A lot of appalling stories are revealed on stage, which the actor will not get away with unless he has a great deal of natural charm.

TWENTY-TWO

JEFFREY BERNARD IS UNWELL AND IN AUSTRALIA

In November 1991, Fiona and I were firmly ensconced in the club-class section of a British Airways flight to my favourite city, Perth, in Western Australia. As always, we landed at about three in the morning and were taken to a lovely house on Cottesloe Beach. The plan was to rehearse for three weeks, have a few days off for Christmas, and open at His Majesty's Theatre in early January.

Ned and Keith had gone out a little earlier to decide on the four other members of the cast. Although any casting is extremely important, it's not quite so crucial with *Jeffrey Bernard* because it is virtually a monologue with interruptions. But our cast was excellent and that always helps everybody's performance.

Happily, I was now back with Deke, who had suggested that I take Tony McGrogan with me as a sort of tour manager. A tour manager is more often associated with a rock 'n' roll tour. Actors don't normally have such a thing, but Deke suggested that as I didn't know who I was going to be working with, and it was going to be a long tour, there was no guarantee that anyone would play golf. That did it. Tony and I had known each other for some time, from the days when we played football together, and more recently from when he was working for RCA, looking after Gerard Kenny.

He was to join us later after spending Christmas at home with his family. My daughter, Hannah, who was then sixteen years old, was also due to come out for the latter part of her school holiday.

It turned out to be an extraordinary Christmas.

A message had come through to the theatre from my old mate and record producer Brian (Benbo) Bennett, who was out there working on an album for Hank Marvin. He and his wife, Margaret, were staying at a place called The Vines, which was a golf resort an hour or so outside Perth, and they invited us to join them there for

Christmas Eve. They had arranged a suite for us and we had a smashing time together. It felt almost decadent to be playing golf on Christmas morning in ninety-degree heat. The fact of being allowed to do anything on Christmas morning that I actually wanted to do was incredible. Brian and Margaret left for home not long after Christmas. Hank, who lived out there with his wife Carol, whom I knew from when we'd both appeared in *The Music Man*, we met up with on several occasions.

Ned had got us all invited to a lunch party over the Christmas period at Alan Bond's house. Eileen Bond, his wife, who was known popularly as Big Red, was an old friend of our producer, Helen Montagu. I phoned up to check that it would be all right to take Hannah. 'Sure, darling, the more the merrier.'

When we got there, I noticed that there were a lot of old Toyotas, Hondas and Subarus parked down the side of the house. I thought how amazing that they had had the forethought to order mini-cabs for our return journey home.

NED SHERRIN: Not only was there a stockade of cars around the house, there was a huge crowd gathered there. Keith and I agreed, 'How lovely, carol singers.'

We rang the bell, to be greeted by loud barks. The door was opened just enough to reveal the slavering jowls of an enormous St Bernard and the scrutinising eyes of Big Red. Once we were identified, the door was flung open and we were given a huge, warm welcome. 'Is this your daughter?' Big Red demanded.

'Yep,' I answered, 'this is Hannah.'

'How old are you, love?' she asked.

'Sixteen,' Hannah replied.

Eileen winked at me. 'She's got huge tits, the boys'll love her.' I nodded, hoping she wouldn't be too accurate.

While we were enjoying the lavish hospitality I happened to mention to one of the other guests how thoughtful it was of the Bonds to order all those cabs for our return.

'Piss off, mate,' he retorted. 'They're all waiting to serve writs on Alan.'

Alan Bond was in serious monetary difficulties at the time. His business dealings had collapsed following investigations into a charge of fraud over the sale of a Monet painting. It was rumoured he owed as much as a quarter of the whole Australian national debt.

HANNAH: Eileen was rich and larger than life. Alan was rather quiet. There were various adult offspring, with their boy- or girl-friends, husbands and wives and babies, and, the centre of attention, the latest Bond grandchild, christened 'Banjo'. They were a bizarre family – over the top, fun and insane. Alan looked on benignly, but then he had his mistress waiting not far away and they all knew it.

There was incredible art everywhere. I'd also noticed a load of paintings, taken out of their frames, stacked by the front door. Naively, I'd first thought someone in the house must have been a very clever artist, they were such brilliant copies. Then I learnt they were the originals, waiting to be repossessed.

The underlying stress was evident over dinner when one of Bond's daughters threw a fork at her father. It missed him, but hit one of the modern works of art. A little later, when things had calmed down somewhat, Alan excused himself and wasn't seen again. We never found out how he managed to escape the blockade. The next thing we heard was that he had made a statement, a day or two later, from New York. I don't know if anyone in the house knew about his cunning plan, but the party went ahead, full steam, until the early hours of the following morning. It took us days to recover, but luckily we were still only rehearsing.

Deke and Jill arrived in time for another Bond bash on New Year's Eve. This time it was open house. Strangers wandered in and out and food was served endlessly. Champagne glasses were piled teetering, high on a sculpture, which Big Red informed us was a Rodin. 'We've another four upstairs,' she added casually as champagne showered down from glass to glass.

McGrogan flew in for the first night. There was a problem with building works going on at Jill and Deke's hotel, and they had to get out for a few days. Without consulting Fiona, I had told them blithely that they could stay with us. Tony was living there too and we had enough rooms, but it did become a little crowded.

So there we were, all cosy in our lovely house on the beach – Deke, Jill, Tony, Hannah, Fiona and myself.

I think this might have been the beginning of the end for poor Fiona and me. Nothing horrifically dramatic happened between us, but I guess I just spread myself too thinly and didn't give her enough time. I was also doing a part that was very demanding and, if anything, slightly larger than Hamlet.

After the dress rehearsal, Ned decided to have a little soirée for cast, company and friends in his hotel suite. He wanted to cook something special for us and the hotel staff were bemused by his requests. It was very hush-hush.

Every other director in the world would prefer to keep you in the theatre till near midnight giving you copious notes, then expect you to go straight home to bed. Ned couldn't wait to get back to the hotel and have a party. Strange odours wafted along the hotel corridors as we arrived and found out why the cooking utensils had had to be so specific. Ned was throwing a 'tripe and wine' party.

Most of us from England had tried this dish at one time or another, but it was a whole new experience for many of the Aussies, and not, it has to be said, a universal success. Ned thought it was hilarious watching the different reactions. It had to be said that the wine, salad and cheese were very popular, and the various pot plants dotted about the room were very well fed.

KEITH WATERHOUSE: It was all hugely enjoyable. I recall the moment a waiter announced to Ned that we had run out of water, and he responded very grandly, 'When we've run out of wine, let me know!'

One of the drawbacks of working with Ned is the risk of getting very fat. He does insist on very good, and sometimes very long, lunches. He and Keith are an odd couple. Keith too enjoys long lunches, but getting him to actually eat anything more than a starter is a huge compliment to the chef. I don't know whether Ned 'does lunch' on purpose, but it has a very relaxing effect on the cast. On some occasions it has a very relaxing effect on Ned as well, but I've only seen him nod off in rehearsals a handful of times! Sometimes during rehearsals he actually directs you, which he will vehemently deny. He is a smashing man and it is always a great pleasure to work with him, although you do have to be careful what you say, otherwise you're liable to end up as an anecdote in one of his books.

Keith too enjoys being there for the rehearsal process. He has perfected the knack of appearing almost disengaged from the action on stage. He sits towards the back of the auditorium, smiling and nodding, leaving you to believe that he has total trust in everything that you do. Then, very quietly, he'll seek you out and tell you a little anecdote which will switch on a light, so that you completely understand how to play a certain scene.

What throws you off guard is Keith's diffident manner. He seems to have absolutely no awareness of his professional standing, and puts everyone at their ease immediately, so that sometimes you forget he is a literary lion with a brain as sharp as a tack.

Between them he and Ned made the whole production a social event, with lunches and dinners and Keith's persistent persuasion to have 'just the one'. In Australia, it was the Chardonnay; usually it's champagne. Keith has a theory, by which he swears – you will never get a hangover from champagne, as long as you don't smoke. He tests it to the full every day, and so far it hasn't let him down.

KEITH WATERHOUSE: There is a peculiar local drinking law in Perth whereby during certain hours if you want a drink, you have to have food.

There was a small restaurant not far from the theatre which we'd adopted as our canteen. We had ordered a bottle of wine and with it came the obligatory sandwich. Dennis had just finished rehearsals and, feeling rather peckish, he decided to sample the food. Suddenly there was a loud warning shout from the back, 'Don't touch that sandwich!'

It turned out the sandwich was about three months old, definitely not to be eaten. It was there simply to fulfil its legal duty.

One of the great joys of doing a play written by Keith Waterhouse and directed by Ned Sherrin is that they are both adamant that the optimum time for anyone to sit in a theatre is two and a half hours, including the interval.

Jeffrey Bernard was also the perfect play for Aussie audiences, because, apart from the slightly stylised presentation, it was about most of the things they hold dear – sex, booze and gambling.

The play opened to great applause. And we had another party! Made memorable by Big Red screeching at the top of her voice, 'They've got the bastard, they've caught the bastard!' It seemed her husband Alan had escaped to some Polynesian resort with his mistress, only to be arrested that day on his return to Sydney.

KEITH WATERHOUSE: Dennis brought to the part a quality of his own, a vulnerability which plumbed the depths of sadness in the role. There is a scene where Jeff is contemplating death, and in his imagination, the friends he has known are with him, awaiting the call of the Grim Reaper. They line up saying graciously, 'After you, old boy.' 'No, after you.' Dennis did it with such exquisite melancholy, it brought tears to your eyes.

And only someone who understood the romance of racing could

deliver the line 'Wait till he gets the sun on his back.' But Dennis could say it, and so could Peter.

Eventually it was time to move on to Brisbane, roughly 3,000 miles away. One of the hidden benefits of touring Australia is that the set has to travel enormous distances by road. This meant that after wrapping in Perth, we had at least ten days' holiday before opening again in Queensland.

We were packed and ready to go and I went into the bedroom to tell Fiona that the cab was about to arrive. She was sitting on the side of the bed, nowhere near ready. 'We can't go yet,' she whispered.

'What are you talking about? Everything has been arranged. Tickets, taxis, everything.'

I sat down next to her. She was adamant we had to stay and sort things out. I was equally convinced we had to go.

'Fine,' I shrugged. 'If that's what you want.' I had no idea what had gone wrong and I still don't. I can only guess that, having been independent for a long time and having held down an exciting and responsible job in television, the prospect of playing the little woman trailing her man across a vast continent was very daunting.

I made certain that she would be OK financially and said goodbye. She didn't move from the bed, crying quietly. As I left, she said, 'I love you, Dennis.' I replied sadly, 'I don't think you do.'

That was the last time that we ever saw each other. Although, after I got back to England, I spoke to her, by chance, on the phone. She had phoned Chris Lewis to check whether she had left a few things at his flat. The conversation was all rather stilted. She thanked me for the money, which she had used as a deposit on a flat. It did cross my mind to ask for her number, but I didn't.

In 1997, I was doing panto at Hackney and I received a letter. I recognised the handwriting immediately. It was from Fiona. It said, as I was local, could I ring her? She wanted to explain to me the reasons why she had acted in the way she had. I didn't respond.

As it happened, the flight to Brisbane was also quite eventful. Tony and I were in club class and the rest of the team were down the back. Notice how my famed sense of democracy goes straight out of the window when it comes to comfort? However, I did manage to persuade the authorities to allow them into the first-class lounge while we waited for our connecting flight. This was a mistake. They had consumed so much alcohol on the flight that their riotous behaviour resulted in us all being threatened with eviction. And only after I had made endless promises to keep them under control were we allowed to board our connection.

Queensland is another great state: the Gold Coast, Surfers' Paradise and a whole new set of golf courses to explore. Brisbane was buzzing. A big Expo was in full swing, the place was heaving with visitors, and we had ten days to sample as much as we could. The hotel was beautiful and we were on holiday.

Then, it was back to work.

While we were playing *Jeffrey Bernard is Unwell*, at the smaller theatre in the Brisbane Arts Centre, Peter Ustinov was performing his one-man show in the arena. As a parting gift, Jenny Ryan, our stage manager, gave me an autographed copy of Ustinov's autobiography, in which she wrote, 'This will have to do until you write your own.' Well, here it is, darling!

Although I still loved doing the play, I found myself thinking more and more about Rula. We'd both given up so much to be together, we had caused so much pain, left behind homes and families. We were still married, we'd shared so much together, so many wonderful times, as well as the bad. I'd been twice married already, and I hated the prospect of another failure.

It was a tough call to make, but I invited her to join me in Sydney.

KEITH WATERHOUSE: To my knowledge, throughout the London run, Jeff had seen the play only once. Whilst he was in the theatre every night, he remained in the bar. Occasionally he ventured into the auditorium but it was only to slump asleep in the back of the stalls.

It was the adulation he loved as well as the free drinks recognition brought – although not always. In London, Jeff was slouched asleep in the bar one evening when the new holiday relief manager marched in and ordered Mrs Matt, the archetypal resident bar lady, to 'get that drunk out of here'.

'You can't,' she answered, 'That's Jeffrey Bernard.'

'Don't be ridiculous,' he retorted. 'Jeffrey Bernard is on stage.' The manager had no idea Jeff was an actual character.

NED SHERRIN: Jeff had been in awe of O'Toole. They were at a lunch meeting, one day, reminiscing about a girl they had both tried to pull, when Jeff suddenly said, 'You won. I married her.'

He also told the wonderful story of being in court about to divorce his seventh wife. Asked who he was citing, he answered, 'Scotland.'

KEITH WATERHOUSE: Jeff was very fond of Dennis; he saw
Dennis and himself as two of a kind.

Jeff had come to Australia specifically to write about the play. The
problem was, he had been commissioned by one English national
newspaper, while at the same time being under contract to another.

He'd timed his visit perfectly. One of Jeff's great loves in life was
cricket. He was in seventh heaven, eating and drinking with the team
in the evening and watching them play during the day. This didn't
leave a lot of time for work. He returned home to find that he had
been fired for moonlighting by the paper to which he was contracted,
and he didn't receive a cent from the paper that had flown him out
there because he didn't write a word.

Rula had flown in a few days before the first night. I was very
nervous. We hadn't seen each other for a long time and I knew we
had mountains to climb. The prospect of being together, facing one
another in a one-to-one situation, on that first day, with nothing to
diffuse the intensity, was a bit too much to contemplate. I felt we
needed a diversion, to re-introduce ourselves slowly.

I thought I had the perfect solution, but how to present it to her
was a delicate matter. I knew she would interpret it as a selfish act,
which in a way it was, but I also knew it would be a wonderfully
exciting and special day, which we would both enjoy and which
might ease our coming together.

On the way back from the airport, I asked her how she wanted to
attack her jet lag. 'Do you want to crash out immediately and we can
go out this evening, or would you prefer to get through the day and
crash for as long as you like in the morning?'

'I don't know, I've just got off the plane,' she said. 'Why does it
matter so much?'

'Well,' I began, somewhat hesitantly, 'we have been invited to the
Sydney Cricket Ground to watch England play Australia.'

'When?' she asked, somewhat dumbfounded.

'Today,' I said, rather too enthusiastically.

'Today? We are trying to get our marriage together, and you want
to go out all day and watch bloody cricket?'

'With you,' I said, trying to inject a hint of romance. Have you ever
tried to make cricket sound romantic? Don't bother.

'I can't believe what I'm hearing,' Rula said in amazement. I tried
to explain the importance of the match, and what a rare opportunity
it would be to see it in such an historic stadium. 'It's all been

arranged,' I added brightly. 'They've laid on private transport, we'll be in an exclusive box, and we have the choice of going at lunchtime for the afternoon session – or later, after their tea break, for the final session. It will be a spectacular day.'

Rula gave up. 'OK, I'll have a lie-down first and we'll go this evening, if we absolutely have to.'

'Thank you.' I smiled. A lie-down wasn't such a bad idea. We knew we were good at that!

The private transport turned out to be a people-carrier. There were about a dozen of us crammed inside. Rula was the only woman. The others all sounded Australian, although, as it turned out, there were several ex-pats who, like me, would be cheering for England. The box was not quite as opulent as I had explained either, but there was hospitality – some not quite brand-new sandwiches and snacks, and we were offered beer, beer and beer, or maybe a little drop of wine . . . 'Vodka and tonic, please,' said Rula, daring our host to refuse. She got her drink, and we sat down to enjoy the match.

It looked like England were in trouble until Botham took five quick wickets and suddenly we were in charge for the rest of the match. The atmosphere was electric. Even Rula was affected, I think.

Aussies hate losing, but the timing of this defeat really hit them hard. This was the tour when the Australian Premier, Paul Keating (a rabid republican) broke all protocol by putting his arm around the Queen. At another event, Botham and Graham Gooch walked out of an evening's entertainment when a female impersonator took the piss out of the Queen.

Suddenly attitudes around us changed. People with whom we'd been drinking happily before the match started asking aggressively what we would think if Australia became a republic and they no longer wanted to be ruled from England.

'You're thirteen thousand miles away. How could you possibly feel English?' I agreed.

'Yeah, right!'

Despite a rocky start, this period in Sydney was like another honeymoon, and apart from those few moments at the cricket, Rula and I were spoilt rotten by the Australians, with boat trips, barbies and invitations everywhere.

Then it was time for her to leave, unfortunately two weeks before me, but it felt almost as if nothing had ever gone wrong with our relationship.

TWENTY-THREE

CIRCLES OF DECEIT

I returned to England and the prospect of another series of *On the Up*, followed by some more *Stay Lucky* and a UK tour of *Jeffrey Bernard*. There was also the small matter of patching up my marriage.

I still had a few things at my Chris Lewis bolthole and I needed to get my head together before I went back to Sheepcote. A couple of days later, I ordered a local taxi to take me home.

Somehow the news got out, and, after a lovely evening of reconciliation, we woke up to a garden full of bloody photographers. The police, it seems, were powerless to do anything. Finally Deke suggested that we get it all over in one 'foul' swoop, by holding an official photo call. They weren't the happiest snaps I've ever had taken.

However, in spite of this wretched new start, life slowly and tentatively got back to an evenish keel.

CHRIS LEWIS: Dennis had stayed with me for most of the year of their separation. He'd arrived with a mountain of gear, including a four foot stack of hi-fi equipment, which was good news for me, as mine had been stolen in a recent burglary.

Shortly after he'd returned to Sheepcote, Dennis called to say he and Rula would be round to pick up his stuff. On the day, I left them to it, while I made coffee for us all in the kitchen. Dennis called, 'I'll leave the hi-fi for you. I've got another one at home. I don't need it.' Then I heard some angry whispering. It was Rula laying down the law again. I walked out of the kitchen to see her carrying the hi-fi amps out to the car. Dennis looked at me and shrugged. Nothing had changed.

I had the great pleasure of seven weeks working with Joan Sims and Sam Kelly et al. in another series of *On the Up*, then it was back up to Leeds for more *Stay Lucky*. There were two notable absentees:

Fiona, and more importantly for the show, Jan Francis, for whom the commuting between Leeds and Kent had become just too disruptive to her family life.

Maybe we should have wrapped the whole thing then, but Geoff and David were very keen to carry on, and because of my love of the atmosphere up there, I went along with them. Basically, I would have gone to read on *Jackanory* if they had asked me.

I had known of Jan's decision to leave for some time. Geoff, David and I had discussed it months earlier, and Geoff had come up with the idea of starting the series with the introduction of a new female character. Susan George was his choice for the role. I had no problem with that. I had known her since we were kids and I thought it would give the show some added kudos, not only because she was quite a big name but also because she had done very little British television. We were soon to find out why.

Susan had been something of a star in the seventies in films like *Straw Dogs*, and had lived for some time in Los Angeles. Sadly, she brought back with her some of the more unpleasant aspects of Hollywood stardom. The first thing she did when she got on the set was to measure our caravans, to make sure mine wasn't bigger than hers. This was the sort of showbizzy bullshit we had successfully kept at bay on *Stay Lucky* and the atmosphere on set curdled immediately she arrived.

I knew it was the beginning of the end when I saw one of our wardrobe assistants coming out of her caravan in tears. I can handle people not being very good at their job, but when they start upsetting my beloved crew there had better be a bloody good reason.

The first episode is always nerve-racking, especially if someone is not very experienced in television and particularly if someone is new to a show. A certain amount of bad behaviour will always be tolerated and understood. But you've got to sort yourself out from then on in.

A couple of days into the second episode, Peter, our production manager, was on the set and I asked him if he'd seen any rushes. He was rather evasive, until I insisted he tell me the truth.

'She's just not cutting it,' he admitted.

It was a difficult situation for everyone concerned. Eventually David came into my caravan and said, 'I'm afraid it's not working with Susan.'

'So what are we going to do?' I asked a little nervously.

'Well,' he said wearily, 'we're talking to her agent about various solutions.'

The problem was that a substantial part of the series had been written around her character. It wasn't possible or practical to recast another actress to take over. It would have meant re-shooting the first two episodes, and that would have blown the budget completely. In the end we decided to continue the character for two more episodes, and write in a reason for her leaving the series and introduce a new female lead.

With great good fortune we were able to cast the lovely Lesley Ash. The moment she arrived, it was evident that we were going to revert to being a happy set once more.

DAVID REYNOLDS: Rula came up for the very last series. They were back together again and Dennis was on his best behaviour. The action was set in Budapest and Rula was cast as a 'countess' character. We thought it would be safer if we made Rula part of those particular episodes and they could be out there together for a month.

It was hard not to laugh when Dennis wanted to sit around and chat with the crew. Rula dragged him off to the opera. Not quite his scene.

However it wold be fair to say that the work went well, and Dennis was terrific.

Back in England, we were up to speed, the show was going really well, when we were all hit by a thunderbolt. Four of us from the crew were playing golf when suddenly we saw Andrew Benson and two of the production team coming to find us. Andrew was looking pale and very grim.

And there, on the eighth tee at Rawdon Golf Course, we heard the terrible news that Geoff McQueen had died.

Geoff wasn't only our writer, he was our great friend. Especially to David Reynolds and me. I had played my last game of football with him, he had given me his old set of golf clubs, we ate and drank together and agreed on virtually everything. We were all totally stunned. Apparently his wife Jan had gone out shopping, and Geoff had said he felt like a rest. When she came back, he was lying on the bed and never got up. He died from an aneurysm, which, at least, had been mercifully quick.

It was the cue to wrap *Stay Lucky*. It was unthinkable to go on without him.

HANNAH: Rula and Dad were together, and there was an uneasy truce between Rula and me.

My decision to spend Christmas with my father in Australia had angered her. She accused me of having divided loyalties over Fiona, which was nonsense. I had met Fiona on only one previous occasion. Inevitably we had spent time together while Dad was working but our relationship was no more than that. I'd gone over there to be with my father. Rula refused to acknowledge this and complained to everyone that not only was I disloyal, but by my action, I had shown no respect for her whatsoever.

A New Year's Eve party was arranged at a nearby pub in Buckinghamshire. Rula insisted it was to celebrate twelve years of marriage. Whatever, we all had a great time. Back home, Rula said something about how wonderful it was, they'd actually been together for fifteen years. I'd had a few drinks and I picked her up on this.

'You can't have been,' I said. 'That means you were together when I was three.'

Rula smiled. 'We've been together a lot longer than you think.' Which to me was really rubbing it in that they'd been having an affair when Dad was supposed to be with Mum. It made me see red, and I stormed out.

Three weeks later, back at boarding school, I received a letter from Rula accusing me of being a meddling little bitch, out to destroy their marriage, warning me not to try to come between them as their love was eternal. It concluded by saying that I shouldn't bother to show the letter to my father, or discuss it, as he was aware she had written it and thoroughly approved.

Immediately I phoned my mother, who was livid. She said she did not believe Dennis knew anything about it, and she was sure he would never allow such a letter to be sent to me. On her advice I phoned my father. He didn't say a word against Rula but I could tell he was furious.

While we were still doing *Stay Lucky*, Vernon Lawrence, head of entertainment for YTV, asked if we had any ideas for future television for me.

Jill Arlon and I had worked together on various ideas for films and television scripts. She had read an article in the *Los Angeles Times* about the punishment beatings in Northern Ireland, which at the time was receiving no recognition at all in Britain, and she was keen to write something about it. We decided then that it would be a good idea to develop a project for me set in Northern Ireland.

I wanted to get away from the type of roles I had been playing on television. I had relished the acting demands of *Jeffrey Bernard*; now I wanted something more testing in a television drama. Setting it in Northern Ireland, with all its divisions and apparently insoluble problems, gave us all the possibilities for tension, excitement and romance. Jill wrote the scenario, which became *Circles of Deceit*.

I was to play John Neil, a retired SAS officer, a haunted man, who is called back to duty after a long absence from the service following the murder of his wife and child in an IRA bombing in Germany. He is a man with nothing to lose, sent undercover to infiltrate a faction of the IRA, in order to track the destination of an enormous cache of Libyan arms. Whilst there he becomes involved with the daughter of one of the IRA hierarchy.

Jill went to Northern Ireland and came back with a huge dossier on the sectarian problems. I think this probably frightened the life out of Vernon. At that time television was quite nervous about tackling certain kinds of controversial subject matter, and that particular punishment-beating storyline was deleted.

However, the character of John Neil was so strong that should *Circles* be the success they expected, the intention was to follow the first two-hour film special with others, taking Neil from the initial narrative set in Ireland on to other missions, where his willingness to put his life on the line and his expertise in military intelligence could be put to the test.

The first film was scripted by Wesley Burrows.

We started filming early in 1993. It was the old team: David Reynolds was executive producer, Andrew Benson the producer, Geoff Saxe the director, with the added bonus of most of our crew from *Stay Lucky*.

The casting for that first two-hour special was brilliant: Sir Derek Jacobi, Peter Vaughan, Clare Higgins and a whole raft of excellent Irish actors.

DAVID REYNOLDS: *Circles of Deceit* showed Dennis in a new light as a thinking action man, as well as calling on all his reserves as an actor in revealing his anguish when the character's wife and child are killed.

It was also a joy for everyone to have the old Dennis back. It was almost as if the Fiona episode had been a last fling and he'd come back more mature and prepared to settle down. He was confident in himself and the work he was doing, and again was the professional, generous and charming actor we all loved. Everyone was thrilled he had come through all his traumas. He was back with Rula and his commitment to work was one hundred and fifty per cent.

From May that year I did a twelve-week tour of *Jeffrey Bernard* all over Britain. We opened in Cardiff with a great new cast – Judy Buxton, Tristram Gemill again, from the Australian production, and a very old friend of mine, whom I hadn't seen for ages, called Dougie Fisher.

Rula and Jeff came down for the first night. This being the first time the play had been taken on tour outside London, it was a very glittering affair.

The only drawback was that we opened on a Tuesday night, which meant we had a matinée the next day. We celebrated into the early hours, but that was fine, I didn't have to get up until midday and it only took a minute to walk to the theatre. Jeff phoned me at around 9.45 a.m. to enquire if I fancied a drink. He explained he was catching a train to Newbury for the races and fancied a tincture or two before he left.

'Sorry, mate,' I said. ' I'm a bit knackered and I've got a bleeding matinée to do in a little while.'

I'm sure he thought I was a complete wimp, and sadly I never saw him again. He died not long after.

It is a truism to say that the second night's show is always an anti-climax.

It is particularly true if the second performance is a matinée. Some plays work at matinées, *Jeffrey Bernard* definitely doesn't.

It opens with a strange modern poem, followed by Jeff waking up under a table in the Coach and Horses pub. His first words are 'shit' and 'fuck'. Matinée audiences are predominantly filled with elderly ladies, and 'shit' and 'fuck' is not the sort of dialogue which generally endears you to the blue-rinse brigade.

One Wednesday-afternoon show in Guildford proved the point. The curtain went up, and as soon as I spoke I could hear the clatter of seats being vacated. Apparently at least twenty-five of the audience left.

At the Saturday matinée, within minutes of the opening, I managed to repeat 'fuck' about fifteen times. When I came off at the interval I was asked if everything was OK.

'Sure,' I said. I had figured that if we lost twenty-five with one 'fuck', with fifteen I could empty the theatre and we could have the afternoon off.

I hate matinées, even when I'm doing a play that doesn't upset anyone. It is an antiquated tradition that is only continued to satisfy the greed of producers and theatre managements. Children's theatre is fine for the afternoons, but most modern adult plays are not suitable and draw very small audiences. Some afternoons don't even earn enough to pay for the electricity, let alone the staff and the actors.

Playing a part like Jeffrey Bernard, which is virtually a one-man show, is exhausting enough with one performance a night, but when you know that the language is going to upset ninety-five per cent of a matinée house, it takes away all the pleasure.

Despite the bad language, the complaint we received in Sheffield was to do with the length of the performance.

To hasten our exit on certain matinées, if I was on my toes, I could cut some of my major speeches without upsetting the rest of the cast, and knock twenty minutes off the show, quite forgetting that in the front of house, they displayed the estimated timing of the end of the show. Some old biddies in Sheffield had taken note of this and complained that it wasn't as long as they had been promised. They hated the play, but they still wanted value for their money. Cancel all matinées!

Croydon, without doubt, is the ugliest town in Europe, with the most horrible theatre I've ever had the misfortune to play. It's called the Ashcroft and poor old Dame Peggy must be spinning in her grave. But it was there that the original producer of *Jeffrey Bernard is Unwell* came to see us.

I was talking to his wife afterwards and she said that she thought I was the best 'Jeffrey' that she had seen on stage.

'Surely not,' I said. 'What about O'Toole?'

'Oh,' she replied, 'Peter was wonderfully mercurial, a brilliant performance, but you are actually the most like Jeff.'

She meant it as a compliment, but bear in mind I was playing a sixty-seven-year-old alcoholic who had just had his leg amputated because of his diabetes and who was famous for being a pest and falling asleep in various drinking establishments throughout Soho. Some compliment!

It was while I was doing *Jeffrey Bernard* in Brighton (another town that has gone right down the tubes) that I was asked to a meeting with the Heather brothers. They had written a funny little sixties musical, which had been quite a big hit in some of the smaller theatres, clubs and pub theatres around Britain, and they wanted to bring it into the West End.

A Slice of Saturday Night was an interesting concept, which also gave me the opportunity to sing again, and I thought it would be fun to do. Sadly it did not live up to expectations and we had a brief but turgid time at the Strand Theatre.

Nineteen ninety-four saw us on the road once more with *Jeffrey Bernard*. This time in Dublin. We had a marvellous time, but surprisingly the Irish press were rather grudging in their praise.

KEITH WATERHOUSE: It was a case of coals to Newcastle. Hostility and a degree of rivalry were expressed: 'You come over here with your play about drunken wits,' someone said. 'We've got drunken wits who could drink your drunken wits under the table.'

I was looking forward to the spring, when I was due to start filming the next film in the *Circles of Deceit* series.

Sadly the television world was undergoing a lot of changes – and none of them for the better – changes that were affecting everyone. Big business had moved in, with accountants and lawyers whose sole interest was the bottom line. 'Streamlining' was the buzz word. Crews were contemplating redundancies, and one of the best-equipped studios in Europe was closed down to make offices for accountants.

The whole industry was being taken over by people with no knowledge, tradition, intuition or real interest in programme-making, and every production was subject to the rule of the cheap buck. For the first time in my life, I met directors, producers and writers who were so disillusioned and disgusted with the way TV was now being run that they were considering early retirement. Historically, no one ever wants to retire in this business. We all want to die on stage, so to speak.

I was made even more aware of just how much the quality of production was being sacrificed for the bottom line by the effect it had on this series. The scripts were definitely not up to standard. The budget no longer allowed for the best, and I was being directed by solid old hacks who had spent their lives directing the odd episode of various series and who were only employed now because they were guaranteed to come in under budget.

On the other hand, it wasn't all that bad compared with what I was going to do next.

For some unaccountable reason, I had let Rula talk me into doing another pantomime. All the pantos I had done previously had been traditional scripts with very good casts. This time we had a 'Gladiator'. The slow decline of television was seeing the proliferation of more and more game shows, including the ghastly *Gladiators*, which was responsible for the rise and glorification of musclebound weight-lifters. Diane Youdal (Jet) was one of these. Actually, we were very lucky, as sometimes she was able to walk and talk at the same time. Diane was pleasant and worked hard, but she had adopted that Californian bullshit jargon, and never used a short word if she could think of a longer one, even if it didn't make sense. She and Rula got on very well. They were both deep into anything 'mystical', and the new bible of the time was *The Celestine Prophesies*.

To make matters worse, we were doing the panto in Reading, where the theatre has to be one of the most depressing arenas in the country. It's so bad, they have even stopped holding the snooker championships there.

We did two performances a day, which allowed time between shows for Rula and me to go shopping! It was my worst nightmare.

TWENTY-FOUR

BREAKING UP IS HARD TO DO

At home, if we weren't openly antagonistic, there was a pervasive sullen silence.

> PAUL YOUNG: My wife and I went to stay at Sheepcote, and it was obvious the marriage was very rocky. I guess I'd have been surprised if it had lasted until they got their free bus passes.
>
> Rula had admitted when they were first together that Dennis' appeal was that he was dangerous and very attractive to women. By her own account she had a fine husband who was also a good father, yet she became involved with Dennis, knowing she was ruining his marriage to Pat. I'm surprised that she was surprised when it happened to her.

Although my indiscretion with Fiona supposedly was forgotten, every day and in every way I was being made to pay, and not just for that – the bitter recriminations concerning the financial pressures induced by the failure of *Cold Justice* continued to be laid at my door.

Rula was doing more and more by herself without any consultation, yet I was expected to ask permission to go and play golf. We were drifting further and further apart, and neither of us and nothing seemed capable of mending the rift. Presents I gave her were accepted, but with little grace and the grudging comment that they were nothing but a means of buying love. That may have been true. One of these so called 'bribes' was a birthday present I arranged for her as a surprise.

We had first met John Blashford-Snell on our very first visit to Australia, for *Same Time Next Year* at some charity event. He was ex-army, but at that time was what he termed an explorer and was in Perth running Operation Raleigh, a scheme which encouraged young people to do voluntary work wherever it was needed around the world.

More recently I had read that 'Blashers', as he was known, was planning a trip to Nepal to seek evidence of an enormous elephant which, it was believed, could be a throwback or related to the great mammoth of prehistoric times.

We, and Rula in particular, had done a lot of charity work for the protection of elephants, so without her knowing, I bought her a place on this trip. It was very successful, they had a fantastic time and Rula came back with a load of photographs of this enormous tusker which really did exist. A second expedition was planned for the following year, and with it the decision to write a joint book about their experiences and findings.

A year later, the book was published and I was invited to the launch for a little added publicity. Throughout the interminable photo call, Rula and I stood side by side and, quite naturally, I would put my arm around her, which she would then shrug off.

Earlier during that year, Rula had been invited by Nicole, our friend from the south of France, to join her in a two-week visit to Tibet. Rula came back a fully fledged Buddhist, and with a real live Tibetan monk in tow.

He turned out to be a Swede who had gone to live in Tibet, and he'd come to England to raise money for an orphanage he was trying to set up out there.

He was a very interesting bloke and a fine guitarist, who played some very passable Pink Floyd. He also was very partial to our better wines. He claimed to be the reincarnation of one of the greatest of Buddhist monks, or was it a Dalai Lama? I assumed that humility was spelt differently in Tibet.

He did not come alone. Our place was soon full of his disciples, who bowed and scraped before him. And he revelled in it. I couldn't help feeling suspicious about the whole thing, especially as there were very few men involved. I made it clear that I had no interest in becoming a Buddhist, and at least he didn't attempt to convert me. He was happy simply to accept our hospitality. Rula waited on him hand and foot. Perhaps I should have converted after all.

His influence lingered long after the time he spent with us. When Rula went into hospital to have a minor operation on her hand, she had to fill out a form with all her particulars, including religion; she put down Catholic Buddhist. I suppose that covered most eventualities.

Sadly, neither of her parents was very well at this time. Her mother was coughing nonstop and getting very weak. Nevertheless, no matter what anybody said, she refused to give up smoking, and I rather admired her for that.

I don't know if there was anything clinically wrong with her father, but he was getting vaguer and vaguer, so much so he had become something of a danger to himself.

This all added to the considerable stress within our house. I think Rula would claim that I didn't care about either of them. She would be wrong. It would be dishonest of me to say that I felt any great warmth towards her father, but I really did care about her mother.

It was a slow year for work. This happens in every actor's life, and what I did do was very enjoyable. At times like this, jobs come in which, under normal circumstances, you would refuse without a second thought, but I still had my *Cold Justice* debts to consider, and when an offer came in to do a soap commercial for a very large fee, I was tempted. It was a series of commercials that another actor had been doing and it was suggested that I should take over from him. Now commercials can be very entertaining. This was not.

DEKE ARLON: It was completely wrong for his career. Dennis recognised this and didn't want to do it either, but there were pressures from home. My advice was against it. This was a classic case of integrity having to take precedent over financial reward, but it stoked the fires between Dennis and Rula.

I had remortgaged the house to pay off the final tranche of what I owed on the film, and we were far from skint, but Rula was frantic when I turned down the ad. She didn't care about the fact that the ad would damage my career; all she wanted was the money. You'd have thought the bailiffs were at the door.

There is only so much you can take of being sneered at for everything you do or are. My friends were boring, my work was rubbish, my lifestyle was crap, I was useless at this and hopeless at that, I was despised because I'd lost all that money, and, to quote Jeffrey Bernard, 'I made her sick'. Rows erupted on a regular basis which ended in a certain amount of flailing around, pushing and shoving on both our parts.

In my experience, men very rarely share their problems with other guys, but I was sitting with an old mate in the clubhouse, feeling particularly low, when he asked me how I was. I knew things weren't great in his home at the time either and I suddenly heard myself saying, 'She's making life so unpleasant, I think she's planning that if it gets bad enough I'll walk out, and she'll keep the house.' Now this hadn't really occurred to me before. It just came out, but I think I might have reached the right conclusion.

I was being blamed for just about everything. I drove Rula to a Harley Street dentist one day and waited for her in the car outside the surgery. When she emerged she had a face like thunder.

'Are you OK?' I asked.

'No. This is all your fault,' she snarled.

'What?' I said, a little taken aback.

'The dentist said I must be grinding my teeth at night and it's down to stress, and that's all your fault.'

WARREN CLARKE: Dennis was the lowest I've ever seen him, he'd lost weight, he was grey. Both mentally and physically, he'd had the shit kicked out of him. Even his sense of humour disappeared, and his personality changed a great deal. Rula was the wrong woman and it was the wrong relationship.

I was asked if I would be interested in doing a tour of a Ray Cooney play. It wasn't one he'd originated but he had translated it from the French and I thought it was very funny.

Deke and I were invited to see a production of a current play of his, prior to a meeting with Ray after the show. We struggled through the first act and made our way swiftly to the bar. Bill Kenwright's brother, Tom, was running the theatre restaurant and he bought us a drink. He warned us the second half wasn't any better than the first but that he'd get us back to our seats in time for the curtain calls. What a relief! I've never been a great fan of farce and this wasn't the best example I'd ever seen, although Ray is a very successful playwright, noted for his very funny actor-proof comedies. 'Actor-proof' means that you can cast a play with the most talentless bunch of idiots but the writing is so good that the audience can't help laughing. *Run for your Wife* is a fine example.

The play which he wanted me to do was called *Fools Rush In*. Ray and I hadn't met before and I felt a bit tentative suggesting that the style of directing or acting we'd seen that evening would not suit the style of this play. I breathed again when Ray concurred that *Fools Rush In*, wasn't exactly a farce, and therefore we could play it far more realistically.

The big carrot for me doing this play was that Eric Sykes was also going to be in it. Eric is a phenomenon. Even though almost blind and very deaf, he continues performing with great zest and originality. Many less physically impaired actors could learn a great deal from him, from his comic timing and technique

I had worked with Eric, briefly, in one of his silent films for television, which he had directed so brilliantly. We had got on instantly, and were delighted to discover that we had both agreed to do this play only on condition that the other did it too.

Seeing Eric on stage, I am sure few people in the auditorium could guess how little he can see or hear. I saw him once in a production of *School for Wives* rushing around the stage like a young gazelle. What I find slightly embarrassing is that, despite his infirmities and the fact that he's in his mid-seventies, I still struggle to beat him at golf! We had a super time on tour even though Gerald Harper was in the show. What a contrast. There was Eric, who was wonderful and brilliant to work with, and Harper, who was neither. Eric nearly hit him on a couple of occasions; I should have let him.

We did the play for a couple of weeks in Leatherhead, then started the tour in Windsor.

Rula and I had always shared a tradition of first-night presents. They could be anything from a single red rose to a piece of jewellery, or something pertaining to the theme of the play. On my first night at Windsor, she bought me four cans of beer and two packets of crisps. I threw them in the bin in front of her. Luckily I was going on tour. Unluckily, I came home on Sundays.

It was on one of these Sundays that I started to suspect that there might be someone else. Sometime after lunch, the phone rang. Before I could get to it, the answering machine kicked in. It was an old mate of mine called Mike Mallinson. Mike was the owner of the Winnebago which George and I had shared on *Minder*. He acted as a sort of hotelier on wheels, and was always around to service the van, and to make sure everything was as we wanted it. He became a friend, and part of the unit. I had kept in touch with him after the series had finished, since when, he had started working for various charities. He also acted as an escort to Rula if ever I wasn't around, and quite often the three of us went out together.

He sounded a little surprised to hear me, he actually wanted to have a word with Rula, but we chatted for a while about my tour, before she picked up the call. A little later I was back at my desk when I noticed the answering machine flashing, indicating that a new message was waiting. I switched it on only to hear the conversation that had ensued between Rula and Mike. The machine had continued recording.

I heard her ask him if he had found someone to go with him to some function. 'Yes,' he said. There followed a blatantly romantic conversation, with Rula betting that whoever it was must have been much younger and more beautiful than she, and Mike saying that no one was more beautiful than her. I went crackers.

'What's going on with you and that spiv?' I spat.

'Nothing,' she said. 'You know Mike.'

'Oh yes,' I said, 'I know him, and I know you. What the fuck's going on?'

Not once did Rula try and defuse the situation by assuring me that nothing was happening. Instead she increased my turmoil by attacking me for listening to a phone call which was private.

Later that same afternoon he phoned again. Again I answered, gave him short shrift and Rula took the call in the lounge. This time, I admit, I did listen in. 'Dennis sounds a little upset,' he said. 'I'll call you back when we can talk.' Again I went to her and asked what was going on between them. Again she didn't try to allay any of my fears, she just persisted in repeating that I had no right to eavesdrop on her phone calls.

'If nothing's going on why can't he talk to you when I'm here?' I demanded. Rula and I knew all about such clandestine conversations. God knows we had indulged in enough of them when we had first started going out together.

I have never been more pleased to get back on the road again. This time to Liverpool!

At Eric's suggestion I stayed on the Wirral, close to where he was staying. We met up with some old chums of his and played some lovely golf courses. But for most of the week I was seething. Finally I found Mallinson's phone number and called him. 'Are you fucking my wife?' There was no point in beating about the bush.

'No,' he replied. 'You know she's been very unhappy recently.'

'And you're cheering her up, are you?' I said. 'I'm fucking unhappy too. But you're not phoning me up, are you?'

It went on in this vein until I hung up, stomach churning with anger.

I returned on the Saturday night to find Rula in a rage. 'How dare you phone Mike? Who do you think you are?'

On Monday I received a letter from his solicitor, insisting on an apology and threatening me that this must never be talked about in the press. I showed it to Rula and binned it.

When the tour ended, I determined for both our sakes to wipe all suspicion from my mind, to make myself believe that nothing had been going on.

Sadly, Rula's parents had died within weeks of each other, and it was around this time that she and most of her family went to Poland to attend some tribute to her father. I met them all at the airport on their return and they'd had a wonderful time.

Rula and I went into truce mode. Not actually being unpleasant to each other and every now and then even being quite nice. Meanwhile, I was asked by an old mate of mine, Paul Knight, to do four episodes of a show he was producing called *The Knock*. This meant quite a lot of location work in Suffolk.

Back home, on one of my breaks from filming, I was shown a lot of family snaps from the recent Polish trip. What I wasn't shown were some pretty pictures I found later. There were about half a dozen of them and they showed Rula and some bloke with a moustache in various romantic poses. My enquiries were greeted with the usual sneers and the excuse that he was just a cousin.

'A kissing cousin?' I suggested.

'That is how we react to each other in our family,' she answered scornfully.

Now Rula has a thing about hands. She claims that they are one of the first things she notices about people. When we were first together in the south of France, one of her favourite photographs was of our hands intertwined. One of the Polish photos showed her hand and that of her 'cousin' in an identical pose, except they were also holding wineglasses. Others were of a smiling couple arm in arm and very close.

When we broke up finally, Rula was most emphatic that it had nothing to do with anybody else, that no one else was involved, that it was all my fault.

Two years later she admitted in an article that the man who had helped her through her agony was the very same one as in those photographs.

HANNAH: That summer I got a holiday job behind the bar at the golf club. Naturally I stayed at Sheepcote. It was absolute hell. The rows were horrendous. Rula and Dennis were arguing twenty-four hours a day, tearing each other apart. I couldn't take it, and in the end moved in with a friend.

Day and night Rula told me how much she loathed me, and that she was leaving. Except she wouldn't go. She wanted the house.

One night the jibes got more than I could bear. It's true I had been drinking, but I was at the end of my tether. I snapped and lashed out.

It is no defence, I know, but it was the only time I ever hurt her. She'd once told me an old boyfriend of hers had tried to strangle her with a telephone cord. I could understand why. No woman, no man, had ever driven me to violence in my life. But now her persistent bullying had goaded me into doing something which I have always despised and of which I am desperately ashamed. I had raised my hand to a woman.

Rula was playing Lady Macbeth at the Stafford Festival. The next day I drove straight up to the theatre, and reluctantly she agreed to see me. She appeared with a black eye. I was devastated. What were we doing to each other? Another fragile truce was declared. We were both away on tour at the time, and distance made things easier.

Before long I got the old routine about how we needed some space and time to get our acts together.

'I'm not moving out!' I said, defensively.

'OK, I'll get a small flat. If I can find somewhere that I can afford.'

I tried again. 'Come on, there's no need for all this, we can work it out.'

'Maybe,' she said. 'We'll see.'

My drinking had escalated. Sometimes it was the only way I could face the worsening conditions at home.

'Is that it then?' I said. 'Is this the end for us?'

'I don't know,' she retorted. 'Maybe after a break we could get back together again.' We slipped into a sullen silence that didn't help anything or anybody. There wasn't even the will to fight.

So our nightmare existence continued, living side by side, but not together, in a stalemate atmosphere of unbearable tension.

One night, after we'd managed a genuinely pleasant evening, we went to bed and I started to get 'romantic'. She stopped me immediately, and said I could forget any hopes I might have of getting back together; her love for me was dead. Through tears of shock and anger, I asked who she did love . . .

'There is no one else involved,' she replied.

We survived like this for the next for four or five months. How, I don't know. I still hoped there was a chance that I could change her mind. She remained isolated in her completely private life. Her family continued to be invited to the house, and I carried on as if nothing had happened, although they all must have known. I even questioned her sister Anna about the man in the pictures. 'Oh, he's just a cousin,' she replied. 'You're so jealous.'

On Rula's birthday in September, I bought her yet another piece of jewellery and suggested we go to Cliveden for a celebratory dinner. I also proposed we invited her cousin, Antek, and his lovely wife Sally. 'That'll be nice,' she said with a shrug.

Dinner was very strained. I tried to make myself agreeable, but I might as well not have been there. I paid the bill, which came to nearly a thousand pounds, and within a week, Rula was gone.

The headline on the front page of the *Mail on Sunday* read, 'MY VIOLENT MARRIAGE TO MINDER'. Rula had struck again. Sadly and embarrassingly, I was not blameless. During our fifteen years together, I had lashed out at her three times. However reprehensible this is, I don't believe it adds up to the non-stop, drunken wife-beating that she and her friendly journalist alleged.

I had stayed overnight with Pat and Jeremy in Devon, having seen Julia in a school drama production. She had been terrific and we'd had a great evening. On Sunday morning the phone rang. It was Pam, the new lady in my life, with news of the article.

PAT: It was a horrible article. Dennis was shocked and very down when he left for London. I was shaking with anger. Dennis had never raised a hand to me or the children. He is not the most perfect of men but he did not deserve that kind of attack. He was also in a no-win situation. Rula was very manipulative and very plausible. If Dennis tried to defend himself, who would believe him?

The girls were distraught. For their sakes, as well as for Dennis', I felt impelled to redress the situation. An interview with the press would have offered the opportunity for a journalist's interpretation or slant on what I had to say. The original article had been sensational enough. I didn't need to capitalise on that by going to the tabloids; I decided to write a letter to the *Telegraph*.

I explained that I had read the article by Rula Lenska in the *Mail* and I had written a letter in response, which I wanted published. They agreed to use it, not on the letters page, but as a feature with an article around it and a photograph. I was hesitant, only because I did not in any way wish to involve my husband, Jeremy. I pointed out that although he was very supportive, it had nothing to do with him. They kept their word.

Because of my husband's job in the legal profession, I was very aware of what it means to be a battered wife and I was incensed that Rula could make such claims. During our marriage, Dennis and I had had a very volatile relationship. But even when I provoked him or threw things, he never retaliated physically. A man doesn't suddenly become a wife-beater, it is already there. Such people beat up all their wives, it is inherent in their need for domination, as it is with women who abuse and bully their husbands.

JULIA: During the separation, Lara and I had stayed in touch. She phoned me that Sunday morning, deeply distressed, to say, 'You should know Rula has spoken to the papers.' She didn't tell me what had been said, just begged us not to be angry with her. It wasn't her fault, but we were too furious and upset to speak to her for a long time.

HANNAH: I brooded over the article all day. I could not believe that even Rula would stoop so low. I could contain myself no longer, and phoned her to ask why.

She claimed it was to protect Julia and me, that she was worried Dennis might hit us. Dad might have shouted if we ever did something dangerous or naughty, but he had never, in our lives, even come near to hitting us. The only one who had was Rula. She smacked us all the time.

WARREN CLARKE: All the friends were very disgusted at Rula's article. I've always refused to take sides with anyone over marital problems, but over this I was appalled. What was amusing was seeing the reply from Pat.

Husbands and wives say things, throw things, but that's not beating someone up in the sense that we all understand it. It was a very dumb move on Rula's part. I believe she now knows she made a huge mistake.

DEKE: Pat's letter created an amazing response from the media, in support of Dennis.

The letter ran as follows:

Dear Sir,

I write this letter on behalf of myself and my two daughters. My name is Patricia Maynard; my ex-husband was Dennis Waterman. We have spent the last twenty-four hours sickened by the interview that Miss Rula Lenska has given to the *Mail on Sunday* which was published yesterday.

I lived with Dennis for over seven years, we had our two daughters, and in the whole of that time he never once raised his hand to me or our daughters: though it is true to say we had a fairly volatile relationship – that is the nature of the man – but violent, NEVER!

My daughters do not wish to see their father's name vilified in this way: he is an exceedingly loyal man and will not defend himself. In case anyone has missed the point, he has never said anything against Miss Lenska, or indeed anyone else.

I cannot understand Miss Lenska's motives for allowing this interview – a couple of smacks, *if* that is what happened, do not constitute being a battered wife: I think it is despicable that she should draw a parallel between herself and those poor unfortunate women who are genuinely abused. My daughters have over the years spent considerable periods of time with their father and Miss Lenska. They never witnessed any violence.

On the morning the interview was published Miss Lenska asked her daughter to telephone one of my daughters to say she had not wanted to hurt them but that she had been 'hounded' by journalists and was forced to give an interview. I too was 'hounded' and indeed offered a substantial sum of money for my side of the story when Miss Lenska succeeded in breaking up my marriage fifteen years ago. I resisted the temptation to say anything. One would have thought that a Polish countess would have had the strength of character to have done the same.

Yours faithfully,
Patricia Maynard.

Rula then did another article the following Sunday, complaining that even some of her friends had turned against her.

These articles were published seven to eight months after she had left me. The final flight had been graphically described by Rula in her first article. In it she claimed how she swept up her teenage daughter and left the family home in fear of her life. After the dreadful night in Cliveden, the situation at home was impossible, and that night, it's true, we had had an evil argument. In my frustration, I had done some damage to a door and even more to my fist, but nothing to Rula or Lara.

What disgusted me particularly about this exposé was that she had gone to the *Mail* only after we had completed the full and final settlement for the divorce.

Throughout all of our negotiations for divorce, Rula had played on my very real shame and guilt. The fact that she had slapped my face

on a number of occasions, including in public, didn't seem to count
for anything. But she insisted that if I contested her demands and
went to court, she would go to the press.

For some time Rula had also been demanding that I give her the
house, her argument being that Pat had received such a generous
settlement. She failed to understand that not only had I abandoned
Pat for her, but I had left her with my two small daughters to care
for. I was hardly going to throw them out on the street.

I had assumed that we would sell the house and split the profit
fifty-fifty. She said no, the re-mortgaging of the house had had
nothing to do with her, despite her being joint mortgagee. She
wanted half the money for the total sale of the house. The mortgage
was my debt. This gave her a huge amount and left me virtually
penniless.

My lawyer advised that if we came to some sort of agreement, Rula
could never come after me for more money at a later date, which
meant I would never have to hear from her again. That sounded like
a very good plan.

Things were almost finalised when she wrote, praising my past
generosity and asking if I would be prepared to give her the part-
finished house in the south of France. My earning potential was far
greater than hers, she argued, and she wanted something tangible to
leave to Lara, should anything happen to her.

By now I was totally worn down by the whole process, and ready
to agree to anything just to get it all over. A few months later I got a
form from her solicitor asking me to sign some papers giving Rula the
right to sell the house in France.

Not content with having taken almost everything she could lay her
hands on, she came back for more and literally plundered the house.
Apart from the initial deposit, Rula had paid nothing towards either
the purchase or the upkeep of the house. Every penny she earned –
and she had earned quite good money – she spent on food, clothes
and Lara and nothing else. The rest she kept for herself. I paid for
everything. Now, with no consultation whatsoever, working on the
formula that what had been ours was now hers, she stripped the
place, even taking hundreds of my CDs.

By the time she had sold the French house, not counting the
paintings and jewellery, she walked away from our marriage with a
substantial sum of money. After a very successful forty-year career,
including fifteen years with Rula, I ended up with barely enough for
a small deposit on a very small house.

When there were no more possessions to take, she tried to strip me of my good name and my career. And followed this up later with yet another piece in the paper saying how she would still like us to be friends.

On reflection, I wonder if a lot of what happened was pre-meditated and worked out a long time before Rula actually left. She would call the police on the slightest pretext, claiming she was scared at the most normal of domestic disagreements. It was so obviously a ploy even the police were embarrassed.

The night she left, the police turned up again, saying that my wife had phoned saying she was worried about me. Both of these visits were completely unnecessary but could serve as incriminating evidence to be recorded in detail in the divorce papers.

TWENTY-FIVE

LOVE IS A PANTOMIME

My marriage was over, the tour of *Fools Rush In* had come to an end. I was living alone at Sheepcote Grange in a state of total misery when I was asked to do the pantomime at Windsor. Lee Dean was producing the show. He had a reputation for doing very good traditional pantos. I had nothing else on. A bleak and desolate Christmas was looming. The theatre was only twenty minutes away, so I thought, I might as well do it.

We had a magical cast and crew and made a huge amount of money for the Theatre Royal, Windsor, which was in imminent danger of being closed down. And I met the lady with whom I now live very happily. Pamela Flint was assistant stage manager on the show.

PAM FLINT: Lee was very excited at getting Dennis Waterman to play Buttons, but when Dennis walked in that first day, we were all quite shocked. He looked like an old man. There was a passing resemblance to the Waterman of *Minder*, but the feisty character was gone. It wasn't just that he was haggard and hollow-eyed; this was a man who looked as if all the life had been drained out of him.

For the first two days he just mooched around, and seemed set apart from everybody. I don't think he'd even looked at the script, and when he came to read, he was very nervous. I felt no attraction for Dennis at the time.

But gradually he began to relax and warm to everyone, and however these things happen, I suddenly began to find him very attractive indeed.

I blame her for kissing me goodnight in the car park; she blames me for, well, everything really. She was a fairly recent divorcée and not really looking for anything that might turn into a relationship. I certainly didn't want anything, except maybe a little loving now and then. Well, we had a little loving now and then, and everything was so calm and easy and natural, we just kind of started to live together. People tell me they haven't seen me so happy and relaxed for many years. Even the demon drink seems to have disappeared. I still celebrate with the best on Christmas and birthdays and other such joyful events, but the forces that drove me to get hammered are all gone.

PAM: By the time the pantomime finished, I was in love with Dennis. But I was convinced that he would go back to Rula again. Understandably he was very wary of talking to me about his marriage. In fact it wasn't until we'd been apart for some time, following the end of the show, that he invited me over to Sheepcote and started talking about what had happened between them. He had clearly been very badly hurt. As we started spending more time together, I noticed that he apologised constantly, at least twenty times a day, for no reason whatsoever. It was like a mantra. This went on for about two years until his confidence gradually returned. A close friend of mine had been married to a control freak, and I recognised all the signs.

I didn't realise just how deeply traumatised Dennis was until the final move from Sheepcote. He had shown very little emotion as he'd packed the few possessions he had left, and he'd hardly spoken as he left the house and we moved into the tiny little furnished flat we'd found. He was very quiet that evening, but when he stripped off to get in the shower, I was horrified to see, from his toes to his head, that his body was one screaming, bright red rash of stress. He was given treatment to help it but his anguish was such it returned frequently. As did the tears.

Dennis professed to hate Rula with a passion. I believe it was a passion that easily could have been translated back into love. I think he might even have gone back if she'd called. What killed everything was the first article.

Any woman can manipulate a situation and goad a man into hitting her. Dennis knew he had been manipulated and he was devastated by it. He was even more distraught that she went to the press. He had always been impressed by her background, and it shocked him that she could behave in such a dishonourable way He was even more distressed that she could be so cruel as to want to destroy him as a man and to damage everything he'd worked for in his career.

It still upsets him, even though he has now reached a kind of plateau where he is content. It has taken almost three years to break down the rigid controls that limited his life. He doesn't have to phone home and report in all the time, he can arrange a game of golf whenever he wishes and friends can visit whenever they like. And the girls can drop in without any previous arrangement.

I was shocked when Hannah came for the first time. Not only was she nervous of me, and guarded in what she said (something we soon put right), she even brought her own food. She never has to do that again.

Something really weird has happened – I now look forward to Christmas. Pam's two children, Matthew and Louise, together with Louise's husband and brand-new baby, join us along with Hannah and Julia. Sometimes we spend it all together with Pat and Jeremy and his kids. It's brilliant.

There is one slight drawback: since I bought Pam some golf clubs, she is starting to beat me, but then everybody else does, so why shouldn't she? As much as possible we go everywhere together. We have never had a disagreement, let alone an argument. It's terrific. I also have the added bonus of getting my daughters back properly.

Stupidly, I hadn't noticed what effect Rula had had on them. Hannah would make any amount of excuses to avoid staying with us. Now Pam and I can't get rid of her, and have no intention of doing so. It's been a lot more difficult with Julia to get back on an even keel. We missed so many years together, but since we broke the barriers and talked, I am determined to make up that lost time and I believe she is too, and the love we have for each other can be openly expressed with no fear of misunderstanding.

I am inordinately proud of them both. They were only the second and third Watermans ever to go to university.

Disturbingly, both plumped for theatre studies! Hannah got a double second at Warwick University in English and drama and has grown into a wonderful actress who is just about to embark as a regular in *EastEnders*. And Julia is in her second year at John Moores University and is doing brilliantly. Musically, she is extremely talented, but now she is talking about being a director. Whatever she pursues, I'll put money on the fact that she'll succeed. Another huge bonus is that they really, really like each other a great deal and I love them both to death. Having said that, I have always loved beautiful women.

JULIA: The other person who suffered so much throughout this damaging time was Lara. We had grown up as sisters and been so close. But for a long time after that terrible article she was left out in the wilderness. Then one day she phoned me. I was still steaming over Rula, but my mother insisted I take the call. It had taken great courage for Lara to make contact again, even though nothing had been her fault. The three of us met for lunch. We had all been victims in one way or another, and we'd gone through a lot together. Lara had grown up a great deal. We'd all learned a lot, and we still loved each other enough, we decided, to rise above the differences of our parents and be friends. We'd been part of each other's lives, we didn't want to lose that again. We meet often now, and she always sends her love to Dad, and hopes he is well and happy. She misses him too, and that means more to him than anything.

My original thoughts were to finish this book back at that fantastic fiftieth birthday party Pam arranged for me. But at this exact moment, I am writing this in a beautiful apartment overlooking the Indian Ocean. I am back in Perth, Western Australia, where Rula and I got married. Added to which, I have just finished an extremely successful tour of *Same Time Another Year*, with Paula Wilcox (I'm not certain I've ever worked with a better actress), which is the sequel to *Same Time Next Year*, the very play that first brought Rula and me to Perth.

So what does all that signify? I'm buggered if I know! What goes around comes around, maybe? All I do know is that my life is back on course, love in all its forms surrounds me, I still enjoy the best job in the world – and even my golf is getting better. I think I feel the sun on my back.

ACKNOWLEDGEMENTS

This is a book about the man, the actor, his life, his career and above all his extraordinary quality of friendship.

So many people came forward to talk about Dennis and everyone counted themselves a friend.

To all those whose warm and frank recollections have added a special dimension to this book we owe a debt of gratitude. A part of them all is in his story and to them all we say thank you.

Jill Arlon

INDEX

Compiled by Derek Copson